T0137568

SOUTHERN GOLD

James Campbell

Order this book online at www.trafford.com
or email orders@trafford.com

Most Trafford titles are also available at major online book retailers.

Printed in the United States of America.

ISBN: 978-1-4269-5614-0 (sc)
ISBN: 978-1-4269-5615-7 (hc)
ISBN: 978-1-4269-5616-4 (e)

Library of Congress Control Number: 2011901027

Trafford rev. 04/18/2011

 www.trafford.com

North America & international
toll-free: 1 888 232 4444 (USA & Canada)
phone: 250 383 6864 ♦ fax: 812 355 4082

CHAPTER ONE

ATLANTA, GEORGIA: September 2, 1864, General William T. Sherman and sixty thousand Union Soldiers marched into the city of Atlanta in close pursuit of a Confederate Army that was outnumbered by a margin of four to one. On this particular day, this part of the Confederate Army was commanded by General Joseph E. Johnston while General Robert E. Lee and his troop were being pushed southward on the east coast near Savannah. Meanwhile, the Confederate troops fought relentlessly to avoid being over-run by the Union troops in Atlanta. But as fate would have it, General Sherman and his troop could smell victory in the air, and it was only a matter of time.

By November, and hundreds of Confederate soldiers lay dead from what became known as the, "Last stand in the south." The Rebels troops were forced to retreat from Atlanta towards Stone Mountain where they made one last stand, but only for a short while before being chased on eastward. But before departing Atlanta, the Union soldiers by orders of General Sherman burned the city of Atlanta to the ground. This of course, was not the typical destruction of a city because the Union soldiers had captured it, it was done in search of two billion dollars in gold that the Confederates had buried somewhere in the city during their last intense battle.

The Rebels troops realized that defeat was immanent, and in their possession was two billion dollars in gold that was donated by southern banks and the French to help finance the war, believing that the gold would bring about a different kind of ending. However, since there was little doubt in the mind of General Joseph Johnston that the war was over, and victory was not going to be in the hands of the Confederates soldiers, the last thing that he wanted to happen to was allow their gold fall into the hands of the Union Army.

In the south east section of the city where the fighting had not become a battleground of the war, the General ordered ten members of his army to dig a hole that was deep enough to bury the gold in a rust-proof vault, and it would never be discovered by the Union troops. The burier detail was done as ordered by General Johnston, and on a piece of brown paper, a faintly hand drawn map by one of the ten soldiers was delivered to the General. At this point, only eleven men knew the exact location of the gold. But again, as fate would have it, the ten soldiers who were apart of the burier detail were killed in the battle, leaving only General Johnson as the sole survival of the gold.

The battle later reached the point of being called, "The March to The Sea" by General Sherman, because as they constantly fought and pushed the Rebels towards the Atlantic Ocean. He wired President Lincoln and said, "I beg to present to you as a Christmas gift, the city of Savannah."

The following year in April of 1865, General Robert E. Lee and General Joseph Johnston realized that they had no place to go but into the sea. On April 9th, the two southern generals surrendered to the northern troops, promising that they would never in their natural lives again pick up another weapon against the Union. But that was not the end of the conflict for General Sherman and his troops who knew they had not captured the gold along with the Rebels. So the question then was being asked over and over again of General Johnston, "Where is the gold?!...What did you do with all that gold?"

The hand drawn map, indicating the exact location of the gold was sent to General Johnson's wife back in Virginia before the surrender, and the Union Army was never able to locate the gold that was buried somewhere in the city of Atlanta. But Sherman was not persuaded by the General's denial of having any knowledge of the whereabouts of the gold, and he continued to pressure Johnston until he finally admitted that the gold belonged to the south, and his Confederate troops had carefully buried it in a place where no Union solider would ever find it. And apparently, he was correct in his confirmation, because a few Union troops went back to Atlanta and dug through the debris for several months after the war, but only to come back empty handed.

General Joseph Johnston was eventually allowed to go back home in Virginia to live out the rest of his life with his wife and two sons. Although he kept the map in a secret place, but he alone knew the exact location where the gold was buried, and he never made any attempt to go back to Atlanta to dig up the fortune. He knew that there were eyes of the government always watching and waiting for him to make such a move.

In 1869, General Ulysses Simpson Grant who accepted General Johnston and General Lee's surrender became President of the United States and the nation immediately found itself faced with a shipwreck of an economy that the government could no longer afford to have troops digging for gold in Atlanta that no one believed they would ever find, he called off the search. General Joseph Johnston died thirty years later, and as far as the government was concerned, the secret to the gold died with him.

**** *145 YEARS LATER* ****

In 2005, a police lieutenant for the Atlanta Police Department named Calvin Gates, the commander of the Red Dog anti-drug squad was hopelessly trying to put an end to the sale of drugs in south east Atlanta. There were all kinds of problems on the south side of the city besides the huge drug trade. There were many other major crimes that had to be dealt with, such as robberies, murders, and rapes that were being perpetrated by gang members. On top of all the problems that the Red Dog squad was facing from the neighborhood and the squad commander was forced to come face to face with the reality of having to deal with his own officers taking payoffs from the drug bosses to be informants, telling them whenever a drug raid was coming their way.

The new information was a serious wakeup call for Lieutenant Gates, for he had been living in a state of denial, refusing to believe many eyewitnesses in the community when he was informed that he had some rogue cops on his squad. Major James Butler, the precinct commander and Lieutenant Gates boss came to a meeting of the minds, "If this thing is ever going to come an end, we must do it ourselves,..." The Major said.

"We cannot allow IA to come in here and do any kind of an investigation,...if we allow that to happen, can we stand to live with what they might turn up?"

"Well, I think as long as we're in the clear, and have no knowledge of what these officers are doing, then we can let the chips fall where they may." Lieutenant Gates responded without hesitation.

Both men were seated in Major Butler's office in precinct three, located on the south side of the city. For the past thirty years, this particular section of Atlanta was considered by anyone who was keeping score as a crime riddled, drug infested hell hole. And the precinct that housed the cops who were hopelessly trying to maintain some form order were often caught up in the middle of trying to be the law enforcers and breaking the laws themselves. In this particular situation, Lieutenant Calvin Gates squad was responsible for controlling the drug trafficking in and out of south east Atlanta, also known as Zone Three, or Little Vietnam. Lieutenant Gates was faced with the reality that his officers whose job was to capture and arrest drug dealers were apart of the problem.

"If we keep Internal Affairs out of zone three, and if I find out who these officers are who are working with the drug boys, and bring charges against them, are you going to stand behind me, James?" Gates asked his long time friend and half brother.

"Goddamnit, Calvin, we go all the ways back to when we were kids, we walked the beat together, me and you. Brothers first of all…Secondly, you're my lieutenant, the commander of the Red Dog squad. If you bring me any evidence that will implicate your people as doing what you're claiming, I will make sure that they get what they deserve.

And I hope the court will send them to prison for a very long time……
Look, my brother, you just bring me the evidence, and I'll stand behind you until hell freezes over…."

Lieutenant Gates was seated in a straight arm leather chair facing the Major… "The only reason I'm asking the question is because I know that some of these officers whom I am suspicious of as being corrupted cops, they are also personal friends of yours. I don't want them running to you for you to save their asses…"

The Major did not respond to Gates immediately, he only stared blindly towards the lieutenant, but not directly at him. "And what make you think that I'm friends with some of your officers?"

"Because I keep an open ear to any and everything that my officers say….You never know what you might pick up…..I'm not saying that you know what they're doing, but I'm just saying when the shit hits the fan, and it will, I can guarantee you that,… you're going to have to take a back seat, or stand down when it comes to them."

The Major again stared into space for a moment before responding. "So, I gather you're referring to Chad Wilson, Bobby Turner, and Danny Porter.?"

"They would be the ones…." Gates rolled his eyes at the Major. "And I do know that these officers have been to your farm out in Mableton on several occasions to family barbeques and so on….."

"Wait, wait,…..So have you, but does that make you guilty by association?" The Major snapped, almost in an angry tone of voice.

"Look, I just don't want you having to decide whose sides you're on when it's all said and done." Gates said softly trying to hold down the tension.

"Lieutenant Gates, my brother, why on God's earth would I do some dumb shit like that?!.....Look, like I said, you bring me proof that these officers are doing what they appear to be doing, and I'll see to it that they get what they deserves, okay?"

Lieutenant Gates stood before saying, "James, I know we were friends before we knew we were half brothers. And I also know that the Chief made me the commander in charge of Red Dog in spite of your objections….. Nevertheless, we're still friends, and I just don't want anything to upset our working relationship…."

The Major stood as well smiling. "The only thing that is going to upset our working relationship is you not being able to prove what you say….. And as far as me objecting to your assignment out here, it was not because I disliked the working arrangement, it was because I figured something like this would eventually pop up, and it might appear to some that you are trying to bring me down so you can take over my job.

I also know how close you and the Chief are too."

Calvin Gates laughed while rolling his eyes once again at the Major. "And you thought trying to talk the Chief out of assigning me to the Red Dog squad would some how save your job?"

"Calvin, everyone in this precinct knows that you and the Chief are best of friends, and the only reason you're in this zone is to try and bring down my command staff, me primarily…..But, that's okay, because I'm still standing as the commander of zone three, and on paper, you still works for me, brother or no brother……"

Lieutenant Gates smiled, but quickly broke it off to a serious glance. "Well then, as long as the paper says I work for you, that's all that matter…." He turned and left the office. As he walked towards the roll call room to prepare for the evening shift which started at 1800 hrs., he passed the three officers that he had been referring to as being on the take from the drug dealers. "Roll call in five minutes, guys!" He snapped to the three officers as they sat in metal chairs in the hallway between Major's office and the roll call room.

Danny Porter was African American, 32 years old, unmarried, and had been on the force for five years. He was born and raised on Atlanta's south side, and knew most of the drug dealers in the zone three precinct area. Porter was also the point man who made all the contacts when there was money to be collected from the drug boys. Porter loved living the life of a high roller. Chad Wilson was white, 35 years old, married with two kids, and lived in a five bedroom home in Austell, Georgia. Chad had an extremely high mortgage to pay each month, and needed the extra cash to help pay the bills. Chad had been on the force for ten years. Bobby Turner was white, 41 years old, divorced after ten years, three kids, and two thousand dollars a month child support payment, and he could not afford to pay that kind of money every month on a cop's salary. Turner was a fifteen year veteran.

All three officers had legitimate reasons for becoming corrupted cops, simply because their lifestyles could not be supported by the jobs they had. Drug money was easy money, and the only thing they had to do was to notify the people who were running the operations whenever the police were planning to stage a raid on their territories. That sounded easy enough to the trio, and no one would ever know that it were them who were doing the tipping off to the drug dealers. That is, until Lieutenant Gates, a 40 year old African American, married with one daughter, realized that the drug dealers could not possibly know every time a raid was being staged unless they were being tipped off.

After doing some checking throughout the neighborhoods, a few of the people in the community who were happy to see the cops doing their jobs, but knew that the same three cops were always hanging around before the raids. They began to talk about seeing the three officers always on the days of the raids. What appeared to have been rather odd when the three cops departed the area, the raids would come later in the evenings, but the drugs boys were gone, or sitting back in the "cut", or in the shadows watching the cops scratching their heads trying to figure out what had gone wrong? And what made Gates job easy as far as knowing who the snitches were, the residents called the three officers by names, Danny Porter, Bobby Turner, and Chad Wilson.

The only thing that Gates needed to do at this point was go back to the same residents and get written affidavits from the witnesses, take them to a judge, which would issue three arrest warrants. However, he was not sure if he could fully trust his boss, and brother, the Major. But he was willing to go forth with his plan as soon as possible.

After roll call and all fifteen police officers had received their assignments, Gates drove out to the location where the witnesses were willing to give him written statements about what they saw his three officers doing. In the housing complex at McDaniel and Glenn Streets, he managed to get five different statements from the witnesses. And when he was done with that, he drove directly to Fulton County Judge Horace Baker's home to get three arrest warrants signed. After he was completed with the warrants, he radioed the Fulton County Sheriff Department for assistance in making the arrests. Of course, he knew that this procedure would not go over well with the Major, but he could not take any chances of allowing anything to go wrong at this point.

Two hours later that evening, Lieutenant Gates advised the dispatcher to have the three officers to meet him at Georgia Avenue and McDaniel Street for a briefing. This particular action alerted everyone else on the squad as to what was about to go down. There had been rumors floating around, but now, they all knew that the rumors were a reality. When the three officers drove up at the location, all in the same vehicle, they were immediately taken into custody without incident, or hassle from the officers.

Although he had done what he believed was the right thing, he was still very much surprised and troubled by the lack of resistance that the trio gave to being arrested. He was worried due to the simple fact that they knew that they were going to be arrested that evening. *So, how could they have known that they were going to be arrested?* There was only one explanation, Major Butler had told someone else, or he had told the officers themselves. However, this was what he had to do, and he did it strictly by the book.

After having their vehicle picked up and carried back to the precinct, Lt. Gates continued with his duties as supervisor of the squad for the remainder of the watch. It was approaching 0100 hrs., it was the following morning when suddenly, there was an emergency call that came through by way of the dispatcher for Lieutenant Calvin Gates. "Lieutenant, I'll patch you in to a secure private line that requires your immediate attention," The dispatcher said anxiously and nervously.

Lieutenant Gate twisted the radio dial to channel 10 where only the caller and the listener could hear the conversation. "This is Lieutenant Calvin Gates, someone on this channel want to talk with me?" He inquired cautiously.

"Lieutenant Gates... Calvin Gates?!" The caller said as if he was not sure as to whom he was talking to.

"Yes!....Once again, this is Lieutenant Gates, who is this?!"

"Never mind who this is, you just listen to what I have to say, chump!"

"Okay, you have my attention, say what's on your mind, chump back at ya.."

"Okay, smartass, I have your pretty wife, and your little girl....Now, Mr. Smartass, if you don't do as I tell you to, they both will die tonight....."

Lieutenant Gates was momentarily stunned to a state of speechlessness. He was finding it difficult to catch his breath, as beads of sweat formed on his forehead. He became extremely nervous, his hand that held the radio-phone shook uncontrollably as he dropped the radio-phone on the car seat. He could not believe what was being said to him. He refused to believe what he was hearing. He slowly picked up the phone again, held it up to his ear. "I hope to God for your sake that this is one of your sick practical joke, because if you lay one finger on my family, I will hunt you down,....and I will kill you with my bare hands,.....do you hear what I'm saying?!"

"I hear you alright, Mr. Police-man......" The caller let out a low tone laugh. "Yeah, I hear you real good, Mr. Police-man......But let me tell you something. And that something is what you're gonna do, and you best get it right. If you don't, the only people you ever loved will die." The caller paused for a few seconds. He then spoke again. "The cops that you arrested this evening, you know the ones I'm talking about?"

Lieutenant Gates suddenly realized what this conversation was all about. "Yeah, I know. They were the only cops I arrested.....Go ahead, I listening...."

"I want you to go to the Fulton County jail, and I want you to drop all the charges, and when you do that, I'll release your family." The caller paused again. "Oh, that's right, you had no way of knowing that they were with me already, did you?"

Lieutenant Gates had to pull over to the side of the street after hearing that. Suddenly, he emerged from the vehicle and stood in the middle of the street. "You sonofabitch!.. If you lay a hand," He stopped shouting because it was doing no good. He said softer. "Okay, listen, I'll do whatever you ask, but I have to know that my family is safe first.....Let me talk to them, please!" Suddenly, he heard a car horn blowing behind him, causing him to jump to the side of his car. "I'm sorry!" He shouted to the motorist.

There was total silence at first, and then there was sobbing from Susan Gates and his daughter, Pamela coming through the phone. Then the caller was back on the phone, "That's all you're going to get, Mr. Police-man.....Now, go do what I told you to do, or you won't be hearing these two crying bitches again."

"Okay, I'll do it,....just don't harm my family!" He jumped back into the car and began to drive like a speed demon heading for the Fulton County jail. Within thirty minutes, he had finalized the release of the three officers. He called the dispatcher again with hopes of getting the number that the caller had used, but the dispatcher could not make the call. He tried to think of someone who had a voice to match the one on the phone, but he had no luck in that area either. He then ordered dispatcher to retrieve the number and make a callback, hoping that caller would answer the phone. Again, there was no such luck. Everything that was tried, he came up empty.

Finally, a call came through again by way of the dispatcher, and she patched Gates in to the caller. "Mr. Police-man, you can find your family on Old Gordon Road just outside the city limits. Turn right on Mead Street, and follow the road to an old abandoned house, they'll be waiting for you." The caller immediately hung up the phone.

"Wait, wait!!" He became frustrated beyond anything that he had ever felt, but this was no time to panic, he told himself. Again, he ordered the dispatcher to try and locate where the call had originated, but there no way of tracing the call. The dispatcher advised Gates of the situation as he raced towards the location that the caller had given him. "Okay, radio, have backup to meet me at the location, I'm on my way there now."

A few minutes later, he arrived at the abandoned house on Mead Street off Old Gordon Road, it was just as the caller had described. The night was pitched black, not even the moon lit sky could help him see any better. He slowly emerged from the vehicle, pulling out his weapon, and walking toward the shack, leaving the car headlights shinning towards the front door of the house.

Stepping up onto the creaky porch, he paused to listen for any kind of sounds coming from the inside. There was not a sound as he continued to move forward. Stopping again in front of the door, he had a gut feeling that something about this whole setup was not exactly as it appeared to be. He reached out with his left hand while holding his automatic in his right hand, and quietly pushed the door open. It creaked loudly as it slowly swung open. From the glare of the high beam headlights, he saw his wife and daughter sitting back to back, and tied to two wooden straight chairs. He wanted to rush in, but instead, he softly whispered their names, "Susan,….Pamela…"

There was no movement, and there was no sound coming from either female. Their heads were slumped down on their breasts as if they were unconscious. He pulled his pocket flashlight from his hip pocket, and shinned to the floor as he carefully stepped closer towards his family. He could not see it, but to him, this felt just like a trap that had set to catch a rat, and it seemed like he was that rat. But he was only a few feet from his family, and he had to find out if they were okay. Therefore, trap or no trap, he had to do what must be done to save them.

One, two, three steps closer, and he would be able to get them out of the old smelly shack. Finally, he was there, standing beside his wife and daughter. He shinned his light down on them, and that was when a wave of terror swept through his body like a bolt of lightening. He suddenly realized that there was blood running down from both women throats onto the flood. They had been murdered as he took one step back and began to scream as loud as his voice would allow him. But then, he realized something else that was not suppose to have been there, it was a red flashing light that was on the opposite side of one of the chairs that was shielded by them when he entered the house. And on that timer it had .05 seconds remaining. "Oh my God!……" He shouted as he tried to shield himself from the blast by pushing over the two chairs and falling on top them.

The massive bomb exploded as it been timed to do causing a combination of fire, smoke, and noise that could be heard and seen for miles away. The old building simply disintegrated into a million pieces, blowing fire and pieces of the structure out on the vehicle that Lieutenant Gates had driven. Shortly thereafter, backup along with fire and rescue arrived on the scene, but there was very little that anyone could do at that point.

CHAPTER TWO

FIVE YEARS LATER: It was twenty minutes prior to the Day Watch roll call at 0700 hrs., and a majority of the day watch officers were gathered in and around the basement of precinct three awaiting for the watch commander to arrive. But it was still early, and the day watch Lieutenant Alvin Clay did not believe in starting a minute before 7 a.m. unless there was a crisis occurring in his zone. On this particular morning, it was early in June, and the temperature was already humming around 78 degrees. In Georgia, it is always difficult to determine June from July, for both months always run into the high 80's, or depending on what county one lived in, it may run up to 90 or more degrees.

The Zone Three precinct was located on the corner of Atlanta Avenue and Cherokee Avenue, the south east corner of the city. And as fifteen Day Watch officers gathered inside and outside waiting for roll call, some were in a chit-chat mode about what had occurred on the beats the day before while others were sipping coffee, trying to get the sleep out of their eyes before their shift began. And then there were still others who were anxious to hit the streets and see what the new day was going to bring them in terms of crime fighting.

It was 0659 hrs., Lieutenant Alvin Clay and two of his sergeants stood before his officers in a calm manner as he normally would do each morning with an eyeball inspection before he began the calling of names of the officers who were scheduled to have been working that day. But then, the building suddenly began to shake violently as if an earthquake was occurring, and there was a loud angry rumbling from underneath the brick structure. And that was when all eighteen officers knew that something terribly wrong was about to happen. It was the building imploding with them inside of it. There was a very loud boom, and everything suddenly was pitched black as fire and a furnace type heat swept through the entire two story building within a matter of seconds.

What had seemed like an eternity took only a few seconds, the explosion was over and done with. And the damage left twelve Morning Watch officers who were waiting outside near their vehicles watching in horror. Of the eighteen Day Watch officers inside the building, only five managed to escape the imploding structure that killed thirteen uniform cops that were trapped inside. The five officers who stood near the rear door were the only ones who were able to escape alive, but even they were badly burned.

The Morning Watch officers who were waiting to change shifts began to scramble, running in all directions, and calling for help to rescue their comrades. Within minutes, scores of fire trucks, ambulances, and others officers were on the scene trying get to the trapped officers. Major James Butler, Mayor Clifford Townsend, and Police Chief Harold Martin were on the scene as well, all trying to figure out just what had gone wrong. No one, not even the officers who manage to escape knew what had happened, or why. As the rescue efforts continued through the morning, city officials and many police officers who were still on the scene, hoping and praying that they would find others alive in the rubble. Obviously, their prayers went unanswered, for every body that they recovered perished in the explosion.

It was around mid-morning when all thirteen officers had been accounted for, and there were none found alive. The Mayor called for an emergency meeting in the middle of Cherokee Avenue with the Chief and the Major of the precinct before leaving for City Hall to give the news media an update on what he speculated to have caused the massive explosion. As they gathered into a tight huddle, the fire department arson investigator approached the group. "Mayor Townsend, Chief, and Major, there's no easy way to explain this situation," The investigator said. "I don't know what type of explosive was used just yet, but as of this moment, I can say that this precinct was purposely bombed."

"What?!" The Mayor snapped angrily, glancing around at the two men standing beside him. "You mean to tell us that thirteen officers are dead, and five more may die, and someone purposely blew it up?......Why on earth, for God's sakes?!!"

"I can't answer that, Mr. Mayor." The investigator responded sharply.

"So, what do you think, was it a terrorist act, or what?!" The Major asked with an unbelievable expression on his face. "There has to be an explanation for this."

"Gentlemen,…all I can tell you at the moment is, that this was no accident. Maybe I'll have some answers for you later in the day. Give me a little time to find out what type of explosive that was used, and maybe I can tell you who would probably use the stuff."

The arson investigator walked away, leaving the three men standing in the street, glancing around at each other searching for some sort of answer. "Listen, until we know what exactly went on out here, and why these officers were murdered, we will give the media only the information that is absolutely necessary.….You men got that?!" The Mayor said in a very authoritative voice. "We do not want this thing to get out of hand."

"Yes, I understand, Mr. Mayor. But in reality, we don't have anything to tell the media.. We're as much in the dark as anyone else right now." Major Butler said.

"Mr. Mayor, I'll put as many investigators on this matter as possible until we come up with some answers, and get the sonsofbitches responsible." Chief Martin said.

"Chief, I don't care how you do it, or who you put on this case, all I want is results! And I don't want it to take two or three months.….I want results like yesterday!"

Major Butler looked at the Chief, then at the Mayor.….. "Look, putting a whole lot of officers on this case, running rampant through the city, locking up anyone who might look like a suspect may not be such a smart idea. The real killers will simply go under ground until things cool off. We need someone who will work underneath the surface. We need someone who can get to the bottom of this thing without causing a lot of fuss."

The Mayor stared at the Major and so did the Chief, and they both asked simultaneously, "And just who do you have in mind, Major Butler?!"

"Well, I'm not sure yet, but if you give me a few days, I might be able to come up with someone who might fit the bill…." The Major said smiling, but only on the inside.

"Major Butler, I'm not doubting your ability to get someone to investigate this case, but if he is outside of the department, how can he possibly help us?" The Mayor asked suspiciously. "And don't even think about bringing in the FBI."

"The FBI, no sir, it never crossed my mind…..But, we're talking about a possible terrorist attack on the police department, and we definitely need someone who has no ties with anyone in the department."

The Chief frowned, not wanting to believe what he was hearing. "Wait a minute!" He snapped. "Are you saying what I hope you're not saying?"

"If you think I'm saying that this just might be an inside job?…..Yes, that's a great possibility, Chief." The Major answered quickly. "I mean, why on earth would anyone want to blow up a police precinct, unless they are trying to cover up something, or get rid of someone? Outside of those two possibilities, nothing else makes any sense."

The Mayor looked at the Chief. "You know, that does make a lot of sense. And you say that this person that you have in mind can come in, and look underneath all the bullshit that we are bound to run into and get to the bottom of this?" He asked the Major.

"Well, I can't make any promises, but I think it's worth a try."

"Do I know this individual, Major Butler?" The Chief asked suspiciously.

"No Sir!" The Major said sharply. "No one that you know, I am sure of that."

The Chief stared at the Major for a moment in a suspicious gaze as if he could sense that the Major was not being totally honest with him. "Now, you do know that I know a lot of people, especially investigators who can handle this type of an assignment. Why not tell us who this person is, and why you think he's the best man for the job?"

The Major smiled. "I rather not do that, Sir…..This is not saying that it will hinder the investigation, but I rather not say, Mr. Mayor. I know you both can understand that."

The Mayor glanced at the Chief…. "Chief Martin, allow the Major to handle this his own way first…..God knows, we have enough on our plates with trying to explain to the media, the families, and the rest of the department as to what happened out here today. Right now, I don't have a clue as to what I'm going to tell anyone, regardless of who the investigator is. If the Major can get us some answers, so be it! Don' you agree, Chief?"

The Chief broke his glanced off from the Major to answer the Mayor's question. "Yes Sir, Mr. Mayor, whatever you say….." Then he began staring at Major Butler again. "If this mystery man of yours causes this department any kind of embarrassment or problems at all, you may want to start looking for another job, Major."

14

15

"Embarrassment!...Problems!" The Major repeated, glancing around at what was left of his precinct. "How much more embarrassed can we get?.... Do you realize that every officer who died in that explosion were under my command?....And that's a problem within itself. Look, I owe it to each one of those thirteen officers, and it is my duty to find the bastards who were responsible, regardless of how I may get it done."

"Well, spoken, Major..." The Mayor said, glancing at the Chief. "Chief, we have to come up with something that the families of the dead officers want to hear besides a lot of mumbo-jumbo.....Not to mention the media, they all are looking for answers that we don't have right now. We need to figure out what we're going to say."

"I totally agree, Mr. Mayor." The Chief said, glancing at the Major once again. "Major Butler, when you decide to get in touch with this mystery investigator, I want to be there when you do, do you get that? Remember, I'll have to sign off on anyone that you bring into the department, okay?"

Without responding immediately, Major Butler thought about what the Chief was saying to him. *Okay, since you want to play that kind of game, well, let's see if you can really handle the truth.* He thought. "Okay, Chief Martin, you're the boss. I'll be in your office first thing tomorrow." He then turned and walked away, returning to a group of his officers who were standing nearby still waiting for any kind of answers or news.

The Mayor stared at the Chief for a moment before speaking his mind. "I get a strange impression that you don't think too highly of the Major's proposal, am I right?"

"You're right, Sir. I think his proposal stinks!....I'm still not totally convinced that some of his own officers are not responsible for what happened here today."

"What?!" The Mayor snapped. "You can't be serious about that, Chief Martin."

"I am dead serious, Mr. Mayor..... And I also think that maybe some of his officers had something to do with the murders of Lieutenant Calvin Gates and his entire family five years ago. We still haven't caught the people who made that happened because they vanished into thin air. And we just might be looking for people who are cops....."

"Okay, I'm hearing that you are accusing some police officers of murdering Calvin Gates and his family. But if that's the case, and if you can prove your hunch, tell me why you haven't arrested these officers?!" The Mayor asked with a stunned look on his face.

"As you already know, Mr. Mayor, knowing something is one thing, but proving it is altogether something different. It was very similar to this precinct bombing, but there was not enough evidence ever found to point the finger at anyone in particular."

The Mayor stood in silent for a moment before saying anything else. Then he said, "That's a scary thought. To know, or to even suggest that we have a bunch of murdering police officers in our department who are willing to kill their own fellow officers. And the question I'm having a problem with is, what reason, for cryin' out loud?!"

"That's the reason why I don't like the idea of Major Butler bringing his own private investigator to look into this bombing. He'll be obligated to find whatever evidence that the Major so chooses."

The Mayor contemplated even more this time. Finally, he said, "Okay, lets' go along with his plan to see exactly who this investigator is…..And, if at any time you become suspicious, I want you to block the Major and whoever he's thinking about bringing in here." The Mayor turned and walked away towards his waiting limo. "I'm holding a new conference this afternoon, and I want you and the Major to be there!"

"Understood, Mr. Mayor….." The Chief responded softly. *Yeah, I hear you.*

By mid-day, leading into the afternoon, the news hotwire was popping hot with the story of the day about the Atlanta Police department. Many rumors were floating around among citizens and police officers alike about what had occurred in the Zone Three precinct. A similar tale was being spun to that of the September 11 attack on New York City. However, Mayor Townsend, or Chief Martin were not buying into the theory of another terrorist attack, especially on a police precinct. They could not put their fingers on just what it was, but this particular bombing did not have the same feel as that of a terrorist attack. Not that either man knew exactly what a terrorist attack felt like, but they had a gut feeling that this was not it.

Mayor Townsend waited patiently in his office for the latest report from the explosive expert who had examined the material found at the bomb site by the fire department arson investigator. It was close to 14:00 hrs., when the two men from the fire department arrived. Chief Martin waited along with the Mayor as the two investigators entered the Mayor's office. Charles Watson was the Arson Investigator and Walter Sutton was the bomb expert. "Have a seat, Gentlemen…." The Mayor said eagerly. "And I hope you have something that will give us some sort of indication as to what happened out there this morning."

As the two men sat next to each other on a small sofa type chair, the bomb expert spoke first. "Well, I can tell you what kind of explosive it was, but I cannot tell you who or whom may have used this type of explosive….."

"Well, just tell us what you know…That's more than what we have now." The Mayor said.

"The device that was used was connected to a time-clock that was set to go off at precisely seven o'clock this morning.." Mr. Sutton explained. "And the explosive itself was plastique connected to C-4…..It was a combination of both explosives. And, in my opinion, the two elements exploding together is probably what cause such a massive fire bomb…..In other words, it's a miracle that anyone got out alive."

"Whoever set that bomb, they were planning for everyone on the day watch to be inside the building when it exploded." Mr. Watson added. "And, for them to have planned the timing, they obviously knew the schedule of the watch change,…."

"Which suggests that this may have been an inside job, right?" Chief Martin asked sharply.

"Yes sir, it could indeed suggest that." Mr. Sutton answered. "But, are you saying that this was an inside job, Sir? And by that, I mean within the police department?"

"Yes, that's precisely what I am saying…But, this is not something that we can prove. So, don't let my suggestion go any further than this office, okay?" The Chief said in very firm voice.

"Yes sir. I mean, no sir….." Mr. Watson said. "But, since you suggested that this could be the work of other police officers, do you want us to extend our investigation among the rank and file of the police department?"

The Chief glanced at the Mayor as the door to the Mayor's office opened, and his secretary peek her head inside. "Ah, Mr. Mayor, I hate to disturb you, but Major Butler is here." The attractive black woman said in a hurry.

Without responding to his secretary, he motioned with his hand to allow the Major to enter. Then, he answered the arson investigator, "Mr. Watson, before we allow any internal investigation by your department, we're going to allow Major Butler to handle the investigation…..As of right now, we're going to keep a tight lid on this whole thing until we see what's going to happen with his investigation."

Mr. Watson and Mr. Sutton nodded in agreement as Major Butler entered the room.

"Oh, I'm sorry, Mr. Mayor, and Chief Martin, I just assumed that you were discussing what you were going to tell the media." He said. *"I don't want these two cooking up anything without me knowing what they're putting in the pot first.*

"Come on in, Major, we were only discussing the findings of what blew up the precinct this morning." The Mayor said. "And we also agreed that we'll hold off on any further investigation until you bring in your man. We're also trying to hold down any and all rumors of this being a terrorist attack, because that's all we need is for the feds to start snooping around with their people."

The Major sat in the only emptied chair which was situated next to the Mayor's desk. "Well, that's really why I dropped by, to inform the Chief that I am heading out this afternoon for the North Georgia Mountains where I hope to locate my friend."

The Chief stared at the Major before speaking. "Wait a minute, where you hope to locate your friend?!.....I was under the impression that you knew exactly where to find this person of yours...."

"Yeah I do. Also, Chief Martin, if your schedule is not too full this afternoon, I'd like for you to ride with me." The Major said with a slight grin, glancing at the two men from the fire department.

"You do understand that we have a press conference this afternoon, and I certainly would like for you to be here, Major Butler." The Mayor said. "After all, Zone Three precinct was under your command. It was your precinct that was bombed!"

"What exactly does, it was my precinct mean, Mr. Mayor?" Major Butler snapped.

The Mayor threw up his hands. "I'm sorry Major, but I'm not sure that with you being in charge of this investigation of your own precinct is a good idea. With that in mind, why not let someone else run the precinct while you run the investigation?"

"No!" Major Butler snapped angrily. "It is my precinct now, and it's going to continue to be my precinct." He said glancing at the Chief. "Was this your idea?"

"Well, ah, I thought it would be best, especially since we agreed that it could be someone within your precinct who might be our prime suspect." The Chief tried to answer with some kind of clarity.

"I'm sorry, I totally disagree." The Major stood, faced the two firemen. "Listen, will you excuse us for a moment? I have something in private to say to the Mayor and the Chief. And I don't think that either one of you fine gentlemen wants to be a witness to what I'm about to say."

Both men immediately stood and left the room. And as soon as they the men were out of hearing rang, the Chief blasted the Major with, "Have you lost your fucking mind, you talking to us like that in front of those two men?!"

The Major sat back down smiling. "Listen, neither one of you want me in front of a camera talking about what I think really happened to my precinct this morning, do you?"

"Major!" The Chief blurted out in anger.

"Chief Martin!" The Mayor shouted. "Look, lets all calm down. We all have to maintain cool heads about all of this…..We all realize that this whole thing was possibly done by our own people….And we certainly cannot allow the media think that we're fighting among ourselves over this matter. So, as far as I'm concerned, Major Butler, you don't to have to be here for this media circus that we're going to have today."

The Chief then stood, walked around to the Mayor's desk. He then turned around sharply. "What exactly are you trying to insinuate, Major Butler by saying that we don't want you in front of a camera talking about what really happened?…..What do you think really happened out there this morning that we haven't already discussed?"

The Major smiled before responding. "Listen, we all have been in this business for a long time. And we all know just what kind of police department we're running here, especially in the Zone Three Precinct. And I know what's being done behind my back."

"Meaning what?!" The Chief snapped.

"Meaning that I know that you two have had me under a cloud of suspicions for the past five years, every since Calvin Gates and his family were murdered.. So, I am not about to allow the killing of thirteen police officers to fall on top of my head as well."

The Chief walked back to his seat. "In other words, are you saying that you would point the finger at me and the Mayor if you thought that we were going make you the fall guy?…..Is that what I am hearing from you?"

"Like I said, I've known both of you for a very long time, and it's no secret around my precinct, or the entire department that I may have had a hand in Gates death….And you're just waiting for an opportunity just like this to throw my black ass under the bus."

The Mayor looked at the Chief before saying, "Major Butler, you have me all wrong, I have thought of doing no such thing. And if Chief Martin had it on his mind, he did not discuss it with me, and that's the truth!"

"I think the Major is imagining things, Mr. Mayor." The Chief added. "And why are you inviting me on this trip with you, Major?....Can't you do this without me?"

"Oh, sure, I can do almost anything in this city without you..... But, I just thought since you have all these suspicions about me, you just might want to see what I have to show you. I promise you that you'll be amazed."

"Chief Martin, I think you should go." The Mayor said. "I can handle the news conference alone…It'll do the two of you a lot of good to take a short trip together."

CHAPTER THREE

The drive to the North Georgia Mountains was approximately a two hours trip, and it gave Major Butler a grand opportunity to speak his mind to Chief Martin about the cloud of suspicion that had been hanging over his head for the past five years. As they approached the turn off to their destination, Major Butler pulled the unmarked city vehicle over to the side of the two lane highway and stopped suddenly. The Chief glanced around at the almost deserted road, wondering why they had abruptly come to a halt. He turned his stare back to the Major who was already staring at him. "What's going on, Major Butler,….why are we stopping in the middle of nowhere?"

The Major smiled before responding. "I just wanted to clear the air before we get to where we are going…." He said.

"Clear the air about what?!" The fifty-five year old Chief was dumbfounded.

"I know that Calvin Gates was a good friend of yours, and since his death you've always wanted to blame me for what happened. But what you're about to see will probably change your mind, and if you tell anyone about my secret, I will personally do to you what you thought I did to Lieutenant Calvin Gates."

"What the fuck are you talking about man!....Have you gone stone mad?" The Chief shouted in anger, realizing that the Major was threatening to kill him as well.

"No, I haven't gone mad, Chief!...But, you cannot get over the fact that I may be innocence of what you've always believed I was guilty of. Do you want to tell me why?"

The Chief paused before trying to answer the question. Finally, he said, "Well, you have to admit that you and Calvin didn't always see eye to eye on very many things. And I also think you may have been under the impression that I was planning to replace you with him. Calvin turned up dead, and you became my suspect, but I had no proof."

Major Butler laughed loudly, but not because what he said was amusing. It was the same thing that he had told the lieutenant before he was killed. "Look, you run the police department the way you see fit, and we as commanders have to follow your orders, or we will find ourselves looking for another job, right?.....So, if you see fit to replace me, or anyone else, that's what you do....However, what I'm about to show you up here in these hills, I don't want you to ever repeat it to anyone what you've seen, okay?"

"And if I do, then what Major Butler?" The Chief asked sharply.

"Or, you will never live to tell anyone else about what you saw." The Major said.

"Are you threatening me, Major Butler?!"

"If that's the way you want to take it, yes I am. But you can't prove that either."

The Chief looked at the Major for a long while before saying anything else. "You do know that you are not the only one that's carrying a gun, right?"

"I know, and you'll have the opportunity to use your gun. But only after you've seen what I have to show you." The Major said smiling. "But let me put it to you another way. If you plan to tell anyone about this, one of us won't make it off this mountain."

"Okay, that's fair enough, I guess….." The Chief said as he thought about what was being said by the Major. "You really would try to kill me, Major Butler?"

"You've known me a long time, Chief, and I don't usually say things that I don't mean." He pulled the gear shift down into drive and they began to travel once again.

"Does this mystery man who we're going to visit know anything about Calvin Gates and his family, what happened to them?" The Chief finally asked as they drove further down a winding two lane road.

"Yeah, you could say that he knew of them." The Major answered quickly.

The Chief waited for something more from his commander, but nothing else came. "Yeah, would you mind telling me just what that might be?" The Chief demanded.

"I could, but then I would have to kill you for real." The Major said smiling.

"Okay, I'll accept that.....So, I'll just wait until we get there to see what all the big fucking mystery is about."

"Yeah, you do that." Major Butler said with a slight grin.

A few minutes later, they drove up a long driveway towards a very large, red brick mansion type two story house, after announcing their arrival at the seven foot tall metal gate. "He's very private apparently. And from the looks of things, he is loaded." The Chief said with a slight giggle.

"Loaded, you mean like having a lot of money?" The Major asked smiling.

"Yeah.... I mean, look at this place!....Only millionaires lives like this." The Chief said with a loud laugh.

"Well, I guess you could say that he's doing all right for himself.... After all, he is a retired banker from New York.....All that he didn't earned, I guess he stole from crooks."

The Chief stared at the Major once again. "Wait, you mean to tell me that we're turning over the most important investigation in the history of the Atlanta Police Department to a fucking banker from New York City?!" The Chief shouted in anger.

Major Butler stared back at the Chief. "Yeah, what's wrong with that?!"

"Stop the car!....Stop the fucking car, Major!....Listen! Now, I've put up with all the nonsense that I'm going to put up with from you....Now, you turn this fucking car around and drive back us to the city.....And, as far as I'm concerned, you can consider yourself fired from my police department...This is totally crazy! You're insane, man!"

"Ah, keep your pants on, old man!....I was only kidding. My God! You're worse than an old woman who's going through the changes. Damn! You're so sensitive." The Major laughed loudly as he brought the car to a halt in front of the house. Before they emerged from the vehicle, he said, "Now, let me do all the talking. You don't say anything until I tell you to."

The Chief did not like the way the Major was acting, or talking to him...This was totally out of his character. But he was willing to go along just to get along. At least until he could find out what was really going on with this mystery man. *And I still just might fire his ass once we get back to the department, just for being an asshole.* He thought.

The two men walked up five steps to a country type porch that extended the length of the front entrance. There were two wooden rocking chairs on each side of the doorway. As Major Butler was about to ring the doorbell, a Spanish looking woman in her middle thirties opened the door. "Good afternoon, gentlemen, welcome to the home of Mr. John Sinclair....He'll be with you in just a moment, he wants to entertain you on the porch."

Major Butler politely stepped back, glancing at the Chief, then back to the woman.

"Okay, we'll wait out here."

"Would you gentlemen like some lemonade? Mr. Sinclair loves it this time a day." The woman said with a Spanish accent.

Major Butler and the Chief nodded yes as they sat next to each other on the left side of the doorway. The curiosity of the Chief was running wild as he looked at the Major and said, "Who is John Sinclair?"

The Major smiled before answering. "Everything will be explained to you shortly, Chief. Just bare with me, I'll give you all the details, I promise."

At that moment, a tall light skinned complexion man stepped out of the doorway following the attractive woman carrying a tray with a pitcher of lemonade and three glasses with ice in them. "Good Afternoon, gentlemen, sorry for keeping you waiting,....I was getting dressed.....I workout everyday about this time." John Sinclair said as he pulled one of the other chairs closer to the two men. The woman set the tray on a table in front of the three men, and she disappeared back inside the house.

"John, this is Police Chief Harold Martin,...." Major Butler said. "I spoke to you earlier on the phone about the situation that we have back in the city, but before you give us your answer, I wanted the Chief to meet you personally."

John extended his hand to the Chief. "I've heard a lot about you, Chief. I'm glad to finally meet you." He said.

Momentarily, the Chief was caught off guard. He glanced at the Major, then back to John as they continued to shake hands. "Really?!.... Well, that's a lot more than I can say about you, Mr. Sinclair. He hasn't told me anything about you until today." He dropped his hand down to the arm of the rocking chair.

"Lemonade, Gentlemen?....My housekeeper makes the best lemonade in Helen, Georgia....." John said smiling. "Now, tell me about what happened back in the city this morning?" John asked as he poured lemonade in all three glasses.

"Basically, it's what you've been hearing all day on the news stations." The Major replied before the Chief could respond. "One, or maybe there were several people who took the liberty of blowing up my precinct, and thirteen of my officers perished in the blast. As of right now, we don't have any clues, or suspects that we can think of. That's where you come into the picture. We want you to come down to Atlanta and give us a hand in finding the people who are responsible."

John looked at the Major, then to the Chief as he swallowed his lemonade. "And just what make you think that I can be any assistance to a city that has several hundreds detectives who could probably do a much better job than I can.....In fact, I don't remember much of what I did as a cop back in New York. Of course, I can remember bits and pieces, but it didn't seem like New York to me. It seems more like it was in Atlanta." John frowned, looking at Major Butler. "Does that make any sense to you?"

The Major did not respond as the Chief looked at him. "What's going on here?"

Major Butler drank a swallow of lemonade before answering. "Chief, hold on to your glass, this is John Sinclair. Except for his height, and physical build, you would never know that this man you're looking at was once Lieutenant Calvin Gates....."

"What?!!" The Chief suddenly rose to his feet staring down at John Sinclair. "I, ah, I thought Calvin Gates was killed five years ago.....And if he was, how in the hell can this man be Calvin Gates? He doesn't look anything like Calvin Gates."

"I know. But, oh boy, it's amazing what a plastic surgeon can do to change someone's facial appearance now days, isn't, Chief?" Major Butler said smiling.

"Do you know who you are, ah, Mr. John Sinclair?" The Chief asked slowly.

"Not really, Chief Martin. Most of what I know is what the Major has told me over the years. Based on what he has told me, Calvin Gates was a damn good cop in Atlanta. John Sinclair on the other hand is a retired cop from the New York Police Department. "

The Chief sat back down turning his attention back to the Major. "How long have you been waiting for an opportunity like this to bring this man out of hiding?"

Major Butler glanced away for a moment. "I'd say about five years." He said.

"However, this man as far as anyone else knows, except for you and I, think that Calvin Gates is dead along with his wife and child. And that's the way it is going to continue."

The Chief was not really convinced that what the Major was telling him everything that he should have been telling him to make this whole unbelievable tale a convincing story. "Hold on just a minute, Major Butler. What you're telling me sounds like a story straight out of some science fiction novel....How do I know that this man, who you call John Sinclair is really Calvin Gates?....Think about it," The Chief pointed to John. "He doesn't know that he was once Calvin Gates, and no one else knows except you."

Major Butler stood walked over to the edge of the porch, sat on the wooden railing. "You're right, Chief Martin, no one except me can prove that he is Calvin Gates, and that's good. But, you can trust me on this, or I wouldn't have brought you all this way to tell you a lie. No, he doesn't remember that he is Calvin Gates. However, his doctors who brought him back to life after that horrible night of watching his wife and kid get blown to bits and pieces, and being blown to hell himself, he is lucky that he is still alive.....And according to his doctors, they believe that one day his memory will return to normal. Of course, when that does happen, I want John Sinclair to be on the job as an Atlanta cop."

During the conversation between the Chief and the Major, John was constantly staring at both men waiting for a chance to say something. Finally, he said, "And when that time come, do you think I will remember who killed my family?"

Major Butler stared at the Chief before answering, "I guess that all depend......"

"Yeah, depend on what?!" The Chief asked abruptly.

"It will depend on whether Calvin Gates saw the people who thought they murdered him along with his family. Or, if there was something that he can remember that led up to the explosion." The Major said. "We all know that there was a phone call, or some other kind of message left for Calvin that told him that the old abandoned house was where he would find wife and daughter. Otherwise, he wouldn't have gone there."

"Who do you think that could have been, James?" John asked the Major.

"Well, you have as about as many suspects in your murder case as you will have in the bombing of the precinct, which could be a few." The Major responded. "John, I'm asking you to do this because I think it will help you regain your memory. Plus, as John Sinclair, no one in the police department, or anywhere else will know who you are, or what you are capable of doing as a cop."

"Amen to that!" The Chief said smiling. "Calvin Gates was one of the best cops on the force….If you can remember anything about being a cop, you will be a force to recon with….You kicked a lot of ass and took plenty names, John!"

"You see, that's why we need this man back in the city, Chief." Major Butler said.

"If this is Calvin Gates, I'll agree." The Chief said, glancing around at the huge house and property. "But I keep wondering, if this is Calvin Gates, how did he become John Sinclair who is obviously a wealthy man?…. Better yet, just tell me what happened the night that he died, and how all of this came to be? Tell me the details."

Major Butler stood from the railing and began pacing the porch while he began to explain the story behind John Sinclair as everyone else looked on, along with the housekeeper, Maria. "On the night that Calvin Gates went looking for his wife and kid, and he obviously found this abandoned house where it was rigged with explosive and was timed to go off shortly after he entered….Even to this day, I don't know how he managed to survive the blast, but somehow he did. It was around four in the morning, I received a call from a neighbor who lived in the vicinity of the blast had heard the explosion. And as he was traveling through the woods to investigate, he found Gates barely alive."

"And you think due to the explosion, he lost his memory?" The Chief asked.

"According to the doctors who cared for him in total secrecy, they said yes." The Major responded.

"And, as far as my new identity, whose idea was that?" John Sinclair asked.

The Major went back to his seat. "Well, I looked at your situation the same way you would have, John. As Calvin Gates, if the situation had been in reverse, you would have assumed that whoever tried to kill me and killed my family, if they knew that I had survived that blast, they wouldn't stop until they completed the job."

The Chief nodded in agreement. "Makes sense to me, John." He said. Then he looked around again. "And all of this….How in the world did you managed to make all of this happen?"

The Major smiled before answering. "When you're in possession of as much drug money as the Red Dogs unit was, it was rather easy….We had over five million dollars in the zone three safe that no one knew about except me and the squad. Of course, when the money came up missing, I told them that I deposited the cash into the city's treasury."

"You took the city's money and paid for a house for man who was supposedly dead and buried?" The Chief asked, glancing at John. "And then, on top of that, the money wasn't even yours to spend in the first place. Major Butler, have you gone and lost your fucking mind?! That's stealing city's money, don't you know that?!"

"Chief!" John shouted. "There is another way of looking at this. As he said, it was my team who had collected this money from drug dealers, right?" He glanced at the Major. The Major nodded, indicating that it was. "Okay. So, you didn't even know that the money was there. Plus, he didn't take the money for himself, he actually save my life, and gave me a new start. Now, what's so terribly wrong with that?"

"That's right, Chief! After all, you of all people should be jumping for joy! Calvin Gates was supposed to have been your best friend, remember?" The Major said, smiling.

The Chief then turned his attention to John. "Yeah, I guess you're right, I should be overjoyed with the idea that my friend Calvin Gates is still alive. And I suppose all of this new identity is going to take some time to get use to." He laughed. "But, Major, you should have told me about this five years ago….And why didn't you?!"

"Well, it was a case of trust, I suppose. And not only that, I was also hoping that John would regain his memory as Calvin Gates, and he could tell you himself."

"And what do you suppose is going to happen when he does remember that God awful night?" The Chief asked in a curious tone of voice.

"All hell is going to break loose, that's what is going to happen!" John Sinclair answered the question for the Major.

The Chief stared at John for a moment. "You sound like you're beginning to remember already, Calvin…"

"I'm not Calvin yet…Or, maybe I'll never be Calvin again. But there's one thing that I do know as John Sinclair, I will get revenge for what they did to Calvin Gates and his family. I owe that much to the old me."

"Now, listen, John Sinclair!" The Chief snapped. "We may be friends, and all that, but I don't want you going around shooting up my city trying to find whoever killed you and your family. Do you understand me?!"

"I promise you, I won't kill anyone until my memory returns, that's a promise."

"How do we know that you haven't already regained your memory, and you're just pretending that you don't remember?" The Chief asked, glancing at Major Butler.

"Chief Martin!" Major Butler said in an angry tone.

"What?!" The Chief said, as if he knew what was coming next from the Major.

"Shut the hell up!....Do you remember what I told you coming up here?"

"Yeah, but you wouldn't dare try such a thing. I'm still your boss."

John suddenly pulled a small automatic hand gun from one of his black cowboy boots and held it in his right hand, pointing towards the floor. "The way the Major and I sees it, Chief, by allowing me to travel to Atlanta to work on the bombing case, this just might trigger something that will help bring my memory back. And we both are willing to do whatever it takes to make that happen, even if that mean leaving you behind in a shallow grave up here on my property." John then pointed the gun at the Chief.

"You see, Chief, we want to be able to count on you not telling anyone, not even the Mayor about what you now know. All the Mayor need to know is that John here will be investigating the precinct bombing, and nothing else." Major Butler added firmly.

The Chief stood, staring at John who was still holding the gun, then at the Major. "Okay, I will do this, but it will be done on one condition,....."

"And what's that?!" Major Butler asked, but he could almost anticipate what the Chief was going to say next.

"If anything happens, I mean anything....This is all your doing, Major. I'll deny having any knowledge of this. I don't care if he is Calvin Gates. You got that?!"

"Chief, I wouldn't expect anything less from you." The Major said as he stood also. "Now that you know Lieutenant Calvin Gates is still among the living, would you like to apologize for keeping me under your committee of scrutiny all these years?"

The Chief glanced at John Sinclair, then looking at the housekeeper. "You can put the gun away, John Sinclair....Look, I'll go along with this little plan of ya'll as long as I possibly can. Although in my book, you both are a couple of con artists of the worse kind.

You've been living very well with stolen money. The Major made your life real cozy up here in these hills." He glanced at Maria who was still standing in the doorway. "Even got yourself a maid, or whatever she might be to you."

"Hey!...Drop it, Chief. The money was drug money, and it didn't belong to anyone. Calvin's squad confiscated the money from a bunch of rotten-ass drug dealers. And it was money that the city didn't know we had. You didn't know about it, and you still wouldn't have known about it had I not told you. So, shut the fuck up!"

The Chief became outraged that one of his commanders was talking to him in such a disrespectful manner. "Who in the fuck do you think you're talking to, Major?!....Do you know I am still the Chief?.....If you don't know, I will politely inform you that I am still your fucking boss! Do I need to fire your ass right now to prove my point?!"

John lowered his gun as he watched the two men go after each other, and he waited to see what Major Butler's response was going to be.

"I'm the one man in the entire police department who knows that since the death of Lieutenant Calvin Gates, you reduced my Red dog squad from twenty-five officers to just five over last five years. You cut my operating budget by two million dollars, and my precinct got the leftover vehicles that other precincts used the year before. And all of this happened after the murder of Lieutenant Calvin Gates who was the commander of the top drug enforcement squad this city has ever had. Now, in my own opinion, who would be the primary benefactor from getting rid of Gates drug squad? And whom do you think would have gained the most by his death? You are the one who practically shut down my precinct to the point of not having the manpower to keep the drug dealers from operating at full strength. All the drug dealings in this city are now in my zone, all because you shut down my drug squad. You have the power do it, and that makes me suspicious of you."

The Chief sat back down. "Is this why you brought me up here?! You actually think that I ordered the hit on my own best friend and his family?...Are you out of your goddamn mind, Major? Why would I do something as stupid as that? For God sakes, this man is my friend." He looked at John.

"No, this man doesn't know who the fuck you are….You could be the one person who's probably making millions by having this man killed." Major Butler said angrily.

"Hold up a second, Major." John said, waving his hand. "Listen to me for a second. Let's not assume anything right now. I don't believe that the

Chief had anything to do with my murder, or my family. But, if I regain my memory, I will know if he did in the course of my investigation, and I'll be more than happy to kill him myself."

"Hey, that's fine with me, how about you, Chief?" The Major asked.

The Chief refused to respond to the question. *Allowing this asshole to come to Atlanta is going to be more dangerous than I first thought.* He said to himself. "Can we leave now that you've got your man?" He said as he stood again. "And I hope to God that you regain your memory, and realize that I had nothing to do with what happened."

"Well, there is one thing that we all know for sure, only time will tell what we all want to know, who killed me and my family. And now, who killed those thirteen police officers this morning in the precinct." John thought about the situation for a moment before saying, "I suppose if I'm going to be investigating this thing, my first question to the both of you, who would benefit most by blowing up a police precinct in zone three?"

The Chief looked quickly at the Major. "Have you made any drug arrests out there lately?" The Chief asked the Major.

The Major studied his thoughts carefully before he attempted to answer. "Yeah, we did make several arrests in the past two weeks. And we found out that all the arrested suspects worked for Summerhill Slim, a well known drug dealer who has risen to power since Lieutenant Calvin Gates been gone from the scene. And now that I think about it, he just might be our leading suspect."

"Just how big is this Summerhill Slim character?" The Chief asked.

"He's the number one man in the drug dealings on the south side."

"That's big!" The Chief said. "And does he pay police officers to be his eyes and ears in the department like they did once before?"

"It's probably worse now than it has ever been."

"I'll be leaving here tomorrow." John said. "Do you have everything set up for me in the city?" He looked at the Major.

"Call me when you hit the city limits, and I'll meet you."

"Good deal...." John said smiling as he stood to bid the men goodbye.

"Is there something that I should know about as far as tomorrow?" The Chief asked.

The Major waved to Maria, and then answered the Chief's question. "From this point on, Chief, the less you know, the better off you'll be."

No further conversation was needed as the two men got back into the vehicle and drove away from the house. John watched the car until it was out of view. *Major Butler was right about one thing, the less the Chief knows, the better it is for him. I can't remember much from five years ago, but the Chief does seems very familiar to me. Is that a signal that my memory is returning? Well, at least, I hope so.* He was thinking.

CHAPTER FOUR

Later in the evening that day, John sat quietly on his front porch staring out across his property along side his German Shepard named Bo, waiting for Maria to finish supper. He could only think of the possibility of regaining his memory some day, hopefully soon as he would return to the city. That much he was looking forward to, but he was not sure if he wanted to become involved in whatever friction that was going on between the Chief and his rival Major Butler. The interesting part concerning him pulling his gun from his boot was pretty convincing he thought. Major Butler had informed him prior to their arrival what to do and when to do it….*Apparently, it worked according to plans.*

So far, he had been told bits and pieces by Major Butler about what had happened to him as Calvin Gates. But it was very difficult trying to picture in his mind, and to see himself as the man that someone went to great lengths to get rid of, including his family. The question of why, was very puzzling. Apparently, that same question was a nagging issue for Major Butler, and he really did believe that the Chief may have ordered the bombing. But now, it was five years later, and a similar, or the exact same situation had arisen again, and the same questions were being asked again of who done it, and why did they do it? This was a question running rampant throughout the police department.

Now, they are bringing me back in as an outsider to investigate what could possibly be two different crimes at the same time. Not that he was against this whole idea of investigating his own murder case, but there seems to have been more to this latest bombing than what been said so far, which was practically nothing. *I asked the question while both men were here, who, or*

33

what would anyone gain from bombing a police precinct? There seemed to have been nothing but a question mark written on their faces as well.

At that moment of his concentration, Maria stepped out onto the porch with a wide smile on her face. "First, let me say dinner is ready." She said as she sat next to John. "Secondly, am I going with you down to Atlanta?"

John returned the smile, reaching for her hand to hold for a moment. "I wish I could take you with me, because I'm going to miss your home cooking…And the reason I want you to stay here, someone has to take care of the house, and Bo. Besides, where I'm going, I can't even promise you that I'll be coming back. If my memory suddenly comes back, I'll be hunting for the people who killed Calvin Gates and his family. Taking you with me will only put you in harm's way, and I don't know if I could stand it if I cause something to happen to you."

"Mr. Sinclair, you'll be back." She said flashing an even bigger smile. "They tried to kill you before, and they failed. Now, you're going back, and there are only two people who really know who you are." She paused for a moment. "But you know, I don't trust, or like that white guy. There's something about his eyes that tells me that he can't be trusted."

"The Chief…..I tend to agree with you. Apparently, Major Butler doesn't trust him either. In fact, he even accused the Chief of having something to do with my death."

"The question is, could the Major be right in his accusations?" She asked.

"Well, I don't think the Major really knows if the Chief was involved or not, but if his suspicion is accurate, I best keep my eyes on the Chief, that's for sure. Or, if someone other than those two learns that I am really Calvin Gates, I will immediately know that it could have only come from one or two men, those two."

Maria stared into John's eyes for a moment. "Do you really want to do this?"

John laughed. "Well, Maria, just let me put it this way, one part of me wants to do it. And then, another part of me is saying no, don't do it…. But, regardless of what my inner feelings are telling me, I owe my life to Major Butler. And he's the only reason why I am going back to the city to do this for."

"But, how will you function? You don't remember anything about the city?"

John smiled again. "Maria, just between you and me, I can't remember a lot at any one time, but I remember bits and pieces of things, and I believe once I get back to familiar territory, and start being around people I use to know, I think a lot of things will begin to come back. I didn't want to tell them that, because I don't want them to know."

"Well, just in case the Chief or some other cop ends up being who you're looking for, I'd like to see the look on their faces when you tell them who you are." She smiled.

John smiled as well. "Yeah, that would be something to see."

*   *   *

The following morning was June 18th, and John Sinclair was on the road early, driving his recently purchased shiny black Hummer H-2 towards downtown Atlanta. In a strange kind of way, it felt a little like going home again although he could not remember much about the city from five years ago. Maria had promised to check on him every day that he was gone, for she hated the thought of her kind and generous boss not coming back to the place where he had not called home for four of the five years. He had been away from the city for a long time, a very dangerous place as far as she was concerned.

Calvin Gates would have been forty-five years old today, John thought. He based that on what he knew about his former self. *When I get to the city, maybe I should celebrate my birthday.* But then he thought better about that, he should at least wait until he found out what deadly situation that he was about to walk into. It was deadly because whoever he was going to be looking for had killed a bunch of cops, and there was no way that a cop killer was going to go to jail without a fight to the end. Suddenly, he could feel the Calvin Gates cop instincts kicking in. *This is going to be fun, I just know it.*

Two hours later, he picked up his cell phone and dialed Major Butler's number. "I know the address, so, I'm just going to go on to the apartment, okay?"

"Okay, I'll meet you there in fifteen minutes. I'm leaving the Chief's office now." The Major said.

The uptown fifth floor penthouse that was pre-paid for twelve months, and was located the in heart of Buckhead, an exclusively rich business and part residential community that was situated north of downtown Atlanta. Buckhead is like a small city within a city. A small rich man's city, a place where only the less fortunate can go visit, shop, go night clubbing, and have beautiful dreams of having been lucky enough to go there. Mostly white, but there were a limited number of African Americans who could afford to live in Buckhead. And now, John Sinclair was among the lucky few.

Reaching the fifth floor, lugging two huge suitcases behind him, he unlocked the door with the key that the Major had given him as they were leaving the day before. John was pleasantly surprised by the exquisite furnishings. *Wow! My friend the Major went all out on this one. But what the hell, when you're spending money that belongs to someone else, who's counting and most of all, who cares?* He thought with a grin.

As he walked from the master bedroom of the three bedroom penthouse, he heard the door opened, and a voice called out. "John!.... Where are you, my brother?"

"Right here, Major…" John said as he entered the living room. "Man, this is almost as nice as my own place." He said smiling. "Oh, I forgot, this is my place."

Major Butler placed a black briefcase down on the coffee table and went over to the bar. "Man, I need a drink bad!....I've been dealing with the press all morning. Everybody wants to make the bombing a terrorist act. They want to believe that Al Qaida has come to Atlanta." He poured himself a glass of straight scotch from a full bottle.

"Isn't that a possibility?" John asked as he poured himself a drink as well.

"Hell no!....The only Al Qaida in this town is a bunch of dirty cops, or some crazed dope dealers who are trying to run the cops out of the area by that nigger Summerhill."

"And that would probably be the famous Summerhill Slim, right?" John sat on the bar stool while the Major continued to stand near the bar.

"You would probably be right. However, we're not ruling out anybody at this point and time. You see, whoever planted that bomb, they knew the exact time that the day watch would be holding roll call. Drug dealers might know when we come on duty, but in order for them to know the exact time to set the timer on that bomb, they found out from cops. Or, those same cops did the work themselves for the drug dealers."

John looked at the briefcase that the Major had placed on the coffee table. "What's in the briefcase?"

"Oh, that's for you…I figured you're going to need some spending money, so, I brought you a couple of hundred thousand dollars." The Major said with a smile.

"So, you're still taking the city's money, I gather?"

"No, that's your money!....The city and the State carried a two hundred thousand dollars life insurance policy on you when you were killed….And not only that, I collected another half million dollars on your wife's and kid's life insurance policies."

John stood with a frown, sipping his drink. "James Butler, my friend, how is it that you are able to do all of this, were you related to me as Calvin Gates?"

"It's funny that you'd asked that question." The Major then walked over to the sofa and sat down. "Yeah, a matter of fact, I am related to Calvin Gates, he was my half brother, which makes you, John Sinclair my half brother."

John did not respond for a moment, instead, he only stared at the Major in disbelief.

"When did all of this happen?" He finally asked.

"Here's what I know. You, Calvin Gates father and my father is one and the same. Since I'm five years older than you, my mother got pregnant by your father. But they never married. My mother then married Will Butler, the man's last name that I have, and your mother married Harvey Gates, our father. So, that's makes us half brothers. And by me being your half brother, I was your only living relative and the insurance companies paid me your seven hundred and fifty thousand dollars."

John began to laugh. "Boy, you're one slick, smooth operator, aren't you?!"

"Hey, you don't remember now, but I taught you everything that I know as well."

"Really?" John sat back down on the stool. "So, just how much did you really teach me, I mean, how much did you teach Calvin?"

"Trust me. It will all come back to you when you get out there on those streets." The Major laughed loudly. "And, you're really going to like who I teamed you up with."

"Really? And just who might that be?"

"Well, I can tell you this much, she's as fine as frog's hair. She has a body that should be unlawful for a female cop to have. And, by the way, did I say she is barely thirty years old? She's young, hot, and sexy. And, did I tell you that she's your partner?"

"Yes, you did, but, just how is she going to assist me in working on this case?"

"Well, first of all, she has a master degree in criminology, which mean, she will be your on hand expert on how deal below and above the law. This of course, will mean that she will come in handy just in case you have to take matters into your own hands."

"Okay, what else can she do?"

"She fired expert on the pistol range, and she's a martial arts expert."

"Let me get this straight, she's an expert in criminal behavior, she's an expert in kicking people's ass, and she's an expert in firing a weapon.....Is there anything that she's not an expert in?" John said laughing.

"Well, as fine as she is, she can't seem to keep a man around any long periods of time. So, I guess she does have her faults. But hey, I think this is a perfect fit for her. She works in the Intelligence Unit, which mean that she knows, and has a profile on all the bad guys in the city. That, you're going to need in order to know who's who in this town.....Although you can't remember, but Atlanta's crime scene has changed drastically over the past five years. In many cases, the drug boys have gone high-tech in doing business. They don't necessarily deal from the streets anymore. They uses computers to send e-mails to their customers, telling them when, how, and where they can purchase their drugs."

"Let me ask you this then, is my beauty of a partner black or white?"

"Well, she's not all black, and she's not all white....She's somewhere in between. Now, to say exactly what race she is?...Hell, I don't even think she knows really. But, the good thing about all that, she's mighty pretty to look at. And to think, she's going to be at your disposal twenty-four-seven. In fact, one of the extra bedrooms you have, she'll be using it when you guys are not working."

"What?!" John snapped. "Why here?.. Doesn't she have a place of her own?"

"Yeah, but you guys are a team now. She has to learn your every move, and you have to know hers. This particular case is like no other case she has ever worked. If, and I said if you have to go after some cops on this case, you have to trust your partner one hundred per cent....You have to know that she has your back no matter what."

John looked at the Major strangely. "What is it that you're not saying, James?"

"What do you ever mean by that?"

"It seems to me that you are using this woman to keep an eye on me twenty-four- seven instead of the other way around. And if that's the case, why did you even bring me in on this case?"

The Major stood, went to the bar and poured himself another drink. "John, let me be perfectly honest with you about this case,…."

"Yeah, please do." John interrupted him.

"Your situation and the bombing of the precinct are as different as night and day. I'm saying that because I'm almost positive that my precinct bombing goes far beyond anything that either one of us could ever imagine."

"You lost me with that statement. What exactly am I getting myself into?"

The Major sat on the other stool at the bar. "I don't know what it is, or why I'm feeling this way, but I have the strangest feeling that this was no Al Qaida bombing, it had nothing to do with drugs dealers, and probably not even cops. It's much bigger than all of that. Now, what that is, I'll be damned if I know."

"So, how do you want me to approach this?"

"Very, very carefully….Look at all possibilities before you and your partner make any moves." The Major said, staring directly at John. "Whatever, or whoever it was that ordered the bombing, they will eventually raise their ugly heads. And when that happens, we want to be ready, regardless of whose faces are attached to those heads."

John poured himself another drink as well. "How much faith do you have in the Chief? I mean, do you really trust him?"

"Trust the Chief?...Yeah, about as far as I can throw him….However, I had to bring him in on this mission, or otherwise he would have become suspicious and presented a major problem for us. But, as far as letting someone else know who you really are, I think he just might run his mouth. However, there's an advantage to that, if he does, we'll know that it came from him."

"By that, you're telling me not reveal my real identity to my new partner?"

"No…. She only knows about John Sinclair. So, let it remain that way."

"Okay, brother, I mean boss." John laughed as he swallowed his liquor. "So, when I'm going to meet my partner?"

The Major glanced at his watch. "She should be here any minute now." As soon as he spoke the words, the doorbell rang. "That must be her now." He slid off the stool and slowly walked to the door. He immediately opened it, and stood before him was a five feet, four inch tall, long black hair, wearing black loose slacks, and a sleeveless blouse. A woman who was as beautiful as the name she answered to, "Seville, we were just talking about you, come on in." He said. "I've got someone I want you to meet."

When she stepped inside the doorway, she was in awe just as John had been when he entered. "Wow!...This is gorgeous. Is this where I'm supposed to be living?" She asked as she glanced to the bar and saw John still seated.

"Supposed to be living?...No, this is where you will be living along with your new partner, John Sinclair." He pointed towards John.

Suddenly, Seville was frozen in her tracks by what she saw. She tried hard not to show that she was even more awe-struck by the handsome creature that she was looking at. "So, you're John Sinclair, the man who I've heard so much about?" She said as she approached him at the bar.

John stood to shake her hand. "I suppose I'm that man, especially if you heard it coming from Major Butler.....But then, he has told me a lot about you as well."

"Really, like what for instance?" She said smiling as she sat on the stool where the Major had been sitting. He continued to stand facing Seville.

"It was all good. Is your name Seville like the Cadillac?" John asked.

"Well, it's really spelled Sevilla, but most people prefer calling me Seville like the Cadillac." She said laughing, glancing at the Major.

"I was just briefing John about y'all assignment, and how I think it could be very dangerous if you don't keep on your toes, and find out as much about your people of interest as you possibly can before making any movement." Major Butler explained. "And just remember, you're assisting John. Although he may not be familiar with a lot of things and places here in the city, but he is still in charge, and you shall give him that respect, okay, Seville, or Sevilla?"

Seville saluted the Major. "Yes sir, boss, will do!" She smiled.

"John, in the briefcase, you will find all your paperwork, badge, ID and so forth. Also, you will find a list of suspects who myself and the Chief feels might be worth looking at as far as the investigation is concerned. And Seville, you already knows what you're to do as far as getting a profile on anyone that you two decide to go after."

John walked over and opened the briefcase as he sat on the sofa. There before him were many neatly stacked and wrapped, brand new fifty dollars bills that amounted to seven hundred and fifty thousand dollars. On top was a brown envelope that contained his official police credentials. *I don't know how he does it, but James Edward Butler should have been a master criminal instead of a cop named Major Butler.* He thought.

"Right now, all we need to do is get the low-down on the people on this list?" John asked.

Seville went over and sat next to John to look at the list as well. She saw all the money which automatically sparked her attention, "Is the cash ours too?" She looked at John, and then to the Major.

"Yeah, that is if John decides to spend his money on you." The Major said smiling. "But if not, you both are being paid very well to do what you're doing." The Major walked towards the door, he then paused briefly to say, "One last thing, this mission is very top secret, Seville. No one is to know what you're doing, or who you're working for. That's the primary reason why you're living here with John. You can pose as girlfriend- boyfriend, or husband and wife, I don't care. But the secret will remain between us and the Chief of Police, okay?" He opened the door and left.

After the Major was gone, Seville was still staring at the stacks of money. "If you don't mind me asking, what's up with all this cash?"

"That's a long story," John responded quickly as he leaned back on the sofa.

"So, we have a long time living together, don't you think?"

"Yeah, but if I tell you, then I'll have to kill you."

"Really?!"

"I've always wanted to say that."

They both laughed loudly.

CHAPTER FIVE

Two days after the arrival of John Sinclair, a group of three men met in the private office of Ethan Johnston, a third generation heir of the General Joseph Johnston, the South Civil War hero who had managed to hide two billion dollars in gold bullions. The Union Army was never able to locate the hidden treasure. Ethan had been joined by two loyal friends, one of which had been able to figure out the exact location where the gold was buried for more than a hundred and forty years. His two partners were Major James Butler and Samuel Houston, a historian who was able to read the map of the late general.

The three men had met to discuss when and how they were going to extract two billion dollars in gold that was believed to have been worth a hundred billions at the present time after over a hundred years of being hidden from the hands of the United States Government. They were aware that if the government could get its hands on the gold before they did, they would not see or hear from their multi-billion dollars find ever again. Therefore, it was imperative that they keep any and all suspicious minds away from the site where the digging was going to take place. *And what better way to do that than to send the only two investigators on the case on a wild goose chase?* Major Butler was thinking as he sat at the conference table with his two partners.

"Major, I'll have to admit, you master minded this entire thing so far." Ethan Johnston said. Ethan was forty-three years old and had made a small fortune as a real estate investor. He was married with two high school boys, and had discovered the map of his great-great grandfather had hidden in the back of a painting that remained in the family for one hundred and forty-five years. "And for what you have done for our effort, you are entitled to a third of the gold."

"That should be about thirty billion dollars, I figured." Major Butler said, for he had already calculated his cut.

"Right." Sam Houston agreed. "And to blow up the precinct with your people inside took guts. And then to send the cops in a totally different direction was brilliant."

"But, how did you managed to bring in a man who has not been around this city for five years?" Ethan asked in a curious tone. "Was the Chief at all suspicious?"

The Major hesitated for a moment. In spite of what the other two men were saying, he realized that he had done a wrong deed that he could never repay. He had actually killed thirteen of his own officers because he wanted to become richer than any man he knew other than Ted Turner. *What a price to pay to be rich?* "John Sinclair is a man who at once upon a time was a very good friend of mine, but as another person. In other words, John was once a good lieutenant who was under my command as Calvin Gates."

Both men were staring at the Major as if he had a third eye in his forehead. "Wait, wait," Ethan held his hands. "You're telling us that this investigator who you managed to get put in charge of this case was a lieutenant of yours, but no one knows him now?"

"Right! Hell, he doesn't even know who he is now." The Major said smiling.

Both men looked at each other, then back to Major Butler. "How in the hell did you managed to do that?" Sam Houston asked with a wide grin.

"Yeah, I'd like to know that myself." Ethan added.

"It was all by sheer luck. At first, I really wasn't sure how we were going to cover up, or disguise the digging for the gold with a bunch of investigators running all over the place looking for clues. But then, I thought about Calvin Gates who was almost killed in an explosion where his wife and daughter were killed. I had to steal millions of dollars from the city to keep him alive and pay for plastic surgeries. Plus, I stole enough money pay for him a new life in North Georgia, and no one knew that he was alive, or knew that I had taken over five million dollars to give him that new life."

"Wow! That's some story." Ethan said.

"I'll second the motion on that." Sam added.

"So, in other words, it appears that this John Sinclair owes you his life, right?" Ethan asked, glancing at Sam.

"Hey, it certainly appears that way to me as well." Sam agreed.

"But, there's only one slight catch...." Major Butler said. "John Sinclair primary purpose for being here is because Calvin Gates loss his memory in the blast. The catch is, by bringing him back to the city, it just might trigger his memory to return."

"You mean bringing him back to the city working as a cop?" Ethan asked.

"Yeah....However, if that does happen he will have another agenda on his hands."

"Another agenda, what do you mean by that?" Ethan asked. "You didn't cause him to lose his memory, did you?"

"No! And that's another story for another day." The Major said smiling.

"So, with John Sinclair looking in a totally different direction for suspects, we can go ahead with the digging as planned, right?" Ethan asked the Major. "I mean, we won't have to be worried by him nosing around the dig sight, right?"

"Not at all...He's going to have his hands full trying to keep from falling in love with the hottest woman on the police department. And they have a list of suspects that will keep them busy as well, because some of them have been dead for years."

"Wait a minute." Sam said abruptly. "You mean, you paired your friend up with a hot female cop who is going to be jumping his bones more than they're going to be out looking a bombing suspect?"

"That's precisely what I did." Major Butler answered with a grin.

"Damn, Major Butler, you're a brilliant ass cop!.....I'm glad you're on our side." Sam said laughing.

"Okay, gentlemen,..." Ethan said as he was about to change the subject. "Now that we've pretty much covered all our bases, I have a few men standing by, waiting for word to start digging. When do you think we should start, Major?"

"We should start as soon as possible, Ethan. With John doing the investigating, the Mayor is going to be busy looking to him for answers. I've already gotten permission from the Mayor and the City Council to begin turning the site into a memorial in honor of the dead officers. In other words, everything we'll be doing out there will look legit, and we'll be able dig up the gold, haul it off, and no one will be the wiser."

"All right then! I like the sound of that." Ethan said laughing. "Pretty soon, we'll home free with billions of dollars in gold. Gentlemen, we are about to be very wealthy men, thanks in parts to you, Major James Edward Butler, our friend indeed."

"Hey, James, I'm glad we came to you with our proposal five years ago." Sam said. "We really didn't know how you were going to react to our plans. In fact, if you had not suggested blowing up the precinct, it would be almost impossible to dig up the vault that's buried right under your precinct."

"Well, when you guys told me the story behind the gold, and about how Ethan's great, great, granddaddy had his men to bury it at that spot. And then, you showed me the map that indicated that the gold was still there, how could I refuse to not be in on something like this? This is an opportunity of a lifetime. As for my officers, I'll be able to give each family a million dollars or more for the sacrifices that were made by their love ones."

"Major, you have a kind heart, but a criminal mind. Why did you ever become a cop in the first place?" Ethan asked smiling.

"I don't know…But, I always believed that an opportunity like this would come along sooner or later. And when you two guys walked into my office that day, and told me what you had discovered right under my nose, well, I figured right then and there, a little collateral damage for two billion dollars in gold was not a huge price to pay. Besides, only I could have figured out how to destroy a police precinct without anyone getting suspicious as to why it all happened.

"Not only suspicious, the feds would be on our coattails trying to take it for themselves." Ethan said in agreement with the Major. "Plus, all we would get out of the deal is a fuck you very much, and our two billion dollars in gold that belonged to the Confederate Army of this great nation would be gone forever."

"Amen to that, my white brother!" Major Butler said. "And I say that without a prejudice bone in my body. Because when it comes down to this much money, slavery, and all that other bullshit just flew out of the window."

"I hear you talking." Sam Houston said in agreement. Sam Houston was a thirty-seven year old University of Georgia graduate with a PhD in Georgia history, and the Civil War. For years, he had studied and traced the whereabouts of the billions of dollars in gold that the Confederate soldiers had collected form white businesses through out the south and

France in order to finance the Civil War against the Union Army. For ten years, he studied the battle of Atlanta and the sudden disappearance of the gold. He discovered that the gold was transported into the city in covered wagons, but when the Confederate Army retreated eastward, the gold was not apart of that withdrawal.

After years of searching for the heirs of the man who was in charge of the gold, he discovered a real estate man by the name of Ethan Johnston. As he began to trace Ethan's ancestors, he realized that Ethan was the third generation heir of General Joseph Johnston. And Ethan had inherited a painting of the Southern General that was hanging in the basement of his home. A hand drawn map of the location of the gold was scribbled on the back on the painting, a place the general knew that the Union Army would never think to look. A hundred and forty years later, they had the map, and they knew the location. The only thing that was left to do now was dig up the vault that contained the gold still in perfect condition, and they all would be very wealthy men.

"Okay, gentlemen, in two days, we'll begin to tear down what is left of the old precinct, dig up our money, and rebuild on the sight a memorial that will be fitting for the real heroes. They gave their lives for us, and as far as I am concerned, building a memorial at our expense is the lease that we can do." Ethan said as he stood.

"Major Butler, I think the city and the families will be proud that you sought a private developer who is willing to donate such a fine memorial for your officers." Sam Houston added as he stood and extending his hand to the Major.

"I really appreciate all that you fine gentlemen are doing in the honor of me and my officers." Major Butler said, trying to hold a straight face as he stood as well.

"And, we'll meet again in two days at the site to get things started." Ethan said.

*   *   *

Later in the evening, another meeting of the minds gathered at Magic City strip club to discuss another matter that had been brought to the attention of Summerhill Slim.

By way of the rumor mill, or the word on the streets, it was being said that the cops were in their initial stage of investigating his drug operation, because the cops believed that he had something, or everything to do with

46

the blowing up the precinct and killing thirteen police officers. He sat in a private boot with two other men who worked for him, as all three men eyes were glued to the five nude women that crowded the boot and danced for the cash they were going to get as tips.

"Listen, I don't give a rat's ass what the cops are saying, or whatever they think! Ya'll know as well as I do that we didn't have a damn thing to do with no damn bombing of a police precinct." Slim lashed out angrily. He patted one of the young women on the buttocks. "Tell them, baby! You know we didn't have shit to do with anything like that. It ain't my style." He said to one of the women while sticking twenty dollars into her garter.

His lead man on the streets was called Mouse, and he sat next to Slim, leaning back on the leather couch as he said. "If you're asking me, Slim, the damn cops blew up their own precinct. We all know it were them who killed one of their own, the cop that in charge of Red Dogs a few years back.....You're talking about messed up! Yeah...."

Slim laughed. "Yeah, that's some messed up shit?!....Fucking cops, man, killing one of their own. And what's worse, he was one badass cop.... But, I'm glad his ass is dead. Now, we don't have to pay all them other assholes cops to keep that badass drug sniffing Lieutenant Calvin Gates off our asses...He was a mean motherfucker!!"

Summerhill Slim was the name everyone knew. His legal name was Jeffery Carter, a thirty-three year old African American who had been in the drug business since he was a teenager. At twenty-six, he shot and killed the then drug kingpin, Coffee Man Kelly for stealing his girlfriend. And immediately afterward, he took over the entire drug business on the south side. Slim took over a highly competitive drug business in a cluttered area that Coffee Man was not able to shake his rivals, and turned it into a multi-million dollar drug empire. Slim systematically did what Coffee Man had failed to do, and that was to kill off the competition. Now, the entire south side territory belonged to Slim.

Slim was well aware of the consequences if the cops were thinking that he and his people were responsible for what happen to the Zone Three precinct, especially from Chad Wilson and Bobby Turner. They were two of the three cops he paid handsomely to keep him in the loop concerning the drug raids that Lieutenant Calvin Gates and his Red Dogs squad were going to pull. However, since Gates ultimately demise, he did not have to pay the three cops off anymore. Although, it was not easy convincing the three cops that he no longer needed their services, and to prove it, he filed a police harassment complaint against the officers with Internal Affairs on several occasions.

Naturally, the harassment complaint did not work for Slim initially. Therefore, he was forced to go to more drastic measures. He set up a sting operation for IA against the three cops. One evening as Slim traveled along Georgia Avenue, he was suddenly pulled over by one of the three cops, and demanded that he hand over enough cash for all three cops. Slim complied with the cop's demand, emerging from his Cadillac, popped open the trunk, reached under the spare tire and came out with three thousand dollars. However, at that precise moment, two plain clothed IA detectives arrived on the scene, and arrested Danny Porter for unlawfully stopping, and confiscating money from a citizen without probable cause. Danny Porter was given an opportunity to resign from the force, or he could fight his case in court and risk going to prison. He chose to resign, but he still keeps in touch with his two friends, Chad Wilson and Bobby Turner.

"What's on your mind, Slim besides all of this hot pussy staring us in the face?" G-Money asked. He was the third man in the booth. G-Money was his street name. His legal name was Gregory Mason, third in command behind Mouse. He joined the family after the cop incident, and he had heard talk of how the cops were being paid weekly salaries to keep them informed and out of jail.

"Nothing man,.....I was thinking about that dirty cop named Danny Porter when Internal Affairs busted his funky ass for trying to take my money." Slim answered with a loud laugh. "Yeah, since them three dudes been out of action, we owned this town, man! Do you two niggers hear what I'm saying?! I'm talking about some real shit here."

"Yeah, we hear you Slim!" Mouse shouted back. Mouse legal name was Michael Wise, and he had been with Slim since taking over the operation. Seven years and counting, and they had made millions in the drug business. And all during that time, they had managed to stay out of prison, in spite of the fact that the police knew what they were doing. They did not need police informants anymore, they were operating twenty-four hours a day, and the police very seldom arrested anyone connected to their operation. Slim had gone high-tech in the drug business, all orders were made by e-mails, and those orders were made in codes, just in case the cops were chimed in on what they were doing.

Magic City was owned by Slim. And he along with his two lieutenants would make nightly visits to the club to get what they called a "Fix". A fix was having sex with as many as four or five women at one time before returning to their headquarters on the south side. "You know, this is a life that I don't ever want to die from." Slim said laughing. "I mean, look at us, we're in our own private boot, in my club with five of the most bad-ass women in the city. We've got more money than God, and we're all young ass niggers. Man, if heaven is anything like this, just let me die now, Lord….But if it ain't, you can leave my black ass right here on earth in this so-called hell hole!"

"I heard that shit, Slim!" Mouse agreed wholeheartedly.

"We're some very rich niggas, and the women love what we've got going. And they love riding these monsters too!" G- Money added, patting himself between the legs.

Summerhill Slim thought of himself as the new "King of the south side", illegal, but still King nonetheless. The Summerhill community was very similar in many ways to the "Black Wall Street" community in Tulsa, Oklahoma prior to 1921. Black Wall Street was a community of African Americans who built the most affluent all-black community in America. That is until June 1, 1921, when a group of very angry, and very envious white men populated mostly by the Ku Klux Klan, burned down more than 1,500 homes and killed more than 3,000 African Americans. Needless to say, what happened in Tulsa probably will never be repeated, but Slim was not taking any chances. Over the past four years, he hired more than fifty armed body guards to patrol the south side in private vehicles, and they reported to his headquarters at least once a day for briefings. The security primary purpose was to make certain that no one entered the community without his knowledge of them being there. That was including the cops.

Slim considered himself, along with many others as the mayor of the Summerhill. There were many black owned businesses that were bankrolled by his powerful organization. Even at the young age of thirty-three, and stood a towering six foot, five inches tall, he was a giant in the business world of Atlanta. He was also the man that the Mayor of the city had to rub shoulders with at election time in order to get the Black votes on the south side. If the word on the streets was that Slim wanted a certain individual elected in city government, and it would need the south side vote to get that person elected. The entire voting south side would cast their votes for that particular individual. The south side was a stumping ground for local politicians, but they all knew that they had to go through Summerhill Slim in order to get what they wanted from the people. Everyone knew that Summrerhill Slim was the man with the connections. Without him, or a word from him, the south side stood still.

CHAPTER SIX

On Friday evening approximately 20:15 hrs., John Sinclair's shiny black Hummer pulled into the front entrance of the Gold Club. The Gold Club was the most elegant, pricy, strip club in the city, and all the big money spenders and big tippers frequent the club on a regular basis to see some of the finest and gorgeous nude dancers in the city. The Gold Club was the one club where politicians, professional athletes, and entertainers alike hung out on any given evening for female companionship and lots of sexual fun.

The valet rushed to the passenger's door first, allowing Seville to emerged, and ran around to the driver's side to allow John to get out. "Welcome to the Gold Club, Sir." The valet said as he handed John a parking ticket and sliding into the driver's seat. John placed the ticket into the inside pocket of his suit jacket. He and Seville then proceeded into the club. Seville was one of the most beautiful women that John has seen in his short life span as she led the way. But as soon as he entered the club, John suddenly realized that there were many more beautiful women in Atlanta because the Gold Club was filled from top to bottom with beautiful women.

"One of the men listed on our list of suspects is the owner of all this." Seville said as they waited to be seated by the hostess. "And this is where anybody who thinks they're somebody hangs out seven days a week.... More money change hands in here than it does at the Federal Reserve." She glanced at John smiling. "Are you impressed?"

"I am very impressed." John said as he glanced around the massive two level paradise filled with mostly male patrons. "And just what we expect find in here?"

"Well, I certainly don't think this guy would blow up a precinct, but he might have heard rumors of someone who know someone who did." She walked ahead following the hostess who was leading them to a table on the far end of the upper level. As soon as they were seated, and before the hostess could say anything, Seville said, "I'm Investigator Seville Patterson, and this is John Sinclair, my partner, and we would like to speak to Mr. Egor Kolenka, the owner concerning a personal matter."

The slim woman smiled politely and said, "Mr. Kolenka is not in the club at the moment, but he should be back at any minute now. And I will give him your message then...Your waitress will be with you in just a moment."

When the woman left, John looked at Seville with a smile. "You seem to know your way around this place, and the people who are in the know."

"Yes, I do. Working in the Intelligence unit allows me to take closer looks at all the major players in this town. And isn't that why we were brought together as a team?"

John did not respond he only stared at Seville. *I've been wondering about that for the past two days myself.* "According to our boss, we are perfectly suited for this unusual assignment, and of course, for each other." He said finally.

The waitress suddenly walked up to their table. "May I take your orders for dinner, or would you like to order from the bar first?" She asked with her eyes fixed on John.

John and Seville placed their orders for dinner and drinks from the bar. Seville then focused her attention on John again. "What exactly did you mean by that comment that you made?.....You don't think that we are suited for each other?"

"No, no, I didn't mean it like that...." He said in a serious tone. "I am of the opinion that Major Butler may have had more than one motive for putting us together. I mean, you're beautiful and single, I'm single, at least I think I am. And he fixed it where we would have to share the same living space. Doesn't that seem rather strange to you?"

Seville thought for a moment. *Now, that you mentioned it, it does seem a little odd that he would have us living together. I mean, John is rather tall and handsome, and most women I know would give anything to go to bed with him.* "Ah, maybe, as he said, we need to be close together on figuring this thing out." She said after a long pause. "Do you have any objections to our living arrangements?"

"Not really!" John said automatically. "In fact, I think it's a great idea....It gives us an opportunity to get to know each other on a semi-personal basis, if you know what I mean."

"No, I don't know what you mean....Why don't you tell me what you mean." She said staring him in the eyes.

At that moment, the hostess reappeared at their table along with a tall, neatly dressed man, in a dark suit, a black shirt with no tie. "This is Mr. Kolenka, the owner." The woman said, then turned and walked away.

The tall Russian stared at Seville for a moment realizing that he recognized her beautiful face. "Seville, my Princess!" He said with a wide smile. "I am surprised to see you here tonight."

John suddenly turned to look at Seville, for he was shocked that the man knew his partner. "You two know each other?" He asked softly.

Seville grabbed John by the hand, and squeezed it. "Yes, this is my old boss. I worked as a stripper while I was in college." She said to John. Then she focused her attention to Egor Kolenka. "It's so good to see you again, Mr. Kolenka. Can you talk to us for a moment?"

Kolenka smiled, as he sat in the seat across from them. "Sure, Seville, I'll be more than happy to talk to you, and ahh.....," He paused, glancing across the table at John.

"Oh, this is my partner, John Sinclair." She said.

"Mr. Sinclair, it's nice to meet you....Any friend of Seville is a friend of mines." He shook John's hand. "Now, what bring you two fine officers to my establishment?"

Seville shortened her smile to a serious expression. "I'm sure you've heard about the bombing of the police precinct a few days ago....Well, we're working that case, and I know you hear a lot of rumors floating through your club. Have you heard any talk lately, or maybe have some ideas as to who might have wanted to blow up a police precinct?"

Kolenka stared at Seville, then at John for a moment. "I heard that it was an act of terrorism. But I'm sure terrorists are not necessarily your primary suspects, is it?...."

"Right, because you know as well as we do that it was not an act of terrorism as we know terrorism to be. It was more of an act of someone, or a group of people, such as drug dealers trying to run the cops out of their neighborhood. Would you say that is a very good possibility?" John asked, cutting him off from what he was about to say.

"Well, I'm sure you know as well as I do that anything is possible." The Russian said. "However, you may want to look within your own department while you're checking out all the other possibilities.....Even some of your own top brass thinks that this may have been an inside job."

"But why?" Seville asked. "I mean, why would a bunch of cops want to blow up and killed their own?....I can't really make any sense out that theory, Mr. Kolenka."

"I didn't say it was a fact." He smiled. "However, if you think that the bombing had something to do with drugs, you may want to start with Jeffery Carter, better known as Summerhill Slim. It would seem reasonable to assume that he may have had something to do with it since he is operating out of that neighborhood."

John suddenly changed the subject. "Did you know a police lieutenant by the name of Calvin Gates?"

"Calvin Gates." The Russian repeated as he paused to think. "Wasn't he the cop who was murdered along with his family in another explosion similar to the precinct?"

"Yes." John said sharply.

"I knew of him, and from what I hear, he was an act of terrorism all by himself." Kolenka said smiling.

Seville looked at John with a curious gleam in her eyes. *Why on earth is he asking about Lieutenant Gates?* She thought, but she refused to ask him why at that moment.

"And why would anybody say a thing like that about the Lieutenant?" John asked, hoping to spark some kind of conversation about Gates.

"Personally, I didn't know that much about the Lieutenant, I only heard things about the kind of cop he was. And as far as I can tell, he didn't take any crap off drug dealers." Kolenka looked at Seville and said, "Listen, Sweetheart, you two can stay as long as you like.....And everything is on the house. I have to take care of some business right now, and hopefully, I'll talk to you before you leave." He stood and left the table.

At that time the waitress brought their food and drinks on a tray, and set the table with their orders. As soon as the waitress was gone, Seville was almost too anxious to ask John, "Why did you ask Kolenka about Lieutenant Calvin Gates?...He's been dead for almost five years now."

"Five years, one month, and twenty-two days." John said slowly.

"Did you know him?"

"You can say that."

"How well did you know him?"

"Well enough to know that his killers are still on the loose. I also know that the people who were responsible, demanded that he let three crooked cops go free before they killed him and his family." *How did I know that?* He asked himself.

"How do you know about that?" Seville asked suddenly as well. "I've never heard anyone officially mentioned anything about some dirty cops being involved."

"Ah, I don't know, maybe the Major may have mentioned it." *It had to have been him.* "Or, maybe I picked it up somewhere else....Anyway, it's not important.....Oh, and the reason why I asked Kolenka, about Gates, for all we know, the same people could also be responsible for both bombings."

"You know, you may be on to something." She said smiling. "I mean, think about it, both incidents occurred to people who worked out of the Zone Three precinct. Wow! Now, that's amazing."

"Come on, Seville, I know that you have wondered about the similarities of the two cases before now." John said laughing.

She then smiled as she thought about it. "I guess I should have, but it didn't cross my mind until you mentioned it.....But, as I said before, you may be on to something, and we just might be able to solve both cases at the same time."

"So, after we are finished here, you want to check out this dope selling Summerhimm Slim dude before heading back in?" John asked.

She smiled. "No, lets get started on him tomorrow....Tonight, lets go back to our place and talk some more about how you know about Lieutenant Gates and the three dirty cops. However, I'll admit that I did hear something about dirty cops involved in that case.

But officially, every time the issue was brought up, it was denied by the Chief. And of course, the Major denied it as well. They both said it was merely speculation that cops were involved, and there was never any evidence brought forth that would link any particular cops to the Lieutenant's death."

"Of course, they would say that." John said smiling. *Did my memory suddenly return for a brief moment? No one ever told me about any cops being involved in my death. So, why did I say it?* He continued to think to himself as they began eating their dinner and enjoying the entertainment.

When the dinner was over for John and Seville, and they had gone into small talking about the way that the evening had gone when Kolenka suddenly reappeared at their table. He said, "Just in case you're interested in knowing, the gentleman that I referred to early this evening, he is now in the club. That is, if you wanted to speak to him. I will be glad to arrange a meeting with him. I'm sure Mr. Summerhill Slim wouldn't mind." He waited for John and Seville to respond.

Seville looked at John for the response. "You want to talk to him?" She asked.

John looked up at the Russian. "Are you sure he won't mind?...After all, this is not official, and he's here to enjoy himself."

Kolenka made a face. "Naw, he's a very nice man, especially when you get to know him." He smiled, glancing at Seville.

"Okay, if you say so. Now, if this nice man gets out of hand, we may have to slap the handcuffs on him right here in your club." Seville added.

Kolenka smiled. "I'll certainly tell him to keep that in mind." He then left the table.

Although it was in their plans to talk to Slim in the future, but they had no plan to talk to him that night. *But since he is here, we may as well see what he knows about the two cases, if anything at all.* John thought. "If nothing else, it will let him and his people know that we're looking into this case." He said to Seville.

Seville looked at John very carefully before asking him her next question. "It is my understanding that you're fairly new to the city. And if that's the case, how much do you know about the cop who was killed five years ago, Lieutenant Gates, that is?"

John did not know how to respond to the question, he only stared back at her without saying anything. Finally, he said, "We'll get to that a little later. Remember, you did say that we were going to talk about it when we get back to our place, right?"

At that moment, Kolenka came back to the table. "Mr. Jeffery Carter would like to meet with you now, and answer whatever questions you'd like to ask."

John seemed confused. "And just who is this Jeffery Carter again?"

"That's Summerhill Slim." Seville said smiling, glancing up at Kolenka.

They followed the Russian to a private spacious room where three men sat on a leather red sofa that rounded the four walls. The tallest of the three stood as the two people along with Kolenka entered the curtains drawn room. Slim smiled at the sight of Seville as if he knew her and was glad to see her again. John also noticed the twinkle in the tall black man's eyes.

He did not say anything though, for he wanted to wait and see if they really knew each other.

"Slim, it's good to see you again." Seville said as she sat first on the sofa across from Slim and his two co-harts. John sat next to Seville, and Kolenka left the room.

Slim then sat back down between his two friends while flashing a wide smile at Seville. "How long has it been, Seville, three, four years, maybe?"

"Five years, Slim." She said without smiling. "I can't believe you lost count."

John was really confused now. He butted in. "You two know each other too?"

"Unfortunately, yes we do." She said sharply. "While I was in college, working here to help pay my way through school, Mr. Jeffery Carter here, and I of course, we dated for about six months. That is, until he became the mayor of the south side."

"No, it was not that at all. You went and became the police! What was I suppose to do? You're a cop! And cops and I don't always see eye to eye. In my business, I can't afford to have cops as friends." Slim said, glancing at his two partners laughing.

John butted in again. "Look, I hate to break up this little love spat, but we didn't come here for a reunion. We came to find out what you might know, about the precinct bombing in Zone Three a few days ago….What can you tell us about that?"

Slim glanced at his two co-harts before answering. "The precinct bombing?...Well, first of all, I, nor we, had nothing to do with any bombing. Secondly, why would I want to know anyone who blows up police precincts? Look, if somebody blew up the precinct, more power to them, okay? And as far as I'm concerned, I don't want to know anyone that stupid. And if I did know someone like that, I'd be more than glad to call the cops on his stupid ass. However, the world is full of people like that, including cops."

"I don't understand…." Seville said. "How do the cops fit in on this?"

Slim leaned back smiling, lighting up a cigarette. "This is old news of course, but a few years back, about five or six years ago, the word on the streets was that some cops wasted one of their own because he was getting too close to them."

"Are you talking about Calvin Gates?" John asked eagerly.

"Yeah, that's him, Lieutenant Calvin Gates, a kick-ass kind of cop. A nigger cop who was getting ready to put the cuffs on some of his own money hungry comrades."

"And you think that's why they killed him?" Seville asked, glancing at John.

"Why else would some corrupted cops murder another cop, and his whole family?" Slim said, glancing at the two officers. "Why don't you two already know this? The case can't be close. Hell, the cops who we believed did the shit are still walking around everyday. Well, one of the assholes got fired a couple of years back, but,......"

"Do you know who those cops are?" John asked suddenly.

"Yeah, but I ain't calling no names, brother man. They don't bother me, and I'm doing just fine without them."

"Do you think there will ever come a time when you might change you mind?"

Slim thought about the question for a moment thinking what was the meaning behind it? "Is there some reason why I would ever want to change my mind?" He asked.

"You never know. Things might be going well for you right now, but who's to say that they won't change somewhere in the near future?....As you indicated earlier, some cops are very dirty, and who's to say they won't try and implicate you in the precinct bombing, and the thirteen officers that died in the explosion?"

Slim glanced at his two friends before focusing on John and Seville again. "What is it that you two want from me?! I told you that I do not know who blew up that rat-hole of a precinct. If I had any idea as to who did it, and before I'd allow myself to get caught up in some shit like this, you damn straight, I'd tell you who did it.....But the problem right now is, I don't know who blew up that building with those cops inside."

For some reason, he sounds convincing. Maybe he doesn't know anything. John thought. "Okay, lets say that you don't know for sure....What if I told you that the same cops who killed Lieutenant Calvin Gates and his family were probably the same ones who blew up the precinct, would you be inclined to agree with that theory?"

Slim laughed. "Hell yeah!...Look man, I've had enough run-ins with those cops until I'll believe anything about the fuckers. Why do you think that black-ass cop got fired that I told the Chief about? Because the nigga was trying to rob me, man! And I set his ass up with the internal affairs guys. They caught him red handed, hands full of cash."

"What was his name?" Seville asked.

"Fucking, Danny Porter that's who!" Slim said grinning. "He should have gone to jail, but the department allowed him to quit rather than take him to court."

Suddenly, there was a major flashback in John's memory. The name of the officer and a picture of his face became vividly clear for an instant. "Oh shit!" He blurted out without realizing what he was saying.

"What's wrong?" Seville asked.

"Nothing, I just remember something important. I guess we should give Mr. Carter and his friends their space."

Slim eyed Seville for a moment. "You know, I'm still available if you want to a try it again." He said with a smiled.

Seville twisted her nose she said, "No thanks. I'll stick with the man I have."

"Oh, yeah, and who's that?" Slim asked not smiling now.

She reached over patted John on the shoulder. "You're looking at him. We may be partners, but we're also lovers."

John almost burst out with laughter, but he held it. "Yeah, she's right, and I don't appreciate you hitting on my woman, Mr. Carter." He stood. "Are you ready, Honey?"

"Now, that's what I call having your cake and eating it too!" Slim said, looking up at John with a wide grin. "Hey, what can I say, Mr. Sinclair? You obviously have the finest partner in the department. And I'll take my hat off to you....I should know."

"Yeah, you should also know that you blew it, remember, Slim?!" Seville said.

"How can I forget a woman like you?....But hey, a man gotta do what a man gotta do.. Plus, I've got a business to run, and lots of money to make. You know how it is."

"Oh, yeah, I know it is all right. But do you call running a drug operation a business?!" She snapped as she stood beside John.

"Hey, it ain't just a drug operation. I'm the only drug dealer in this city that's worth his weight in gold. And besides, I can pay both of ya'll salaries for the next ten years. Do you know any other business man in this town besides Ted Turner can do that?"

"No, I guess not....." She said smiling. "But you just remember one thing, Slim, my old friend. Me, and my partner just might be the cops who will bring you and your empire down to the ground one day....You see, you might be all mighty and powerful for the moment, but time eventually will bring us all back to reality, including you."

Slim laughed loudly as he stood as well. "Listen, sweetheart, you and your cop friend here don't have enough juice in those pretty little badges you wear to bring me down. I'm connected all the way to City Hall, and don't you forget that, okay?"

"We'll keep that in mind when you and whoever it is in City Hall that you are talking about is placed in the cell next to yours', okay?" John said.

Slim did not respond as John and Seville left the VIP room, he only stared at the woman he once considered his "First Lady". *That old man just doesn't know what he's got on his hands. He can't handle a woman like that.* He thought as he began to smile as the two cops disappeared in the crowd of people. "Damn, that's one fine bitch!!" He shouted out in disgust with himself for allowing her to disappear from his life.

"Yeah she is, but it seems to me like she has other plans right now." One of the men in the room said.

Slim slowly turned to his friend who made the comment. "And who asked you?!"

They all laughed as they waited for their dancers to come and perform for them.

Once inside the Hummer and John drove the speed limit back towards their penthouse, he glanced at Seville. Then he said slowly in a casual tone. "I guess being a beautiful woman has its advantages, wouldn't you say?"

"Not as much as you would think." She said fast and sharply. "Me being beautiful hasn't got your attention yet, I see." She smiled.

"Oh, it got my attention, but I'm a little reluctant because we're partners, and we have a job to do, remember? And if we get involved romantically with each other, it might place our mission in jeopardy."

"And that's your opinion, I'm guessing?"

"Yes, that's my opinion. I mean, don't get me wrong, I've thought about it many, many times, but,…."

"But what, you're afraid of what Major Butler might say or think, right?"

"Well, that's one way of looking at it, I guess."

"And who's going to tell him that we are we are sleeping together every night?… After all, it was his idea that we live in the same house. Are you going to tell him?"

"And just why would I do something like that?"

"I don't know. You sound as though you and the Major are lovers or something. Or maybe he's going to spank you for being a naughty boy." She laughed.

"Just hold on, you're really taking this thing much too serious. I am not gay, and the only thing the Major and I have in common is,….." He suddenly caught himself. *Damn! I almost said that he saved my life five years ago.* He thought.

"And what is that?" She asked in a curious tone.

He tried to laugh it off by saying, "We, ah, grew up together. And, we've been very good friends for a long time."

She stared at him for a moment. "You know, it's strange that I've known the Major for five years, every since I've been on the force. And not once he has never mentioned you as a friend. In fact, the first time I heard him call your name was when he asked me would I be partners with you?"

"Really?…..And just how did he explain who I was then?….."

"He said that you were a retired New York cop, and Atlanta was hiring you to work on this case." She smiled for a moment. "And, he said that I would find you to be a very attractive man, and I would like working with you."

"Really?" John said smiling.

"Really." She responded with a smile.

"Well, I guess that settles it, we are the perfect match for each other."

"I guess it does." She laughed. "Does that mean we can date each other in the privacy of our own house?"

John laughed. "Don't you think that you might be a little too young for a man like me?" He smiled.

"Like I said earlier, if you don't tell anyone, I certainly won't."

"Well, I guess that answers all of my questions."

"That's right. And you have no more excuses. That is, unless you like living in the same house with me, and still refuse to be my lover."

"Your lover….That sounds rather personal, and freaky."

"Good. Now, we can run through our expensive pad buck naked as much as we want to. That is, if you don't mind. It sounds like fun to me."

John laughed, glancing over at her as he turned into the parking lot of their penthouse. "Okay, I'm with you all the way. Whatever you want me to do, I'll do it."

"Good!" She said laughing. "Now, that's freaky!"

CHAPTER SEVEN

Ten days after the precinct bombing, Attorney General Mathew Foster called FBI Director Paul Morrison and gave the orders to look into the situation in Atlanta. In his opinion, the bombing of precinct three and the killing of thirteen police officers was an act of terrorism. And as far as he was concerned, the FBI as well as Homeland Security should look into the matter to make certain that the enemies of some foreign nations such as Afghanistan, Iraqi, or even the Iranians had not invaded this country with their destructive tactics.

Special Agent Harvey Hill sat in the Chief's office to discuss the role that the FBI would play in the investigation. "Chief Martin, we're not here to step on anybody's toes." Special Agent Harvey Hill said calmly. "But I have been given orders that came from the Attorney General, maybe even from the President that the FBI and Homeland Security should look into this situation."

The Chief was seated with both elbows on top of his desk. He was angry because no one told him, or even asked him could the FBI take over his investigation. It was not that he wanted this tragedy lingering any longer than necessary, but it might, or probably would cause his department some serious embarrassment if it was discovered that some of his police officers were involved in any kind of way. That would not be good news for the media to get its hands on, or for the families of the deceased officers to find out.

"Listen, Special Agent Hill, I too, want to get to the bottom of this horrible mess, but with the FBI involved is only going to make matters worse." The Chief said. "What I mean by that is this, your people are going to be running all over this city, shaking every tree, looking for every possible lead that may, or may not be out there. I don't want this town turned up side down by the Feds. Besides, we have a man working on this case who is not really connected with the department, and I think he is going to get to the bottom of this thing on his own, without the help of anyone else."

Special Agent Hill sat forward in his seat. "Who is this man? Or better yet, what kind of investigator is he, if he's not, as you say, really connected to your department?"

"I am not at liberty to say. All anyone need to know however, that he's out there, and he's in plain sight. But yet, he's invisible to anyone who may be concerned."

Special Agent Hill leaned back in his chair. "Now, what exactly does that mean? Is he a ghost of some kind?" He smiled, but he was dead serious.

"Agent Hill, the only thing that I can tell you is this,….please don't get in his way. I know this man, and he's not one to be toyed with. He takes his job very serious."

"And so do the FBI, Chief Martin!" Special Agent Hill stood. "If this order hadn't come from the top, I could care less as to how you and your people handle this case. But since it did in fact, come from the top, we'll do what we have to do, and I'll hope that you and your department will work with us." He started to leave, but paused. "And by the way, will you kindly inform whoever this 007 Secret Agent is that you have out there, not to get in the way of the FBI….I don't want to be forced to make this a federal case. Because if we have to do that, it will mean your people will not be allowed to come anywhere near this investigation. And that also goes for you top secret agent." He turned and left the office.

Sonofabitch! Who does he think he's talking to? This is my fucking city! I'm the one who call in the FBI if they are needed. They don't just come into my office, my city, and take over. What the fuck is going on?! He thought in anger as he continued to stare at the door that agent closed behind him. He immediately picked the phone and dialed Major Butler's cell phone. "Major, you need to get to my office ASAP!" He hung up.

Fifteen minutes later, Major Butler arrived at the Chief's office wondering what was going on, or what was on the Chief's mind. He knew from the tone of his voice that something was not right. As he walked into the Chief's office, closing the door behind him as he asked, "Yes, Sir, what going on?....You sounded as if there is some of kind emergency." He sat in the chair that the FBI agent had sat in.

"We've got a slight problem on our hands. The FBI wants to look into the precinct explosion." The Chief said, throwing up his hands. "I don't know what brought this on, but the U. S. Attorney wants them as well as the Homeland Security on this case."

"I know. They think that it might have some connections with a terrorist group. That's all it is." The Major replied smiling. "It's no problem, let the FBI look anywhere they want to look, or investigate anyone they want to investigate. They won't find a thing.

I have the perfect situation planned for any outside investigation. First of all, they will have to depend on the information that we hand over to them before they can do anything.

Secondly, I have the perfect man in to do that job for the department."

The Chief stood, walked around his desk, glancing down at the Major. "So far, what have Gates,…I mean John Sinclair come up with?"

Major Butler looked up at the Chief with a stern gaze. "Listen, Chief, for whatever you do, do not let Calvin Gates names slip out of your mouth around anyone else except me. The worse thing you can do right now is allow anyone to know who John Sinclair really is."

The Chief suddenly returned to his seat and dropped down hard. "So, what's going to happen when his memory finally does comes back?.... According to you, his memory could pop back at any time now."

The Major smiled. "Well, if it does, he'll be looking for the people who murdered his family instead looking for the ones who bombed the precinct, that's all."

"And that could mean what?" The Chief asked with doubt written on his face.

The Major rubbed his chin. "Well, that could mean that he'll probably go after the three cops he that arrested on the day he was killed. And even if he does, he still won't interfere with what we're doing. In a few days, you'll be worth a hundred million dollars just for going along with the program."

"I sure hope you know what you're doing. This whole little scheme of yours could blow up in our faces, and all our asses will end up on death row."

"You know what your problem is, Chief?" The Major asked as he stood.

"No I don't know, but I'm sure you're going to tell me anyway."

"You worry too much about the wrong things."

"The wrong things!...Do you call what we did over there in your precinct the right thing? If I'm not mistaken that was about as wrong of a thing as anything can get."

"As we always say, it was collateral damage. Collateral damage, Chief! Sometimes good people die for the right reasons. And as we both know, we've paid our dues for a very long time trying to keep this city safe. But, at the end of the day, at the end of our careers, what do we get? We get a fucking measly pension that we can't live on. And as statistics have shown, we'll be damn lucky if we live five years after retirement. Now, be honest with yourself, Chief, do you really want to go out like that?"

"Okay, so we did it for the money. The only thing I'm saying to you, I just want to be able to spend a hundred million dollars when this is all said and done. But with the Feds breathing down our necks, I don't want anything to go wrong. No more killing, no more nothing except digging up that gold, you hear me?!"

The Major smiled as he leaned on the back of the chair. "Yeah, I hear you. But now, you hear me, and you hear me good. For the amount of money that we stand to make with what we're doing, if it takes killing someone else to get where we want to go, they will have to become just another collateral damage. It's just that simple."

The Chief stood. "This officer that you plan to use to feed the bogus information to the FBI, who is that, may I ask?"

"The fact of the matter is, I have two officers in mind. They are the same cops who Lieutenant Gates was going to arrest for being in the pockets of the drug boys five years ago, Chad Wilson and Bobby Turner. Danny Porter got himself fired."

"Can you trust them to do the right thing?" The Chief asked with a worried look.

"Yeah, and they'll fit right into the plan that I have in mind."

The Chief walked closer to the Major, placing his hand on his shoulder. "I'm sure you think you know what you're doing. And for all our sakes, I sure hope you're right."

"I have been right so far. Everything has gone as I have planned it, right?"

"So far, things have gone as you've planned them, so far."

"Just because the Feds are in on this case doesn't mean a thing. How can they find a terrorist group when there is no terrorist group? However, while they are busy looking for terrorists, it will give us the time we need to put the gold somewhere safe."

The Chief smiled. "Man, I like the sound of a hundred million dollars."

"Then, all you have to do is to continue to play Chief, and don't say anymore than you have to about the bombing, okay?" The Major said as he turned to leave.

"Okay, this is your show, and as you said, you've been right so far."

"Good! Then, let me handle this." Major Butler said as he left the office.

Chief Martin went back to his desk as he continued to analyze the situation that he was willingly participating in. No one was forcing him to be apart of this masterminded, murdering scheme of Major James Butler and friends. *When the Major first approached me with the idea of a buried treasure underneath the precinct, I thought he was crazy. But that was before I saw the map that the Confederate General drew before he died of natural causes. I was convinced that for a hundred million dollars, I could turn my head and look the other way while they blew up the building. I didn't want to go along with the killing of innocent police officers, but the Major figured that this was the only way to cause the city to focus on something else other than the real reason why they were digging in the spot where the precinct once stood.*

Once the gold is on its way out of the country, and finding the culprits to the bombing reaches a dead end, I am going to retire from this hellhole. And then, my wife Mary and I will quietly disappear into the sunset on some small deserted island. Hell, I can buy my own island then. He smiled as his thoughts ran wild for several minutes. But then, another crazy, but fantastic idea ran through his mind. *What would happen if I convinced Ethan that he really doesn't need Major Butler any longer? The precinct is no longer an issue. I can now become a partner instead of being a mere watchdog. Then we can eliminate the Major, and I will be line for a third instead of a hundred millions. I wonder would Ethan go for my idea. But why wouldn't he? It's less people and more gold for everyone else. I would go for my idea. But, wait a minute. I've got a better idea.* He began to smile as his thoughts became clearer. He clasped both hands together. *Brilliant!*

Driving away from police headquarters, heading west on North Avenue, and approaching Peachtree Street, Major Butler began to think about the conversation that he had just had with his boss. *Bringing the Chief in on this was the only way we can pull this thing off without him getting suspicious. However, I don't trust him at all. He's the kind of asshole that if the pressure gets too great for him, he'll tell everything that he knows. And that's one thing that we cannot afford. Ethan and Sam both agreed with me that if he begins to talk crazy and start getting shaky, we will have to eliminate him before he can tell anyone else what is going on. Nevertheless, as of right now, we need him, and we will allow him to live as long as we can trust him. A liability we don't need.* He thought.

Major Butler suddenly decided to look in on John and Seville to see what kind of progress they were making. He called John from his cell phone to make sure that they were in. "John!" He said when John answered. "Listen, I'm in the neighborhood, and I'll be stopping in at your place in about ten minutes."

As he had promised, ten minutes later, he was standing in front of the door ringing the doorbell. Seville opened the door and greeted the Major. "Hi, Major Butler!...So, you decided to show up and see if we're earning our pay, right?"

As he entered the doorway, he laughed as he said, "Not really. But I do want to give you and John heads up on what is happening with the investigation."

John entered the living room from the kitchen as Seville closed the door. "Is something going on that we should know about?"

The Major sniffed the aroma coming from the kitchen. "What's for dinner? Man, that smells mighty good." He sat on the sofa as John sat on the bar stool across the room and Seville sat on the sofa with the Major.

"John is a very good cook." Seville said. "Did you know that he could cook like that?"

Major Butler looked at John with a smile. "No, I didn't know he could burn like that.....If I had known you could cook, I wouldn't have hired you a housekeeper." He said laughing.

John looked at the Major, then towards Seville. "You didn't hire her, I did." *Why did he have to say that?* He thought.

"What housekeeper?" Seville asked curiously.

"Oh, that's just a little joke between John and me." The Major said quickly. "But he does have a housekeeper."

"Oh, so that's the female that calls everyday?" She asked John.

John smiled. "Yeah, that's Maria. She wants to make sure that I'm safe down here in Atlanta."

"So, you are some kind of like a big shot up there in New York?" She laughed.

"Yeah, I guess you can say that." *She thinks that I'm living in New York, and that's good.* "Anyway, what's going on with the investigation?" He asked the Major.

"The FBI is snooping around, because they believe this may be an act of terrorism.

They shouldn't be a problem for you guys, but I wanted to let you know just in case you happen to bump into them somewhere….They are aware that we have someone on the case, but when the President tell the Attorney General to do something, then, the shit rolls down hill from there."

"Well, we have talked to some people, and for some crazy reason, they're all pointing their fingers at the police department." Seville. said. "They think this might be connected with Lieutenant Calvin Gates case."

The Major looked at Seville, then at John. "Really?!" He responded quickly. "Well, this is what we've been thinking all along. But the problem is, we don't have a clue as to who the officer is."

"We do now!" John said. "Do you know a cop named Danny Porter?"

"Danny Porter, sure I know him. He was in my precinct. He was also one of Calvin's Gates officers on the Red Dog squad. But who gave you his name?"

John was about to say Summerhill Slim.

But Seville cut him off. "We don't want to say who just yet. Our informant thinks that his life might be in danger if he gave us his name, or the other names."

"Are you saying that there are others involved?" The Major asked, pretending that he did not have a clue as to who the other two officers were. "This is very interesting. But needless to say, this information goes no further than right here with us! Regardless of what you may hear, or find out, I want to be the second one to know about it, okay?"

"You say Danny Porter worked in your precinct, and our source is saying that he was apart of whoever killed Lieutenant Gates and his family. That makes me believe that if others were involved, then, they too worked in your precinct as well." John theorized.

Major Butler stared back at John. "Listen, John, I know you want to find out who killed Gates as much as I do. But, the fact of the matter is, we have a much more serious case on our hands, and finding whoever was responsible for blowing my precinct and killing thirteen of my officers is your primary mission." He glanced at Seville. "I don't want you two to get ahead of yourselves. Once we find out who was responsible for the bombing of the precinct, then we we'll go after whoever were responsible for Gates murder. Am I clear on that?"

"Perfectly clear Major." John said as he stood and headed back to the kitchen to check on his food.

Major Butler looked at Seville. "Do not let him get off this case to look for someone else who he thinks may have killed Lieutenant Gates." He said in a whisper.

"We're on the primary case." She said sharply. "But what's up with him and Lieutenant Gates anyway?....Were they very close or something?"

Major Butler smiled. "You could say that. Yeah, they were very close. Damn near like brothers, you could also say."

"Really...." She responded sarcastically. *There is something about this Lieutenant Calvin Gates that they are not telling me.* She thought.

Major Butler quickly changed the subject. "What's he cooking?"

"He's preparing a Chicken Creole with Chili cream sauce and Broccoli. And I'm not sure what else he's whipping up in there." She answered.

"So, in other words, John doesn't allow you in the kitchen?" He laughed.

Seville did not find his comment amusing. "No, that's not it at all. We take turns on cooking. I'll cook tomorrow."

"Okay, I didn't mean to ruffle your feathers." He said quickly. "So, where does your investigation to takes you next?"

"Well, since our source seems to think that Danny Porter may be linked to the precinct bombing, we're going to see if he has a good alibi for the morning of the bombing....Who knows, it just might pay off if we can push the right buttons."

"Now, that sounds like a plan to me." He stood. "Listen, tell John that I'll call you guys later in the week, okay?"

"Aren't you going to stay for dinner?" Seville asked as she stood also.

"Well, I would like to, but I just remembered that I have a meeting this evening with some of the family members of the deceased officers."

John suddenly re-entered the living room. "Are you leaving so soon?"

"Ah, yeah.....But I'll tell you what," He looked at Seville. "I'm inviting ya'll out to my place for dinner real soon. Is that okay?"

Seville and John said simultaneously. "Sure, we'll be there, just say when."

As soon as the Seville closed the door behind the Major, she turned and John was standing directly behind her. "What's wrong?" She asked as she moved even closer to him. "You want to drop down right here on the floor and make love to me now?"

"You know, this really doesn't seem like work, does it?" He said smiling.

She smiled back while staring up at him. "No, it doesn't, but who's complaining?"

"But then, as soon as we hit the right nail on the right head, we may have more on our hands than we may have bargained for."

"You got that right!...." She walked around him back to the sofa. "But, let's not rush into this thing. I kind of like hanging out with you. And if we find our killers too fast, the case will end, and we'll both go back to our own little worlds, right?" She sat again.

John moved over to the sofa and sat next to her. "Yeah....But maybe, you and I can stay in touch with each other after it's over with. Or, maybe you can come up to where I live and spend time with me and my housekeeper. I mean, who knows?"

She reached over and held his hand. "We've been living together for almost two weeks now, and we haven't done what the Major put us together to do."

"Oh yeah, and what's that?" John looked surprised.

"Come on, John, you can't be that lame! You know as well as I do that the Major had a reason for putting us together like this....I mean, we're like husband and wife, and we can do anything that we want to do, have sex, sleep together, or do whatever. Do you know any other cop teams, female-male partners who are paired up like this?"

"No, I don't. And the Major put us here in this place to do exactly what?!"

"Besides screwing our brains out, I'm really not sure. But, I keep getting this weird feeling that something is going on with this case that we are not being told about."

John moved closer to her. "Like what?"

"I can't think of anything. But all of this,..." She glanced around the room. "All of this fancy apartment, he giving you all that money, and we're allowed to do pretty much as we see fit. It's too perfect! Something about this is not what it's cracked up to be." She stared at John for a moment. "Don't you agree that this just doesn't feel right?"

I guess I've been so preoccupied with my former life until I didn't think about anything else. "You know, you just might be on to something." He stood. "But while we're trying to figure it out, let's eat, the food is getting cold.

They both headed off to the dining room laughing.

CHAPTER EIGHT

The dinner date ended and the love making began as they had hoped it would. Seville and John for the very first time got off to a roaring start with their love making in the shower. And it continued until late into the night. As far as John knew, he had not been with a woman in five years. But his loss of memory did not have any ill effect on his ability to satisfy Seville beyond her imagination of what an older man could do for her in bed. As their bodies melted together in a sweet sexual bliss, John's mind began to have flash backs of his former life as Calvin Gates having sex with his wife Susan. And in the middle of a total black out of what he was doing and where he was, he began to called his wife's name, "Susan, Susan,...I love you so much." He whispered to Seville.

Seville's eyes opened wide, staring up at John. *Who in the hell is he talkin' to, calling me Susan?* She thought. "What did you say?" She asked softly.

John suddenly stopped what he was doing. "What?!" He snapped. "I didn't say anything. Did I say something?"

"Yes you did….You called me Susan. Who is Susan?" She insisted as she pushed him over to the side.

He stared at the ceiling for a moment trying to remember. "Susan." He repeated. "I don't know,…" He said slowly. *But I do know who Susan is. She was my wife.* "Seville, I am so sorry. I was so caught up into the moment until I totally forgot where I was."

"And wherever you were, apparently, you were fucking Susan instead of me."

"No!..." John said quickly. "It was not like that at all. I ah, I have these flashbacks sometimes." He paused before trying to explain. *I can't tell her who I really am,* "Maybe one day we'll sit down and have a long talk about this Susan that I called you."

"Well, who is she?" Seville leaned over John, staring into his eyes. "Was she someone you were madly in love with? I mean, you said that you loved her very much. She has to be someone you know very well." She paused for a moment. "John, I'm not angry with you, I just would like to know who she is."

John immediately climbed out of bed, put on his robe. "Come with me. Let's have a drink on the terrace, and I'll try to explain as much as I know about myself and Susan."

Seville got up as well, grabbed her robe from the arm chair on her side of the bed. "I definitely want to hear this." She followed John to the bar and then out to the terrace.

They both sat in recliners facing towards downtown Atlanta. The skyline was as beautiful as it was amazing as they gazed out at the glittering lights of the skyscraping office towers and hotels. "I had forgotten what it look like at night." He said.

"From up here, it's a beautiful sight. It's so peaceful, and quiet. But down there on the streets, it's like all hell has broken loose." She said, glancing over at him. "Now, tell me all about this mystery woman and you."

John sipped on his liquor before responding. "Five years ago, I was married to the woman who was named Susan. I had not remembered her name since then, until now."

Seville stared at John before asking her next question. "What do you mean by until now?....I don't understand what that mean."

"Until now mean that I can't remember anything that happened in my life pass five years ago, including my wife Susan. Tonight, while we were making love, I saw her in my mind. And for reasons unknown to me, I called out her name. I don't know why."

Seville leaned closer to John. "What are you talking about?! I still don't understand what happened to you five years ago." Suddenly, she stopped talking. She stood up and stared down at him in total fear of what had abruptly entered her mind. "Wait, are you trying to tell me that after five year of no memory, you're Calvin Gates?"

"Yes, that's what I'm saying." He answered, watching the expression change on her face. "Of course, I don't look like Calvin Gates, and I don't sound like Calvin Gates. But I am Calvin Gates." He waited for her to catch her breath and take her seat again.

Finally, she sat back down with an unbelievable gaze in her eyes at him. "I don't believe you! If you're Calvin Gates, the Major would have told me. Why didn't he tell me that a dead man who once was Calvin Gates is now walking around as John Sinclair? A dead man who just screwed me silly, but he is alive and kicking, how can that be?"

John smiled as he patted her on hand. "You can never tell anyone. The Major is the one who saved me, and protected me just in case the killers tried to finish the job."

"Who am I going to tell? And even if I did, who is going to believe that you are Lieutenant Calvin Gates? Nobody!" Suddenly, she stood again and pulled her chair closer to him. "Now, if you are who you say you use to be, tell me how did you survive, and how did you become John Sinclair?"

"First, you tell me how did you guess that I am Calvin Gates?" He asked curiously.

"Well, first of all, when I first came on the department, that was all everybody was talking about, how Lieutenant Gates and his family were murdered. And then, there were those who thought it may have been an inside job. I took it upon myself to read the incident reports that were made available to me a few months later after I graduated from the academy. The reports mentioned your wife and daughter. Your wife's name was Susan, and your daughter was Pamela. And when you said Susan was your wife, it all came together. Five years ago was when it all happened."

"So, in reality, you know as much about me as I do right now."

"That's probably true. But I want to know how did you survive the blast, and how did you become John Sinclair?" She paused for a moment to collect her thoughts again.

"Major Butler! He's the key to everything, isn't he?"

"He is the key!" John said smiling. "He saved my life. It was he who made sure that I got a new face, new name, and a new start."

"But, how?...Or should I say, how did he do it and no one else knew about it?"

"It's a very long story, and I can't wait to make love to you again."

She laughed softly. "Listen, Buster, you're not getting back in this until you tell me everything. At least, tell me all that you know. Plus, we have plenty of time for that."

John laughed loudly while he sipped on his liquor. "Mostly what I know is what the Major has told me. Every once in a while, I'll remember bits and pieces about what happened to me on the night I went looking for my wife and daughter. Then things will get fuzzy in my mind again. *I remember getting a phone call telling me to release the three cops that I had arrested for informing drug dealers about impending raids that the squad was going to make. And I remember they kidnapped Susan and Pamela, and I was told where to find them once the cops were released from jail.* He was thinking. Then suddenly, he began staring at Seville strangely as if she had vanished from her seat. "I can remember everything that happened the night I was killed." He said finally.

She stared back unbelievably. "What do you mean by you can remember what happened the night you were killed?!" She repeated reluctantly.

"I mean, I finally know what happened. I can remember the cops who I arrested. And I also remember getting a phone call telling me to release them from jail, or my wife and daughter would die. But, whoever called me knew that they were already dead."

"Wow! You're just now able to remember that after five years?" She asked.

"Yes." *But maybe I didn't want to remember any of it until now.* "The doctors who put me back together warned me that this might happen once I came back to familiar surroundings. They said that my memory might come back in bits and pieces, and then it all might come back all at once. I think for all these years, I have been afraid that what I might remember would be so horrifying until I didn't want to remember any of it."

"Now, this is some strange shit!...." She stood, walked over to the railing, looked on the street below. "First, we made love, and you called me your dead wife. And out of nowhere you suddenly get your memory back after five long years. What kind of game are you playing, John Sinclair, or Calvin Gates, or whoever the fuck you are?!" She turned to face him with anger written on her pretty face.

He stood and walked closer to her, he held her hands. "This is no game. Until now, none of what I just told you could I remember." He looked up to the sky. "However, you can't tell this to anyone, not even the Major."

"But he saved your life! Why don't you want him to know?"

He let go of her hands and stepped towards the railing. "I would like to find out just what is going on as John Sinclair. Besides, Calvin Gates is dead and buried along with his family. So, why don't we just allow him to remain dead?"

She smiled. "Okay, Calvin Gates is still dead. So, what do we do now, John?"

"What do you mean?" He reached for her again, pulling her closer to him.

"I mean, if you know what happened the night you were killed, doesn't that change the game plan as far as what killers we're looking for?" She kissed him lightly.

He thought for a moment. "It could, but our focus is still on the precinct. We have to learn as much as we can about that bombing. Right now, it's like you and I are looking for a needle in a haystack. We don't have any suspects in mind. There is no kind of evidence to speak of. We really need something to go on! How are we suppose to find a mad bomber by asking a dumb-ass drug dealer, or a strip club owner? Maybe they don't want us to find the people who are really responsible."

Seville rolled eyes at him. "Boy, one minute you get your memory back, and the next minute you've got a whole new theory about this case. So, now you're beginning to see that we could be doing nothing but chasing after shadows."

"Well," John let her go again, and walked back to his seat. "The Major and the Chief drove two hours north of to get me involved in this case when they have investigators right here who could be doing a much better job. I had no memory of anything here in the city. So, why come that far to ask me to work on this case?"

"Maybe the Major figured that you owed him a favor." Seville said as she too   returned to her seat.

"Yeah, that's one reason, but that was not the reason they wanted me involved." John then laughed. "You know, he even threatened to shoot the Chief if he told anybody who I was."

Seville leaned forward. "You're kidding!"

"No I'm not! And it seemed that the Chief was literally forced to accept this whole idea of bringing me back to the city to work on this case."

"Okay," Seville began to theorize. "Let's say the Major wanted you particularly to investigate his precinct bombing. And the Chief didn't go along with that idea. But what do the Major have on the Chief to force him to go along with bringing you back?"

"I don't know." He paused for a moment. "But I know one thing, I think we are about to find ourselves involved something that may go a whole lot deeper than just the precinct bombing."

"You think?" Seville smiled.

"Yeah, I think."

" So, what if, we find out something that may, or may not involve the Major?"

"He's my friend. He saved my life, and gave me a new one. I guess the question would be, do we walk away from it all, or let the chips fall where they may? I can, and will walk away. But you on the other hand, you're a real cop, which mean, you cannot just walk away, or turn your back. You have to do whatever the law says do."

"Thanks a lot! I mean, he's my friend too. Think about where we are right now. It's all because of the Major. He has given us the chance to do something great for the city. Just what that is, I'm not really sure. But, he also gave you and me an opportunity to meet, whereas, otherwise we probably would have never met. So, let's not focus on him too much. Let's hope our investigation takes us in a different direction."

John smiled as he downed the last of his drink. "Hey, I am all for that. I mean, the man stole five million dollars for me, how can I go against that?"

"What?!" Seville snapped as she rose from her seat. "Five million, American dollars, all for you?....And how on earth did he managed to do that?"

"Trust me when I tell you, there's a lot about the Major that you don't know."

"Well, based on what you've already told me, nothing that you can say from this point on will surprise me about Major Butler." Seville said with a smile. "However, looking back on what you can remember about your friend, the Major, why do you think he brought the two of us together? And more importantly, why did he bring you back after five long years of you not knowing who you were, or anything about your family?"

"Bringing me back is still one big mystery." He said with a grin. "And putting us together is a bigger mystery. He could've paired me with anyone and it would not have made a difference with me in the beginning. However, as far as this case is concerned, starting tomorrow morning, we'll begin looking for some real answers."

"So, where do we start?"

John thought about the question for a moment. Then, he said, "We certainly don't want to start with the Major, because he will know that we're suspicious. I would suggest going to the man who at one time was a close friend of mines."

"Yeah, and who would that be?"

"Chief Martin." He laughed. "You know, I feel very strange after all those years of not knowing who I am, and not knowing my ass from a hole in the ground. And suddenly, I'm getting it all back in a real rush. I can remember everything from the birth of Calvin Gates to the rebirth of John Sinclair. I am here, but I am also there." He looked at Seville in a strange but serious manner. "I guess the question is now, can I really trust you to be totally loyal to me, or will you go back and tell the Major everything?"

"Tell the Major everything." She repeated as if she was not sure how to respond to his suspicion. "And what make you think that I would do a thing like that?"

Again, he laughed, but cutting it short. "Now, that I am getting my memory back, I am also able to see things a whole lot clearer than I did before. And you must admit that the Major handpicked you, got you living here in this expensive place with me twenty-four-seven….That was no accident. He wanted you to report back to him on everything that we did, right?"

She stared at John with unbelievable eyes. Then, she broke into a smile. "Okay, maybe some of what you're saying is true, but not all of it."

"Okay, then break it down and tell me which part is true."

She let out a loud sigh before responding. "Yeah, I was handpicked, as you said. And yeah, he suggested that I live here with you. And, I was to report our progress on the case…..But, he has already made that clear when he was here. But as far as we having sex, that was not apart of the deal. We came to that conclusion on our own."

John stood, walked to the railing, he looked over the edge. He then turned to Seville. "So, were we put on this case to solve it, or simply pretend that we're looking for someone that probably doesn't even exist?"

Seville stood also, walked closer to him. "John, listen to me. Yeah, at first, I thought that this was a case where we were supposedly playacting everything. But after looking at this whole thing with a third eye, I am beginning to believe that we both are being used while there is something more sinister is being done. And, I am willing to go along with you all the way to find out just what is laying beneath the surface."

John smiled. "Okay, Ms. Sevilla Patterson. As I said, tomorrow, we'll start with the Chief. And if that doesn't work, we'll just have to go straight to the horse's mouth, the Major."

Seville grabbed his robe and pulled him to her. "Are you sure that you want to do any of this?"

"I'm just as sure as you are that you want to hang with me after we both know that the Major put you here just to keep an eye on me."

"So, then tomorrow it is, we go look for answers."

"Tomorrow, we look for answers."

"But tonight, we're looking for love making in the bedroom, wouldn't you say?"

"That's the best thing you've said yet." He paused, glancing away, then back to her. "I want the truth. Have you ever slept with the Major?"

She did not pull away, she remained close to him as she answered, "No!...I have not slept with the Major, have you?"

"What?!" John asked in half shock, he could not believe what he was hearing.

"You heard me, John Sinclair! Have you ever slept with the Major? And don't you dare act as if men don't do that shit. There are one million gay men in the city of Atlanta, and you two just might be among that number. You did say he stole five million dollars for you, am I right?....I mean, you did say that, didn't you?" She laughed loudly.

"Yeah, but that was not because we're gay, or anything like that. As far as I can recall, James Butler is a married man with several kids."

"And what does being married have to do with anything? Nothing! In fact, being married makes it easier for a man to be gay, because most people don't believe married men are gay. But I know otherwise."

"Okay, okay! Yeah, five million dollars is a bad example, I'll admit. But he did that out of kindness, and the goodness of his heart. Not because we are gay."

Seville threw her head back, looking up at him. "Okay, I believe you. But do you believe me when I tell you that the Major and I never slept together?"

"I do now." He said laughing.

"Good! And now, let's get down to our business at hand."

As they were strolling through the living room holding hands, they allowed their robes to drop to the floor, and they began to embrace one another right there.

CHAPTER NINE

It was around 10:00 hrs. the following morning. Instead of going to see the Chief as they had previously said they would, John decided that he wanted to see one on the men whom he believed had either killed his family, or knew who did. That man was Danny Porter who was now working as a security guard at the West End branch of First Atlanta Bank. John felt very comfortable talking to people who probably knew who may have killed Lieutenant Calvin Gates and his family. He felt this way because none of the people he recognized, they did not recognize him. When they drove the black Hummer into the bank's parking lot, Seville spotted a security officer standing near the front entrance watching bank customers as they entered and departed the facility.

"Is he the one we're looking for?" She asked John, pointing towards the officer.

John squint his eyes looking through the windshield. "Yeah, that's our guy. I'll never forget that sorry looking bastard." John smiled as he placed the gearshift in park position. "And to think, he was one of my best officers."

They got out of the vehicle and slowly approached the entrance where Danny Porter was standing and chatting with a young woman who had just walked up also. As they approached the non-police uniformed officer, Seville pulled out her badge and ID, holding it up. "Officer Danny Porter, I'm Officer Patterson, and this is Investigator John Sinclair. Can we bother you for a few moments with a couple of questions?"

Before answering the question, he eyeballed both cops from their heads to their shoes. "I don't recognize either one of you as being cops." He spouted bitterly. "And, why don't you tell me why I should be answering y'all questions, Miss Police Officer? ...I haven't done anything, not recently at least. I've been right here all day long. In fact, I've been here all week."

"Is there some place we can talk besides here in front of the bank?" John asked.

Porter glanced around. "Why, something wrong with right here? I don't have anything to hide. So, if you want ask me some questions, you either ask them right here, or no place at all. Don't think I don't know my rights, I was a cop myself."

"Yeah, we know that you were a police officer at one time." Seville said.

"Okay, Porter, have it your way. What do you know about the murder of Lieutenant Calvin Gates five years ago?!" John asked immediately.

Suddenly, Porter eyes widened, and they began to dance in his head. "Who?!"

"Come on, Porter! Don't play like you don't know the name. Lieutenant Gates, he was your Red Dog Commander before he was killed five years ago." Seville said.

"And there are people who think that you, along with some comrades of yours, either killed Gates and his family, or you hired someone else to do it." John added.

Porter eyes were still dancing as he moved to the side of the entrance way. "Step over here." He said.

"Ah, I think we may have pushed the right button, John." Seville said glancing at John with a smile, then back to Porter.

As soon as they were in place away from the entrance, Porter said, "Listen, I don't know who killed the Lieutenant. Yeah, he was my lieutenant, and there were guys on the squad who didn't like the way he was running things,……."

"Did that include you, Danny Porter?!" John snapped,

"No!....Not me, I liked Gates. He was a good man. He was by the book kind of guy, if you know what I mean. But I didn't have any problems with him." Porter pulled out a cigarette from his shirt pocket and lit it up, his hands were shaking.

"Are you nervous, Porter?" Seville asked after she noticed his hands trembling. "You don't know who killed Lieutenant Gates although you worked with the man, and you were there when all of what happened went down….Why don't you know who killed him?....I bet I can tell you who killed him. You and the two other police officers who were taking cash payments from a young drug dealer named Jeffery Carter, better known as Summerhill Slim."

Porter stared at John first, then, he looked at Seville. "Who are you two?!"

"I'm John, and this is Sevilla, better known as Seville." John said smiling. "Lets' talk for a moment about another matter that is very similar to the Gates case. I'm sure you've heard about the precinct bombing a couple of weeks ago. And who are the first people comes to mind when you think about that situation?"

"A precinct blown to hell, and thirteen cops killed in the process." Seville added.

Porter waved his hands. "Wait, wait a minute! Back up!...You said I was there when it all happened. I was where when all of what happened?!" He stared at Seville.

"Our sources tell us that you and your comrades were arrested by Lieutenant Gates, but because someone had kidnapped his wife and daughter, he was forced to release the three of you. That's when he went searching for his family in an abandoned house, and it blew up with him and his family inside. I'm sure you know all about that. And if you were not present when it occurred, it was all on the news." John explained to him.

Again, Porter appeared stunned by the information that they were spouting to him.

The news networks did not report that three officers had been arrested prior to Gates being killed though. How could they know that? Porter thought. "Look, I don't know what you two are talking about. And, as far as I'm concerned, y'all are as crazy as some of those other cops down there." He started to walk away.

"Wait!....We're not finished with you." Seville said in a high pitched tone.

"Porter paused for a moment. "Oh, yes you are. I'm not saying anything else. And if you want to ask me any more questions, you'll have to ask them to my attorney."

"No, Danny Porter, the next time you see us, we'll have an arrest warrant for you and your friends for murder." John said.

As they turned and began walking back to their vehicle, Porter rushed inside the bank and immediately picked up a telephone at one of the emptied desks, dialed a number and said, "We need to talk!"

John and Seville sat in place for a few moments watching to see if Porter would come back out of the bank to check and see if they had left the parking lot. "What do you think he's doing?" She asked, glancing over at John.

"If I had to guess, I'd say he's probably making a phone call to someone telling them what we said." He smiled. "And if that's the case,...." He paused.

"And if that's the case.... What were you going to say?" She asked with a confused look, glancing back and forth at the bank door.

"If that's the case, someone may want to know how much we know about the arrest of the three cops. And that we know someone made the phone call to Gates that night."

Seville blinked several times before saying, "I don't understand,... explain."

"Did you see the expression on his face when I said Calvin Gates got a phone call telling him to release the three cops? And then, I said, Calvin went searching for his wife and child in an abandoned house when it blew up killing all three. And I said that this information was all on the news?... Well, I lied about that part, because I don't know."

"You lied about the information being in the news media. And what else?....."

"I am sure there were only two people who knew about the phone call, Calvin Gates and the person who called him."

Seville stared at John for a long moment before responding. "Okay, you're saying that you and the caller are the only two people who knew. So, who was that caller?"

"I don't know who made the call. But I know the one person who knew that I had made the arrests of the three cops." He paused again.

"Yeah, and who was that?!"

John hesitated to answer. *I am not fully convinced that I can trust Seville all the way. What if she goes back and feed everything to the Major who was the only person who knew that I was going to make the arrest on the three police officers?* He was thinking. "I rather not say at the moment." He finally said.

Seville suddenly opened the door and started to get out. She had anger written on her face. "If you don't trust me by now, John Sinclair, you never will!....Plus, I refuse to be the partner with a cop who doesn't trust me."

"Wait!" John snapped. "Close the door." After she closed the door, he continued. "Okay, I trust you. But you must understand what I have gone through for five years of not knowing who I was. And now, my memory is back, and I'm beginning to think that the man who saved my life was the same man who betrayed me, or set me up to be killed.

That's not a pleasant thought. Then, he fixed me up with the most attractive woman in the department, only for her to make sure that if I do begin to remember, to let him know."

"Okay, I get it. But I don't get it!" She said sharply. "Why would he set you up to be killed and then save your life…He gives you a new identity, and steals five million dollars for you. Then he brings you back to work on a case, knowing that one day you might remember who you are? I want to know! You tell me why would he do all that crazy shit for you?! That's the craziest damn thing I've ever heard of, John Sinclair!"

They suddenly realized that Danny Porter had emerged from the building by the rear door, and trotting to his personal vehicle, a Chevy Avalanche. "I didn't expect this, but I think we may have spooked our boy." John pointed to the rear of the building.

"Wonder where he's going?" She buckled her seat belt.

"I don't know, but I don't think we're going to be surprised." He said smiling.

The Chevy Avalanche pulled out of the rear parking lot and onto Lee Street, turning right and traveled towards Interstate 20. John maneuvered the massive Hummer onto Lee as well and began to follow Danny Porter's vehicle. After entering onto the expressway, Porter drove at a high rate of speed for approximately two miles, and then immediately exited off onto Interstate 85, and headed south. He traveled for another two miles, and exited again onto University Avenue. Turning left on University, heading east towards Capital Avenue, and then turning into South Side High School parking lot. He came to a halt next to an unmarked police vehicle that was waiting for his arrival.

When John saw the vehicle turn off University Avenue and stop, he immediately pulled over to the side of the street, making sure that they had a clear view of the two vehicles. The second vehicle was a black Ford Crown Victoria, the typical color and model that all high ranking police officers drove. "Who do you think he's talking to, the Major?" Seville asked.

"Can't tell from here…." He unbuckled his seat belt and got out. "I'm going to try and get a closer look, and maybe hear what they're talking about."

Seville immediately moved over into the driver's seat, for she wanted to be ready to move fast if John was spotted by the two men. John slowly walked as quietly as he could between two warehouse type buildings, through an open fence that led to the edge of the parking lot of the school. At the edge of the paved lot, John stood behind a large oak tree that was about a hundred feet from the two vehicles. He could not hear the conversation, but he could clearly see that the man Porter was talking to was not Major Butler. Instead, it appeared to have been Chad Wilson in a captain uniform. *Chad Wilson has been promoted to Captain? Wow! He sure climbed the power ladder fast in the last five years. He was only a patrolman when I arrested him.* He thought.

The conversation lasted only a few minutes, because Porter had left the bank unsecured. The two cars dispersed and left the school's lot heading in different directions, with Porter traveling north on Capital Avenue. Chad Wilson turned right on University Avenue and traveled east from their location. As John walked back to his vehicle, he was relieved to know that the man who met up with Porter was not the Major. This particular meeting did however meet his suspicion that the three officers that he arrested five years ago were in some way responsible for the death of his family.

"Did you get close enough to see who Porter met up with?" Seville asked as he got back into the vehicle on the passenger's side.

"Yeah, but it wasn't the Major." He said in a disappointed tone.

"Well, at lease we know that the Major was not involved with what happened to you, I hope." She said with a smile.

"That goes for me as well." He said smiling. "But let's face it, anything and anyone that was in Zone Three at that time could have been involved…. As Porter said, I was not the most liked supervisor. I went strictly by the book, which is not always a popular thing to do."

"So, who was in the other car?"

"Chad Wilson, he was one of the other two cops I arrested."

"You want to follow him?" She started up the Hummer.

John shook his head. "No, I think we should pay the Chief a visit as we planned. Maybe he might be able to shed some light on how Chad Wilson went all the way from patrolman to captain in five years. I mean, he's no genius cop."

"You mean the police officer that you arrested is now a captain?"

"You got that right!" John laughed. "I was there for ten years and barely made lieutenant. Chad must be kissing some mighty big ass."

"Either that, or he was rewarded for getting rid of you." Seville joked as she stirred the vehicle in the direction of police headquarters.

Ten minutes later, they were pulling into the covered parking lot of police headquarters on Ponce DeLeon Avenue, north east side of town. After parking, they rode the elevator located in the lobby to the fifth floor Command Section. Flashing their ID cards and badges to security as they entered, they were allowed to pass on.

They were told by the Chief's secretary to wait a few moments until the Chief was finished conducting his business with someone else. When he was concluded, he called them into his office. John and Seville sat in the two leather arm chairs that were facing his desk. He looked at both officers before he asked why they wanted to meet with him. The Chief was assuming that John was still suffering from a loss of memory, and only knew what Major Butler had familiarized him with. "I was informed that you two are making serious progress on the case." He said, knowing that he was fabricating, *but what the hell?* He thought. *They don't have a clue as to what is really going on.*

"We are here to hopefully clear up a little misunderstanding." John said.

"A little misunderstanding. Sure will, if I can." The Chief quickly responded.

"The misunderstanding is about why exactly did you and the Major bring me back into the city to work on a case that you already have investigators who are more qualified than the both of us together?" John asked.

"It seems like you and Major Butler wanted us to chase after shadows and ghosts rather than the people who actually blew up the precinct." Seville added.

Again, the Chief stared at the two officers. Then he looked directly at John. "You don't remember any of this, but John, once upon a time you and I were good friends."

Seville looked at John as if she had no idea what the Chief was referring to. "What is he talking about?"

John smiled. "He means that in another life, we were so-called best friends."

"Okay, so you knew each other in another life. But what does that have to do with us chasing after our own tails?" She asked, casting her light brown eyes up at the Chief.

"Young lady, do you want to be on this case or not? I mean, if it's your wish to return to your assignment, I'll grant it right now." Chief Martin barked at Seville firmly.

"No!" John snapped. "What she meant is; why don't you, who were my best friend in another life, tell us what is really going on. Not one thing that we can determine about this bombing case makes one ounce of sense. Think about it, why in the world would anyone want to blow up a precinct full of police officers, if they were not terrorists? We're running around looking at drug dealers, and club owners. The drug dealers had no fear of cops in Zone Three. A club owner on the north side has no connections with cops on the south side. So, with that in mind in both instances, none of the people on our list of suspects fits the profile of a mad bomber."

The Chief rocked back in his chair, and he then rocked forth again. He was trying to think of something that would sound remotely feasible that made the impossible sound sensible. Finally, he said, "Listen, what we have here is an unfortunate situation. A situation that the Mayor and I agreed not to let the general public know about, especially the news media." *I have to make this sound good, or they are not going to buy it.* "Several weeks ago, we received notice from the gas company that we had a serious gas leak in the area of precinct three. They brought in crews to locate and repair the leak, and as far as we knew, they had fixed the problem. But apparently, they didn't repair it."

John and Seville stared at the Chief with their mouths dropped open. Seville finally asked after she managed to pick her jaw up off the floor, "Are you trying to tell us that this whole crazy mess of a bombing is the results of a faulty gas line?!"

"Hold up for a moment, Chief." John said. "If it was an accident like you say, why try to hide it from the media, or anyone else?...Just tell people, especially the families what really happened. Wouldn't that be a lot easier than staging a phony investigation?"

They're buying it. It might even work with the Mayor and the media. That way, the feds will have no choice but to leave this investigation to my department. "Yes, I hear what you're saying, and it would make a lot more sense. But the city just can't afford to pay out only God knows how much money to the families in lawsuits, especially if they find out that we knew about the leak before the explosion."

"So, this is all about the money that the city can save by letting people believe that this was some kind of terrorist act, is that what you're saying, Chief?" Seville said.

"You got it, young lady!" The Chief responded firmly. "And by the way, what is your name? The Major didn't tell me about you."

"My name is Sevilla Patterson. I worked the streets for two years before being assigned to Intelligence. And the Major thought since most officers don't know me, I'd be perfect for this assignment with John."

"That was good thinking by the Major." He smiled. "Now that you know the real truth, I trust that this information will remain the utmost of secrecy with you two."

"The secret is with us, but how are you going to convince the FBI that this was a simple case of a faulty gas line?" John asked. "They are bound to bring in their own experts to make sure this was really the fault of a gas leak, and not terrorists."

"We're not going to try to convince the FBI of any such thing. We want the FBI to keep thinking that it was a terrorist act. When they don't find anything to suggest otherwise, case closed. And you two can go back to doing whatever you were doing before all of this came about." The Chief smiled again. *I think I just solved the biggest puzzle since General Sherman burned down Atlanta looking for the gold.* Leaning forward on his desk, he was looking very confident that he had cleared up any and all misunderstandings. "Have I cleared up everything for you two?" He glanced at his watch. "If so, I have a lunch engagement in twenty minutes. You know how these things are."

John and Seville stood. John then remembered Chad Wilson. "Oh, there's one other thing, Chief. And I'm sure that this was your decision to do it, but how did Chad Wilson move up in rank so fast? I saw him wearing captain bars today."

As the Chief stood, he looked complex by John's question. "Chad Wilson!" He pretended to not recognize the name. Then he said, "That Captain Chad Wilson! Okay, now I know who you're talking about now. He was highly recommended by his superiors after passing the captain's exam. In fact, he has been a captain about two months now."

"I was just wondering, because if I remember correctly, he was a bribe taking uniform police officer five years ago. And now, he's a high ranking commander."

Just the words, '*if I remember correctly*' coming from John's mouth made the Chief a bit anxious to find out if his memory had came back. He waited until John and Seville turned to leave his office before saying anything else. "Ah, Lieutenant Gates!" He called out sharply, hoping that John would suddenly turn and answer to Gates.

John and Seville did stop however. John turned slowly and casually said, "If I remember correctly, Lieutenant Gates was killed about five years ago. Do I remind you of him, Chief Martin?"

Chief Martin smiled and said, "Yes you do, John....Yes you do." He then watched the two as they departed his office.

As soon as they were on the elevator going back to the first floor, Seville asked, "What was he trying to do by calling you Lieutenant Gates?"

"He was trying to see if I had regained my memory."

They did not talk again until they were back inside the Hummer and the engine running. "Did you buy that crap about the faulty gas line causing the explosion?" Seville asked.

"No, did you?"

"No, I didn't!....But why is the Chief lying about this whole thing? That bullshit about having to pay out millions to families in lawsuits doesn't wash with me either."

"You and I agree. Nothing that he said made any sense whatsoever. But something is going on out there at precinct three to cause that much collateral damage. Maybe it's time that we take a closer look at the place that causing everybody to send us on this wild goose chase as if we are a couple of rookies, or just fell off the watermelons truck."

"I heard that, but do you think that's a wise thing to do?" Seville asked as she began to drive the truck away from the parking deck.

John looked out of the window as he answered. "Maybe it's not wise. But they came to North Georgia to get me. I didn't ask to come here, and I certainly didn't ask to work on this case." He turned back to Seville. "But, I am glad they did ask me to come. I'm working with a gorgeous woman, and I got my memory back. What more can John Sinclair and Calvin Gates ask for?"

"Well, John Sinclair, do you want to reconsider, or keep chasing ghosts. Because if we mess around and dig in the wrong spot and discover something that we're not supposed to discover, we're going to be in big trouble. If they are willing to kill thirteen police officers with one blast, what do you think they're willing to do to us?"

"Probably kill us twice as fast is my guess." John responded with a laugh.

"Then, maybe we should do what they want us to do, don't take this too serious."

John rolled his eyes at her. "Are you getting cold feet on me?"

"No, but I don't want to end up like those thirteen officers either."

"Boy, they've really got you spooked. I mean, we're only theorizing."

"John, I'm not spooked. But I see the handwriting on the wall. Look, the Chief lied to us for a reason, and if you and I go out and find something to prove that he's lying, you do know that he's going to be highly pissed off? And that my friend will be our asses!"

John laughed loudly. "Baby, you sound like we're looking for the boogieman or something.....Okay, let's say you're half-way right, and we find something that we're not suppose to find. What can they say?! Hey, this is what they hired us to do, find evidence of who bombed the precinct, right?"

"Sure you're right!"

"So, what is the problem?" John leaned over and kissed her on the jaw. "Look, just hang in here with me on this. If we run into something that doesn't look right, we'll back away, and get the hell out of Dodge. And we'll keep chasing ghosts, okay?"

Seville smiled, "Okay...." She continued driving towards the precinct site. But there was no doubt in her mind that they were going to find something or someone that was not on their list of suspects.

CHAPTER TEN

Approximately 12:20 hrs., Chief Martin was about to meet with Ethan Johnson for lunch at a downtown eatery called the Peachtree Sidewalk Café. The street side seating arrangement gave the Chief ample opportunity to have lunch with his soon to be business partner, and say hello to other customers and people who were walking along Peachtree Street. But before Ethan arrived, he called Major Butler on his cell phone to alert him concerning the conversation that he had just had with John and Seville. "Major Butler, I just wanted to give you heads up on a change of plans."

The Major was standing nearby the dig site at Grant Park, the spot where his precinct once stood. "Yeah, what change of plan is that, Chief?"

"Calvin Gates and his partner came by to see me, and they wanted to know what was going on? I told them that the precinct really blew up due to a faulty gas line, a simple accident case. And I think they bought it." He said in a very low tone of voice.

The Major was silent for a moment as he glanced up and saw the black Hummer headed in his direction. "Okay, I think I see them coming now, I'll take it from here."

Ethan arrived as the Chief was placing his phone back into its pouch. "Ah, Mister Johnston, I'm glad to see you." He stood momentarily to shake Ethan's hand.

"I'm a busy man these days, Chief, what is it that you wanted to see me about?" He asked as he sat down to the small iron table covered with a green flowered cloth.

Before their orders were taken, the Chief said, "I want to talk to you about including me in as your partner. I want a share just like everyone

89

else." He glanced around to make sure that no one was within hearing distance.

Ethan blinked several times before even thinking about responding. "And what make you think that you can call me down here in a public place and ask me something like that?...Do you have any idea what's at stake here, Chief Martin?"

"Yeah, it's about a whole lot of money. Much more than what I am being given to keep my mouth shut."

Again, Ethan looked around to see who may have been watching. "First of all, I did not bring you in on this. That was the Major's idea. Secondly, if you have a problem with what the Major is giving you, then, you need to take that up with him." Ethan started to stand. "I think this meeting is over."

"What would happen if I told the Mayor what really went down out there?"

Ethan eased back down into his chair. "You wouldn't dare, you sonofabitch!" He whispered. "But then, if you do tell the Mayor, you'd be implicating yourself as well."

At that moment, the waitress came to their table to take their orders. Ethan spoke first. "Nothing for me, please."

Chief Martin felt comfortable with the position that he had placed Ethan in. "Ah, I'll have a club sandwich and tea, please."

As soon as the waitress turned around and left the table, Ethan spoke again, "Listen, you redneck, peckerwood, sonofabitch, I am not somebody you want to be fucking with. I will not stand by and allow you to blackmail me by threatening to blow this entire operation. If you care anything about your life, you'll take what the Major is giving you and keep your mouth closed. Or you may find yourself floating in the Yellow River."

The Chief smiled. "And speaking of floating in a river, what if your partner, the Major finds himself floating in the Yellow River? Would that give me a bigger piece of the pie then? You know I can make that happen."

This time, Ethan stood up, leaned on the table to within a few inches from the Chief's face. "If you harm one nappy hair on Butler's head, I'll make sure that you'll never wear that blue uniform ever again. Do you understand where I am coming from, Chief of police, Martin?" He then walked away leaving Chief Martin staring at his back as he left the outdoor eatery.

Sonofabitch! I don't think he has a clue as who he's fucking with. I'll show him. Chief Martin thought in anger. His plan to convince Ethan to get rid of Major Butler had failed. And as Ethan had plainly said, there was no way that he could tell what really happened to precinct three without implicating himself as well. *It seems to me that the Major has really made an impression on Ethan. A white man talking about killing one of his own for the sake of a black man, what in the hell is the world coming to?* His thoughts continued.

Approximately three miles from the eatery, John and Seville stepped out of the Hummer simultaneously that was parked next to the Major's car on Atlanta Avenue. The Major stood across the street next to a fenced in, canvas covered area that was designed to hide the huge digging equipment. He walked casually, but slowly across the street to meet John and Seville. "What's going on with my two favorite cops on the force?" He said smiling. "Let me guess, you two have fallen in love, and you came all the way out here to tell me that you're getting married sometime in the near future, right?"

John glanced at Seville at the same time she was looking at him. They both automatically responded, "No, that's not why we're here!" And then John continued with, "And if that does happen, we have you to thank for it."

The Major did not like the sound he heard in John's voice. It was sharp, snappy, almost sounded as if he was angry about something. "Wait a minute, John. Don't tell me that you two have had a fight all ready. What did she do?"

They waited until he crossed the street before replying to his question. "Rather than asking all the dumb-ass questions, why don't you answer a few for us, huh?" John said, still in his angry sounding voice.

I definitely don't like the sound of this. He thought. "Yeah, sure, what is it that you two want to know?" He leaned again the Hummer as he glanced around at the vehicle. "Man, this is a damn nice vehicle! When I get some money, I'm going to buy me one just like it. What do you think about that?"

John looked at him. "You want this one? I mean, it was your money that bought it.

Thanks to you, I've got enough cash to buy two more." John looked at the covered up site as the sound of digging equipment roared with power. "What's going on here?"

The Major glanced at the site. "Oh, that. I didn't tell you guys about this, did I? But anyway, I convinced the Mayor and the Chief that this spot should be turned into a memorial site for the fallen officers. That's the least the city can do for a group of fine men and women who were just coming to work to do their jobs."

"Are you going to include Lieutenant Calvin Gates on the memorial?" Seville asked.

"Most definitely, Sevilla! He died in the line of duty just like these other officers."

He paused for a moment. "Now, I know you two didn't come down here to talk about a memorial plot for Lieutenant Gates did you? So, what gives?"

John dropped his head for a moment before answering. "Well, we've been thinking about this whole investigation situation, and nothing about it seems to make any sense. And we just met with Chief Martin just before lunch, and he said,....."

"He said that this was an accident due to a faulty gas line." Major Butler finished John's statement.

"Yeah.....But is that really what happened, Major?...You can tell us the truth."

"That's really what happened. But we kind of gave the impression that it was a terrorist attack, or some pissed off drug boys, or even a bunch of angry, dirty cops."

"Kind of gave the impression?! I think you did a very good job of making people believe that this was in fact an act of terrorism....." John sounded even angrier now. And he was pissed off about the fact that he, more so than Seville had been led down a blind alley. As far as Seville was concerned, he was still not one hundred per cent convinced that she was really who she say she was. *But like everything else, only time will tell what side of the fence she is standing on.* He thought while staring directly at the Major. "So, since you brought me into whatever it is that you and the Chief are trying to cover up, what are we suppose to do now?"

The Major paused for a moment, glancing in both directions of Cherokee Street. "Listen, the both of you....." He snapped in a very firm voice as if he was getting very agitated with the way they were approaching him with their concerns. "I want you to do what I asked you to do in the first place. And by all means, stay the hell away from the Chief...Look, all we're trying to do is the right thing. And at this moment, it is to build a memorial site for thirteen dead police officers. These were officers who gave their lives because of a damn faulty gas line.....Now, as far as you two are concerned, I want you to go through the motion, act like you're investigating a very serious terrorist attack, okay? You can do that, right? Because that's what I want you to do for me, okay?!"

John looked at Seville as she was staring back at him. Then, John said, "Okay, we'll do what we have to do to make this look as official as possible. Look Major, the only reason we brought this to you in the first place is because we became suspicious about the way this thing is set up. First, you tell us one thing. Then the Chief tells us something that is totally different. We're getting very confused by all the bullshit! Now, you and the Chief need to make up your minds as to what lie you're going to tell, okay? You have to understand, if Seville and I go out here and arrest someone for terrorism, or for blowing up the precinct just for the hell of it, and the courts finds out later that this was the result of a gas line leak, the city is till going to be facing some serious lawsuits."

Major Butler suddenly tried to laugh the situation off. "Okay, you've got me there! John, that's why I love you, because you always looking out for my best interest." He said looking at Seville with a wide smile. "Don't you just love this guy?!"

Seville glanced at John. "Yeah, he's cool! In fact, when this is all over with, I think we just might hook up on a serious basis."

"Are you really?!" The Major snapped, making his grin even wider. "You see, I knew I was picking the perfect partner for you, John. Like I said, I want to be the best man, okay?" He turned to look at the dig site. "Look, you guys go do what you're getting paid to do, find me some bad guys, even if you have to lock their asses up on GP." He then walked back across the street, entered into the closed gate, guarded by a uniformed police officer. The fence that surrounded the site was totally covered from spectators.

John and Seville got back into the Hummer, neither fully understanding what the Major had said, or expected for them to do. But they did know slightly more now than what they knew before. For whatever reason, they along with everyone else outside the Chief and the Major knew very little about what had really happened. More importantly, why had both men lied about the bombing in the first place? *But maybe at the time of the bombing, they didn't know that it had been a gas line that had erupted.* He thought as Seville continued driving. "Where to now, partner?" She asked, glancing at him.

"Let's go to the west side and have lunch with some of the home folks."

"By that, you mean black folks, right?"

"Yeah, that's right. The last time I was out there, we were still running things."

"Well, that's all changed in the last five years....White folks and Indians have moved into the city, and they have now taken over the west side."

"Wow!....That was fast. Five years, and black folks are out of business?"

"You've got it, just like magic." She laughed.

Seville drove back towards downtown on Capital Avenue, turning left on what was now Martin Luther King Drive, and they traveled west bound until they got to the west side. Once on the west side of town, John remembered the days and nights that he patrolled the old neighborhood in a single man car. As a young officer, he built a straight cop's reputation by arresting anyone who violated the law, including politicians. He was so impressive at one point in his career, the department promoted him to detective first class just to get him off the streets. "Man!...I remember the days out here." He finally said as he took in the sights of several emptied buildings, which was once upon a time were booming businesses. "What happened to all the black businesses?"

"Gone with the wind!...And nobody knows the troubles I sees." She hummed.

"Gone out of business, just like that? Now, there must have been a good reason for that many people to just go out of business."

"Yeah, there was a very good reason, it was white folks and Indians with money."

"And they sold out just like that?"

"Hey, you've heard the old saying, 'money talks, and bullshit walks.'" She smiled as she turned into the parking lot of the 'This Is It Restaurant.' "Now, this place is still owned by black folks, and maybe a couple of others out here. But that's about it. I figure in about another year or two, everything over here will be Indian or Chinese owned."

John chuckled out loud. "I can't believe black people would sell out like that."

"Well, it's either that, or you're going to spend a whole lot of money to bring your business up to a standard where you're going to attract other than the black clienteles."

"And you're saying that the black business people didn't want to do that, or could not afford to do that?"

She chuckled as she opened her door to get out. "Probably, a little bit of both."

"Wow!....I guess I have been away from the city much too long."

"Yes, you have, my sweet....Yes, you have." She said they walked towards the front door on the restaurant.

As soon as they walked in and were being escorted to their table by the waitress, Seville spotted Summerhill Slim sitting two tables over from them. She smiled and bumped John on the arm. "Look who's among the living." She nodded towards Slim.

John acknowledged his presence by nodding in his direction. In spite of seeing Slim in the restaurant, the smell of the soul food quickly grabbed their attention more than the drug dealer. While they waited for the waitress to return and take their orders, Slim stood and joined John and Seville, leaving his two companions at the table. "Mind if I cop a squat for a breeze?" Slim asked before sitting.

John glanced at Seville for a definition of what he had said. "He wants to sit for a moment." She explained.

"Oh, please do." John said.

Slim sat down, and wasted no time getting to the reason why he had joined them. "You know I own the Magic City Club down town?"

"John doesn't, but I do." Seville said. "So what, are you inviting us down to see your women do their thing?"

"No, Sweetheart, that's not why I mentioned my club." He smiled, for he still had feeling for Seville. "Anyway, the last time we talked, you guys were investigating the bombing of the precinct, right?"

John nodded. "And, do you know anything about it?"

"Maybe I do. There were a couple of guys in my club two nights ago, spending lots of cash and drinking heavy. Of course, they also had loose lips. I overheard them say to my girls that they had bombed a police precinct a while back. And it started me to thinking, these two nut jobs must be the ones you're looking for."

"Wait, wait!" John said immediately. "Are you saying that you overheard two guys talking about bombing a police precinct?!"

"Yeah, you heard right! Not only that, these two grease-balls said that they had been paid a lot of money to do it. They didn't say how much money, but it was a lot."

"Do you have any idea who they were, or where they came from?" Seville asked.

"No, but I can tell that they're staying in a motel out on Fulton Industrial. Their names, I can't tell you. They hired two of my girls for the night."

"Black guys, white guys, or who were they?"

"One black guy, and the other one was a white dude." Slim smiled. "From the way they were talking, it seems as if they were to suppose to leave town shortly after the bombing, but they decided to stay around town for a while. Bad idea I'd say."

John looked at Seville. "If we can locate them, it's a good idea that they stuck around. But if we can't find them, it may have been a bad idea."

Slim started to stand. "They shouldn't be too hard to find, only a few motels in that area. You just might find them." Slim wink his eye at Seville, then left their table.

The waitress reappeared at their table, they ordered quickly, anticipating going out on Fulton Industrial Blvd. to look for the two men who claimed they had bombed Zone Three precinct "What do you make of that? You think they lied through their teeth to impress the women?" Seville asked. "What if they are telling the truth, then what?"

"I don't know. But let's find them first, and then we'll decide on what to do."

As their food was being placed on the table, Seville began to glance around the café as if she was in deep thought. She was in a complete world of her own for several moments. She remained there until John noticed that she in another world. "What's going on in that head of yours, are you're on to something?" John asked curiously.

Before speaking again, she began to eat, but suddenly, she stopped, holding the fork in her right hand. "Not that I believe every word that comes out of Slims' mouth, but let's suppose he's telling the truth about the two men. The question now becomes, who, why, or what could possibly be so important about that precinct to make someone pay a couple of butt-wipes a lot of money to blow it up?"

I was thinking the exact same thing. He thought to himself. "That's what we're going to find out when we leave here." He said. "Someone for hire blew up the building, and they were told to get out of town, but they didn't leave. They're still hanging around, getting drunk and talking about what they did. Slim overhears their conversation." He suddenly stopped his theorizing. He got up and went over to Slims' table. He remained standing as he looked down at the three men. "Let me ask you Slim, did you by some chance mention the conversation you overheard to anyone else besides us?"

Slim stared at John for a moment while he thought about who else had he spoke to about what the two men said. "Yeah, I did. Why? Does that make a difference?"

"No, no, the question is not why, but who did you tell?" John insisted.

"I told one of the asshole cops who I used to pay off every week, Chad Wilson."

"And while you were casually mentioning the two men, did you just happen tell him where he would be able to locate them?"

"Yeah, I did…But, what's wrong with that, the cops need to know that, right?"

"Well, let's hope this cop is not the asshole you say he is." John turned and went back to his table. He pulled out forty dollars, dropped the two twenty dollar bills on the table. "I think we need to get out to that motel as soon as possible."

Seville did not respond, she immediately stood and they raced out of the restaurant towards their vehicle. Seville drove out of the lot onto the main street of Martin Luther King Drive, and headed west. Three miles west, they entered Interstate 20 and continued driving west. Approximately ten minutes later, they exited off onto Fulton Industrial and began looking for motels in the area. They went to two motels front desks with no luck of two such men being registered. The third motel that was located about a mile south of Interstate 20 was Motel 8. There, the two men fitting their description had been registered there for several weeks.

The motel clerk led the pair to room 107 on the first floor where the two men were staying. The clerk knocked prior to opening the door with a master key if there was no answer. Inside, they found what John and Seville were hoping to prevent from happening. The two men, one black, about forty years of age and appeared to be about six feet tall. The second man was white, a little shorter, appeared to be in his mid-forties. Both men had been shot multiple times at close range. They were sprawled on the floor in blood.

Seville radioed the dispatcher to announce what they had found. A homicide unit was on the scene within a matter of minutes. Homicide Detectives, Richard Thomas and Alton Gomez immediately began conducting a homicide investigation. They were wearing the procedural attire, dark suits and dull looking ties. The senior detective was Richard Thomas, and with a pen in one hand and a note pad in the other one, he casually approached John and Seville who were now standing a few feet away from the crime scene observing, and trying to get that dead smell out of their noses. "Are you two with the APD?" He asked, glancing back and forth at Seville and John.

"Yes, we are." John responded.

"Did you find the bodies, or did someone call for you on this case?"

"We are working another case, and we received a tip that these two characters may have had information pertaining to our case." Seville said. "But, as you can see, someone else got to them before we did."

Detective Thomas suddenly readjusted his stance. "Exactly what kind of case are you working on?" Before they could answer, he followed up by saying, "I don't think I remember seeing you around the department before." He was looking at John. "And here I am thinking that I knew most of the investigators, or at least seen them around."

"Ah, I'm on loan from the New York Police Department." John said quickly. "I've only been in Atlanta for about three weeks."

"NYPD you say? You're a long ways from home. And you're working on what?"

"I didn't say, and I probably won't say." John said as he glanced at Seville.

"And neither did I, and won't say." She replied sharply.

Detective Thomas studied the pair for a moment, for he was not sure what to make of them being there on the murder scene. And he certainly did not know what to think of them not answering his question concerning this case. "Maybe you need to talk to our boss, Captain Chad Wilson before leaving the scene."

"Maybe you need to call our boss, Major James Butler." Seville said.

Suddenly, his facial expression changed for the better. "Oh, you're working for Major Butler?....Which mean you're working on the precinct bombing case?"

"Yes….." John said. "Is there anything else that you need from us?"

"No, no,….If I need to ask you anymore questions, I'll contact Major Butler."

"Now, you do that, Detective!" Seville said as they turned and began walking away headed back to their vehicle.

Detective Thomas called out, "And by the way, I do know you, Officer." He was looking at Seville. "You used to work with Intelligence, right?"

"That's right!" Seville answered, motioning with a thumb up.

Detective Thomas watched as they drove away, heading back onto the main street. He took out his cell phone and speed dialed a number. "Captain, are you familiar with a John Sinclair, a detective from the NYPD working with a Sevilla Patterson, one of ours?"

"No! And what kind of case are they working on?!" The voice shouted back.

"According to them, they're investigating the precinct bombing case."

"Don't worry about them, unless they know something about who popped those two out there at the motel."

"They said they were on their way out here to the motel to question the victims about the bombing, but apparently someone else got to them first."

"Okay, when you wrap it up there, have another chat with those two officers to see how much they really know about your victims."

"Will do Captain!....Ah, one other thing, Sir…They say they're working for Major Butler. Should I go through him first?"

"Why go through him? You don't need his permission to talk to these officers about an ongoing homicide investigation….Find them and see what they know!"

"Yes sir!….." Detective Thomas flipped his phone shut and continued with the investigation.

CHAPTER ELEVEN

It was around midnight when the backhoe hit something that sounded like metal. With bright lights illuminating the area, the three man digging crew along with Ethan and Major Butler knew that they had hit pay dirt. But then, neither man wanted to get too excited before actually seeing for the first time with their own eyes the treasure that they were seeking. One of the diggers jumped down into the massive hole to examine their find. With a hand shovel, he moved dirt away from the top of the metal box. As he swept the dirt away, it appeared that they had finally reached the vault that the Confederate Soldiers buried with the two billion dollars in gold inside. "I think we found it!" The digger yelled.

The Major quickly turned and went to the gate where the police security guard was standing. "Listen, no one, and I mean no one can come within fifty feet of this area."

"Yes sir!" The guard snapped.

When the Major returned to where Ethan was still observing the digger who was still trying to work his way to a door that led to the inside of the vault, Ethan said softly.

"Major, I think it's only fair that I warn you that Chief Martin wants to eliminate you as a partner, and bring him in to replace you."

Major Butler stared at Ethan in a surprised manner. "What?!" He snapped.

"Maybe he's only trying to blow smoke up my ass, but I think he's possibly dangerous….So, all I'm saying is, you might want to keep your eyes on him. A hundred billion dollars is a lot of money, people will do some crazy things for that kind of loot."

Major Butler smiled at the thought of doing crazy things. "Yeah, we should know."

At that moment, the digger waved his hand, indicating that he had found the vault door. "I've got it!" He yelled again.

Ethan and the Major both jumped down into the hole with the digger. Before them was a huge dirt covered box setting upright with a single door facing out. There was also a huge lock that had secured the vault door for a hundred and fifty years. Ethan examined the vault for holes that may have rusted out the metal due to its years in the ground. But to his amazement, the vault was in good shape, and was still strong enough that they knew immediately that the lock would have to be broken. "Get a hammer and break the lock." Ethan told the digger anxiously.

While the digger was gone to fetch a hammer to break the lock, Major Butler looked at Ethan and said, "What do you think I should do about the Chief?"

Ethan smiled, glancing at the vault. "If the gold is still here, and if everything goes as we've planned it, we cannot afford to be stopped by someone who wants to risk exposing this entire operation. If we have to, we need to get rid of him just like we did everyone else. Killing one more cop won't make any difference now."

"Well, apparently, that's what he has in mind for me." The Major said smiling.

"Apparently so.....And if the gold is here, the quicker you get rid of him, the quicker we can get to the next phase of moving this gold out of this hole."

"You think he has some of his people watching?"

"What do you think?....For this much gold, and if I were him, I'd have the entire department watching every move we make. From this point on, we must be very careful in everything we do, because we never know who might be watching."

"And don't forget the Feds either. They've been searching for this gold for over a hundred years with no luck." Major Butler said jokingly.

"And you're right. We definitely have to keep our eyes open for those assholes! This would definitely put a feather in the FBI's hat."

At that moment the digger jumped back into the hole with the hammer. The Major and Ethan stood back while the digger struck the lock with one solid blow and it fell to the ground. All three men anxiously began to tug and pull on the door until there was enough room to get a good look inside with a flashlight. Ethan shined the light and was shocked beyond belief by what he saw. He was blinded by the still bright color of the gold bars that were still stacked neatly away from the door. "Oh, My God!!"

"What's wrong?!" Major Butler snapped as he stood directly behind Ethan.

Ethan moved out of the way, handing the Major the flashlight. "See for yourself."

Major Butler took the flashlight and looked inside, scanning the light from wall to wall. "Oh my God is right!!" He stood back with a wide grin on his face. "We are some very rich men!!..Really, really rich men!!" He then handed the light to the digger for him to get a look at the treasure that had been buried there for a hundred and fifty years.

After the digger had gotten a glance, all three men climbed out of the hole with a look of excitement written all over their faces. All five men congratulated each other for a brief moment. Ethan immediately called the historian, Sam Houston, the man who was responsible for pinpointing the exact location of the buried gold. "Sam, it's really here! It's right where you said it would be." He listened to Sam for a moment. He then said, "Okay! Very good!... Listen, we're going to bring out some more officers to guard it until we can get it out, load it up, and be on our way." He shut his cell phone off.

"What did he say?" The Major asked Ethan.

"Okay, he's been on the phone all day, looking for new buyers." Ethan said as he motioned for the digger to check on the other two men. Ethan and the Major walked out of the fenced in area to further discuss the latest details. As soon as they were across the street, Ethan said, "Okay, here's is the latest, we've got three solid new buyers, they are Hong Kong, Russia, and Cuba. They're willing to pay three times our original offer."

"Wait a minute, did you say three times?!" The Major was suddenly incoherent.

"Three times!" Ethan repeated softly. "That mean we will have more money than we can ever count or spend. Now check this out. Today on the global market, gold is valued at one thousand dollars an ounce. And there's about ten million ounces there."

"That's the coolest shit I've ever heard in my life!" The Major did a little dance.

""Okay, it's going to take us a couple of days to get everything set up." Ethan began to explain. "We'll use a cargo plane to fly from here to Miami two days from now. We will then load it onto a larger cargo plane there and we'll take it into Hong Kong, maybe Russia, or Cuba. However, in the meantime, I want you to increase the security here to at lease seven of your officers until the shipment is hauled away from here."

"Where are we flying out of here from?" The Major asked.

"Charlie Brown Airport…..From the county we will draw less attention by flying out of the city from there." Ethan looked around at the three men who were standing nearby. "I want these men here early tomorrow morning. We need to get this gold out of that vault as soon as possible before anyone gets suspicious. As far as the Chief is concerned, you may want to take care of him as soon as possible." Ethan then went to a waiting car and got in the passenger's seat, and the vehicle sped off.

The Major immediately began making calls to officers who were standing by waiting for his call. "Be on location in one hour!" That was his message to all of the officers. Then he went to the lone officer who was still guarding the gate. "When the other officers arrive, you are relieved. However, my orders still stand for them as well. No one will go into the memorial site under any circumstances. You got that?!"

"Yes sir, Major." The officer said.

The Major then went to the digger who had actually had seen the gold. "I want you to stay here just in case something happens that is not supposed to happen. I'll be close by just in case you need me…."

"Are you expecting something to happen?" The man asked out of curiosity.

"There is a lot of gold down there. And there is one person in particularly that knows what we have here. He would do anything to get his hands on what's down there. But right now, I'm going home and check on my family, and I'll be back soon."

The Major departed the dig site to do as he had stated to the digger. And as he drove home, he was constantly checking his rearview mirror, making sure that no one was tailing him. He was taking Ethan's warning to heart now that they had dug up the gold. *I believe if there is any way possible, Chief Martin is going to try and intercept the gold for himself. Yeah, he could easily do just that. After all, he is the Chief, and he has the authority over the entire police department, and he could order the SWAT team, or any number of officers to try and take over the site for himself…*He was thinking as he drove faster and faster towards his home.

Fifteen minutes later, he was pulling into his driveway. But as he turned into his driveway, he immediately saw an unmarked black Ford parked at the entrance. *What the hell is this?* He thought. As he pulled up next to the Ford with his weapon in his hand, he could clearly see that it was Captain Chad Wilson. The Major rolled down his window and angrily barked out, "What in the hell are you doing here in my driveway, Wilson?!"

Chad Wilson got out of his car and walked around and got in on the passenger's side of the Major's car. The Major put the vehicle in park, slowly turning his head to Wilson, and asked again. "Why in the hell are you parked here in my driveway?!"

Wilson lit a cigarette. "We need to talk….." He looked at his lit cigarette. "Do you mind if I smoke?"

"No, Wilson, just as long as you blow your smoke out of the window, and not in my car." He rolled down all the windows.

"Anyway,…" Wilson continued. "The two men that I told you about who I believe were responsible for the precinct bombing, they were found shot to death today. Do you know anything about that, Major?"

"I heard something about it over the police radio today…." The Major sounded surprised. "I was wondering who could have got to them before I did? In fact, I was planning to have my investigators look into it to see if they could get some information out of those two." The Major stared at Wilson for a moment. "Why are you asking me do I know anything about who may have killed them?!"

Wilson blew smoke out of the window. "Well, the way I'm figuring it, these two clowns had been around town since the bombing, so said my sources. And no one had thought anything about these two monkeys until I told you about them. And now, they turn up dead. It just seem mighty strange that one day I inform you about them, and the very next day, both men are shot multiple times at close range. They knew their killer."

The Major narrowed his eyes at Wilson. "Are you implying that I might be the one who killed those men, Captain?"

"No sir! I wouldn't do that."

"Well, it sure sound like you are. And if that be the case, you best remember who made you, and who put you in the position that you're in. I put you there! But I can also take you out of that position. Do you get my meaning, Captain?"

"Yes sir, I certainly do." Wilson suddenly changed the subject. "Ah, Major, the real reason I'm here is not because of the scumbags who blew up the precinct, but because I heard that there may be a contract out on you, placed by the Chief."

"What?!" Major Butler snapped in total surprise. "So, the Chief sent you here to tell me that or take me out yourself?!"

"No, sir, not me!…He's bringing back Danny Porter to do the job."

The Major smiled. "So, he's hiring an ex-cop to kill me so there won't be any ties to the police department, or him, is that right?" The Major smiled some more. "So, why are you telling me this? You don't have any loyalty to the Chief anymore, do you?"

Chad Wilson laughed. "Yes I do! But I'm more loyal to you. As you said, you put me in the position that I am in. And that's why I've decided to let you know what he is planning to do, just in case you want to turn the table on his ass."

The Major thought about what all of this would mean to their plans concerning the gold. "I'll tell you what Captain, I might decide to allow him to live, at least for a couple more days. But in the meantime, you can make up whatever lie you want to as far as Porter taking me out of the picture, because it will never happen."

Wilson thought for a moment longer. "Ah, let me ask you one other thing, Major. Who is this guy asking all the wrong questions about who killed Calvin Gates?"

"I don't know any guy who would be asking the wrong questions about Lieutenant Gates. Who are you talking about?"

"The same male and female investigators who I believe say they are working for you. They went after Porter earlier today, and then later on, they are the ones who discovered the bodies out on Fulton Industrial this afternoon. According to Porter, these two knows an awful lot about what happened to Lieutenant Gates. To be honest with you, they know a little too much to not have been around five years ago."

"Okay, I know who you're talking about." The Major finally admitted. "Yes, they are my investigators and they are working on the precinct bombing case, period. As far as the Gates case, they were just fishing for information, they don't know anything."

"Oh, I just wanted to know." Chad Wilson began to open the door to get out of the car. And as he was stepping out and closed the door behind him, he turned around and leaned back into the car window with a weapon in his hand, he said, "What I told you about the hit and that how Danny Porter is coming after you,….well, guess what?"

"Yeah, you really had me worried there for a moment." The Major said smiling.

"Well, I lied! I came here to kill you!" He pointed his automatic weapon at the Major and started to pull the trigger. But the Major suspected all along that he was the hit man. His was weapon already aimed at Wilson. He pulled the trigger two times rapidly.

"Yeah, bastard, I know you lied….." The Major said as Chad Wilson fell backward to the ground and fired several rounds in the air. The Major ducked down into the car to avoid being hit by a stray bullet.

A few moments later, the Major's wife Carolyn along with their two daughters ran to the door, looking to see what was going on. When Carolyn saw her husband getting out of his car, and another man lying in the driveway, she rushed out to see if her husband was all right. "James! Are you okay?!" She shouted. "I heard gunshots, what is going on, and who is that?!" She pointed down to the dead man laying face up on the ground.

As the Major walked around the car, he waved for his wife to stay back just in case Chad Wilson was still alive. "Stay back, honey! This man came here to kill me, and I don't know if he's still alive or not."

Carolyn held on to the girls and stood a few feet away form the crime scene. The Major called 911 on his cell phone. "Yeah, this Major James Butler, and I just shot another police officer who were here at my home and tried to kill me…..Send an ambulance, a homicide team, and notify the Chief." He closed the phone. The dispatcher knew the address of all high ranking officers home which came up automatically on the switchboard for the operators to see whenever their cell phones were used.

Within fifteen minutes, everything that was needed on a crime scene was parked in the driveway of the Major's home, including several news media cameras with lights shining everywhere. Major Butler did not see the need to answer any questions until he was interviewed by the investigators. But while he waited for the investigators, his mind was on the gold as well as he knew what had to be done now as far as the Chief was concerned. Even before the gold was out of the ground, stupid Wilson showed up at his home for the sole purpose of killing him for the Chief. But the one question that was lingering on his mind, why would Chad all of a sudden turned against him for the Chief? *Why?! I wonder did the Chief tell him about the gold?* He thought.

"Major Butler, I just want to ask you a few more questions about what happen here." The lead homicide investigator said as he entered the Major's home while the Major and his wife Carolyn held hands sitting in the living room.

"Detective Crawford,…." The Major said. "In the first place, I was shocked to see the Captain waiting for me in my driveway. But then, for him to get out of his car, and walk to my car and pull his gun in an attempt to kill me was even more shocking. I've never witnessed anything like that in my entire life. He could've harmed my family."

"And you have no idea why he would come after you like he did?" The detective asked with an amazing look on his face.

"Detective, not a clue!" The Major glanced at his wife. "You know, at first, I thought he was joking. But when he said, 'I'm here to kill you. I knew that was no joke."

"So, you already had your weapon out?"

"Yes I did!….Like I said, at first, I had no idea who or why he was in my driveway. I pulled my gun out, and I placed it between my legs, hidden from sight."

"So, in your opinion, you think that the Captain had it all figured out. Kill you, get back into his car and drive away. Then, everyone would assume that some street thug had it in for you, and your murder would go unsolved pretty much like a lieutenant of yours who worked for you five years ago?" The detective asked a far reaching question.

The Major looked at his attractive younger wife once again. "Yeah, we can assume that this would have been a similar situation.…..Not only that, I practically lost my entire day watch three weeks ago in an explosion.….I mean, damn! What can I look forward to happening next?!"

The detective stood. "I think that will be all for tonight, Sir….I will notify the Chief, and let him know what took place. I'll be in touch with you sometime tomorrow."

"Thanks Sergeant, I wished that I could have avoided this, but there was no way." The Major said as he stood with the detective. "If there's anything I can do to make this any easier for his family, let me know." He shook the officer's hand as he escorted him out of the door. *Don't worry, Sergeant, you'll have another homicide to investigate real soon.* He thought as he watched the last of the news media and the investigating teams leave his driveway.

CHAPTER TWELVE

"*According to the police public relationship officer, Major James Butler shot and killed a fellow Atlanta police officer, Captain Chad Wilson last night. Details of how this horrible situation occurred are not available at this time….. We will bring you more as this story unfolds, Lisa.*" The on the crime scene reporter Justin Mason said.

At that moment, John walked into the bedroom wearing a white robe and a towel around his neck. "What was that all about?" He asked with a toothbrush in his mouth.

Seville, who was now fully dressed, turned to John, and started staring at him in a wide-eyed stare. "I don't know, but this whole thing is getting weirder by the day…..   Apparently, the Major shot and killed Captain Chad Wilson last night."

John almost choked on his toothbrush as he muttered, "What?!"

"That's what is being reported on the news just moments ago."

"Are you sure you heard that right?"

"I know what I heard, and they showed the Captain's picture. Yeah, I'm sure."

At that moment, the doorbell began to ring. Since she was already dressed, Seville went to the door to see who was there. She gave a quick peek through peep hole. She opened the door and waited for the two plain clothed detectives to state their business.

"Good morning, Ms. Patterson. Remember me? I was the investigators at the Fulton Industrial motel yesterday, and if it's not too much trouble, may my partner and I come in and ask you a few more questions about the murders yesterday. By the way, I don't think you met my partner, this is Detective Alton Gomez."

"Seville only stared at the two plain clothes officers before responding, "So, what is it that you think we can tell you now that we didn't tell you yesterday?"

"Seville, why don't you let these fine officers in?" John said as he walked up behind her. "They're only trying to investigate a couple of homicides."

Seville stepped back allowing them to enter. As soon as they were inside, she closed the door and joined John on the sofa as the detectives remained standing. "You're welcome to sit down, guys." John said waving his hand towards the adjoining sofa. Detective Thomas sat while Gomez remained standing.

"Look, I'm not going to beat around the bush. I checked you two out after you left the crime scene the yesterday. Sevilla Patterson, you did check out as being one of us. But you, John Sinclair, I can't find no record of you anywhere in our database. Not even with the New York Police Department, as you claimed you were a member there once upon a time.... In fact, no one there knows anything about a John Sinclair."

"So, what are you trying to say, that we made him up, or that he's a ghost?" Seville asked smiling. "I mean, you're looking at him, and he's right here."

"No, that's not what I'm saying...." Thomas said. "But, what I am getting at is, until a few weeks ago, John Sinclair didn't even exist anywhere. Not with the APD, or the NYPD. How do you explain that, and yet, you're here at the APD working as a cop?"

John glanced at Seville, "First of all, I told you at the murder scene that Major James Butler would answer any questions that you may have about who we are, and what we're doing. And that same game plan is still in play at this moment. You know who Sevilla is, but not me. And I am sorry about that. If I revealed to you my real identity, I'd be forced to eliminate the both of you. And I definitely don't want to do that."

Gomez came closer to Thomas, but still standing. "Mr. Sinclair, or whoever you are, this is a very serious matter. We have two people murdered by bullets from a .10mm hand gun, the same caliber of guns that we use, which could have possibly been fired from a police weapon."

Seville held up her hands. "Lets get a few things straight right here and now!...First of all, John has not carried a weapon since he's been here. But he will from this point on. Secondly, I'm the only one who carrying a .10mm, and I damn sure didn't kill those men. The third thing, John Sinclair is with me, who happens to be a cop. And Major Butler assigned him with me, which mean, regardless of his name, what business is it of yours to be checking him out anyway?! Tell me, who died and put you two in charge?!"

"Ms. Patterson!" Detective Gomez said. "We're only trying to get to the bottom of a double homicide, that's all. Now, you can either answer our questions here in this fine place you have." He glanced around the room. "Or, you can answer them downtown."

"And by the way, Major Butler killed our commander of homicide last night. So, it doesn't seem like the Major is in a position to speak for anyone but himself." Detective Gomez said with a slight smile.

"And what exactly is that suppose to mean, is he being charged with murder or some other old nasty crime?" John asked suspiciously.

Before Detective Gomez could answer, the doorbell rang once again. Seville slowly rose to see who was interrupting their spirited conversation. She did not bother to peek this time, she simply jerked open the door and was about to bark out the question of *'What do you want?'* when she suddenly realized that it was Major Butler standing at the door. "It's about time you showed up……We were just discussing you. Why don't you come on in and answer these gentlemen questions."

When Major Butler entered living room with Seville walking behind him, he saw the reason why they had been discussing him. "Good morning, gentlemen!" He said as he sat in the arm chair that was in between the double sofas. "I've always heard that when you talk about the devil, he'll surely appear. I guess I must be the devil in the flesh."

For the investigators, the scene suddenly became somewhat uncomfortable. They could feel the tension in the room as they were about to be forced to explain why they were there in the first place. "Ah, not the devil at all, Major." Detective Thomas said. "We're following up on a double murder investigation that Officer Patterson and Mr. Sinclair discovered yesterday at the motel. And we had some questions about Mr. Sinclair's identity. It seems that before two or three weeks ago, he was non-existence."

Major Butler smiled. "Really? And why did you feel the need to search out the identity of Investigator John Sinclair?...Are you telling me that his identification card, his badge, and the word of his partner are not sufficient enough for you, Detective Richard Thomas, and you too, Detective Alton Gomez?"

"Well, ah,…." Detective Thomas, 35 years old African American started to say, but stuttered while speaking. "Everything they showed us was in order, just making sure."

"I see….." The Major said. "Now, what was the discussion you were having about me?" He glanced at Seville who was sitting besides John again.

Gomez, 33 years old Hispanic, this time tried to explain. "Well, the news about what went on at your home late last night is all over the news, and we wanted to inform your officers that you might be answering a lot of questions about how it all went down."

John abruptly turned to the Major, searching his facial expression for a response as well. But the Major's only response was, "I'm not at liberty to discuss that matter since it was your commander who was the victim. And the case is still under investigation."

"Yes sir, we understand!" Thomas said. "We were not discussing what happened."

"Good!....And if there is no other questions, then I suggest that you wrap up this investigation in your office." The Major said as he stood.

Both detectives knew that this was their signal to leave. Thomas stood, and he along with Gomez moved quickly towards the front door. Again, Seville followed the pair and swiftly closed the door behind them as they left the apartment. She immediately returned to join John to begin what they called getting to the bottom of a stinking mess.

As the Major sat down once again, he began to explain. "Listen, I know it's all over the news, and I know that you know that the dead man used to be one of my best officers. But what happened last night, or early this morning was an unfortunate situation. The bastard was waiting at my house to kill me! I had no choice but to do what I did."

John stood, went to the kitchen, poured himself a cup of coffee and returned. "You want some coffee?" He asked the Major.

"Yes, I need a cup after what happened last night." He answered politely.

Seville immediately stood, went to the kitchen and poured her and the Major a cup of coffee each. "Sometimes, I think he forgets that I'm not just his partner, I'm his roommate, not the maid." She said, glancing down at the cups that she had in her hands.

The Major looked at John with a question mark on his face as he was handed his cup. John went on to explain. "She means that I should have gotten us all coffee."

The Major smiled. "I can see that you two are working out well." He sipped the hot black, sugarless coffee. "Anyway, although last night was the first attempt on my life, I am sure that it probably won't be the last attempt."

While Seville held her cup with both hands, she popped the question, "Major Butler, pardon my expression, but what in the fuck is going with you?!"

John was looking directly at the Major as well. "Yeah, and that goes for me too.

Look, you brought us into what seems to be something right out of a mystery novel, and I think it's about time you come clean on what is it that we're really up against here?"

The Major stood he was a bit nervous about what he was going to say. "Look you two I brought you together for a damn good reason. Seville, I thought you'd make John an excellent, beautiful, young partner." He smiled as he paced back and forth holding his cup. "John, you have enough money to make you and Seville a very good life up there in them hills. And if everything goes as planned, I'll make sure that you'll have a lot more."

John then stood up. "Wait, wait! What in the hell are you talking about?! James Butler, my half brother, you're making no fucking sense! Now, you need tell us what it is you've gotten yourself mixed up in, and tell us now."

He turned sharply towards John. "No! The only thing you need to do right now is pack your things and go back to Helen. You and Seville forget about this case, leave this city today, because if you keep looking for something that isn't there, you're going to get yourselves hurt or even killed….This is for your own good." The Major thought about what John had said about being half brothers. "So, you're remembering who you are?"

"Yeah, I know that I am Calvin Gates. But that's not what we're talking about. We were talking about you, and whatever it is that's going to get us all killed."

The Major sat down again. "Sit down, John, Calvin, or whoever! Look, besides my wife and daughters, you're the only family I have in the world. And when I tell you that there are some things better left unknown and unsaid, you better believe me!"

John sat down next to Seville again. "Okay, everything you've ever told me, or done for me so far has been like a blessing from God. But now, you're scaring the shit out of me and her.…You need to talk, man! And tell us what is going on. What is wrong with the three of us battling against your problem? I think we can whip the shit of out it."

The Major laughed. "John, there are some things in life that are worth fighting for. They're even worth dying for. And trust me when I say this, whatever I'm involved in is worth all of that, and then some. But, there are other people in the police department, in the city of Atlanta who knows what I know, and they are willing to kill me, and anyone else who stand in their way to get their hands on it."

John looked at Seville with bucked eyes, for he could not imagine what the Major was talking about. She was constantly staring at the Major with squinted eyes. "Okay, let's say we do as you say do." Seville finally said. "And, what almost happened last night becomes a reality, you end up dead anyway. How do you suppose we are going to live with ourselves knowing that we could have done something to prevent this from happening?"

The Major stared at both of them for a long while before saying, "I want you both to understand something very clearly, this is not a request, this is a fucking order! You're no longer on the case. John, you no longer work for the Atlanta Police Department. Seville, you are fired! Go get married, have some babies, and stay put until I call for you to do otherwise, okay?"

John was not satisfied with the information they were receiving. "Can you tell me this, why was your old friend, Captain Chad Wilson, out at your home waiting to kill you?

I mean, you can't tell us why you think this man who was once your friend come gunning for you? After all, he used to work for you and me. So, I knew the man as well."

"Here's what I will tell you, John and Seville." He smiled. "I brought you two together to work on a case that I knew was a lie. We all know that the bombing of my precinct was the fault of an old building with a leaky gas line. At the time, we wanted to pretend that a bunch of drug dealers, or a group of terrorists, or even a bunch of corrupted cops were the blame. But we knew all along that was a lie. Now, the truth is out, the Mayor will be making the announcement this afternoon. The city is the blame for what happened to those thirteen officers who died in that building. And the city will pay out millions in a major lawsuit to the families."

John glanced at Seville again. "But that still doesn't explain the attempt on your life, what's up with that?"

The Major wanted to get up and leave. He felt that he had said enough. But then, he decided to drop a bomb on John. "Okay, you want to know

why Chad Wilson came after me last night? Okay, I'll tell you why.....
Chad Wilson suspected that I knew that he was one of the people who were
involved in your family murders, and that we all know what happened five
years ago. In other words, he was simply trying to shut me up for good."

John suddenly sat back on the sofa with an unbelievable gaze in his
eyes. Seville stared at the Major. She could not believe the words that he
had just uttered from his lips. "So, you're saying that Chad Wilson and
the two other cops John arrested that day are the same ones who killed his
family?...But why are you telling it now?" Seville asked.

"Look, I didn't have the evidence that I needed to prove they did it.
But apparently Chad Wilson thought that I did." The Major said. "And
the two men who were killed at the motel, they were the ones who set the
bomb in the old abandoned house. And because they were back in town
to collect more money to keep quiet, they were killed because of what they
knew. I mean, everybody have absolutely gone crazy with killing!"

"And none of this had anything to do with the precinct bombing?"
John asked trying to connect the dots.

"Not at all!" The Major said. "And see, that's why I am telling you two
get out of town. These people could know that you are really Calvin Gates,
and they'll be coming after you again real soon. And I do not want to take
any chances of having to bring you back from the dead again, John."

Seville looked at John with a smile. "He does make a lot of sense,
John."

John stared at Major Butler for a long while before finally admitting
to himself that it did sound logical. Then he said, "How do you plan on
stopping whoever else it is out there?....And what about the other two
jackasses whom I arrested with Chad Wilson?"

The Major stood. "If the information that I received is correct, I'll
be able to make an arrest real soon on those two. I just hope that I don't
have to kill them as well." He walked toward the door. "Listen, you two
don't have to leave town right away, but just stay away from the police
department and this case, and you should be okay." He opened the door.
John got up and walked to the door, leaving Seville behind on the sofa.
The Major glanced upward to John who was slightly taller. "Obviously,
you have something else you want to say."

"How did you guess?" John said as they both stepped outside
the doorway, closing the door behind them. "Listen, as John Sinclair,
everything you said in there, I would be inclined to go along with it.
But as Calvin Gates, I'm not really buying into this so-called mysterious

bombing, terrorist attack, and now a faulty gas line. As I said in there, James, you need to tell me exactly what is going on. You're not being up front with me. And this bullshit about packing my bags and heading back to the hills, well, that ain't about to happen no time soon."

"John!" The Major said, patting him on the arm. "Whatever is going on, it does not concern you and Sevilla. Listen, just trust me on this one, I've got this!....But I will tell you this much, if anything does happen to me, the first asshole you should start looking at is the Chief. Now, that much you should know. Stay here if you must, but don't do anything until you hear from me, okay?"

John stood there at the doorway watching the medium size black man as he strutted away down the five flights of stairs into the parking lot, whistling a tone all the way. *For a man who just killed his so-called friend, and now talking about if something happen to him, look at the police chief first, he is awfully damn happy.* He thought. John turned to go back inside the apartment only to discover that Seville had been standing there with the door open listening to what was being said. "How much did you hear?" He asked.

Seville smiled as she went back and sat on the sofa. "I heard enough to know that you are not leaving. Nor, are you leaving this investigation. Now, with that said, how are you planning to proceed?"

He also smiled as he closed the door and sat next her. "Very carefully, my dear..." He shook his head in disbelief. "Now, here's a man who saves my life. I should have been dead along with my wife and kid. But out of nowhere, this man finds me in a wooded area almost dead, carried me to a private hospital, hires the best doctors in the country to give me a new face, and then he worked his magic some kind of way to steal five million dollars from the police department to give me a new life,....."

Seville continued his statement. "But why won't this same man now tell you what is going on with him and the department, and whoever he's involved with?"

"Very good!" He said. "Not that I don't trust him, but I think Major James Butler is up to his eyeballs in some real shady stuff. I'm willing to bet a half million dollars on that it has something to do with the precinct bombing. And if those two men who were killed did in fact blow up the precinct, then the Major knows who killed them."

Seville suddenly stood. "Wait! You just hit on something. Okay, before we found the two dead guys, we talked to Danny Porter. Danny Porter in turn talked to Captain Chad Wilson. Chad Wilson then goes to the

Major's home and waits for him. The Major comes home and find Chad waiting. They talked. The talking gets out of hand and guns are drawn. The Major gets off the first shot killing Chad Wilson."

John sat there for a few seconds thinking about Seville's theory. "I think that is pretty close to what really happened, except for one thing…."

"And what's that?"

"If Chad Wilson, the Major, and Danny Porter are all connected, why would Chad Wilson go gunning for his old boss?…Remember, it was the Major who recommended that Chad be promoted to Captain. More importantly, why would Chad and the Major argue about who killed two the punks who were going around bragging about they blew up the precinct? No, that theory doesn't really do it for me." He smiled. "However, I do believe that they were connected in something. And it wouldn't be the first time."

Seville went back to the kitchen to pour her and John another cup of coffee. When she re-entered the room, she handed John his cup. "You said it wouldn't be the first time. Are you talking about your own situation?" She asked.

"Yeah!….It's now beginning to bother me that a high-profile case like mines was, and the department just closed the case without even interviewing one suspect. There were suspects all over the place, including your old boyfriend, Slim. Although at the time he was coming into his own, after killing off the big fish to take over the business."

"Wow!" She said. "I'm sorry about what happened to you and your family. But I didn't know about that. When I dated Slim, I was a stupid college student thinking that I had some big time business man. But, as it turned out, he was nothing but a drug dealer.

I know that it seem like it was a bad choice of men, and it was. But when I applied to become a police officer I let him and all his money go. However, in spite of what we think we know about the Major, we still don't have one ounce of evidence that he's involved in doing anything wrong. Even if we did know, and even if he was standing right here, and admitted that he's involved in whatever is going on, what in the world could we do about it?!" She sat down again next to John. "Don't answer that, I can answer it for you, not a damn thing! And don't forget what he said about the Chief. So, who do we go to if the Chief is dirty too, the Mayor?"

John laughed softly. "Damn woman, you sure do ask a lot of questions. Legally, we can't do a thing. He took me off the case, and he fired you. So, we're sitting here in a nice apartment, rent paid for a whole year. I've got a lot of money to spend, and we really don't have to do a thing to do except have a good time, just you and I. We may as well."

Seville laughed along with John. "Yeah, all that sounds mighty good. But that's not what we're going to do, now, is it, Mr. Big spender?"

John shook his head. "No, we're going to pay Danny Porter another visit, and then we're going to locate Mr. Bobby Turner, the third officer who I arrested. If the Major thought that Chad Wilson was apart of the people who killed my family, then the other two cops were right there with him."

Seville stood. "I'm ready if you are. Get dressed and lets make some noise. Oh, by the way," She turned and went to her bedroom, and immediately returned with a flat rectangular black box. She handed it to him. "This is for you. It's just a little something to take care of my baby when I'm not around." She smiled.

John hurriedly and opened the box. With the box opened on the coffee table, John surprisingly stared down at a Walther PPK .38 9mm Parabellum. He smiled as he picked it up and held it with both hands. "This is beautiful, Seville!" He said with a wide grin.

"She holds one round in the chamber, and fourteen more in the magazine." Seville said. "I've got a feeling that you're going to need all of them."

John stared at her for a moment. "If I do, it will be for my wife and baby girl. My daughter would have been twenty years old today." He looked sad for a moment.

After John got dressed, they both left the apartment not knowing what they were going to find, but whatever it was, they were ready for it. Now that his memory was rapidly returning to normal and to the night that he could not save his wife and daughter, revenge for what happened to them was more on his mind than anything else.

CHAPTER THIRTEEN

Approximately 11:00 a.m. that morning, the Chief met in a special meeting at City Hall with the Mayor and the two investigators from the fire department who had originally found the explosive material at the scene of the precinct bombing. This was more of a meeting of the minds than anything else. The Mayor and the Chief wanted to be absolutely sure that they all were on the same page when the Mayor gave his press conference about the bombing in about an hour from then.

The four men sat around the rectangle conference table in the Mayor's office, waiting for the fifth man, Major Butler. "Did you let the Major know about this meeting, Chief Martin?" The Mayor asked, staring directly at the Chief.

"Yes sir!...I called him just prior to my arrival, and he said he was on the way. He should be here any minute now." *I really don't care if he shows up or not.* He thought.

"Anyway, gentlemen, just to make sure that there are no slip ups. Are we all in agreement that the explosion was caused by a faulty gas line?" The Mayor asked.

"Yes sir, Mr. Mayor." Both Charles Watson and Walter Sutton responded.

"And just to let you know why we're giving the press this false statement is because, if we don't do it this way, we will have the President and everybody else in Washington telling us how run our city and this investigation." The Mayor said.

"We already have the FBI snooping around…" The Chief added. "And as far as I'm concerned about this investigation, the Feds can leave. We do not need them."

At that precise moment, Major Butler walked in after being told by the secretary that the group was waiting for his arrival. "Morning, Gentlemen!... Sorry I'm late. I had a meeting with a couple of my officers….Hope I didn't miss anything." He sat next to the Chief facing the Mayor.

"No, you didn't miss a thing Major Butler." Mayor Townsend said. "By the way, how is that old school gym working out as a temporary precinct for your people?"

"Just fine, Mr. Mayor….The men, and women of course are finding that it's a good place to work out without having to travel out to the police academy."

The Mayor smiled. "Good!" The Mayor glanced around the table. "Now, as we all know, or have heard about the situation on last night involving Major Butler, is there any way possible that Captain Chad Wilson was involved in the bombing?"

Before responding, Major Butler glanced at the Chief. "Maybe you should ask the Chief about that one, Mr. Mayor." He said with a smirk.

The Mayor looked at the two investigators. They knew what that look meant. It was for them to leave. They got up and walked out of the meeting. As soon as the door was closed behind the investigators, the Mayor looked at the Major. "Now, what the hell was all that about, Major?!"

The Major leaned on the table. "Mr. Mayor, all I know is Captain Wilson was sitting in my driveway waiting to kill me. And according to the things he said convinced me that he was sent there by someone in the department to do the job."

The Mayor frowned. "Are you saying it was someone in the police department?"

"Like I said, his words were, he was there to kill me." He again looked at the Chief. "And if he was not sent there by someone in the department, what other reason would he have to kill me?...None that I can think of."

"Major, you and I need to talk in private, because I don't know anything about what you're talking about." The Chief said.

The Mayor looked at both men. "No!...Whatever the problem is, we can discuss it right here in my office. I want to know what is going on between you two."

"There is nothing between us that a little private talk can't straighten out." The Major said.

The Mayor looked at both men for a moment. He was dismayed by what he was seeing between two of his best in the department. "Okay, I'll tell you what, I trust that you can work this out, and get to the bottom of this mess.....Because if I have to step in, neither one of you are going to like my solution. I hope you understand my meaning."

"Yes, Mr. Mayor, we both understand." The Chief said.

The Mayor watched both men leave his office looking as if they had discovered something that they were not expecting. As soon as they were down on the ground floor, the Chief could not wait to discuss the situation at hand. He motioned for the Major to follow him to a corner of the building out of hearing range of others. As soon as they were in position, the Chief snapped, "Listen, goddamnit! I know you were insinuating that I had something to do with Captain Wilson trying to kill you.... Yeah, I admit that it did cross my mind, and I probably would have, but I didn't..."

"Wasn't it you who suggested to Ethan that I should be eliminated, and he should replace me with you?" Major snapped back.

The Chief looked off for a moment. "Yeah, I told him that....But, I had second thoughts about it. Look, we're in this together, and we're this close to pulling this thing off." He held up two fingers, measuring a small distant between the fingers. "I'm satisfied with my cut. Because when the shit hit the fan around here, and it will, we better be as far away from this town and country as we can get. You and I can't be fighting over whose cut is the biggest, because if one of us goes down, we all go down."

Major Butler thought about what the Chief was saying. "Well, if you didn't hire Chad Wilson, somebody else close by sure as hell did!"

They both looked at each other with the same thought. "If I didn't, that only leaves one other person who knows about the gold, and that's Ethan." The Chief said smiling.

The Major shook his head. "No, Ethan wouldn't double-cross me like that. He knows, without me, he can't take that gold anywhere. I'm the key to this whole thing."

"Key, or no key, you need to keep your eyes on that cracker! Don't you know you're dealing with a third or fourth generation man whose granddaddy fought in the Civil War? It was his ancestor who tried to keep people of your race in slavery!"

Why am I listening to this asshole?! The Major thought. "Look, that was a hundred and fifty years ago, it has nothing to do with anything today. Why are you trying to turn this thing around to make it look like Ethan is the bad guy?....I still think you had something to do with what happened last night." Major Butler started to walk off, but suddenly stopped. "And if I had to put my money on it, I'd bet that it was you who had Calvin Gates and his family killed too."

The Chief rolled his eyes at the Major. "And what make you say a crazy thing like that?.... Calvin was my best friend. But it doesn't matter what you think, he's still alive."

"Yeah, he is, but his family isn't."

"How do I know you didn't do it? Calvin Gates and you were at odds. And if I can recall, he suspected you and your cut-throat goon squad as corrupted cops."

"Yeah, have it your way." The Major said as he walked off to his car and drove away leaving the Chief standing there. *You are a first class asshole, that's what you are.* The Chief, while still standing there in the lobby of City Hall, used his cell phone to make a call. "Okay, you're next up, and let's not make the same mistake again. I want this asshole dead!....In fact, I want them all dead. I don't care how you do it, call for backup if you have to, but that gold will not to leave this city, do you understand me?!" He closed his phone and left the building. *Why should I be taking a handout from that fucking Butler when I can take the whole damn thing? Then, I can be the richest ex-police chief in the free world.* He thought as he headed back to the department.

A few minutes later, Major Butler pulled his vehicle to a halt at the site where the so-called memorial was being built, and immediately got out and casually walked over to where Ethan was standing with the three diggers. Ethan suddenly turned to the Major and said, "I heard what happened last night. I told you this was going to happen. Listen, I don't trust that fucking Chief of yours. And as far as I'm concerned, he's planning anything and everything to keep us from moving this gold."

Major Butler nodded in agreement. "I know. But he's blaming what happened on you. But then, I know that's bullshit!"

"Okay, I told you what you had to do. If we don't kill the bastard today, he might ruin the whole damn operation. Not only that, we have to bring in the trucks tonight, and we have to get this gold loaded, and moved out of town immediately!"

"Don't worry about the Chief! You bring in the trucks, get them loaded, and I take care of the rest." The Major said with a laugh. "Hey man, we're almost there. It's just a matter of a few more minor details to be taken care of.

Ethan grabbed hold of the Major by both arms. "James, I'm depending on you. We can't let this asshole put a stop to something that we've gone through hell to get our hands on. Plus, our very lives depend on what you do to put a stop to Chief Martin. I can't go to prison and lose a hundred and fifty billion dollars in the process. Too much planning has gone into this operation."

"Like I said, don't worry, it's a done deal." *I have the perfect plan to stop him.*

He thought as he went back to his car. He was prepared to do whatever needed to be done to avoid being stopped now. But he knew that this could very well turn into a street fight with blazing gun fire between his side and the men who were hired by the Chief. However, at this stage of the game, neither man could afford to allow anything to stop them now, especially the nutty-professor as police chief. The problem now was that the Chief wanted the whole thing for himself. *There is always a greedy bastard in the bunch.*

The original plan was, once the gold was loaded onto two separate trucks, half and half, just in case one truck did not make it, they would still have half of the gold. Once the gold left Charlie Brown Airport for Miami, the Major's plan was to have his hired guns to eliminate the Chief in a mysterious hit as he was leaving his office a day later. This would eliminate any suspicion towards himself for he was certain that Mayor Townsend would temporarily appoint him to the position of police chief. Thirty days later, once the gold was in its new location, he and his entire family would suddenly disappear. He would leave behind clues that would indicate that he and his family had been kidnapped, murdered, and leaving behind no evidence of where the bodies were.

By his way of thinking, since Chief Martin wanting to take over the gold for himself, moving up the timing on his death was as simply as calling his people into action a day early. It was a possibility that things were going to get ugly, but that was the cost of doing business. Not only that, now that the planning had gone this far, it was impossible to stop it, or put things on hold. There was a timeline on everything they were doing.

Once the gold reached its destination, he along with Ethan and Sam would make the money transactions, and then the cash would be wired to

Australia where the three partners would meet up after thirty days to split the cash. The plan was perfect according to their calculation. However, the only fly in the ointment was Chief Harold Martin.

While driving towards downtown, Major Butler made a call to the men who had taken care of the mouthy bombers at the motel. "Listen, as we discussed earlier, the job is not over until that plane touches down at our secret location, and not a minute before. I want you to call in more men to make the haul tonight." He listened for a moment. "Yeah, so did I.....But our plans have changed, we have to move tonight, or we may never move. Too much is at stake to have the slightest thing go wrong now." He paused to listen once again. "Once the plane is in the air, I have another job for you, and I will pay one million dollars to each man when the job is done...." He closed his phone.

Now that this part of his business was done, he only had to make sure that John and Seville were in a position to not interfere. In spite of what he had told them earlier, he knew Calvin Gates well enough to know that he was not going to walk away from the case that he was working on. So, he had to make sure that he stirred them away from what was about to take place with the gold. He flipped open his phone and made another call to John and Seville. "John, the Mayor is about to give a news conference at noon. Why don't we meet up for lunch at Mary Mac's on Ponce around two, okay?" He closed the phone with a huge smile. *Now, this is what I call smooth operating.* He thought.

At noon sharp, Mayor Clifford Townsend stood at the podium in the atrium of city hall to give his speech to the media about the precinct bombing. Mayor Townsend was the first white mayor to be elected in the city of Atlanta since early 1970's. And if he wanted to get re-elected, he knew that he had to clear the air about this particular incident, or his chances were slim to none. In the past three weeks, the press had speculated that the explosion was either the work of terrorist, or possibly an inside job. He wanted to make sure that the public knew that it was neither.

Coming in on the tail end of what happened the night before, two high ranking officers getting into a shootout, one killing the other was making it very difficult to make anything sound legitimate or convincing. But Mayor Townsend was anxious to give it his best shot. It was like the city was falling apart from within, and there was nothing that he could do to stop the bleeding. "Ladies and gentlemen of the press, and to the citizens of this great city of Atlanta, I stand before you this afternoon to apologize for all the rumors and talk of terrorists that has been running wild throughout the city of Atlanta. I'm apologizing because that's all it is, idle gossip and false rumors.

"Atlanta, Georgia is probably one of the safest cities in America, if not the safest. But, I do take responsibility for the lives loss in the explosion. It was an unfortunate accident that was caused, not by corrupted police officers, drug dealers, or even terrorists. It was caused by my not making sure that the city's buildings were properly inspected and made safe for our employees to work. A faulty gas line was the culprit in this this tragedy. And I, the Mayor of this great city take full responsibility….. Thank you."

The Mayor did not respond to any questions, he turned swiftly and left the podium followed by two plain clothed police officers. The media shouted for answers to their many questions, but Mayor Townsend refused to give them what they wanted.

Instead, Major Butler took the heat by answering several questions before rushing off to make his lunch date with John and Seville. This of course, was the least he could do, the Major figured. After all, what did it mean to him? It meant that within the next thirty days, he would suddenly vanish and no one would ever see or hear from him again.

To him, it was like playing out a role in an adventure movie where three adventurous men who had discovered a treasure that was too large to fathom. And now, all three men were about to sail off into the sunset and live happily ever after.

In this case, the means really did justify the end. He had done something that was totally deplorable, downright wretched in the minds of others if they really knew what had happened that morning. Now, it was up to him to make sure that no one outside of the people involved ever knew what really happened. And that meant taking the Chief out of picture, because all three men knew that if they allowed the Chief to live, even if they managed to get away with the gold, he would let the world know what took place.

A few minutes after leaving city hall, Major Butler pulled into the parking lot of Mary Mac's restaurant on Ponce DeLeon Avenue. Seville and John were already seated in the rear of the eatery. When the Major joined them, Seville and John immediately saw what appeared to have been gladness written all over his face. As soon as he sat down, John asked in a soft tone, "Why are you so happy this afternoon? The news conference must have gone the way you, the Chief, and the Mayor wanted it to."

Major Butler glanced at the both of them. "You know, this is a very beautiful day. And tomorrow is shaping up to be even more beautiful. And by the way, yes it did."

"What, did you also hit the lotto or something?" Seville asked. "Oh, but then I forgot, you have access to the city's confiscated drug money, don't you?"

"That's right, but that's not the reason why this is a good day." The Major said, glancing around for the waitress. "Man, I'm starving!....Hey, lunch is on me."

After lunch was served, and the chit-chatting was over, the Major became a bit more serious. "Listen to me, the things that I said this morning, I want you to forget about that. You guys got a job with the Atlanta Police Department as long as you want it, okay?"

John smiled as he swallowed his ice tea. "What changed your mind?"

"Let's just say that a whole lot of things are going to change in the next thirty days. But right now, I'm not at liberty to talk about them."

"Why, what's all the secrecy, Major Butler?" Seville asked in an irritated voice. "When you put us together, you acted like your life depended on you informing us of things that we should know about. But for some reason, you don't think we're important enough to know what you know anymore. Remember, you brought us into this situation."

"A matter of fact, my life does depend on me keeping what I know a secret." He said after swallowing his food. "But, that's not to say that you are not important. By no means!....Look, you two are the most important people I know besides my wife and kids. In fact, when I'm gone, I will leave instructions on how to find me and the family. I'll have something big for you." He laughed loudly.

John did not speak for a few moments he only stared at the Major. Finally, he said, "Are you and the family leaving town on vacation or something?"

"You could say that, but not for a while....Not at least for thirty more days."

Suddenly, John changed the subject. "Do you think it's going to do any good to question Danny Porter and Bobby Turner, now that you've killed our third suspect?"

"By all means!....Listen, Porter and Turner are the only link to whoever ordered the hit on you and your family. It's because of them that the hit was put in place."

"We know where to find Porter, but where is Turner working these days?" Seville asked. "We haven't seen him around."

"You'll find Turner working in Property Management. He's a sergeant now. But, if I were you, I'd wait until they both get off work. That's just in case you may have to beat the crap out of them." The Major stood before finishing his lunch. "Anyway, I've got to run. I have a lot of work to do. And when you do find the answers, you may be totally surprised to know as to who was really behind the hit on you, John."

John leaned back in his chair. "I'm sure I will be....But why don't you tell me just in case these people turns up dead before I get to them."

"No, that will take all the fun out of seeing the expression on your face when you find out.....Besides, I owe it to them not to tell you." He laughed again.

"Funny thing though. Now that I have my memory back, I keep getting this strange feeling that it was you who ordered the hit. After all, those three were friends of yours. And they would do anything for you. Even commit murder, all for you."

"Well, apparently they weren't the friends you thought they were. I killed the ring leader last night in my driveway." He walked away. "Go figure that one out."

John and Seville sat and stared at the Major as he walked away. Finally, Seville said, "You know, I'm beginning to dislike him more and more everyday. And I don't care if he is your friend, or your brother who saved your life....Something is definitely wrong with that uppity black bastard!... How do you stand him?"

"I was just getting ready to say the same thing to you!" John said. "But I'm also wondering, if he didn't order the hit on me and my family, then who did?"

Seville smiled. "Looking at it from a Calvin Gates standpoint, it could have been anyone. You made a lot of enemies out there five years ago. And you certainly can't rule out Summerhill Slim."

John could only stare at Seville for he knew all too well that she was right. Then they both burst out in laughter. "Well, you certainly got me there!" John said.

"It seems like I know Calvin better than I know you, John." She said smiling.

CHAPTER FOURTEEN

The situation had grown to the point where everybody was leery of everyone else. There was an old saying about gold. "Gold will make fools out of men, and fools will eventually destroy themselves." Major Butler was trying hard to concentrate on how he was going to get rid of the Chief without bringing a whole lot of suspicion on himself. Once the Chief was out of the way, he would become the temporary chief. Then he would disappear like magic. But having time to think about the after-affects, the plan did not seem so brilliant after all. What had seemed to have been a foolproof plan had more holes being blown into it with each passing hour.

As he sat at his desk in a back office at the old gymnasium on Pryor Road, he rocked back and forth as he continued to contemplate what his next move would be. Suddenly, there was a knock on the door. "Come in….." He responded.

Sergeant Frank Logan, an evening watch supervisor who was in charge of the security detail at the old precinct site entered his office. The younger man closed the door behind him. He appeared to have been in his early thirties. "Major, I just wanted to bring you up to speed on what's been going on at the memorial site." He said as he sat in a straight chair facing the Major's desk.

Major Butler looked at the sergeant with his eyes bouncing back and forth. "What's been going on?" He was biting his lip and was somewhat confused.

"Well, for starters, we've had several strange looking people hanging around all day. They didn't come near the site itself, but they've been riding by and looking as if they were expecting something to happen."

Major Butler frowned. "Strange looking people, strange in what way?" He asked.

"Well, they didn't look like people who lives in the neighborhood. I saw at least five or six different men riding by repeatedly."

These were people obviously working for the Chief. He thought. "Sergeant, this is a life or death situation. You and your men stay alert and don't let anyone or anything get near that site without getting my approval first. You got that, Sergeant?!"

"Yes sir!" Sergeant Logan said sharply. "But sir, it's only a memorial site for the dead officers, how come you're saying that this is a life or death situation?"

"Sergeant Logan, don't worry about how it became a life and death situation, you just make damn sure that no one, and I mean absolutely no one enters that site!...Do you understand that?"

" Yes sir. But, does that goes for Chief Martin as well?"

"That goes especially for the Chief!" The Major snapped bitterly.

"But sir, how do you expect for me and my men to stop the Chief?....I mean, he is the chief of police.... And what he says goes! He can fire all of us on the spot!"

"Listen to me! Don't worry about losing your job. I'll take care of that. I don't care if you have to put his ass in handcuffs and arrest him. You stop him! Do you hear me?!...

And by the way, that is a direct order. I want you to follow it to the letter."

The Sergeant started to stand, but hesitated. "Can I ask one question, if you don't mind, sir?" The Sergeant gave the Major a quick smile. "What's down there?"

"Sergeant Logan, there are some old bones of Confederate Soldiers that we discovered while digging down there. We want to haul them out of there to a safe place before we let the world know what we have. That's all." Major Butler falsely explained.

"That's all?!" The Sergeant was baffled. "Well, if that's the case, why is there so much hush-hush, and all the secrecy about a bunch of dried up bones?"

"Sergeant Logan, you ask too many questions." The Major said. "Now, go follow my orders and stop worrying about what's in that hole, okay?....

After tonight, you won't have to worry about securing the location any longer. We're moving those old bones tonight to a safer place. Tomorrow, you can go back to your regular assignment."

Sergeant Logan nodded and then left the office still a bit confused. But he was still not quite willing to take the Major at his word about what was in the hole that seemed so valuable. But what could he do? He was not in a position to disobey a direct order just to look at a bunch of hundred and fifty year old bones. Nevertheless, he was not really sure what he was going to do if the Chief suddenly showed up. *I guess that's a bridge I'll have to cross when I get to it.* He thought as he was leaving the precinct.

Major Butler continued to sit and stare at the wall and the file cabinet in his office. He was beginning to dislike who he had become. He was now a murderer, he was a liar, and he was a thief. But he was too far gone now to second guess himself. There was no turning back. *But, I did it for the money. I did it for a reason that most men would give their lives for. At least, I'm still alive. And if I can find a way to secretly get rid of the Chief, I'm home free.* He was thinking. Then suddenly, the one thought that had been in the back of his mind all day long. John Sinclair was the answer to his problem. *I know who set him up to be killed five years ago, and I will say, it was the Chief.* He smiled as he leaned back in his chair. He had now come up with the perfect solution to escape any suspicions that he might bring on himself. If he convinced Calvin Gates that the Chief was the one who had someone to kill his family, Calvin would kill the Chief by night fall.

John Sinclair would later be arrested for the murder, and he could then be clear to follow through with his plans. *I love it when a plan comes together.* He thought. He had almost pointed the finger at the Chief earlier at the restaurant, but had refused to do so. He knew that Calvin Gates and the Chief were very close friends. *But how close will they be when I tell him what I know? I hate setting John up like this, but I have no choice. And telling him that Danny Porter and Bobby Turner were also key suspects in the murders, John will kill all three, and would be charged with three counts of murder. Of course, I alone will hold the key to the evidence that will be needed to clear him. But by the time his trial comes up, I'll be long gone. I hate that my half- brother and a man I love dearly will have to suffer such a dreadful fate as being charged with murder. But it is crunch time, and I'm the one who is doing the crunching. He'll eventually be set free.*

Across town at police headquarters sat Chief Harold Martin who had his own thoughts of how he was going to pull off the biggest heist in the history of the south. *I am fifty-five years old, and I'm too old to go to jail.*

And then, on top of that, I'll be going to jail for something that I had no part in doing. I'll be going for not arresting that black bastard who planned this whole thing. If I allow him and his two friends to get away, they will be rich beyond the human imagination, and I'll be a distant memory. Or I'll be back here with a few crumbs and a real risk of going to prison for the rest of my life.

How will I explain to the FBI how they managed to blow up my own precinct, killing thirteen of my officers, dug up all that gold, and I had no clue as to what was going on? This whole scheme is going to hit bottom like a rock falling off Stone Mountain. At best, I will be sitting on death row with the rest of those assholes. There is no easy solution of coming out of this thing smelling like a rose. Therefore, I will have to kill them all as soon as possible, take the gold for myself, and disappear just like they are planning to do. If it will work for them, it will work for me as well.

At that moment of contemplating his plans, his secretary buzzed him. "Chief, Sergeant Turner is here to see you." She said.

"Okay, Susan, send him in." He said with a smile. As soon as Bobby Turner entered the office and closed the door behind him. "Sit down, Sergeant Turner." The Chief said. "Listen, I know what I told you earlier, and that was depending on what these bastards do. Well, as of right now, it appears that I'm going to be left holding the fucking bag, while those assholes fly off into the sunset to live happily ever after. No, fuck that!

We're going to be the ones leaving them holding the bag, and facing murder charges. You and I, we'll be the ones somewhere in another part of the world living like kings. Our wives won't even know where we are. Now, what do you think about that?!"

Sergeant Turner smiled. "I think it's sound very good, sir!.....So, you're saying we're going to have to leave our wives behind?"

"That's only for a little while, Bobby." Chief Martin said grinning. "Listen, for a while, no one can know where we are, what we've done, or why......And as far as the gold that we're going to take from those assholes, no one can ever know what happen. Now, did you get in touch with your people like I asked you to?"

"Yes sir, they're standing by waiting for the word. I've got five, well trained ex- military men who will hi-jack anything, anywhere. They all are from out of the State."

"Very good, Sergeant.....Now, the only problem right now is, they're expecting for me to do something. Therefore, they've been very quiet about when they're going to move the gold. But the one thing I know for certain, they'll be moving tonight. Or it might be tomorrow night. But what the hell! It really doesn't matter, Bobby. I want you and your people out there whenever they decide to move it. I want that gold for myself!"

"Consider the gold yours, sir!" Turner said with a slight grin.

"Good, we don't want anymore slip ups like we had last night."

"I understand, Chief. There won't be anymore slip ups this time."

"There better not be......" The Chief said as Sergeant Turner departed his office.

*   *   *

"Slim, this is Seville, I need you to do me a favor later on this evening." She said into her cell phone.

"Yeah, and what's that?" Summerhill Slim asked as he sat in his home office of his south side mansion.

"Can we stop by your place, and we'll discuss the matter when we get there?"

Slim laughed before answering. "Yeah, come on by, I want to see your pretty face again anyway...You said we,...are you still with that fancy old dude, the cop?"

Seville glanced over to the passenger's seat at John. "Yeah, I'm still with the fancy old dude, the cop. I mean, why shouldn't I be, he's my partner?"

"Yeah, just thought I'd ask.....You never know, I was hoping that you would have dumped his ass off somewhere." He laughed loudly.

"So, you've got joke today, huh? Not a chance, Sweetie."

"Ah, baby, I was just funning with you.....Yeah, come on by, I'll be here." Slim closed his cell phone as he pointed a finger at G-Money who was sitting across from his desk. "Tell the guys we've cops coming by, make sure everything is cool."

G-Money got up and rushed out of the office to the courtyard where Slim had several of his expensive automobiles parked and four bodyguards stood nearby talking among themselves. "Guys!...Look sharp, we've got cops coming by."

Ten minutes later, Seville pulled the Hummer into the gated driveway of the white brick three stories mansion. She stopped the vehicle in front of the house on a circular driveway where a doorman stepped out to the car and opened the doors. "Mr. Carter is expecting you." The elderly man said.

Seville glanced at John as they were escorted into the huge foyer surrounded by huge expensive paintings on the walls. "My, my, my, it's amazing what drug money will buy you when you've got half of the police department on your payroll, isn't it?"

John smiled as they continued to follow the elderly black man to where they met Slim in his office. Slim played the part of a big shot businessman very well. He stood immediately as they entered his office. "What a surprise! I didn't expect you two to be calling on me, at least not this soon." He pointed to the smaller leather sofa in front of his desk. "Please have a seat."

John slowly looked around, admiring all that he saw. "How do you do it, Slim?" He asked politely.

Slim smiled, pretending not to know what John was referring to. "How do I do what, Mr. Sinclair?"

"This!....This house has to be worth at least four or five million dollars easily. How do you manage to stay in the drug business, living like this, and not go to jail?"

"A former drug dealer.....I am a legitimate business man. I have three night clubs and five music stores throughout the city. I pull in over ten million dollars a year. And the last time I checked, none of that is against the law.....May I offer you something to drink?" He glanced towards Seville first.

Seville glanced at John before she responded. They both agreed on brandy and coke. The house man sharply turned and left the room to get the drinks. While they were waiting, John said, "Yeah, I suppose you have a point, if what you say is true."

Slim was leaning back in his soft leather chair as he threw both hands in the air. "Hey, check me out if you like. I ain't got nothing to hide from the cops or anyone else. I'm clean in every direction. But then, I'm sure you didn't come out here to check up on me, because if you had, you'd have shown a search warrant at the gate, right?"

"Right!" Seville said with a grin. "But, what we want you to do for us might be a little out of your league if you're going straight these days."

Slim suddenly leaned forward. "Yeah, what do you want me to do?"

"Like kidnapping a cop and bringing him here and interrogating him." John said.

"Well, he's really not a cop. But he's the same cop you got fired a few years back." Seville explained. "Danny Porter."

"Danny Porter." Slim repeated, loving the thought of kidnapping a cop for the cops. "Why bring him here to my pad?"

"Because if you bring him here, he'll be convinced that he might not live to get out of here if he doesn't cooperate." Seville answered.

"I like the sound of that. And besides, I owe that cop a good ass kicking anyway."

"Not only do we want you to give him a good ass kicking, we want you to beat some answers out of him at the same time." Seville said.

Slim stared at both cops for a moment. He was wondering why had they come to him? At that time, the house man who had gone for drinks suddenly re-appeared carrying a tray with a bottle of brandy and three cans of coke and some ice. He placed it on the desk and asked Slim, "Will there be anything else you want me to do, sir?"

Slim nodded with his head indicating no. The man turned and left the room, while a bodyguard stood at the office door. "Now!" Slim said as he leaned across the desk pour himself a drink. "This is some of best brandy in America. I had it imported all the way from France." He glanced at Seville smiling. "Anyway, now you say that you want me to do all of this for you, but what's in it for me?"

Seville stood and poured her own drink, mixing it with coke. She glanced around.

"From what I can see, there isn't much we can offer you except the satisfaction of knowing that you're doing me, rather us a favor." She sat back down next to John.

Slim laughed. "Five years ago, that would have been music to my ears, especially from you. But now, I mean, you're a cop, and the way he's looking at you, you're a cop's woman." He glanced at John.

John then stood to pour his drink. "Come on, Slim, lets cut with the bullshit! We need your help. Now, you're either going to help us or not, without making it personal."

John sat back down next to Seville, took a sip, and gave Slim a toast.

"I don't know who you are, or where you came from, but you're one smooth motherfucker!" Slim said with a half smile. "And I like that in a man. Any man who can snag the most beautiful woman I've ever known must be something special. And because of that, I'll help you two niggers."

Seville smiled at Slim, glancing at John. "If Slim say you're smooth, trust him, you are very smooth!" She then focused on Slim. "Thank you. Maybe one day, we'll be able to return the favor."

Slim leaned back. "Okay, where do I find this asshole of an ex-cop?"

John glanced at his watch, it was 15:31hrs. "Right now, he's still at the bank in the West End. Anywhere between five and six, he should be leaving there headed for home. But, we don't want him to get home. We want to take him somewhere in between."

"You want to kidnap an ex-cop in broad daylight?" Slim asked suspiciously.

"Yes." Seville said. "We know it's risky, but he knows something that is very important to our investigation. And we must find out what that is."

Slim shook his head. "Wait, I don't understand. What is it you think he knows?"

John stood. "Okay, first of all, we talked to him yesterday about a dead cop named Calvin Gates. He then met up with Captain Chad Wilson to discuss our meeting with him. Last night, Chad Wilson was killed by Major Butler. Now, I don't know how, but I think all these cops know who killed Calvin Gates. Plus, these were the same two cops, plus, Bobby Tuner who were taking bribe money from you. I'm sure you remember them."

Slim rocked forward, leaned on his desk as John sat back down. "Man, this sound like some crazy shit! It sounds like something right out of one of those James Bond movies. However, I know this Major Butler, and if there ever was a cop that you don't want to fuck with, it's this dude, man!"

John frowned when Slim said that. "Why would you say that?"

"Look man, the Major been running things around here for years! And as far as I'm concerned, if this Calvin Gates was killed by anybody, the Major did it….Not only that, the damn so-called precinct bombing, there is no way in hell was that some kind of accident. A gas explosion my ass! The bastards blew that building up themselves…Now, what the hell for? That's what I would like to know."

"So, you're saying that you believe that the Major was behind the bombing of his own precinct as well?" Seville asked, glancing at John.

Slim stood up. "Have you been out there yet?!...C'om on man, it's like Fort Knox over there. There are cops everywhere. And they won't let anyone near that place for it to be nothing but a hole in the ground. And all the cops I saw, they work for the Major."

John stared at Seville. Suddenly, they both knew that Slim had just put the spotlight on some untold reason why the precinct was bombed, and why they changed their stories about what caused the blast. "So, what's in the hole?" John asked Slim.

Slim turned and stuttered, "What, what is in the hole?!"

"You heard him the first time, what's in the hole?!" Seville snapped.

CHAPTER FIFTEEN

At 18:35 hrs., Danny Porter drove his pickup south on Lee Street towards Sylvan Road. He had just left the bank, stopped by the liquor store on Lee Street, picked up a six pack of beer for the evening, and he was headed home. He stopped for the traffic light at the corner of Lee Street and Lucile Avenue, signal lights on to turn left onto Sylvan Road. He turned left when the light changed to green, crossed over the railroad tracks to travel east. At the corner of Sylvan and Harper Street, he stopped for a stop sign. Then suddenly out of nowhere, two black Mercedes S-500s' pulled in front and back of his truck. Two men wearing masks bailed from each car running towards his pickup with automatic weapons drawn. One man shouted, "Get out of the truck, or you're dead."

Porter slowly raised his hands, not understanding why he was being ordered by a group of armed masked men to get out of his truck. *Am I being car-jacked?* He asked himself as he looked around at the cars that they were riding in. *Naw, I don't think so.* He started to go for his own weapon that was on the front seat, but the man on the right side of the vehicle with his own weapon pointed into the window, motioned to let it be. "Do y'all know who the fuck I am?!" Porter yelled as another man yanked his door open.

"Naw, we don't know who you are, and we don't give a shit either!" The man shouted back as he pulled Porter from the truck. "And don't be a fucking cute guy either, or we will kill you right here."

"Look, I ain't going no fucking place until somebody tell me what in the hell is going on, man?!" Porter yelled as he pulled back, falling against the truck.

Another man who was standing on the side of Porter slammed the butt of his weapon to the side of Porter's head. Porter dropped to his knees and the two men dragged him by both arms to the back door of one of the Mercedes, and shoved him into the rear seat. Another man climbed into the driver's seat of the truck and all three vehicles sped off eastward towards Highway 166.

Fifteen minutes later, the three vehicles pulled into the courtyard of the mansion as John, Seville, and Slim looked on. "Take him to the guesthouse!" Slim commanded the two men who dragged the still unconscious Porter out of the back seat of the Mercedes. Inside the guesthouse, Porter was seated in a straight chair with his head slumped over. And as John began to have memories of what happened to his family, he was anxious to get some answers out of Porter any way that he could.

A glass of cold water was plashed into Porter's face to bring him around by Slim. "Wake your silly ass up, Porter!" Slim shouted. "We didn't bring you here to sleep."

Porter shook his head several times before realizing where he was. He immediately stared into the faces of Slim, Seville and John and three other men who were standing in the background. In the guesthouse, Porter was seated in the living room, facing the front door. John pulled up a chair and sat directly in front of him. Seville remained in the back of Porter while Slim stood with his arms folded next to Porter looking on.

Porter looked at John, remembering that he was the same man who had visited him at the bank. "I remember you. You were at the bank asking questions about Calvin Gates. Who are you?!"

"I'm Lieutenant Calvin Gates…Five years ago, you along with Chad Wilson, and Bobby Turner worked for me on the Red Dog squad. And you three also were taking pay-offs from this man, Jeffery "Slim" Carter." He nodded towards Slim.

Slim leaned down in front of Porter looking at John. "You are Calvin Gates?! How is that possible? Calvin Gates is dead."

"Yeah, how is that possible?!" Porter repeated as he started to stand up.

"Sit your ass down!" Slim yelled at Porter. "Don't make me tie your ass to this chair." He then turned his attention back to John. "Are you really Calvin Gates?"

"Yes, I am Calvin Gates. Yeah, I know, I don't look like myself, but it's me."

"Well, if you're Calvin Gates, then you should know that these three bad cops were the ones who everyone in the department thought were behind your murder. Or, what they thought was your murder."

"That's why I had you to bring him here. I already know that he was apart of what happened to me and my family. He also knows who ordered the bombing of the house that my wife and daughter were in......But then, now that I remember, they were already dead when I arrived."

Porter's eyes dotted back and forth between Slim and John. "Why did y'all bring me to this place?" He attempted to stand again. Slim snapped his fingers for two of his men to tie him to the chair with a rope that they had nearby.

"We tried to treat you with a little respect since you were a cop and all." Slim said. "But no, you want to stand up. I don't know where you think you're going. I've got bodyguards all over this place."

"Yep, he's right about that." Seville said from the rear of the room.

As soon as the men had tied Porter to the chair, John continued. "Listen, you may as well get the monkey off your back, because I'm only concerned with who gave the orders to kill me and my family.....Whoever that may be, I'm going to kill that person. You, on the other hand, I just might let you live. But that will depend on how convincing you are. So, you may as well do yourself a favor. Tell me what I want to know."

Porter looked at John in a very strange manner. *The voice might be that of the Lieutenant, but the face, he doesn't look anything like Gates.* "Listen, I don't know who gave the orders. When you came back to the jail and released us, I went straight home. I was just glad to be out of jail. And, later that night, I received a call from Wilson saying that somebody had called him and said that you and your whole family were dead."

"So, who called Chad Wilson and told him that I had been killed?" John asked in a firm voice. "And if I think you're lying to me, I going to kill you right here."

"He didn't tell me who had called him. And if he knew, he never told me."

"And in five long years, you never thought to ask him who made the called?"

"Look, we all knew that regardless of who blew up that old house with you and your family inside, it was an act of revenge. And we were going to be the prime suspects for your murder. All we wanted to do was get as far away from that case as possible. That's why we all transferred out of zone three."

"So, why did the department stop the investigation?" Seville asked as she walked around to the front of Porter.

"Well, the Major and the Chief agreed that there was so little evidence until it was impossible to find who did it." Porter paused for a moment still staring at John. "If you survived the blast, how did you manage to escape?... Or better yet, how did you make this change into John Sinclair?"

"That's a long story, and who I've become is not as important as to why I become John Sinclair. So, you don't know who gave the orders to kill me, and you don't know who rigged the explosive, although it was done because of you three?"

"Look man, you were our supervisor, and we knew sooner or later that you were going to find out and it was going to end badly. As you said, we were taking pay-offs from drug boys. And you caught us red-handed. We should have gone to jail. But I don't think either one of us would have gone as far as murdering you and your family. It was your job to supervise your men. And I don't know who wanted us out of jail that badly."

"The people who didn't want you guys to spilling your guts about who else were on Slims' payroll." John turned and looked at Slim. "Who were they, Slim?"

Slim ignored John's stare for a moment. Then he muttered, "Who were they in relation to whom or what?"

"Slim, stop the question with a question bullshit!...You know exactly what and who he's talking about." Seville snapped angrily.

"Oh, am I the one being interrogated now?" Slim asked with a laugh.

"No, you're not being interrogated. I just want to know who else were on your payroll that had enough juice to order a hit on me and my family, that's all." John said.

Slim walked over and sat in an arm chair across the room. "Listen, you didn't hear this coming from me, okay?" He finally said.

"Okay, we didn't hear it coming from you." John said smiling.

"At the time when you and your Red Dogs gang-busters were knocking down all drug dealers doors except mines, not only were these assholes were on my payroll, but both of your bosses were picking up cash from me as well." Slim said as he glanced back and forth from John to Seville.

"So, you're saying that the Major and the Chief were taking cash from you as well?" John asked anticipating the answer would be yes.

"Yes, that's what I'm saying!"

"So, rather than transferring me from the squad, or firing me, they figured it was better that they killed me instead." John said to Slim.

"Killing you, I'm not sure who, or how that even played a part. But, the way I figured it, when you arrested those guys that day and placed them in the county jail, the big dogs knew these dudes would eventually cut a deal to save their own asses."

"It makes perfectly good sense, John." Seville said. "And the only way they were going to stop you from bringing down a whole lot of cops, including the Major and the Chief, they were forced to eliminate you."

"Right!" Danny Porter snapped. "Look man, I told you, we didn't have anything to do with killing you and your family. It happened the way she said it did, obviously."

John stood and began to pace the floor in front of Porter. "Yeah, it sounds logical that way. But, it doesn't explain why the Major saved my life if he's the one who tried to kill me. I am still dealing with that part of the equation. And then, he turns around and steals all the drug money that we had confiscated to set me up with a whole new life and identity." He turned and looked at Seville, Porter, and Slim. "Does that part make any sense to any of you?"

Slim shook his head. "Now, that's some crazy shit, too crazy for comprehension."

Porter said, "No, I don't understand it….."

Seville smiled before she said, "Did you ever think that maybe he had a change of heart after he had done what he did?....I mean, you, his brother, your wife and daughter, maybe he just decided that he wanted give something back to you to make up for what he had taken away from you."

Slim looked at John. "As crazy as it sounds, she does have a point."

John was still pacing. "He's going to give me my life back for killing my wife and daughter." He shook his head. "That's one hell of a trade off, don't you think?!"

"But there's only one other way for you to find the truth,…." Seville said.

"Yeah, and what's that?" John asked as he took his seat again.

"Beat the truth out of the Major before you kill him."

Slim immediately stood. "You want my boys to take care of him for you?" He asked smiling.

"No, this is something that I'm going to have to do myself. In fact, I owe it to my family to take care of it." John said.

"Can you kill a friend after five years, the one who saved you life?" Slim asked.

"Base on what we know already, he was the bastard who tried to take my life. And he took the lives of my loved ones…Yes, I can kill the sonofabitch!"

Suddenly, one of Slims' men who were not in the guesthouse briefly knocked on the door at the same time he was opening it and rushed in. "Boss, you ain't going to believe this shit that's on the news! Turn on the television!"

Everyone's attention was on the big screen television as Slim picked up the remote and pushed the on button. It was a "News Break" on the evening news. The announcer spoke; "Breaking news just in from our on our scene reporter." The Reporter: "It is not clear exactly what happened, but from what we know at this moment, Major James Butler, a twenty year veteran on the Atlanta Police Department was apparently traveling alone on this stretch of highway near his home when he apparently for some unknown reason, lost control of his vehicle, and plunged down this thirty feet embankment. The vehicle struck a tree, burst into flames and immediately upon impact, the car exploded. The Major was trapped inside and died on the scene instantly. When we know more on what caused this terrible accident, killing one of the department's top commanders, we'll get back to you."

Everyone in the guesthouse was completely stunned, flabbergasted beyond words. They took their seats wondering what a strange turn of events that had taken place at the very moment that they were discussing the man. "Wait a minute, what just happened? I can't believe what I just heard, it's no way!" John finally said.

Slim rolled his eyes towards Seville. "That beat any damn thing that I've heard of."

"Hey, you guys!" Porter shouted. "Y'all can cut me loose now. We know who killed your family. Although it's a little late, but maybe he got what he deserved."

John stared at Porter for a moment. "Let him go!" He said. "The man who held the key to what happened to me and my family is now all of a sudden dead himself. This shit is getting crazier by the day."

"Well, we still have the Chief." Seville said. "He was just as much involved as the Major was."

John stood. "I guess the Chief is our next stop. He'll be at the crash scene."

John thanked Slim and for all that he had done as he and Seville got back into the Hummer and sped out onto the main street and headed towards the crash site where they knew they could certainly find Chief Martin. Fifteen miles across town to Cascade Road off Interstate 285, they began to slow down due to the heavy traffic in the area. John glanced at his watch, it was 19:35 hrs., and it was still daylight. When they arrived on the scene, they walked for another fifty yards to the actual crash site. They spotted the Chief standing in the middle of several uniformed police officers who were trying to figure out what had happened. The news media which consisted of several cameras and reporters were getting bits and pieces of what they thought had happened to Major Butler.

When the Chief looked up and saw John and Seville, he turned and walked over where they were standing. "I'm sorry, John." He said glancing around at the surrounding. "As you can see, this is a deep curve, and the best that any of us can figure out, he must have loss control of his vehicle, and ran off the road. It's just a very tragic accident as far as we can tell right now….We've had many such accidents in this very curve."

John and Seville stared down the embankment at the still smoldering car, it was totally burned to a shell. "How were you able to identify it as being the Major's car?"

"We were able to check the tag number that fell off on impact." The Chief said. "That's his car. But as far as he's concerned, we still haven't positively identified the body. We'll have to do that from his dental record. But we know it's the Major."

Again, John looked around the wooded area. "The Major lived in this area, right?"

"Yeah, he did, about a mile from here. I've already sent a man to his resident to inform his wife, pending identification of course…..Why you asked?"

"Well, putting myself in the same situation, I would know how dangerous this curve is, and I would have slowed down. But the way this apparently happened, the Major didn't apply brakes at all. He just simply ran off the road as if he was asleep or already dead."

The Chief stared at John for a moment before he too glanced up and down the road. "You know you may have a point. But as of right now, unless something really jump out at my investigators, and say this was more than just an accident, we don't have anything else to go on."

John smiled. "Oh, I didn't mean to imply that there was some sort of foul play. But, it does make one wonder, especially by him traveling this road everyday, twice a day."

The Chief forced himself to smile. "I understand….He was our friend, and that's a natural reaction, especially after,…." He cut his statement short.

"Go ahead, especially after what, Chief?!" John immediately asked.

"Especially, after what happened last night." The Chief looked away for a moment. "You did hear about the shooting last night where he ended up killing a fellow officer?"

"Yeah, I heard….." John suddenly kicked a small rock in the road. "Anyway, the main reason why we're here, I heard when Calvin Gates and his family were murdered, you and Major Butler were on Summerhill Slims' payroll. And after hearing that, you are now my number one suspect for the planning of those murders. Are you willing to comment on that?" John and Seville waited for the sky to suddenly drop on their heads.

"And just where did you get all of your information from?" The Chief finally asked after carefully glancing around to see if there was anyone close by who could possibly overhear their conversation. "Before you answer that, you may want to think about the consequences of your statement."

"And what fucking consequences are you talking about?! I don't work for you." John said angrily, trying to hold his voice down. "What you need to be worrying about is what's going to happen to you if I what I'm hearing is correct."

"Trust me, John, your information is incorrect. And if you want to discuss this any further, you need to pick a better place and time than this right here."

John glanced around at the news media. "Why, are you afraid that the cameras are going to pick up on what we're talking about?"

"Listen, I can easily say that your former boss was responsible for whatever happen to you, which he was. But what good is that going to do any of us now?" Chief Martin said, glancing down the embankment at the burned wreckage. "Listen, when you get your memory back, you need to start looking at the possibility that you brought that whole damn thing down upon yourself."

Before John realized what he was doing, the Calvin Gates suddenly appeared and came out with a right hook to the side of Chief Martin's jaw. The Chief dropped to the ground on one knee in pain. John abruptly turned and walked away as Seville helped the Chief back to his feet. Then she walked away as the several reporters who saw what had just happened ran over to him with questions. Two officers who also witnessed the knock-down attempted to stop John, but Seville showed up and flashed her badge. "It's okay, he's a cop." Then she suddenly turned around and ran back to the Chief. "By the way, Chief Martin, he has gotten his memory back." She then ran back to their vehicle.

Reporters and officers alike who had just witnessed the so-called attack on a police chief were stunned by the Chief's reaction. He stood, bushed himself off, smiled for the cameras, and said, "It was nothing, it was just a misunderstanding....He's a very good friend of mines....." He watched the Hummer as it drove off. *I don't have time for him at the moment. He'll just have to wait.* He thought as he pulled out his cell phone and dialed a number. "Get over to where they are digging, and shut it down! I don't want nothing or anyone in or out of there until I get there." He closed his phone and began answering questions for the media.

CHAPTER SIXTEEN

It was 20:00hrs. later that evening by the time the Chief's men arrived on the scene of the bombed precinct. Several men got out of their cars and began to stare at what was once a canvas enclosed restricted area that was now reduced a mere hole in the ground, and all the security personnel were gone. "Where did they go?" Sergeant Bobby Turner asked no one in particular as he turned in circles. "Where in the fuck did everybody suddenly run off to?!" He shouted in disgust.

One of the men who were with him responded, "Maybe whatever it was that they were guarding, they loaded it up and took it with them."

Sergeant Turner could see that for himself. He stumped his foot several times. "Hell, I can see that! But the question is still the same, where did they go?!" He paced the street in front of where the precinct use to be, and thinking about what the Chief was going to say when he learned that Major Butler had out smarted him again. *But how could he? The Major was found dead just a couple of hours ago in a burned out vehicle.* He took out his cell phone and dialed the Chief who was wrapping up a news conference with all the local TV and radio stations. "Chief, there is no one here......"

"What do you mean, there is no one there?" The Chief asked as he drove back downtown to his office.

"Just what I said, Chief, there ain't no fucking body here! And whatever it was they were guarding, it's gone as well."

"Sergeant!...I want you to take your men and get out to that damn Charlie Brown Airport as soon as possible. I'm on my way, I'll meet there." He closed his phone and headed for the airport. *I knew I should have killed that goddamn Butler when I had the chance, and took the gold for myself. Now, those two asshole partners of his jumped the gun by moving the gold hours early. They must have known that my men were going to hijack the trucks on their way to the airport.* "Goddamnit!!" He cursed while he was thinking about what happened to the gold. He turned on his blue lights and siren and floored the accelerator increasing his speed towards the county airport.

As far as Major Butler was concerned, there was no doubt in the Chief Martin's mind that he was dead. The Major had saved him the trouble of having to do the job by killing himself in a car crash. His only question now was, how was he going to collect his hundred million dollars that was promised to him by the Major if the gold was gone, and Major Butler was dead? His only hope now was to catch Ethan Johnston and Sam Houston before they loaded the gold onto a plane and vanished like the wind.

Even if he caught the plane before taking off, he knew that he would have to arrest Ethan and Sam and force them to honor Butler's promise. Any other way, it would bring too much attention to the gold itself, and how it came into existence. If that happens, there would be many serious questions asked about the precinct bombing and the thirteen officers who were murdered because of the gold. *No, I can't allow that to happen. With Major Butler dead, if anything goes wrong, I'm the only one left to take the fall.*

It was a few minutes later, the Chief and three car loads of uniformed police officers stopped at the security gate at the Charlie Brown Airport. The Chief was leading the way at the security gate as he immediately began to quiz the guard. "I'm looking for some trucks, possibly two with at least four white males, two driving, and two riding shotgun or guarding the contents…..Have you seen anyone like that?!"

The black female guard checked her in-and-out log sheet to make sure that she had allowed such vehicles to enter the private and chartered aircrafts air field. "Yes I have, about two hours ago." She said.

"Do you know exactly where the plane they were headed to is located?"

"Yes I do…." The guard hesitated to say any more.

The Chief was getting impatient. "Where?!…Where is it goddamnit!?"

"The plane took off about thirty minutes ago. The trucks are still parked in hangar number four. And who exactly are you?!" The guard asked but she got no answer.

The Chief immediately floored the accelerator, spinning off towards hangar number four with the other three cars speeding off right behind him. There was no doubt in his mind that Ethan and Sam had pulled the slickest getaway of all times. And the worst part about the whole thing in his mind, there was nothing he could do about it now. Major Butler was dead, the gold was gone, and he was left holding the bag of explaining to the Mayor what was going on with the building of a memorial monument.

Racing to hangar number four, and all vehicles coming to sliding halt in front of the hangar door. Everyone got out of their cars and rushed for the double doors on the hangar. Several officers pushed the doors open, only to find two white, two-ton panel trucks parked inside the hangar. No one was in or around the building. A few moments later, two airport security cars with two men each drove up to the hangar to investigate the business of the Atlanta Police.

A short fat security lieutenant approached the Chief first. "Sir, ah, Chief Martin, can we help you find whoever or whatever you're looking for?"

The Chief turned around and pointed at the trucks. "We are here to arrest the men who drove here in these two trucks. And do you know where they are now?"

The security boss glanced around at all the other police officers. "Ah, a gentleman by the name Ethan said to give you this." He handed it to the Chief a white envelope.

Chief Martin took the envelope and began reading the note inside. *Chief Martin, I know this is not what Major Butler had in mind. But you must understand our situation. I just could not afford to have a man like you creating a problem for this operation. So, I hope you are able to handle all the questions that you will eventually get thrown at you. Sorry for the trouble we caused you. Ethan,* "That sonofabitch!" The Chief cursed softly.

"Anything wrong, Chief Martin?" The security guard asked.

"No, nothing is wrong." The Chief said, glancing around the hangar. "Do you know where the plane was headed to?"

"Well, their flight plan said they were headed to North America, somewhere around Ontario Canada....But I have my doubts about that of course, just my opinion." The security guard said.

"I believe you." The Chief said before turning around, pointing to his officers to load up and depart the area. He suddenly realized that there was no one that he could turn to figure out what his next move would be. Then suddenly he thought. *Wait a minute! I still have John....Or Calvin Gates, my old friend. Either way, I can trust him. If I can confide in him about what happened, I think he would be willing to look for Ethan and Sam. But where would he look?* It was a good question, but he had no answer.

*   *   *

Two days passed, John and Seville remained close by their apartment, they were out of ideas as to what they were supposed to do next. The Major was no longer running the show. John sat quietly for two days while Seville went out shopping at Lenox Mall both days. He pondered the whole situation from start to finish. Major James Butler was a very complex man to say the least, he told himself. If what Slim had said was true, the Major arranged for someone to kill him and his family, but failed to complete the job. The Major then turns around and saved his life, hid him in the north Georgia mountains for five years with a complete new identity and a very comfortable lifestyle, after he stole five million dollars from the precinct safe and created him as John Sinclair. Why?

After five years, he recruits John to come back to his old job, but under a bogus investigation. He brought John back into the city for a reason other than the one that he laid out for him initially. And then, the Major made sure that John was comfortable in the city by renting an expensive penthouse for a year in advance. Then he recruited a beautiful roommate for John to make sure that he was not bored with his new assignment. John looked at this mind boggling situation from every angle possible, and there was still nothing that he could see that gave him a clear answer as to why the Major had done the things that he did. Not one thing, except for the fact they were half brothers. But even from that angle, none of what he was looking at made any sense to him.

Suddenly, he remembered the hole in the ground at the old precinct. Maybe that was where the key to this puzzle was hidden. He immediately got dressed and caught a taxi downtown to his old precinct. Seville had taken the Hummer to do her shopping.

When the cab arrived at the site, the rain began to pour down heavily. He told the driver to wait while he climbed down into the twenty-five foot hole that was left open. He began slid in the mud as he struggled to get inside the deep trench. Once down in the trench, he was shocked to be standing face to face with an open vault door large enough to drive his Hummer into. "What the fuck is this?"

He stepped inside of the huge vault which also shielded him from the rain. He turned in circles, looking up and down the four walls trying to figure out what had been secured in the steel box for at least a hundred years, he figured. He scanned for evidence on the floor and walls, spotting traces of gold smeared against the walls. He rubbed with thumb and index fingers together trying to get a feel of what exactly he had discovered. Finally, he had figured out what had been hidden in the vault, it was gold. It was a lot of gold. It was enough gold to kill an entire day watch of thirteen officers for in order to dig it out. *Gold! So, this is what all the fuss is about, gold! That's why the Major couldn't or wouldn't talk about what he was doing. It was all about the gold.*

While standing inside the vault, he could hear a rumbling outside of the metal box, and it sounded like dirt falling on top of the vault. He started to run out because he had a bad feeling that something was happening and it was not good. As he started for the door of the vault, dirt began to slide down over the box, covering up the door. "Holy shit, I'm being buried in this fucking box!" He tried desperately to climb through the mud, but he could not. Suddenly, there was only one thing to do, he grab hold of the door that was opened to inside and began to close it to keep the mud from sliding inside.

He began yelling for the cab driver, hoping that his yelling could be heard. He began calling for help. "Hey!...Hey!...Somebody help!... Somebody help, I'm down here!"

For several minutes, the cab driver did not notice anything happening because he was listening to the car radio. But then he glanced over towards the site, thinking that his passenger had been in the hole for a long while. Then he realized that the hole was being covered up from the wet mud sliding down. "Oh shit!" He got out and raced over to the trench that was completely covered up now. He turned in circles trying to figure out what to do next. "What I'm going to do?" He wanted to call for help. He pulled out his cell phone to dial 911 when he spotted a tractor with a backhoe attached to it. He had driven one in the past. That was it. It was the only way to save his passenger. He ran approximately a hundred feet to the tractor, climbed on top of the machine with the key still in the ignition. He started it up and drove toward the trench.

John was almost in panic mode as he continued yelling for help. Once again his life was flashing before his eyes, telling him that he was about to die. Sooner or later, the air was going to be sucked right out of that vault, and he was going suffocate in the metal box. "God, if you're listening, send somebody to get me out of here!....Hey God, you did it before, you can do it again." Suddenly, he could hear the backhoe banging on the roof of the vault. "Oh Lord, you did it!...You did it!"

The cab driver operated the backhoe like a true professional as he maneuvered the hoe back and forth moving the dirt from the top, and then from the front and sides of the vault. After about fifteen minutes, the driver had pulled enough dirt from the door of the vault to allow John to climb out onto the hoe and was lifted to solid ground. As soon as John was on pavement, he shouted to driver, "Thank God, and thank you driver!....Man, I thought I was a goner for a while there. That was too close."

As the driver climb down from the hoe, he said smiling as the rain continued to pour down, "I use to operate one of these things. I wasn't going to let you die."

John, who was muddy from his waist down, grabbed the cabbie and hugged him. "I knew I picked you for a reason. And I started once to drive here by myself. Man, what a bad idea that would've been."

"Boy, you can say that again!" The cabbie said looking down in the hole with a smile.

Both men were drenched from the falling rain before they realized how hard it was raining. "Well, I guess you better take me back where you found me, my friend…." John said to the cabbie. "By the way, what's your name?"

"Fred,…Fred Thurman….."

"I'm glad to know you, Fred Thurman….I'm John Sinclair."

"Did you try using your cell phone?" Fred asked out of curiosity.

"Fred, I was so damn scared down there, I didn't even think about my cell phone… Besides, I probably couldn't have gotten any service down there anyway."

Fred laughed. "You're probably right."

Both men got back into the cab and headed back to Buckhead. When they arrived at the apartment, John ran inside, to get a reward for the cab driver for saving his life. He went into his briefcase and took out at least ten thousand dollars in bills, and ran back downstairs, handed the driver the cash. "Hey, I know there is no value on the human life, but I just want you to know I appreciate you for being there to save my life." John turned and walked away.

The driver shouted out to John. "Hey, you don't owe me for doing what anybody would have done!" He saw that John was ignoring him. He dropped the cash down on the seat beside him and slowly drove off still watching John as he ran back up the stairwell.

As soon as John entered the apartment, Seville was walking into the living room, and was suddenly startled by the sight of John. "What on God's earth happened to you, baby?!"

"First, I'm going to take a hot shower, put on some dry, clean clothes and I'll tell you all about it then."

"Well, since you put it that way, I guess I'll take a shower with you."

John and Seville showered, made love, and prepared a late night dinner before they sat down to the dinner table and began to talk about her shopping spree before they got into what happened to him to cause such a muddy mess. "Now, are you going to tell me what happen to you, or better yet, what muddy hole did you fall into?" She asked.

John laughed just thinking about how the cabbie had dug him out of the trench. "Well, I went over to the precinct to see for myself what the big secret was all about."

She was eating, but she suddenly stopped to comment, "Judging from the mud you were covered up in, I suppose you found just what you were looking for."

"I think I really did discover the secret.....And we would've never guessed that this whole thing at the precinct is about gold. In my opinion, gold was the reason why the precinct was blown up, and thirteen officers were killed in the process.

Before commenting again, she stopped eating to laugh. "You said gold. And just how much gold would it take for somebody to blow up a police precinct and kill thirteen cops?" She stared at John as if he had loss his mind for making such a statement. "And even if it were true, where did the gold come from?"

"I don't know! But, believe me when I tell you, there is a big-ass vault buried in the ground under the precinct, and it probably has been there since the Civil War." He stopped talking. *Civil War gold? No, it can't be that.* He thought to himself.

"So, you're saying that the precinct was setting top of a gold mine, and someone finally found out about this gold, and blowing up the precinct was the only way to get to it?....Is that your theory for the bombing?"

"Have you ever read the history of the Civil War?" John asked as he stopped eating completely.

"No, but I have a feeling that you have." She said smiling.

"Well, I have. I had the occasion to read about it during my five years of not knowing who I was. On September 2, 1864, General William T. Sherman along with sixty thousand soldiers marched into Atlanta. They outnumbered the Confederate Army by a two to one margin.....Not so long before Atlanta became the turning point of the war, the Confederate Army had collected close to two billion dollars in gold from mostly the French Government, and the white business people throughout the south. This gold was to help finance the Civil War for the south.....

"However, as Sherman and his men fought their way into the city and from the scouting reports they knew that the Confederate Army was hauling a ton of gold loaded on four or five wagons...You see, Sherman wanted the gold as much as he wanted to win the war. I mean, in reality, they didn't give a rat's ass about freeing the slaves, or capturing General Lee. They wanted that gold. And when they could not find the gold, General Sherman ordered Atlanta to be burned to the ground....He did not want a building left standing without that gold being found. They burned the city to the ground."

"Wait, wait!" Seville cut him off. "The Confederate Army had over two billion dollars in gold in 1864. And General Sherman wanted the gold for himself and the Union Army..... So, what happened to the gold?"

"The Confederate soldiers obviously buried the gold somewhere in the city before they retreated. The Union Army searched, and burned the entire city looking for the gold, but they never found anything that looked like gold. And to this day, no one knew where the Confederate Army buried the gold, or how much gold they really had."

Seville stared at John with an unbelievable stare. "Until now....?"

"Until now...." John agreed.

Seville thought about John's theory for a while before it really sank into her brain. She even poured her and John cups of coffee before she continued. "Just for the sake of argument, let's say you're right about what you're saying. The questions now become, who blew up the precinct, who was it that dug up the gold, and where is the gold now?"

"That's the billion dollar question....."

"And my next question would be, was the Major in on this whole gold theory of yours? Was the gold the reason for him saying if anything should happen to him, our number one suspect should be the Chief?"

John stared for Seville for a moment before saying, "He did say that didn't he?...I wonder how much does the Chief really know about that accident? You know, he did look at kind of strange when I questioned the fact the Major lived on that road, and it didn't make sense to me for him to be speeding and missed that curve in broad daylight."

"So, you're thinking that maybe someone ran him off the road?"

"Yeah, I'm thinking that way." He looked to the ceiling for a moment. "He and I didn't always agree on things when I was Calvin Gates and working for him. But James Butler was a very careful and clever man. He was too smart to speed along a dangerous road. Why would he?....Was he rushing home for some reason? Maybe we need to talk to Carolyn, his wife. She would know if he was rushing home or not."

Seville stood, walked around the table to where John was seated. She reached down and held his hand. "Let's talk about this gold for a minute." She pulled him to his feet and they walked into the living room and sat on the sofa. "In 1864, the Confederate Army buried a couple of billion dollars in gold. We're talking about a century and a half ago. What would that same gold be worth on today's market?" Seville asked.

John began to calculate in his mind as to what he imagined the value of gold would be worth at the present time. "Here in the States, maybe fifty or sixty billions, but trying to get rid of that much gold here in America would be very difficult without raising a lot of red flags. That's including the Federal Bureau of Investigation....You have to remember, this is gold that is still listed as missing with the federal government. Think about what has taken place in the passed few weeks. The precinct blows up, thirteen cops are killed. Someone digs up the same spot where the precinct once stood, and from that spot two billion dollars in gold are now missing. No way!....The entire City of Atlanta would be under marshal law if that much gold is suddenly floating around this city." John laughed. "Everybody from the Mayor on down would be under investigation. The FBI would have a field day on the local cops trying to figure this thing out."

Seville smiled. "Okay, so we're back to the Major,....was he involved?"

"Maybe so, and then maybe not.....But there's one thing that we know for sure, we'll never find the answer to that particular question now."

They both leaned back on the sofa and began to allow their thoughts to simmer on what their questions might have been if Major Butler was still alive........

CHAPTER SEVENTEEN

Friday morning, July 15, John and Seville were among several thousands of mourners who had come out to pay their last respects to the remains of Major James Edward Butler. The services were held at the Cascade Baptist Church on Cascade Road. John was hoping to chat with the Major's wife Carolyn before she was overwhelmed with reporters wanting to ask questions about the suspicious nature surrounding the accident.

Chief Martin was seated down front of the church near the family as everyone felt the pain of having loss a friend, a colleague, and a mighty fine cop.

When the services were complete, and many people in attendance were headed in their separate directions, FBI Special Agent Harvey Hill approached Chief Martin at the grave site to pose a question. "What if I told you, Chief Martin, that our people found evidence that the precinct was in fact blown up with C-4 explosive, although you and your people claimed that it was a faulty gas leak?"

The Chief looked at the agent with an unbelievable stare. "Are you people still on this case?!....Look, you and your boys may as well pack up whatever it is you brought into this case and leave. There is no investigation to be done. There was no terrorist act of any kind. So, this situation is none of your business. It's a matter for the police, okay?"

"A few days ago, we also discovered that something was dug up out there. Do you care to elaborate on what that something was? I see that whatever it was has been removed and the area has been covered over again."

Chief Martin walked away from the grave site to avoid anyone overhearing their conversation, and the agent followed him for a short distant. The Chief then turned and stood face to face with the agent. "Listen, first of all this is the wrong place and the wrong time to be talking about that situation. Why don't you have some respect for the dead, you over-zealous bureaucrat!"

The agent dropped his head momentarily, before saying, "Speaking of the dead, do you believe that the dead can talk?"

"What?!" The Chief snarled angrily, but he was thrown off by the question.

"You know, the dead can say things after they are long gone...."

"What are you talking about, Agent Hill? Why don't you make some sense!"

"Okay, then let me get to the point." The agent said smiling. "Two days ago, I received by mail a handwritten letter, written by the Major before he died. He apparently suspected you, or someone in your department as trying to kill him."

The Chief stepped back. "You have a handwritten letter by the Major saying that I wanted him dead? Agent Hill, obviously someone is trying to create a problem. Or, they are playing a cruel joke on you. Major Butler and I were good friends. We've known each other for twenty years. Why in the hell would I want to see my own commander dead?"

"Would it be because somebody found gold buried underneath the precinct three building?!" The voice came from John Sinclair who had walked up to where the Chief and the agent were standing.

The agent suddenly turned around to John and said in a stutter, "Gold, gold,... what gold?!" He frowned, looking at the Chief.

The Chief immediately tried to stare John down with a frown on his face, which would indicate to John not to say anything about gold. "John, may I introduce you to FBI Special Agent Harvey Hill."

"So, you're with the FBI?.....And why would the FBI be interested in the bombing of precinct three?" He paused. "Unless, there was some gold out there that they figured belonged to the federal government and not the finders."

Agent Hill shouted firmly. "What in the name of God are you blabbing about, man?!" He turned back to the Chief. "Who's the fuck is this joker?"

The Chief shrugged his shoulders. "Never saw him before in my life... I thought he was with you."

John laughed. "You know, if we weren't standing in the middle of a cemetery during a memorial service, I'd knock you on your ass again."

The Chief smiled. "Agent Hill, this is a good friend of mines, Calvin,...I mean, John Sinclair. And he was assigned to the precinct case to keep everybody up to date on what's going on...." He looked at John. "And you say you found gold?!" He laughed.

"No, I didn't say I found gold. I said somebody found gold all right, but it wasn't me." John said, smiling at the Chief.

"Wait, wait," The agent held up his hands. "There's that word again, gold. What gold are you two talking about?"

The Chief looked at John. "Yeah, John, why don't you tell us about this gold you keep babbling about, I mean you've got my interest going now as well."

John looked at the two men, one who had doubt written all over his faces. And he knew that there was no need in trying to explain anything further about the gold. "Never mind, you wouldn't understand anyway." John turned started to walk away.

"John!" The Chief said. And as John turned around to see what he wanted, the Chief said, "The next time you punch me like you did, I'm going to have you arrested..." He rubbed his left jaw smiling. "I was wrong for saying what I said. Sorry about that. Anyway, I'm interested in hearing what you have to say about this gold theory."

"Yeah, that goes for me too." Agent Hill said.

"Apparently, a whole lot of gold was buried in Grant Park about a hundred and fifty years ago. The exact location was underneath the precinct. Someone obviously pinpointed the exact location, and they blew up the precinct to get to the gold." John paused and waited for a response.

"And you know this to be a fact, how?" The Chief asked suspiciously.

"Because I was in the vault, and I saw with my own eyes that gold had been there."

The agent glanced at the Chief. "Could this have anything to do with what we were talking about earlier? We know C-4 was used to blow up the precinct."

"So, you think that the Major's accident was no accident, and it may have had something to do with this gold that John is referring to?" The Chief asked.

The agent glanced around at the grave site before saying, "Isn't it ironic that we're standing near the grave of the same man who wrote me a letter talking his death. Now, he's dead, and out of the blue, your own man is talking about gold. Chief, there is a connection. But why would he want the FBI to investigate you is a mystery to me…..."

"Oh, really?!" John snapped. "Funny thing about that, he said the exact same thing to me a few days before he was involved in that so-called fatal accident. Chief, not that I am accusing you of anything, but I think maybe we need to talk about why you and the Major really brought me into this case."

"And in the meantime, Chief Martin, I am going to look further into this situation about some loss gold…And I'll be getting back with you in a few days." Agent Hill said as he turned and walked away.

As soon as Agent Hill was out of hearing range, the Chief focused his attention on John again. "Why in the hell did you have to bring up the subject about gold while I'm talking to the FBI?!...Look, I am doing everything that I can, Calvin Gates to get these bastards out of my hair."

John smiled before answering. "First of all, I don't believe that Major Butler ran off some damn curvy road and killed himself…I don't believe that. He lived in the area, and he knew the road like the back of his hand. Now, you tell me that you really and truly believe that he died due to that accident?"

The Chief smiled. "Well, if I say no, you're going to say that I had something to do with his death. And if I say yes, you're still going to say that I had something to do with his death. You're going to blame me regardless of what I say."

"Yeah, simply because he accused you before he was killed! Now, you put yourself in my place; who would you believe, a dead man who knew that he was going to die, or the man that the dead man accused of killing him?"

"Calvin, I know how this must look to you." The Chief started to say.

"Call me John, please. I've gotten use to that name." John interrupted him.

"Okay, John…..I know how this must look. But, I swear on my mother's grave that I had nothing to do with James' death….Look, once upon a time, we all were friends. We all went through the academy together. And we all rose through the ranks together."

"Yeah, but look at you. You're Chief! Is that because you're white and we were not? I have often wondered about that one."

"John, why are you bringing race into this? This has nothing to do with you being black, or me being white, or anything else. Look, I loved both you guys. You and James were like my brothers, black brothers!" He laughed softly.

"Yeah, that's real funny, huh?"

"No, but it's strange how you can draw race into all of what has happened in the past five years…..You are trying to accuse me of having something to do with what happened to you. But I had absolutely nothing to do with that."

"Okay, you made your point." John said as he glanced around for Seville. She was still having a conversation with Carolyn Butler at the grave site. "What I need to do now is get to the bottom of this whole crazy mess. And I would like for you to give me the authority to look further. I need some answers, Chief!"

The Chief hesitated for a moment. *I hope I won't regret doing this.* He thought as he said, "Okay, I'm going to do as you ask…But, I want you to report to me on a daily basis….I want to know what you know at all times. And I want to know how you're going about doing it… That goes for your partner as well."

John glanced back in the direction of Seville. "I'll make sure that I tell her you are concerned about us and how we're doing things."

Both men walked off in separate directions as the service was coming to an end.

When John met up with Seville, he said, "How's Carolyn taking it?"

"Pretty hard, she still can't believe he's gone." She said, glancing back at the limos as they departed the grave site. "I can't believe he's gone either…I mean, he had that kind of affect on people. His personality could overwhelm you."

John gave her a quick smile as they walked back to their vehicle. "I know what you mean…..Maybe that's why we need to pay the medical examiner a little visit."

"Medical examiner,…what for?"

John stopped momentarily, glancing around at the grave where his half brother was now buried. "Sometimes, you get a gut feeling that things ain't always what they seem to be. And right now I'm getting that feeling. Do you know what I'm saying?"

She laughed. "Not exactly, but why don't you explain it to me."

"Well, it means, we're going to make sure that if James Butler died in that crash. I want to make damn sure that it was the crash that killed him, and not a bullet, or something else caused his death before he ran off that road."

"So, you really think that he was dead prior to the accident?"

"Yes I do. And I'm saying that because of what I found in the hole. Think about it, a lot of gold is floating around out there. Many people are going to die because of it."

"Do you think the Chief is behind what's happening now?"

"Especially the Chief.….Hell, Seville, I am not convinced that he didn't have the Major killed. Even the Major suspected that he would attempt to kill him…Remember his last words to us?….If something happens to me, the Chief is your prime suspect."

"Yes he did say it." She replied.

They started walking again toward the Hummer as Agent Hill met them at the vehicle. "Mr. Sinclair, I want to have a word with you before you leave." The agent said.

John paused while motioning to Seville to start up the truck. "Do I have to guess?"

"No you don't.. First, I believe what you said about the gold. And secondly, I think Major Butler had something to do with the bombing of the precinct. I also think that the Chief knows a lot more than he's telling me or you about his death. I received a letter written by the Major, and it stated that if anything should happen to him, we should investigate the Chief first.….Now, here you come along talking about some buried gold that has been there since the Civil War. In my opinion, that's more than a reasonable suspicion that he knew someone was going to kill him to get their hands on that gold."

John smiled as he walked around to his side of the vehicle. "Okay, so go and arrest the Chief on suspicion of murder."

"It's not that easy. First of all, we have to have proof that a murder was committed. And secondly, we must have proof that it was really gold buried under the precinct?"

John smiled. "Right now, it seems that on both counts that neither one of us can prove that either one took place. First of all, the Major is dead, and all he left behind was a note saying to suspect the Chief, but no proof. And, if there was gold buried under the precinct like as we both suspect, the question now becomes, where is it now?"

"Well, that's what I wanted to talk to you about…..I know you're working on this case, and I know you're not going to allow it to drop just like that. So, I would like for you to keep me in the loop on whatever you come up with."

"Keep you in the loop…." John repeated with a smile. "That's funny. Those were very similar words the Chief used. He wants to know my every move from this point on. The FBI on one hand, and the Chief of Police on the other hand, how can we go wrong?"

Agent Hill smiled. "I'm sure that maybe Major Butler viewed his situation from a similar standpoint. Look where it got him……Listen, all I'm saying is, if what you're saying is correct, and I don't have a reason to doubt that it is not, you and your partner need to be very careful. If my counting is correct, that's fourteen cops, plus the Captain that the Major shot and killed. It seems to me that this gold you know about is rapidly turning into a cop killing orgy.

John glanced inside the vehicle at Seville. "Yeah, we'll be careful." He turned to get into the Hummer, but paused to say, "This is kind of like having a murder scene where there is no body. And we've got a lot of suspects, but no evidence."

The agent waited until John got into the vehicle before responding. "That's what makes it so scary. We don't know who to call a suspect. And, the only man who might be considered as a prime suspect seems to have all of his bases covered."

John stared at the agent for a moment. He knew that he was referring to the chief. "You do know there is no such thing as the perfect crime, right?"

"Yeah, I know….But try telling that to the people involved."

"You make a good point. But I have a feeling that this craziness that appears to be a mystery right now will unfold and show its ugly face, sooner or later."

"I heard that." The agent stood back as Seville stirred the vehicle away from his position down a winding road in the cemetery towards the main street.

As John relaxed for a moment, Seville said, "I took the liberty of calling the medical examiner…. He's expecting us…."

He smiled. "How did you know that's where I wanted to go right now?"

"Because John, it's the only question mark that's written on your face." She responded with a laugh. "Remember I'm a cop too, and I'm dying to know who it is."

She is a cop, and I have to keep reminding myself of that fact. Plus, she's a damn good cop. He thought. "Somehow, I keep forgetting that you're a cop. It won't happen again." He said. "And by the way, how is Mrs. Butler taking the death of her husband?"

"She's taking it very well, I must admit….."

John glanced at her with that same question mark written on his face. "You must admit?…. You make it sound as if you were surprised….."

"A little….I was looking for a woman and her two kids to be all broken down with grief and suspicion that someone may have killed her husband. But instead, what I got was a woman and her two kids who appeared to be smiling at times. Or, maybe they have learned how to treat death as a good thing in a good way."

"Yeah, and what way is that?"

"The Bible says we should cry, or morn when babies are coming into the world, and rejoice when people are leaving out. In other words, be happy when someone dies."

"And you think that's really what it is, or she has some other motive for not feeling grief for her dead husband?"

"And what other motive would there be, Mr. Detective Sinclair?" She smiled.

"Other motive; I wouldn't think when it comes to Carolyn, she would have any kind of motive….She really loved her husband. However, when I was Calvin Gates, she and I knew each other very well. In fact, back then, she would always tell me that if anything ever happen to our spouses, we would marry each other." John said smiling.

"Really now!" Seville said, glancing over at him. "Okay, you both are now without spouses. So what's keeping you two from following through with your plans?"

"For one thing, I'm not Calvin Gates anymore. Secondly, I think I like you now."

"Oh, so you don't suppose the Major told her you survived the explosion?"

"No, and we're going to keep it that way."

"Hey, just asking….." Seville laughed. "Did you ever screw your friend's wife?"

John looked at Seville strangely before answering. "Not that I can ever remember. I mean, we were close, but not that close."

Seville pulled into the parking lot of the Fulton County Medical Examiner's office.

John and Seville had no idea as to what they were expecting to find at this point. They both knew that if there was any kind foul play that caused Major Butler's death, Dr. Karl Bostic would have already alerted the Chief. *But there is nothing wrong with asking a few simple questions just to make sure that they had covered all the bases.* He thought.

Dr. Bostic was a white male in his early fifties and looked to be very fit for his age. He was six feet tall, with a thick graying mustache, a balding head, and wore thick wire rimmed glasses. He escorted the two cops to his office that was separated by a wide window overlooking the examination area. Seville sat in a leather chair while John stood next to her. John led off the conversation by saying, "Ah, Dr. Bostic, we don't want to take up too much of your time, and we know that this is after the fact, seeing how Major James Butler is already buried and all…. But, we'd just like to know, if there was anything that may have seemed a little out of place, or suspicious about the accident?"

Dr. Bostic opened a brown folder that he had placed on his desk. "Besides the fact that he was burned beyond identification, no, there is nothing that I can put my finger on as being suspicious, or out of place…. However, I will say that I haven't seen too many bodies that were burned to that extent."

"By that, you mean this was a little out of the ordinary?" Seville asked.

"Well, yeah, but not to the point of making me believe that this was no accident."

"So, there was no way of knowing if Major Butler was shot, or forced off the road prior to the vehicle crashing and catching fire?" John asked.

"There is no way of knowing if any of that took place…But that's not to say that it didn't happen the way you explained. Of course, there was no bullet found on the scene."

"So, someone could have killed him before the car ran down the embankment, hit a tree, caught fire, and burned like crazy?" Seville asked.

"I've learned that in this business, anything is possible….Now, I will say this, you two are the first to inquire about whether he died in the accident, or was killed before the accident." Dr. Bostic said.

"Is that unusual, especially in a situation where a police officer is involved? I figured that the department would want to make sure that this was just an accident and nothing more." John said as he took a seat next Seville.

Dr. Bostic hesitated for a moment. Finally he asked, "Are you two working on this case for the department, or who?"

"Yeah, we're with the APD." John said quickly, glancing at Seville "Why, is there something wrong?"

"No,…it's just that the man was buried today. Now, you two are here looking for a possible crack in what was reported to have happened. That's a little on the unusual side, don't you think so?" Dr. Bostic was feeling a bit uneasy.

John sat back in his chair, crossed his legs. "Dr. Bostic, maybe you're unaware of all the things that have gone down in past few weeks, and months…But there are a lot of unanswered questions that's surrounding Major Butler. First, there was the precinct bombing that killed thirteen police officers. Then, the Major killed another police officer who was also one of his close friends. Now, he's dead, ran off a road that he was very familiar with. When you put all of that together, what comes to your mind first?"

Dr. Bostic thought about it for a moment. "I see what your point."

"Oh yeah, what's our point?!" Seville snapped.

"Well, you have doubts about what really happened out there on that road." Dr. Bostic responded. "And like you said, since Major Butler seems to have been the key to everything that has happened over the past weeks and months, it causes one to wonder what's really happened to the Major? Was it an accident? Did someone force him off the road? Did someone kill him first then place him the car?"

"And is he really dead?" John blurted out of nowhere. "Can you positively say that the remains that were buried today were the remains of Major James Butler?"

"Yes!…." The doctor responded sharply. "I can positively say that the remains were those of Major James Edward Butler…." Dr. Bostic paused for a moment. "What are you driving at, you think that the Major is still alive, or he faked his own death?!"

Seville looked at John as well. "Yeah, what are you saying? Are you're saying that you don't believe that he's dead?"

John shook his head. "Look, I don't know what to believe right about now. But I do know that something is really, really wrong with this situation. It stinks like hell!"

"I'll agree that it all look suspicious, but I examined the Major's remains myself. His dental records match perfectly. I don't blame you for being a little suspicious, but to say that the remains that were buried today belonged to someone else are highly impossible." Dr. Bostic said as he stood. "Now, if you don't have any more questions, I'd like to get back to work."

John and Seville stood and left the examiner's office convinced that maybe the Major had in fact killed himself. John of course, became suspicious after thinking about what had happened to him. Only a few people knew that he was still alive, and no one recognized him as the former Calvin Gates.

Instead of taking their vehicle, they began to stroll towards downtown to Central City Park where they bought ice cream cones and sat on a park bench. John had some crazy thoughts running through his mind, and he could not understand why he was thinking in such a way. He wanted to sit out in the open air and discuss his thoughts with Seville. As they ate their ice cream, he stared at the younger woman wondering where would she go, or what would she do when this situation was all said and done? While thinking about what he wanted to say, he glanced around at the many people who were sprawled on the green grass, or just simply walking through the park.

"When we find out what the truth really is, are you going back to your old assignment, or will you ask for a transfer?" John asked with a smile. "I know the Major said you were fired, but apparently that no longer apply."

Seville smiled. "I don't know....What will you do, go back to your quiet little farm up in North Georgia, to your annoying Spanish speaking housekeeper?"

John laughed. "Maria is not annoying!...She's simply making sure that I'm still alive, and doing okay, that's all."

"Yeah, but she calls all during the day and night, even when we are making love, she's calling her boss to see if he's okay, bitch!...."

"Are you jealous?"

"No, I'm not jealous!" She smiled. "Ah, a little....But, John, have you ever considered coming back to work? I mean, now that the Chief knows who you really are, you can get your old job back...Look, we both hate that the Major is dead, but it could work out better for the both of us now that he is dead." She stared at him for a moment.

John laughed and looking towards the sky because what she just said was funny. "What if I told you that the Major is a live and well, would you believe me?"

She wanted to say something but she could not find the words to say at that moment. Finally, she said, "And just how do you know that?"

He stood up. "Look at me!....Five years ago, I was Lieutenant Calvin Gates. Today, I'm private citizen John Sinclair. The only way anyone knows that I am Calvin Gates is because I tell them. And even then, they are having a hard time believing me. Now, the same man who masterminded my secret identification with a new face, a new name, and a whole new lifestyle is now dead, or supposedly dead. Why couldn't that same man who was so brilliant at turning me into someone else, do the exact same thing for himself?"

"Wow!" Seville snapped as she stood also. "I had forgotten all about that. And you're absolutely right. If he could do it for you, he certainly could also do it for himself....And his reason for becoming a new completely different person is,......"

"How about two billion dollars in gold....." John completed her statement. hey both stared at each other laughing. "The Major is still alive." They both said.

"And, that's why Carolyn was acting so calm, cool and collective." Seville said.

"Wouldn't you be calm if your man was apart of a two billion dollar gold heist?"

"No doubt about it!" Seville said laughing. "But hold on there, Long Ranger....." Seville sat back down on the park bench. "Now that we both believe that he's still alive, so how do we go about finding the new Major James Butler?"

John took his seat as well. "Now, that's another billion dollar question." He frowned with a serious thought coming into his brain. "The gold was worth two billion dollars century and a half ago....Today, it's probably worth fifty times that much. Or you can make that a hundred billion dollars question." He laughed.

CHAPTER EIGHTEEN

Several days had gone by before anyone spoke about gold again, especially Chief Martin. And when he did speak, he spoke to his one number man in wrong doings as of late, Bobby Turner. He had gone over all the possibilities of where Ethan could have taken the gold to get the highest price for it. There was a buyer in Japan who was paying more than a thousand dollars an ounce. And then there was a Russian buyer who was in the gold buying business and was paying two thousand an ounce. However, knowing who was paying what price did not tell him anything about where Ethan has taken the gold. And just because Japan and Russia were in the buying business did not mean that Ethan had traveled to either place.

"Did you hire some people to find Ethan and his partner?" The Chief asked Turner.

"Yes sir, they all are staying in a downtown hotel." Turner replied.

The two cops were standing out front of a city owned car wash waiting for their vehicles to be washed and waxed. The Chief was desperate to locate Ethan, and he had placed a million dollar bounty on the heads of Ethan and Sam Houston, the historian. Chief Martin firmly believed that the two men would return home after the sell of the gold. After all, no one could tie them to anything, whether it was the bombing or the gold. They were totally invisible now that Major Butler was dead.

"So, what are you planning to do once we locate these people, Chief?"

"I want them located, and I want them arrested for the mass murder of thirteen police officers. That will only take place if they refuse to give me my split of the money. I estimate that to be about thirty billion dollars….." The Chief laughed. "You see, Bobby, the feds are looking for some terrorists, and I will hand them two of the biggest terrorists in the business, dead of course."

"So, in order to stay alive, they will be forced to hand over the money or the gold?"

"Exactly!…." The Chief stared at Turner. "I tried to make a deal with that fucking Ethan Johnston,….I told him that I would take care of Major Butler if he would give me the Major's share. But he refused. Now, the Major is dead, and now I will get my share."

"But, you didn't kill the Major, did you?"

"No I didn't, but Ethan doesn't know that. As far as he's concerned, I kept my promise, and now I want my share of the money. Or, he will never live to spend a dime."

"So, what do you want my people to do first?" Turner asked.

"Our Investigator John Sinclair, he's getting to be a pain in my ass! He knows that the gold was buried underneath the precinct. And I'm afraid if we allow him time to figure things out, he and that little bitch that he's working with could be trouble. We definitely do not need their kind of trouble."

"Aren't they supposed to be working on this case?"

"So?! But they're cops who could get us both sent to prison if they're given time to figure this whole thing out." He laughed. "Listen, John Sinclair is Calvin Gates! You do remember Lieutenant Calvin Gates, don't you?! You know, he was the cop who was smart enough, and brave enough to send three of his own drug men to jail, you included." He laughed again. "My, my, my, if we hadn't kidnapped his family and forced him to release you guys, you would probably still be in prison today."

Turner looked confused, he was not sure that he heard the Chief correctly. "You said John Sinclair is Calvin Gates? He doesn't look like Calvin Gates. What happened?"

"The strangest shit I've ever seen, the one man who planned Calvin's murder was the same man who saved his life and gave him a new identity."

"What? But, why would he do something like that?!" Turner was really confused now. "I don't understand that. Major Butler tried to kill Calvin Gates, successfully killing his wife and daughter, but had second thoughts and saved Calvin. That's insane. But how is it that this John Sinclair doesn't know what took place as Calvin Gates?"

"The way I understand it, Calvin Gates was in a coma for a whole year. And when he woke up, he was John Sinclair, and had no recollection of his former self, that is until a few days ago, apparently."

"Until a few days ago?! Are you saying that he knows who he is now?"

"According to that female detective, he does. And that's the danger in him being alive. Eventually, he's going to figure out who made that phone call demanding that he release you guys from jail."

Suddenly, Bobby Turner became very nervous, as beads of sweat began to pop up on his forehead. "That Major Butler, a sonofabitch! Why would he not just let Calvin Gates die with his family as we had planned?!"

The Chief smiled. "Well, the only reason that I can think of is the fact that they have the same father, which makes them half bothers sort of speak. Other than that, I don't have a clue as to why he did it. In fact, I didn't even know about it until a few weeks ago. He's the reason why John Sinclair is on this case now. He needed John to cover his tracks with a fake investigation while we dug up the gold, and escaped with it."

"Now, he's dead, and the other two assholes pulled a fast one on you." Turner wiped his face with his handkerchief. "Yeah, we must get rid of Calvin Gates, again."

"Don't forget the female, she probably knows what he knows by now, and we may as well get rid of her as well. You can bet your sweet ass, if he knows, she knows."

"Yes sir, I have someone special for her."

"You do, who?!"

"Her name is Kim Lee, a Bruce Lee kind of kick-ass bitch."

The Chief smiled. "I like the way you think, Bobby...."

At that moment, a worker came from the rear of the shop to let them know that their vehicles were ready. Turner and Chief Martin got into their cars and sped off in different directions. As far as the Chief was concerned, everything was all set to go into overdrive. All there was left to do now was to wait for Ethan and Sam to show up at their residents. It had been more than a week now, and it was a sure bet that the two men were going to be coming back to Georgia pretty soon. And when they did decide to show up, his people would be there waiting to intercept them.

The only problem he was anticipating, would he be able track down the money before killing Ethan and Sam? By the time they arrived back in Atlanta, there was no doubt in his mind that the money that they had collected would be in some foreign bank where the IRS or the FBI could not put their hands on it. But would he be able to force them to talk? *I know the answer is no. So, how do I get my hands on the money?* He thought. They had gotten away with the gold, and he was left out in the cold without collecting one dollar of that he had been promised by Major Butler. Now that the Major was dead, Ethan did not feel that it was his responsibility to pay the Chief anything.

It seems that everybody keeps pissing on my head, and telling me it's raining. Sooner or later, the FBI is going to try and tie me in on the bombing and to Major Butler's death. If the Feds are able to do that successfully, I'll spend the rest of my life in prison and I will not collect one thin dime out of the whole ordeal. What a bitch! The Chief was thinking as he returned to police headquarters.

*   *   *

Since John and Seville first met, she had tried to get him to meet her parents. John refused the request, for he knew that he was only five years younger than her father, and he did not like the idea of screwing a woman whose parents were about the same age as he. "John, being forty-five these days is the new twenty-something, okay?" Seville said with a laugh. "You're only fifteen years older than I am. So what?...Big fucking deal."

"I just don't want your folks thinking that I can't get a woman my own age. They are probably hoping that you end up with some fine outstanding younger man who's going places in life." John said as he glanced at her as she stirred the Hummer toward her parent home in southwest Atlanta.

"Look, John Sinclair, it ain't my folks business who I sleep with, okay?....Besides, as far as they know, you're my partner, remember?" She thought for a moment. "Of course, I did tell them that we were living in the same apartment. Does that mean we're sleeping together to them?"

"Well, I guess we'll find out real soon, won't we?" John said smiling. He stared out of the window for a little while thinking about his half brother, James. "You know, the more I think about what the Major did for me, the more I am beginning to believe that he may have masterminded this whole gold caper as far back as five years ago."

"Why do you think that? Of course, that's not to say that he didn't." She asked.

"It goes back to him saving me, and making sure that I was given a new life. He stole five million dollars just to help me give me a new start. Now, the question is why? And how was he able to do all those things and nobody even knew what he was doing?"

Seville laughed. "He did it the same way he planned his own death. He did it in a way that no one can prove otherwise. James Butler is apparently a criminal minded genius. And you already know the only way you're ever going to find out his new identity is if he walks up to you and tap you on the shoulder and say, here I am."

"Yeah, like that's going to happen."

"Well, I wouldn't be too sure about that, he just might when everything has cooled down. You have to remember, he already know that you're not going to turn him in to the authorities. You owe him your life."

"You see, that's why I'm saying that he may have planned this whole thing five years ago.…..He gave me my life back knowing that the day would come when I will have to return the favor." John chuckled. "Now, that's what I call a fucking genius!"

"So, you agree that the man has outsmarted everybody except you and me?"

"I do agree. And like you said, he could walk pass me today, and I could not positively say that it's him. Yeah, James Butler is one brilliant asshole." John suddenly realized something that he had not seen in his theorizing picture before. "Pull over for a minute." He said startling Seville.

She immediately pulled the vehicle over to the curve and stopped. "What is it?!" She snapped.

He turned to her and kissed her on the lips. "We've overlooked a very important piece of the puzzle with our assumption that the Major is still alive,…."

"We did, and what's that?"

"Okay, in order for him to pull off such a magical trick, he needed help. If the body in the burned car was not his own, he would need a replacement body. And where would he most likely find a body available that no one would miss?"

Seville smiled as she responded, "The morgue!"

"You're exactly right, the morgue. Which mean, if this situation is as I think it is, he needed help to get a body from the morgue and place it in the car.….."

"Which mean Dr. Bostic knows a whole lot more than what he told us." She completed his statement.

"Right!….In fact, I believe that if I'm correct, the good doctor may have also helped in making sure that the body was identified as that of the Major."

"Wow!" Seville said as she started to drive once again. "You know, you may have stumbled your way into solving the crime of the century. But, to pull off a caper this big would mean that the Major is not working alone. Again, he needed big time help to bomb the precinct and dig up the gold. So, who helped him?"

"You're absolutely on the money again, Seville. Who helped him is right. But think about this for a moment; gold from the Civil War, buried underneath the police precinct, how did a black cop know that the gold was located in that particular location?"

"He didn't. Someone else knew that the gold was buried there."

"And that's why it was so easy for the Major to go along with blowing up the precinct, killing the officers. He was convinced that the gold was there by someone else."

"Wow! But who convinced him? It certainly wasn't the Chief....." Seville smiled as she turned into the driveway of her parent home. "We're here!

John felt a little more at ease by the time they arrived. He felt better because he suspected that his brother was not dead. But on the other hand, he felt sorry for the men and women who died in the precinct bombing because the city had built the zone three precinct over the buried treasure more than twenty years before. At the present time however, he did not want to concentrate too much on his thoughts, it was time to deal with Seville's folks, at least for the next hour, he figured.

John glanced at his watch as he emerged from the vehicle, it was 17:15 hrs., and at that point, he had no idea what Seville and her parent had planned for the evening. Seville did not bother to ring the doorbell, she used her own key to open the front door of the red brick front, two stories, up scaled, six figured home. "Mom!...Dad! Where are you guys?!...We are here!"

Suddenly, a rather tall, middle-aged handsome man along with a fair skinned woman about the same age appeared in the foyer from the family room. "Hi, Baby!" The woman shouted as she rushed to Seville and they hugged as if they had not seen each other in months. "My baby, we've been wondering when you were coming home."

The man walked over to John and shook his hand. "I'm Walter Patterson, Sevilla's father, good to meet you. We've heard a lot of good things about you."

"You have?" John responded with a chuckle, glancing at Seville. "She never told me that she discussed me with her parents."

Seville's mother, Gloria then grabbed John by the shoulders and hugged him. "Sure she does. I'm Gloria and she tells us everything, including the case you two are working on." She paused for a moment. "Wasn't that sad about y'all boss? He was a nice man. Walter and I met him once when he came to recruit our baby for this assignment."

They all walked into the family room where Walter had already set the bar with glasses and ice for drinks before dinner. John began by mixing his own drink of brandy and coke. Then he poured Seville a gin and tonic. The mom and dad drank red wine. It was obvious to John that Seville had told her father a lot about him, with exception of his real identity. It was also clear that mom and pop were chopping at the bit, eager to ask him questions about himself.

As they all sat on the circular brown leather sofa, Gloria began to quiz John by asking, "John, how long have you been a detective?"

John smiled as he sipped his drink. "Ah, I'd say about three months, give or take a few days."

"Mama, John is a retired lieutenant from the New York Police Department. He's on loan with the city of Atlanta to work on the precinct bombing case." Seville explained. "That was the reason why the Major recruited me to work with John."

"John, I can only imagine coming from New York to Atlanta has been a real exciting experience." Walter said. "I bet you've seen a lot of action in your career, huh?"

John smiled. "Yeah, I guess you could say that, Walter...You know, once upon a time, we use to think that New York was a big city with big crimes, and Atlanta was a small country town with small crimes. That is certainly not the case today. Atlanta is a big city with a huge crime problem, just like New York."

"Well, how are you two coming along with your case, or, are you permitted to go into details about it?" Walter asked.

"Right!...We're really not at liberty to discuss our case." Seville said. "You saw what happened to Major Butler! I mean, we're really beginning to think that his accident was not an accident. Maybe it has something to do with the precinct bombing."

Walter frowned, glancing at his wife. "What, are you saying that the precinct explosion wasn't an accident as the Mayor and Chief said in their news conference?"

"Well, right now, we really don't quite know what to think about anything." John said. "But, the one thing that we do know is there are a lot people dead, and they all seem to be connected with the explosion of the precinct."

On that note, they all rose to and went into the dining room for dinner. John now had more confident in Seville now than ever before that she was not playing both sides of the fence. In the beginning, he was not sure of her, or what to think about what role she was playing. At one point, it seemed that she had been hand picked to work with him just to keep an eye on him for the Major, making sure that he did not venture too far down the wrong path. But now, she appeared to have been up front with him and was on his side in what they had discovered so far. And the one thing he was certain about was that she was just as shocked to learn of the Major's death, or supposedly death as he was.

After dinner, they all sat around and small talked on a variety of topics without Seville's parent becoming suspicious that they were more than just partners in working crimes. The time finally arrived for goodbyes, and Seville taking her usual position by sliding in on the driver's side and stirring the vehicle back onto the main street. As beautiful of a woman as she was, she did not take a back seat to anyone when it came to driving. After going through a rigorous pursuit driving course in the academy, she fell in love with driving vehicles such as a Hummer.

On the other hand, John loved the idea of her being able to handle herself when it came to driving. It may have been a severe case of paranoia, but for some reason, he felt better when she was driving. It allowed him to check his side mirror as they traveled along the streets of the city. Such as the case at that moment; he was staring in his side mirror at the headlights of a vehicle that seemed to have gotten on their tail as soon as they left Seville's parent home. At that moment, he refused to mention the fact for fear of setting off an alarm in Seville. *Let's see where this is going to take us.* He thought.

They did not know it at that moment, but they had become a liability to Chief Harold Martin. And whether he was dead or alive, they also had become a liability for Major James Butler. As Seville had mentioned earlier, John was now guilty of possibly solving the biggest crime of the century. And if his theory was correct, the FBI was willing to hear what he had to say about the traces of gold that was found in the vault buried underneath the old precinct. The FBI wanted to know what he knew…

CHAPTER NINETEEN

As soon as Seville pulled into the parking lot, John motioned for her to stop. She stopped quickly before the tailing vehicle could see him getting out of the Hummer. "Go ahead, I'll catch up!" He said.

"What's going on?" She inquired fearfully.

"Nothing, just go!" He insisted.

She drove on to her parking space, wondering what was going on. The trailing vehicle was a custom built, standard government vehicle. The driver pulled into the parking lot shortly after Seville had parked. As the driver stopped in an opened space, John rushed to the Ford sedan on the driver's side with his weapon drawn. He motioned to the driver to roll down his window. The driver obeyed the command as Special Agent Harvey Hill got out on his side. "FBI!" He said, holding up his badge and ID. "We just want to ask you a few questions, John Sinclair."

Seville walked up behind Agent Hill. "Not until you put your hands on the roof of the car." She placed the barrel of her gun in the small of his back.

The agent did as she commanded. "We are with the FBI! We just want to talk, that's all." He looked at John. "Your partner?!"

John nodded. "Oh that's right, you two haven't met yet. Meet Seville Patterson, Agent Hill." John holstered his weapon. "He's okay, Seville, I know him."

Seville holstered her weapon as well and stepped back from the agent. "Now, what brings you two boys up here in our neighborhood?" She asked.

Agent Hill turned to Seville and said. "Is it okay if we go inside and talk?"

Seville looked at John for his okay. "Can we trust the FBI?"

John stepped back from the car. "Yeah, I think we might be able to trust these two." He said smiling.

The driver of the sedan parked in one of the vacant spaces and the four rode the elevator up the fifth floor. When they were inside the apartment, John invited the two white agents to have a seat while Seville changed clothes into something a little more comfortable than the street clothes she was wearing.

Once Seville was back into the living room, wearing jeans and a pullover, she sat on the sofa next to John facing the agents. Agent Hill introduced his partner. "This is my partner, Special Agent, Fred Jennings." He glanced at his partner. "A couple of weeks ago, the director of my office here in the Atlanta asked us to look in on this so-called terrorist attack on your precinct three…..Now, we've concluded that this case has all the making of being some kind of inside job for something more sinister."

John smiled while saying. "So, I take it that you believed my little theory about the gold by using the term more sinister?"

Agent Fred Jennings was in his mid-forty's, who had the look of an agent. Close cut hair, neatly cut inexpensive blue suit, and the usual highly shinned black shoes. He spoke. "After you told Agent Hill that you found traces of gold buried underneath the precinct, we began to dig into that old urban legend of the lost gold of 1864……"

Agent Hill took it from there, "Hypothetically, let's assume that the gold was never found by the Union Army at the end of the Civil War. And let's also assume that the Confederate Army successfully hid the gold, and it was never found until now. The only way anyone could have known that the gold was buried there, it was by someone who had a map of the buried gold. That mean whoever buried the gold, also drew a map."

"And while we're assuming, let's also assume that the map was found by a third, fourth or fifth generation descendant. That descendant then found someone who was able to pinpoint the exact location, which was at the spot of the precinct." John added.

Seville looked at the two agents smiling. "It would take something of that magnitude of wealth to make Major Butler murder his own men in cold blood. But why blow up the precinct with the officers inside? Why didn't he just wait until the precinct was emptied? That is, assuming that the Major was involved at all."

"Well, I suppose we'll never know the answer to that question,..." Agent Hill said. "But I suspect it was done to create a diversion, to make everyone think, or go looking for a group of terrorists while they were busy digging up the gold. And the way things look now, whoever took the gold away from the site may have gotten away with it."

"With the demise of the Major, we don't have a clue as to who we're looking for." Agent Jennings added.

This was rapidly developing into a serious, top rated mystery case that no one could figure out. Sure, they figured that Major James Butler was a key player, but only because he was not there to defend himself. And sure, they had come to a conclusion that two billion dollars in gold had been buried underneath the old precinct. But other than that, they sat there staring at each other. John and Seville did not dare to mention their own theory about the Major. And even if they did, the FBI would not be able to locate a man who no longer existed as himself.

John knew first hand how the process had worked for him. If he had a family, they would not be able to recognize him. Both agents suddenly stood. "It would be a big help to us if you could keep your ears to the ground, for anything that may pop up." Agent Hill said. "Are you two married?" He glanced around the apartment.

"No, this is our living arrangement while we are working in on the case." John explained.

"But then, when this is all over with, we just might get married, Agent Hill." Seville said smiling.

Agents Hill and Jennings laughed as they turned and headed for the door. Jennings opened the door and stepped out on the walkway first, and Hill followed, closing the door behind them. At that moment, almost in silence, a thud sound was made, and blood spurted from the back of Jennings' head. A second thud sound was made, and this one went through Hill's chest. Both men dropped to the cement floor outside of the apartment.

Upon hearing someone yelling and crying for help outside of their doorway, John leaped to his feet and rushed to the door. He slowly opened it, peeping out first to see what was going on. Glancing down, he saw the horror on the face of the bleeding Agent Hill. He could barely mumble, "We've been shot!"

John quickly open the door wider as he shouted to Seville, "Dial 911!..Dial 911!..They've been shot!!" He suddenly pulled his own weapon, crouching down and pointing outward, looking for the shooters as he turned in a complete circle. But he spotted no one in or around the balcony, the elevator, or the steps leading down to the ground. He stood and leaned over the railing, looking for anyone on the move, or getting into a moving vehicle. Still, he saw no one.

After making the call for help, Seville joined John on the apartment landing where the two agents lay badly wounded. John could tell that Agent Hill was in bad shape, but he was still alive. But as he checked Agent Jennings, he saw the head wound, and there was no pulse, it was obvious that Agent Hill's partner was dead. "Is help on the way?" He asked Seville.

"Help is on the way." She responded. "Did you see the shooter?"

"I didn't see anything! Apparently, whoever it was, they were on foot. No vehicle left the parking lot. The shot must have come from a high-powered rifle at a distance."

Seville ran back inside the apartment to get a towel to place over the chest wound of Agent Hill to stop the bleeding and the wound from sucking air while they waited for an ambulance to arrive. And as they waited along side of the suffering and deceased agents, John could not help but think that maybe the shooter was possibly waiting for he and Seville to step out of the front door. Maybe the real targets were them instead of the agents. He wanted to believe that maybe it was all in his mind, but how could the shooter have known that the FBI agents were going to be at their apartment that late in the evening? There was no way for whoever did the shooting could have known. The shooter obviously hit the wrong target. And if that was the case, would he try again?

A few minutes later, so it seemed, every cop on the north side was crawling around the parking lot five floors below along with two ambulances. Other federal agents were on the scene to take over the investigation. It was like a mad house for a while for John and Seville. They were being asked a thousand questions by the FBI as to why the agents were visiting their apartment, and who could possibly wanted them dead? They wanted to know what questions the agents had asked, and what kind of answers they were apparently given. Finally, the director of the Atlanta office arrived on the scene. He was Paul Morrison who had been with the Bureau for twenty-five years.

"Listen, don't talk to the media, or your own department until I give you the word, okay?" The Director said to John and Seville while they sat quietly in their apartment. "There's a whole lot going on that I don't understand about this case. And I don't want the media blowing this story all out of proportion on something that might not be true. And then again, it may be true…Do you two get my meaning?"

Both John and Seville nodded and then rolled their eyes at the director as he left the apartment. A few minutes later, Chief Martin rang the door bell of the apartment. John refused to open the door, staring at Seville. "I guess the Director is coming back to arrest us for murder." He muttered loudly.

After several rings, Seville got up and opened the door, and to her surprise, Chief Martin was standing there looking very unhappy to see them still alive. But suddenly, he began acting as if he was glad to see them. "John, what on earth happened up here?!" He said as he entered, closing the door behind him, looking at Seville. "What happened, Sevilla?!"

Seville glanced at John. "We've been ordered by the FBI not to talk to anyone, not even you." She said as she sat next to John again on the sofa.

Chief Martin sat down in the arm chair facing John and Seville. "I'm your boss, you have to talk to me. I ask the questions, you give the answers. It's as simple as that."

"I'm afraid not, Chief!" John snapped as he stood. "You see, somehow, all of this mess that you and Major Butler got me involved in, I think your ass is sitting right in the middle of it. And I don't think whoever shot those agents were shooting at them. They were trying to kill me and my partner. Problem is, only one man knew where we lived."

The Chief suddenly stood. "Ah, cut the fucking crap, John, we all knew where you two lived." He sat back down. "Listen to me my friend, Calvin. I hate to be the one to break the bad news to you, but you and Detective Patterson have been played since day one. But then, I was played right along with you."

"Stop!" Seville shouted. "What the fuck are you talking about?! And what do you mean by we've been played since day one?"

"Yeah, I'm just dying to know that myself." John added.

"Okay, John you have your memory back, right?"

"Yeah, I know who I am. What does that have to do with what we were saying?"

"Well, haven't you wondered why the Major saved your life and not your family?"

Before John answered, he looked at Seville strangely. "Yeah, I wondered, and…?"

"You were more valuable to him alive than dead." The Chief said smiling.

"Okay, so I'm alive, and now he's dead. Just tell us what's going on here!"

"What's going on here is what you figured out for yourself….It has been about the gold all along. He knew five years ago that the Confederate gold was buried underneath his precinct. And it took him all this time to figure out how to dig it up, haul it away and no one would ever be the wiser."

"But you knew!" Seville snapped. "And you still allowed him to blow up that fucking precinct, killing all those police officers. How could you, Chief?!"

"No, no, that's not the way it happened." The Chief said hurriedly. "I was just as much in the dark as Ray Charles. I didn't know anything about the gold until you brought it to my attention at the grave site. Then, I began to look into it. And low and behold, I discovered that my Commander and my friend had pulled off one of the most devious acts of murder and mayhem that any one man could have ever committed."

"And you really believe that the Major acted alone?" Seville asked smiling.

"Sure I do. When you look at all the things that he has done over the past five years, the man was capable of doing anything, including getting away with all that gold."

"Well, if that the case, then you don't believe that the Major is dead?" John asked.

"Well, yes, but no….Because there's no evidence that he's alive."

"But, if he's dead, then who took the gold?" Seville asked.

The Chief suddenly realized that he had spoke too soon, or too much about the gold. Then he began to backtrack to throw the blame somewhere else. "Well, I don't know who took the gold. But I'll tell you this much, whoever took off with the loot, I won't rest until their asses are behind bars. There's nowhere in this country can anyone hide that much gold without alerting someone. Somebody knows something, and my people will monitor every gold transaction that takes place in the United States."

"There's only one problem with that idea,….." John said.

"Yeah, what's that?" The Chief asked.

"If the Atlanta Police Department put the word out about a couple of billion dollars in gold floating around out there somewhere, and the holders are looking for a buyer, every nutcase in this country is going to be searching for that gold."

"And then, instead of having thirteen cops death on your hands, you'll have a whole lot more to deal with." Seville added. "As you've already witnessed people are dying and doing unthinkable things because of that gold."

John got up and mixed himself a drink. He looked at the Chief. "Are you on duty this evening, Chief?"

"Yeah, I'm on duty. But what hell, I'm the Chief. I can have a drink if I want to." He said with a laugh.

Seville stood and went to the bar with John. There was a look on John's face that told her the he had something on his mind that he had not mentioned yet. "I know that look, what's up?"

"Listen and learn." John whispered. He carried the Chief his drink and sat on the sofa again. He waited until Seville had gotten back to her seat. "Chief," John began. "As I said earlier, what just happened here tonight, I don't think for one second that it was meant for the FBI. I believe those two bullets were meant for me and my partner. With that said who would profit most by killing the two of us, and having us off this case?"

The Chief looked at Seville first, then back to John. "I suppose that is a trick question?....And by the way you phrased it, you really believe that someone in the department had something to do with it, right?"

"No, it was not a trick question." John said quickly. "But this one is a trick question; who in the department wanted me and my family dead five years ago? Was it you, was it the Major, or who would benefit most by eliminating me and my family?!"

The Chief held his glass with both hands, rolling it back and forth. "Calvin, are you sure you want hear my answer to that question? If not, I'll leave right now."

John stared at the Chief. His hesitation to answer the question was making John angrier by the second. "Just answer the damn question, Chief Martin."

Chief Martin leaned forward before beginning his response. "Up until what happened to you and your family, you and I were very good friends. I assigned you to the Red Dog Squad because I knew that you could get the job done. Major Butler objected to that assignment, but I said, I'm the Chief, and I can assign whoever I damn well please, to wherever I want to. Of course, you know what kind of reputation you built for yourself and your men. You became the most feared cop out there in that God-forsaken place.…..

"You became too good! So good until cops and drug dealers alike were complaining. They said that you and half of your men were on the take. But as far as you were concerned, nothing was ever farther from the truth. The only thing you were guilty of was locking up the bad guys. But that was only half the problem,.….Major Butler was a man after your own heart. He wanted your reputation and your beautiful wife. But she wouldn't have any parts of him. As a result, he began plotting to have you removed from the squad and from his precinct even. But I wouldn't allow him to reassign you. I told him that you were the damn best cop on the force, and if he didn't like it, I'd remove him and promote you to Major to run precinct three."

John sat there quietly, motionless, almost like a statue. He was more than stunned to hear that something was going on between his half brother and his wife. John suddenly stood, pulling out his weapon at the same time that he threw his glass up against the wall, spattering glass and liquor everywhere. "You're about one second from me putting a bullet in your fucking head!....Now, you tell me that this bullshit about my wife and my half brother is a lie. Or, I will shoot you right here in this apartment."

Seville stood as well. "John! No, John, you can't do that.…Lie, or no lie, you can't shoot the Chief, not here, not now!" She placed her hand on top of the gun, lowering it.

The Chief remained seated as he lowered his head. "Calvin, I know what I'm saying is not something you want to hear. But the truth is the truth.…..
And I clearly asked you, are you sure that you want to hear the truth?...Your answer was yes! Now, if the truth hurts, so be it. I can't help that."

John realized that Chief Martin was only telling him what he asked him to tell. "Okay, you're right.…I lost my temper, I'm sorry for that." He sat back down, putting his weapon back into his waist band. "Go ahead with what you were saying."

"Are you sure?" The Chief asked again.

"Yeah, I'm sure, talk man!"

The Chief leaned back in his chair. "Listen, Calvin, I know you've gone through a lot, and I don't want to pretend like I know how you feel.…But, as your friend still, I feel like I can tell you now what happened five years ago. I figure with the Major being dead, the truth need to come out…You should know what happened that night."

"How do you know what happened to me that night if you wasn't there yourself?" John asked with a suspicious stare.

"Look, I've had five long years to figure all this out. No, I was not there when it happened, but over the years, the people he was trying to protect are the same ones who told me everything that happened."

"And they were, Danny Porter, Chad Wilson, and Bobby Turner?"

"Yes…..Anyway, maybe you didn't know it back then, or maybe you just overlooked some things because he was your brother. But Major Butler was one of the most corrupted cops in the department, probably in America. Now that I know he was behind the bombing of the precinct, I'm sure of it." The Chief said with a slight smile.

"So, you're saying that the Major killed my family, but saved me…. Why?!"

"Well, like I said, the only thing I can come up with is that he probably didn't mean for that to happen. Your family that is, but things got out of hand. Maybe your wife discovered that it was him, and the only way to keep her quiet was to kill them both…."

"But, along with the three cops I arrested, you as well as the Major were on Summerhill's payroll. Do you care to elaborate on that?"

The Chief looked away for a moment. "Look, both of you, I'm not proud of some of the things I've done, but I'm no killer. I didn't murder your family, believe that!"

"Okay, if you're no killer, why then would the Major tell us, and write the FBI a note saying if anything happens to him, you are our number one suspect?" John asked.

"Because he was a no-good, low down, sonofabitch, that's why he did it. Look, Calvin, I don't know who y'all father was, or his mother, but whoever they were, or are, they reproduced a rotten-ass human being when they gave birth to that bastard!" The Chief said with a smile. "No offense, I know he was your half brother."

"None taken….." John said. He thought for a few moments. "Obviously, a dead man can't haul off two tons of gold, so who did and where did they take it to?"

"I don't have a clue." *Yeah I know, but I am not telling your ass. That is my gold, and come hell or high water, I'm going to find Ethan. And when I do, he's a dead man. So far, everything I've planned to get my hands on that gold has backfired. But, not this time. I am going to have my people to keep a close eye on you two, now that you know that gold is involved. And just in case that sorry-ass Butler is faking his own death, I'm going to be the one who put the handcuffs on his ass for murder. My day is coming.*

"Chief! Are you all right?!" Seville asked, seeing that his thoughts were gone.

"Oh yeah," He sprung to his feet. "Listen, I'm going to go and have my people to give the FBI a hand on catching their killer." He hurriedly and left the apartment.

"Wonder what suddenly popped into his head?" Seville asked smiling.

"Don't know, but it must have been good." John said as he leaned over and kissed Seville on the lips. "Thanks for intervening. I almost killed that bastard!"

"That's what partners are for."

CHAPTER TWENTY

Before calling it quits for the evening, Chief Martin called Bobby Turner on his cell phone while driving back downtown. "Sergeant, meet me at the corner of Fulton Street and Capital Avenue ASAP!"

Five minutes later, the two men met at the location, across the street from the old Atlanta Braves Stadium in an empty parking lot. As soon as Turner drove up, the Chief beaconed for him to come to his car. "Get in!" The Chief said in a very angry voice.

As soon as Turner got into the car, Turner said, "I'm sorry about that, Chief. They shot the wrong people."

"You bet your sweet ass they shot the wrong people! I told you to make sure that your shooter, whoever he is, knew his target! What in the hell happened this time?!"

"We thought we had the right target until we heard on the news that it was the two FBI agents." Turner replied in a nervous tone. "But, we'll make sure that we get it right the next time."

The Chief thought about what had been said at the apartment. "There won't be a next time. I've changed my mind about killing those two."

"Why, what happened?" Turner asked. He was confused.

"They said something that made a lot of sense." He looked at Turner smiling. "What if Major Butler is faking his own death? And what if he show up later, and no one recognizes him? Except, maybe there is one person who will know the real Major."

Turner frowned. He was completely puzzled. "Chief, I know I'm not the brightest person in this car, but will you tell me what you're driving at."

The Chief smiled. "Never mind what I'm driving at. Just know this, if Major Butler shows his new face anywhere in this city, there's only one man who will be able to identify him….That man you were suppose to kill tonight."

Again, Turner was still puzzled. "Okay, let me get this straight, you think that Major Butler is faking his own death. And for whatever reason, he's going to reappear. And John Sinclair is going to know who he really is… But, how will John Sinclair know him if he's going have a new look?"

The Chief laughed loudly. "Do you have any idea who John Sinclair is?"

"Yeah, he's really Calvin Gates!"

"And for your information, if Calvin Gates is John Sinclair, he'll recognize the Major. Remember, it was the Major who gave Gates a new identity."

"And you think he's using the same plastic surgeon as Calvin Gates did?"

"Exactly, and that's why I figure John will easily know who the new Butler is."

"Wow, that's amazing!….." Turner said staring out of the car down the street. "And I am still amazed that Gates survived the explosion. How did he get out?"

"I don't know how he survived, and I don't care how he survived. If, and when I give you and your nitwits another opportunity to kill John Sinclair, please kill the right person the next time. For now, he's thinking that his half brother was tapping his wife, and that's the reason he wanted Calvin Gates dead so he could have her for himself."

"And he believed that shit?" Turner asked smiling.

"Well, right now, Calvin Gates will believe anything if he thinks that it is going to lead him to whoever killed his family. The man is desperate to kill whoever killed his wife and kid. I could see it in his eyes. And that's why we cannot allow him to get too close to us. He just might remember what good friends we really weren't."

"So, you really don't want him to know that it was you and the Major who plotted to killed his wife and child?"

"That's right! I mean, why would I want him to know that, Turner?! And don't let that shit ever utter from your lips again, you got that!"

"Yes Sir!…..But you know, and I know, if it comes down to him killing the Major, he's going to know that it was you also, because the Major is going to tell him."

"Bravo for you, Sergeant! That's why the bastard has to die! There is too much at stake to allow this poor sonofabitch looking for revenge to remain alive. We have enough on our hands figuring out where all that money is. Why is that? Your people let the gold get away. And I definitely don't need to worry about the likes of Calvin Gates!"

"I understand, Sir." Turner responded in a humble manner.

"Good!....Now, get out of my car, go find that bunch of brain-dead people you hired, and make sure they stake out the right house where Ethan lives. Can you do that?!"

"Yes sir, I can do that......What about Calvin Gates and the female?"

"Yeah, those two....I want eyeballs on them around the clock, even if you have to use regular officers. Sooner or later, if the Major is still alive, he's going to make contact with Calvin, I'm almost sure of it. And when he does, I want you and your people to be there to nab his ass." The Chief paused, staring at Turner as he got out of the car. "Please don't screw this up like you've done everything else!.....I mean, how do you let two trucks loaded with all that gold get away? Frankly, I don't damn know. But your people managed to do just that. Now, if you mess this assignment up in any kind of way, I'm going to kill you and your family myself....Do you understand me, Sergeant?!"

"Yes sir, Chief! You can count on me, and I won't screw up this time, I promise you." Turner closed the door and went back to his own vehicle.

"Yeah, I've heard your promises before." The Chief said as he drove off.

Bobby Turner sat there for a few moments thinking about the fact that Lieutenant Calvin Gates was still alive. It was difficult to believe. For five years, he and his fellow officers in crime thought that he was dead. Then he began to think about the overall situation that they were facing along with the Chief. *First, it was Calvin Gates thought to have been dead. Now, he is alive again. Then, there was the bombing of the precinct because there was gold buried underneath it. Later, the Major killed Chad Wilson. Now, the gold is gone and no one seems to knows who took it. Next in line was Major Butler being killed, but the Chief is not sure if he is really dead or not. It's time for me to get into another line of work. This shit is going to get me killed, or I am going to end up in prison for life.* He started up the car and drove off.

Back in Buckhead at the penthouse, John and Seville were still up talking to the director of the Atlanta office of the FBI. He had returned to try and clear up why the two agents were at their apartment in the first place. "I know what they were working on as far as the bombing of the precinct is concerned. But I am not clear as to why they were here talking to you, Detective Sinclair, and you, Detective Patterson." Director Paul Morrison said.

"The reason we think, we are also working on the precinct bombing from a local standpoint." Seville answered. She was now sitting on the floor next to the sofa working on her laptop computer. "The only thing we can think of, they wanted to know what we knew that would help them in their investigation."

The Director sat in a chair facing John and Seville. "Listen, I know it's getting late, and I don't want to take up too much more of your time. But I am sure you both understand how these kinds of situations are. And by the way, Special Agent Hill is going to make it, I think. He's not out of the woods yet, but thanks to your quick action, he didn't lose too much blood."

"Thank God for that." John said. "But, as far as the investigation is concerned, we all tossed around a few ideas as to why the bombing took place. Speculations were all we had, no evidence whatsoever. We all agreed that there is a lot crazy stuff happening."

"Was the mentioning of gold apart of your speculations? You do know the old folklore tale of the Confederate gold that was left behind before the South surrendered?"

"Yeah, we discussed it, but like you said, it's only a myth. Why would anyone in their right minds bomb an entire police precinct, killing a dozen cops in the process over something that is no more than a myth?"

"I don't know, John, I really don't know. Whether it's a myth or not, it was widely reported that the gold was never found by the Union Army in 1864."

"Yeah, we heard that too. But, if the gold really does exist, and a century and a half later, someone discovered it, that would be reason for all that has occurred," He smiled, glancing down at Seville. "Wouldn't you say so, Seville?"

She paused for moment, looking up at the Director. "I am working on line as we speak about the lost gold. There was gold carried by the Confederate soldiers. However, after the end of the war, the gold was never found, according to public records."

The Director stood. "Anyway, I just wanted you two to know that Agent Hill is going to make it. Agent Jennings, he was a good agent, and we all are going to miss him." Director Morrison walked ahead of John to the door. "Listen, John my agents are going to find the shooter. And I wouldn't be a bit surprise if those two bullets were meant for you two. So, be careful out there." He gave the warning is a soft voice.

"We believe that as well…." John said. "You be careful as well, Sir.."

Several agents were standing near the door as Director Morrison opened the door.

"We found the location where the shots were fired, and we combed the entire area. The shooter is long gone. But that doesn't mean that he, or whoever it was won't return. So, I'll say to you and your partner again to the both of you, keep your eyes open, someone believes that you are getting too close to the truth to what is really going on."

I wonder what truth that might be? Is it the truth to who killed my family, or is the truth to who murdered thirteen police officers? He thought as he closed the door behind the director. He went back to the sofa and joined Seville who was now sitting on the sofa.

"What did you find out on the buried gold?" He asked.

She smiled. "Okay, here's what I think is the real root to all of this gold craziness. General Joseph Edward Johnston was a West Point graduate, and he was a soldier in the regular army. But he resigned his commission as a brigadier general from the regular army in 1861. And later that same year, he was appointed to a brigadier general in the Confederate Army. Later in the war, Gen. Johnston was given command of the Western Theater which he controlled the entire Western sector of the southern region.

"In 1864, General Johnston strategy was to make a strong defensive stand against General Sherman's advancement to Atlanta. In May of that year, Sherman began his offensive march toward Atlanta, winning every battle. Johnston's Army of Tennessee fought a gallant battle but they were forced to retreat all way to Atlanta as Sherman's Army out maneuvered Johnston's troops in every battle." She paused.

"What's wrong?" John asked.

"Well, due the out maneuvering by Sherman's Army on General Johnston's troops, President Jefferson Davis removed Johnston from his command. But by the time the President replaced Johnston with a Lt. General John Bell Hood, General Johnston men no longer had in their possession the two billion dollars in gold that had been collected from the French Government and the southern businesses. The gold that was carried in several covered wagons had suddenly vanished. However, Sherman suspected that the gold was hidden in Atlanta. And he staged a mad hunt for it. He burned Atlanta to the ground, hoping he would force somebody to tell where it was hidden…..." She paused again.

"And, go on….." John insisted.

"Well, no one knew at that time. Obviously, somebody eventually discovered the whereabouts of the gold, and I suspect it was a descendant of the late General….He and his wife had two sons. And he had a brother named Charles Clement Johnston. And if he left a map indicating where his men had buried the gold, it was probably one of his descendents, or someone from his brother's side of the family. And of course, his brother was a U.S. Senator representing Virginia."

"So, we're looking for someone who is related to the sons or the brother of General Johnston. And it is believed that before his troops surrendered, they hid the gold so Sherman would never find it, although he torched Atlanta looking for it?" John asked.

"That's the way it went down. And after all these years, people are still looking for the lost gold of the Confederate Army. But until now, no one knew where it was buried.

First, the south had in their possession two billion dollars in gold while they were losing the war to the north. But, before the Confederate Army retreated from Atlanta, they figured out a hiding place that no one would find the gold, even if Atlanta was burned to the ground in their search. Now, here we are one hundred and fifty years later, someone approaches Major Butler with this map which indicated that the gold was buried underneath his precinct. The Major bought into the idea of being rich beyond his wildest imagination, and someone devised a plan to blow up the precinct while officers were still inside to make it appear like a terrorist attack, or later an accident."

John was getting excited just by believing that they had finally figured out exactly what happened and why. "Okay, lets say there are two or three people involved in this, and the gold is evenly split, these guys are richer than rich! However, with that much gold, they will have to have a buyer outside of the American borders…..The gold was transported outside of the United States." He stood and turned to Seville. "The Major faked his death in order to make a clean getaway, and no one would be the wiser."

"What about his wife?"

John snapped his fingers. "Wife?! You're right, what about Carolyn? She must know something about all of this." He paused as he sat back down. "We'll pay her another visit tomorrow, she knows where her husband is. Remember, you said she was acting real calm at the grave site? That's why. She knows he's not dead, and this whole mess about blowing up the precinct and killing cops was all about the gold."

"Okay, I am with you on everything except for one factor that you didn't mention." Seville said. "The Chief.....How could such a plan be carried out right under his nose and he not know anything about it?..... And, did you buy that crap about your own brother trying to kill you and your family because he couldn't have your wife?"

"Hell no!....No way. James and I didn't always see things eye to eye, but he would never try to make it with my wife. And even if he did, why try to kill us all off, then, turn around and save me? That shit didn't make sense, and he knew it when he said it." He smiled. "Now, as far as him knowing about this gold, somehow, someway, he knew about it. But knowing the Major as I do, James Butler pulled a fast one on everybody."

"And what do you think about the shooting tonight?"

"It was meant for you and I, and it had something to do with the missing gold."

"Why us, we don't know where the gold is?"

"Now, that's a good question, I can't seem to find an answer for that one."

Seville stood up. "Listen, baby, I don't want to stay here tonight, let us check into a hotel, just to be on the safe side."

John stood as well and headed towards the bedroom. "Let's go! You don't have to ask me twice. I think we'll take the Presidential Suite tonight."

Within minutes, Seville drove onto Peachtree Street traveling south towards downtown for the Plaza Hotel. As she stirred the vehicle along a still busy lighted streets, she glanced at John and said, "I think when this is all over with, you and I should take a long vacation, and lets try to forget that we ever heard anything about gold."

John's mind had wandered off into another direction. "The Chief is involved." He said softly.

"What did you say?" She asked, not understanding what he was saying. "Are you listening to me, John Sinclair?"

"Look, we're headed to a hotel for security reasons. Why didn't the Chief offer to let some of his officers guard our apartment? Maybe it was him who wanted us dead."

"John, what are you talking about?" Seville was confused at first. Then she thought about what he was saying. "You're right, he got up and left like his tail was on fire, and he never said once that he would have some of his officers to stay in the area just in case. He's a lowdown bastard!"

John smiled. "Ah, what were you saying about a vacation?"

"Never mind, we'll discuss that later....First, we have a lot of loose ends to tie up, and a million questions that need answering. Right now, we don't know who we can trust. The only name that hasn't popped up is the Mayor. So, where do we go from here?"

"Right now, we go to the hotel. In the morning, we're going to see my sister-in-law. Hopefully, we'll get a few of those questions answered from her. After that, who in the hell knows where this gold trail might lead us."

"Okay, you're the boss."

"Really now? I thought you were the boss."

"We really have to work on your communication skills." She said laughing while glancing up into the rearview mirror. "There's a car back there, and it has been there since we left the apartment. So, who's the fuck is it this time?"

John looked back and he could see that the vehicle was several car lengths to their rear, but traveling in the same lane and at the same rate of speed as they were. "We can't be this lucky, twice in one night. No way!.... Maybe it's just a coincident, speed up and try lose them to see what they do next."

Seville did as John suggested, she climbed to a speed of 50 mph in a 35 zone. At two different intersections, she ran the red lights, and so did the trailing vehicle. They both knew at that point that they were being followed once again. "Okay, so we're being tailed, what do you want to do now?" She asked John.

"Keep moving! Lets' get on the freeway, we'll have a better chance of losing these clowns on the Interstate. This baby will fly."

"Or, we may have to shoot it out!" She said as she turned off Peachtree Street onto Collier Road heading towards the north expressway.

"You really want to shoot somebody, don't you?" John asked her smiling.

"Hey, this is why I became a cop in the first place, to shoot bad-ass folks." She said laughing. "I was only kidding about that. But, if the bad guys are the like the ones who shot those two agents, then I'm all for killing the bad guys."

John turned and look again, the tailing vehicle was several hundred feet back, but there was no doubt in his mind that they were in for some serious action. "Well, from the way things are looking, you just might get your wish."

Within minutes, Seville was pushing hard towards Northside Drive. Northside Drive immediately intersected with 75 north and south. "North or south?" She asked.

"Go south!" John shouted, glancing back.

Down the entrance ramp and onto the freeway south, Seville floored the Hummer, climbing up to 100 mph in a matter of seconds. But that was nothing for the trailing car as it matched their speed and then some. As they approached the downtown connector of I-20 east and west, the pursuing vehicle was right on the bumper of the Hummer as their speeds were well over a 100 mph. Seville's skills as a driver was much more advanced than John could have imagined. She was good at what she did as the trailing vehicle tried on several occasions to pull up on the side of them. Each time, she would swerve to force the tailing car back or into the next lane.

As the I-20 east ramp was rapidly approaching, she had to make a decision whether to take the ramp, or continue straight on I-75. But she waited, and as the trailing vehicle attempted to pull up on her left side once again, she slammed on the brakes, causing the Hummer to smoke its' tires, skidding to almost a dead stop. She then turned its wheel to the right for the exit ramp, and flooring the accelerator heading up the off ramp. Other traffic on the freeway went sliding and skidding in all directions trying to avoid crashing.

The pursuing vehicle could not stop in time to make the off ramp. And as the driver of the pursuing car tried to make a similar adjustment, he suddenly caused a massive traffic jam, car after car crashing into the rear end of another vehicle. A fully loaded eighteen wheeler came barreling down the freeway in the same lane that the pursuing vehicle had came to a sliding halt. Immediately the driver realized that he and his one passenger were sitting in the lane of the overloaded truck that was not able to stop. The driver struggled to get out of the way, but they had nowhere to go. The big rig careened into the much smaller vehicle like a bug smashing into a windshield and pushing the car sideways several hundred feet down the freeway as it exploded after the impact.

On the ramp to I-20 that circled above and over I-75 freeway, Seville stopped the Hummer and they both got out and observed the crash that took place below. As they emerged from the vehicle and stood on the side of the ramp looking down on what was later described as a crash that caused two fatalities. "Wonder who they were? And why they were chasing us?" Seville asked John as they drove away heading to the hotel.

"I guess we'll never know the answer to that question. Did they teach you how to drive like that in the academy?" He said out of total admiration.

She smiled. "The academy taught me how to chase cars. But that back there, I picked that up on my own. Plus, I know that the Hummer is one of the safest, maneuverable vehicles in the world. Anything that the Army approves, it's good."

"And here I am, thinking that you're just another pretty face in the crowd."

"Well, you know what they say about looks, don't you?......"

"Naw, why don't you tell me what they say about looks….."

"Well, there are several sayings, but the one that always seems to fit me is, 'You can't tell what's in a book by looking at the cover. And then, there is another one that I like, 'Looks can be deceiving. That's sounds more like me, wouldn't you say?"

"Well, I think in your case, they both fit you perfectly." John grew silent for a moment as he and she carefully entered the hotel from the rear entrance. "You know, I'm beginning to feel that you are becoming very valuable to me."

Seville immediately stopped in her tracks, grabbing his arm. "And what exactly does that mean?"

John smiled. "Well, it means that you are becoming too valuable for me to just let walk away from when this is all said and done. I just may have to take you with me."

"John Sinclair, are you trying to say that you're in love with me, huh?"

He looked at her strangely. "Now, I didn't say all of that. However, I like you a lot more now than I did when I first met you."

She smiled. "Okay, I'll take that as a maybe, or possibility." She walked on ahead of him to the elevator.

He smiled as he watched her twist her buttocks walking to the elevator. *Lord, don't let me fall in love with this young woman…My heart can't take the kind of loving that she puts on a man for a long period of time. It's been hell already!* He thought.

CHAPTER TWENTY-ONE

After a night of FBI agents getting shot and one died, and later a car chase that ended in death, John slept through the remaining darkness like a baby. It was around ten the following morning when he awakened. For the past few months, he had been waking up to the sound of Seville's snoring. But this morning, there was no sound of Seville anywhere in the strange looking room. He reached over in an attempt to rub her naked bottom half, because she always slept in the nude and on her stomach, the buttocks were not there. He slowly opened one eyes, then both eyes to see if she had gotten up before him, and she had.

Down near the lobby in the hotel fancy restaurant, Seville was seated at a table in back of a crowded eatery, watching the entrance just in case John came in. Across the table from her was seated Summerhill Slim. She had made the call early that morning for him to meet her at the hotel. To her, things were getting way out of hand with all that was going on without an explanation as who was behind it. She wanted answers, and she knew that if anyone in the city could give her a straight answer, Slim could and would.

She was dressed in a black two piece jogging outfit, while Slim wore one of his usual flashy suits, a white shirt without a tie, and his mouth sparkle with a gold tooth every time he smiled. "Look, you need to give up this bullshit of trying to be a cop, and come be my woman again where you can make some real money in one of my clubs."

"Slim, you and I both know that will never happen…." She said firmly. "Besides, we are already richer than rich. All we have to do right now is, wait until the Major resurface, make sure that everything is still cool, and I'll get our money."

"But suppose that nigger put you in a trick like he has done everybody else, then what?!" Slim asked, glancing around making sure he kept his voice low. "Look, every since he approached me with this get really rich gold idea, things have been going crazy! People getting killed, cops killing each other! Are you sure he's still alive?"

"He's alive!…. Look, everything so far has gone as planned, until last night. Someone killed an FBI agent and wounded the other one, this was not apart of the plan. And what's worse, we think the bastards intended targets were John and me. Now, the feds know that, and they are going to be keeping close tabs on John and I…We can't have the FBI following us around like that. I need you to find out who has put a hit out on us. We need to remove that threat immediately."

"Hell, Seville, that ain't no problem, I can tell you who that is right now!" Slim said laughing.

"Yeah, who is it?!" She stretched her eyes over her sunglasses.

Slim answer was interrupted by the waitress who brought breakfast and placed it on the table. As soon as she was gone, he said, "Your boss, the Chief." He smiled. "Look, the Major brought this turkey in on the deal in order to pull this thing off without a hitch. But as some white folks are accustomed to doing, the Chief wanted a bigger slice of the pie. But the two other white boys are saying, no way! ….So, this greedy pie eater is trying to get rid of the other players and take all the gold for himself." He paused for a moment to eat. "But there is only one problem with that idea." He continued. "The Chief doesn't know where they took the gold, and he doesn't know what off shore account is being use to hold the amount of cash that will be deposited into."

"So, right now, he has nothing. All he knows is that the Major is gone, and the gold is gone as well." Seville said.

"That's the way it's looking. But, why is he trying to take out you and John?"

"That's why I called you…..I need you to find out who is working for him, whether they are cops, or whoever, I don't care, I want to know!"

"And when we find out, then what?"

"I want them all dead! Can you do it?"

Slim smiled. "For you, yeah, I'll do it. But, for your boyfriend the cop, they'll be doing me a favor if they would kill his ass."

"Slim, get the job done! I promise you, you will be paid very well for your troubles, okay? And don't worry about my man, the cop, he's doing just fine."

"And don't forget about the two shit-heads at the motel, that's an extra million, five hundred thousand for each one to be exact."

"Don't worry you'll get your money."

"What about the asshole who's giving the orders to kill?"

"You mean the Chief?.....Don't worry about him, the Major will deal with him when the time comes." She started to stand with the intent to leave.

Slim held up his hand. "Hold on, stay a little while longer, I want to ask you something."

"Slim, I have to get back up to my room before he wakes up." She eased back down into her chair. "What do you want to say to me, Slim?!"

Slim laughed softly. "What's going to happen when your cop boyfriend finds out that he has been misled by you all along? Wonder what he's going to think about you when he learn that you and his brother set him up to be the fall-guy if the shit really hit the fan?....I'm just wondering, when will you really tell him that the joke is on him?"

Seville pointed her finger directly into his face. "Let me tell you something, Slim, maybe that was the plan from the beginning....Maybe that's the way the Major thought it would work out. I didn't plan to fall in love with this man, but I did. And I'm going to do whatever it takes to protect him. As far as the Major is concerned, well, he's too rich to be concerned about what happen between John and me. And you are too."

"If John is really Calvin Gates, he'll figure it all out sooner or later."

"Well, if he does, let's hope he'll be too old to do anything about it."

"And you really think you're in love with this already old man?"

Seville stood again. "Slim, you just do the job that you're going to get paid to do and leave my love life for me to handle, okay?" She walked away.

"You know there's only one man for you, and that's me, baby!" Slim said as she was walking away.

"In your dreams!...You had your chance, and you blew it, baby."

Slim stood, dropping his napkin on the table. "When your partner figures out what's going on, you'll be running back to me begging like a little bitch!"

Seville stopped in her tracks, wheeled around and burst back to Slim and stood face to face with him. "If you ever let the word bitch come out of your mouth directed towards me, I will stab you in your fucking heart!... Do you understand me, tall-ass nigger?!"

Slim did not speak he simply stared down at the much shorter woman. *And I believe she mean what she is saying.* He was thinking before finally saying, "Okay, I didn't mean anything by saying it.....But you do know that you'll be back, don't you?"

"Not if you were the last dick swinging." She snapped, then turned and walked away again.

"Damn, baby, that's cold!" He said as he watched her disappear from the eatery.

"And then you're going to stab me in my heart? Shit, you're a mean-ass woman!" He laughed as he sat back down and continued to eat his breakfast. *Bitch!!* He thought.

Seville hurried back to their room on the twentieth floor, for she was certain that John was probably awake and wondering where had she ran off to without waking him first? When she entered room 2040, she saw John seated on the side of the bed watching a local news broadcaster reporting on the series of auto crashes on the freeway that cost the lives of two people, one who was a former Atlanta police officer. "What's going on?" She asked she closed the door behind her.

John looked at her strangely. "The car that was chasing us early this morning, hit by the tractor trailer, one of the people in that vehicle was Danny Porter."

"What, Danny Porter?!!." She sat down next to John on the bed. "Man, this is weird! Think about it, the same cops you were going to arrest, and the same ones who were probably responsible for the death of your family, now two of them are dead. And the third one will probably get nailed soon if things keep going the way they are."

He smiled before saying, "Yeah, one more to go. And to think, I didn't have to lift a finger towards either one of them." He stood. "I'm going get a shower and we're going to head out to the Butler's house." He looked down at her. "Where've you been?"

She stared at him for a brief moment. She wanted to tell him everything that she and Slim had talked about. She also wanted to tell him that she knew for a fact that the Major was very much alive. *No, let's play this by ear. When he really starts trying to figure things out, maybe then I'll confess, but not before.* She thought before saying, "I was downstairs following up on a tip that might help us figure out who was behind the shooting and that car crash….I think maybe, I have the answer,…."

"Yeah, let me guess, would it be someone that was connected to the Major?" He asked figuring that he knew as much, he chuckled.

"More like the Chief, I think he wants the fortune for himself. And he think that we might know a bit too much about the gold, and who has possession of it."

"If he was thinking that we knew who has the gold, then why try to kill us? That makes no sense. It would make more sense if he just simply asked us what we know."

She stood, and pulled his towel from around his waist. "You know John, for a man who is fifteen years older than I am I think we're going to make a great couple." She glanced down at his penis. "And for an older guy, you still have a whole lot to offer a younger woman in the sex department."

John pulled her closer. "And you said all of that to say what?"

"I said all of that to say, I love you." She said as she pulled him down on the bed on top of her. "Can we make a baby?"

John stared at the beautiful woman for a moment before responding. "Are you telling me that you want to get pregnant by me, right now?"

"Yeah, right now I want everything that's in you to make a baby right now. I want to get pregnant with your baby right now."

John stood up again, picking up his towel and placing it back around his waist. He smiled. "Maybe in our future, we might consider a baby, but as of right now, there are too many things that we as cops are still trying to figure out. Trying to get you pregnant will only complicate things more than they already are. Let's hold off on making a baby until this is all over with." He turned and headed to the shower.

Seville pushed herself up with her elbows to watch him as he got into the shower.

She was not really sure how she was going to approach him with the idea that she, along with the Major's wife Carolyn knew all about the planned accident, and the body that was placed in the burned car that was identified as the Major. She also knew the plans about Ethan and Professor Houston who had gotten away with the gold that was now setting in a safe place in another part of the world. The way it had all boiled down to at this point; outside the United States, a bidding war was being waged for rights to buy the gold. It was a good market to buy all the gold to stabilize a shaky economy all over the world.

For the holders of the gold, it really did not matter who the buyers were, or for what reason. They only wanted to do business with anyone who could come up with the most money. She knew however, that if John went along with the fact that Major Butler, his half brother had purposely killed thirteen police officers in order to become a part of the biggest gold heist in the history of the country he too might become very wealthy for all his troubles. If he did not, he would have to suffer the consequences.

But for the moment, it was no time to risk everything they had done thus far just to let John in on what had become known as the best kept secret in the world. A few minutes later, John was showered, dressed in a casual shirt and slacks, and standing in front of Seville waiting for her to come around from her deep thought. "Ready?" He asked.

She stood, kissed him on the lips before heading for the door. "That's for the baby we're going to have in the near future." She said as she peek through the peephole, and then opened the door.

"Are you still thinking about having a baby?" John asked smiling as they rode the elevator down to the lobby.

She chuckled. "Oh, you thought I was joking?"

"No, not really joking, but I didn't think you were all that serious either…..Come on, you need a younger man, somebody who is your own age for this idea of starting a family. Hey, I haven't fully recovered from losing my wife and daughter yet."

She pulled herself close to him. "Don't worry, I'll give you all the time in the world…..But I want to be with you when you do fully recover."

John pulled back. "Now, you know my housekeeper Maria isn't going to like this one bit….You do know this, don't you?"

"Trust me I can handle this Maria chick, okay?" Seville laughed loudly.

As soon as they stepped off the elevator, she could hear her police radio quacking with a BOLO (Be on the look out) for a black Hummer that was believed to have caused the accident on the south freeway in the early morning hours. "They're talking about my truck." John said as they hurriedly turned the corner in the lobby and rushed to the parking lot that was still down one flight of stairs from the lobby.

As soon as they opened the door leading to the parking lot, they spotted a patrol car running the registration of their vehicle. They paused for a moment. "Think we should go back?" She asked John, glancing around to see if there were any other cars in the area.

"Naw, we can talk our way out of this one…..Follow my lead. Besides, we are cops ourselves, you know." John led the way over where the police unit that was parked in front of the Hummer.

"Oh hell, I forgot about that. We are cops." She repeated catching up with him.

When they reached the patrol car, John walked to the officer's side of the car. "Is there a problem, Officer?"

Suddenly, he paused from talking into his police radio. "Are you John Sinclair?"

"Yes I am….Why, am I wanted or something?"

"No, nothing like that….Unit-One has just advised me that you and your partner are under cover officers."

John frowned. "Unit One?"

"The Chief!.....Anyway, we got a BOLO on a vehicle matching the exact description as the one you're driving. But, apparently, Unit One has made the decision that it was not your vehicle that we're looking for."

"You sound as if you're in doubt of what Unit One is saying….." Seville said.

The officer stood up from his seat in the car. "No, not really….It just that the tag number that the witnesses gave this morning is the exact same as this one." He shrugged. "Oh well, it won't be the first time a witness gave out the wrong tag number." He got back into the car. "Hey, you guys have a good day." He drove off.

"You have one too, Officer!" John and Seville said together.

"I see your so-called friend the Chief is trying to look out for you." Seville said smiling as they both climbed into the Hummer. "I wonder why?"

"You better believe, whatever his reason is, it was strictly for his own benefit and not ours'." John said. "But it was mighty white of him to call off his dogs."

As they drove away from the parking lot with Seville still doing the driving, she suddenly thought about something that she had forgotten. "Danny Porter was one of the people killed in that wreck, how do you suppose he fit in as far the shooting of the FBI?"

John smiled, glancing out of the rear window to see if they were being tailed again. "At this point, I don't know what to think anymore." He didn't see any vehicle that would indicate they were being followed. "From the night that everybody thought I died with my family, it has been one long crazy mystery to me. None of the pieces seems to fit the puzzle that would give me a sense of logic at the end of this story."

She chuckled. "Do you really think there's ever going to be an end to this story?"

"I don't know.....But what I do know is that the gold that the Major and whoever helped him dig it up are the keys to the puzzle. And, whenever we ever find the Major, or whoever he is calling himself now days is the answer to the puzzle."

"But will that also solve the puzzle as to who killed your family?"

"Somewhere between the remaining cops who are still alive, Bobby Turner, Chief Martin, and my half brother, James, one of those three killed my family."

"What's going to happen if you find out that it was your half brother, so said the Chief? He made that claim. But can you imagine killing your only living relative?"

Only living relative....I haven't used that phrase in a long time. But how does she know that? Did James tell her that he was my only living relative? Oh well, maybe he did, I don't know. He thought before answering her question. "Ah, that's a difficult question to answer. "If it's true, my wife and my daughter are both dead because of him. Will I be able pull the trigger to kill him after he has saved my life, and was able to do all that he has done for me? I really don't know......" He thought for a moment. "If you were me, could you kill your only living relative, which happen to be your brother?"

She smiled, glanced at John. She decided not to answer the question.

After twenty minutes of driving, Seville pulled into the driveway of Carolyn Butler's home where they were greeted by the front end of a U-haul truck that was parked in the driveway. "Seem like she's moving out." Seville said.

"It certainly looks that way."

They got out of the Hummer and entered the front door of the newly built red brick, two story home as three men were busy loading the truck with furniture from the inside. Carolyn met the two cops in the partially vacated living room. "I'm sorry that I failed to inform you that I'm in the process of moving when you called earlier. But, I've been so busy trying to get things organized with the movers until it completely slipped my mind."

"That's okay,....we just wanted to ask you a few questions pertaining to the Major, it won't take long." John said.

Carolyn nodded with her approval and led them to another part of the house which was the Major's study. When they entered the wood paneled walls room, they all stood for a moment, fascinated and mesmerized by the many plaques, certificates, and letters of accomplishments, which all were an indication, or evidence that Major James Edward Butler was an outstanding police officer from the very first day he joined the Atlanta Police Department until that fateful day he died. John even saw pictures taken of himself as Calvin Gates with the Major that were taken during their glory days in Zone Three.

"Wow!" John exclaimed loudly. "I've forgotten about those days."

Seville nudged John on the arm. "John, how could you know about those days, being from New York and all?" She gave him a half smile. *Shape up big boy. You ain't supposed to know about any of this.*

"Wow! You're right, what I was I thinking?" *Man, I keep forgetting that I'm not Calvin Gates anymore.* He thought.

"Did you know my husband before coming here from New York Detective Sinclair?" Carolyn asked John.

"Ah, yes. I knew him from his visits to the Big Apple a few years ago. So, since I was retired there, he asked me to come here and work on the bombing case of his precinct, along with Detective Sevilla."

Carolyn smiled as they all sat down on a huge sofa in the study. "He talked about you a lot after the bombing. He thought very highly of you, Mr. Sinclair. And he would say that if any man could track down the people who were responsible for that horrible situation, you could."

While John was sitting there listening to Carolyn talk about her husband, he was remembering how he had not visited his own place of resident since he had regained his memory. He looked at Seville, "And by the way, don't let me forget to pay a visit to the house where Calvin Gates used to live…"

"Calvin Gates!" Carolyn snapped surprisingly.

"Ah, yeah, I was told a lot of good things about him by your husband." John said.

"Really?" She said, glancing at Seville. "My husband hated Calvin Gates guts! If Calvin were still alive, I'd say that he caused my husband to drive off that road."

John readjusted his seating. "Wait, Mrs. Butler, I thought your husband and Lieutenant Gates were very good friends. In fact, they even worked together didn't they?"

"Yes they did. But Lieutenant Gates was a very dedicated and ambitious man! Not only that, he was also my lover and my husband knew it. They hated each other."

John suddenly stood up. "What?!....Are you saying that Lieutenant Calvin Gates was in love with you?....And your husband, Major James Butler knew all about it?"

"Yes!...For five long years, I've suspected that my husband had Calvin Gates murdered along with his family for what he believed was going on here."

John's head began to spin in circles. Seville saw what was happening, she stood and grabbed hold of John's arm. "John, are you okay?" She whispered as she pulled him back down with her to his seat.

"What's wrong? How well did you know Calvin Gates?" Carolyn asked strangely.

"I didn't know him!" John said sharply. "I mean, after hearing all those wonderful things about Calvin Gates, and what a dedicated family man he was, I can't imagine him being involved with another woman, especially the woman who married his brother."

Carolyn smiled with memories of their love affair. "It was not that simple, Mr. Sinclair. Calvin and I were sweethearts back in middle school and high school. He graduated a few years before I did, and he went off to college. Four years later, I was dating James, and I got pregnant with James' child. Picking up where we left off in high school with Calvin was not my intention, it just happened. At the time, I didn't know that they were half brothers, not until a few years later. It was after Calvin and I were heavily involved again. But, we both were then married to someone else."

"And both men ended up on the same police department. Both men rose in rank, and both men ended up working in the same precinct?" Seville asked.

"Yes....And by that time, our secret had somehow gotten back to James. But he never let on that he knew. That is, until Calvin wanted to arrest James along some other officers for being involved with a group of drug dealers in his area."

"So, you think your husband had Calvin Gates murdered, along with his family because he wanted revenge for what he knew about you and Calvin's affair?" John asked.

"Yes, that is exactly what I think...But I couldn't prove my suspicions, so I just let it alone. I mean, after all, it was all because of my love for Calvin."

John observed Carolyn Butler very carefully while he tried to remember ever having a love affair with her. From the way she looked at the moment, he was sure that she was once a very beautiful woman. Even now, probably in her mid-forties, she still had an attractive face and a sexy body. Until now, he thought he had his complete memory back. But based on what she had said, he knew that he was still a long ways from remembering all that had happened years ago and beyond. "Tell me, Mrs. Butler, why are you telling us this about your husband? You should have told the investigators this story of your suspicions when the murders occurred five years ago." John finally said.

"Like I said, what proof did I have then? None! And I still don't. But, I can tell you because both men are dead now, and the police sure can't arrest a dead man."

"So, you really believe that your husband died in the car accident?" John asked.

"Why wouldn't I believe it?... He is dead, right?" She asked suspiciously, glancing at Seville.

"Well, that's why we came to see you. We are not totally convinced that he's dead. We think he may have faked his own death." Seville replied cautiously.

"Really, he faked his own death?! And what would be his motive for doing that?" "You don't seem too surprised, Mrs. Butler...." John said while glancing at Seville.

"Surprised... No, I am not because it's totally ridiculous! My husband is dead! And he ain't coming back... Bottom line... Period... End of story!"

John glanced at Seville again, he figured she wanted to say something about the gold, but she ignored his glance. Then he decided to ask about it himself. "Before your husband death, did he mentioned anything about discovering some Confederate gold that was buried underneath his precinct way back when before the end of the Civil War?"

She smiled as if she was not surprised again. "So, this is really what the visit is all about, isn't it? It's about the gold.....And just for your information, Mr. Sinclair, you're not the only ones who have been around here asking the same questions about gold."

"Oh really, who else been here?" Seville asked anxiously.

"Let me see, the Chief has been here, the FBI has been here, and a few other crazy looking men were here. They all were asking me about this gold you're talking about. I will tell you just like I told all of them. I don't know anything about any gold! And if you think that's why James faked his own death because of that gold you're talking about, well, Mr. Sinclair, that's must be one of those little secret that he kept to himself, because, he didn't tell me about it. Or, he must have plans to spend it with some other woman."

John looked at Seville. "I think we've heard all that we need to hear, don't you?"

Seville smiled. "Yeah, John, I think we found out something that is more valuable than the gold." She stood and headed for the door. "Thank you, Mrs. Butler!" She said.

John stood along with Carolyn. He shook her hand. "Mrs. Butler, can you give me a description of Calvin Gates, if you don't mind." He asked out of curiosity.

She stared at John for a moment before answering. She frowned as she looked at him, going from his head to his feet. "Sure, I can tell you that…. You know, he had your build, your height, in fact, you kind of favor him. But you are a lot more handsome than Calvin was." She smiled, as she turned and walked away. "Goodbye, Mr. Sinclair!"

He smiled as he watched her enter another part of the house. Then, he remembered something that was important. "Mrs. Butler!" He called out.

She stopped and came back. "Yes!"

"I was just thinking,…." He glanced around the house. "If I remember correctly, you and James have two daughters, right?"

"Yes, why you asked?"

"Well, I see you're moving. Hope you don't mind if I ask where you and the girls are headed for?"

"We're selling the house, and we're leaving in two weeks for Paris, France. And when we come back, we'll be moving on the north side of town." She stared at him for a long time once again. "You really remind me of Calvin Gates…." She laughed. "Is there anything else you want to know, Mr. Sinclair?"

"No, I'm good….Thank you, Mrs. Butler, you've been very helpful." John turned a walk away.

CHAPTER TWENTY-TWO

Two days after the incident on the south freeway, the Mayor was about to blow a gasket, he was almost angry to the point replacing his Chief of Police. He had called an emergency meeting with Chief Martin in his office on a Wednesday afternoon in the middle of August, the second hottest month of the year. "I remember growing up in this city back in the sixties. Atlanta was called Hot-Lanta back then. Atlanta, like many southern cities that had serious racial problems, and black folks were demonstrating, rioting, looting, and doing whatever it took to bring about equality. Today, Atlanta is the most post racial cities in America. Right now, we're the most violent cities in America."

The Chief was seated in front of the Mayor's desk wanting to say something in his defense. He held up one finger to speak, but the Mayor ignored him.

"In the last two months, or should I say, from the time of the explosion of precinct three, we have had one incident after the other, and they all involved police officers in some kind of way.....Chief Martin, whatever is going on in your department, it has better ceased immediately, or you'll be looking elsewhere for another job.....Now, what is it you have to say about this?! And it better be damn good!"

"Mr. Mayor, everything that you've said is absolutely correct. But there is a good explanation for everything that has happened over the past few months. I realized that I have not operated a model department, but there are things that have occurred that I had no control over." *I'm at a point where I must clear myself with the Mayor. If I don't now, and this whole gold issue becomes public knowledge, I'm going to be right in the middle of it all with no one to blame.* He was thinking as he tried to explain himself.

"Chief Martin, do you have any idea that from where I'm sitting and as far as the local news media is concerned, I'm sitting on the damn hot seat? The news media wants answers, and I don't have any answers! You need to give me something that will sound logical. Something that will make the police department seem like I've got someone in charge who knows what in the hell he's doing, and what is going on!….."

Chief Martin nodded in agreement. But as far as sounding logical, he was not too certain about that. "Sir, like I said, it was out of my control, and you're not going to believe what I am about to tell you. But, I can truly say that every word is true. Now, as far as the media is concerned, they probably won't buy into it anyway because it's going to sound like some wise old gold tale that someone made up for his grandchildren."

Mayor Clifford Townsend stared at the Chief with an unbelievable stare. "What the fuck are you talking about?!"

The Chief glanced over to the table that setting behind the Mayor with a pitcher of water in it. "Mayor Townsend, may I have some water?"

The Mayor rocked back in his chair. "Sure, go ahead….."

When the Chief filled the glass with water, he sat back down, facing the Mayor, he turned up the glass and gulped the water down in one swallow. "Mr. Mayor…." He began.

"When the precinct was bombed, we all thought it was a terrorist attack or something of that nature. Remember the Major and I went out and brought in an independent investigator because we wanted to keep the FBI out of it…..Well, the FBI did get involved as you already know. And we came up with this story about a gas line leak that actually caused the explosion for the purpose of the FBI…But, that was not the case."

The Mayor suddenly rocked forward. "That was not the case? What are you saying, Chief Martin, that we deliberately lied to the media for reasons other than what we said?"

"My investigators have now uncovered a plot to blow up the precinct, and killed thirteen innocent police officers because someone discovered that a ton of Confederate gold was buried back in 1864 and it was directly underneath the precinct."

The Mayor's mouth dropped wide open. He was frozen in place. He was speechless. And what he had just heard did not even register on his brain until moments later. "Tell me that what I just heard you say was a fucking joke!"

"It's no joke, Sir! Gold was actually found buried underneath Zone Three precinct. Right there in front of Grant Park....Remember the Civil War, Sir? Robert E. Lee and his men actually buried two billion dollars in gold way back in 1864. And no one ever found that gold until now."

"Chief Martin, you're sitting here in my office and telling me that you actually believe that two tons of gold was buried in Grant Park, and it has been buried there in the ground all these years, until now? Is that what you want me, and now the news media to believe?!" The Mayor stood, poured himself a glass of water and gulped it down. "Chief Martin," He went back to his seat. "Okay, lets' say this wild tale of yours is true. And lets' say that the gold is actually buried underneath the precinct, and we went public with this wild story, do you have any idea what kind of chaos we'd create in this city?!"

The Chief slid forward in his seat. "Mr. Mayor, the gold is no longer there. It's gone, and we don't have a clue as to who stole it, or where they have taken it."

The Mayor was a bit confused. "Okay, the gold has already been dug up and taken. And now, you don't know who took it, and where they have taken it to? Well, hell, now ain't that just fine and dandy! Can you answer me this, do you know who's involved?"

"That's what I've trying to tell you! That's why the Major was killed, because he was the mastermind behind the whole thing." The Chief smiled, thinking that he had the Mayor convinced. *Oh yeah, I've got him thinking my way now.* He thought.

"But, how could Major Butler know that the gold was buried underneath his own precinct?.....Did someone discover it by accident and told him about it?"

"In a way, yes they did. The man who contacted the Major had a map, drawn by the man who actually buried it. This man was a General in the Confederate Army."

"Are you talking about General Lee?"

"Yes sir! General Robert E. Lee himself."

The Mayor stood again and walked from his desk. "Chief Martin, even if this is true, who do you think is going to believe it without having the gold to show them?"

Chief Martin turned in his chair to face the Mayor. "Well, Sir, that's going to be a problem, because I don't have a clue as to where the gold is, or who stole it."

"We could say they stole it. But we don't have any idea who they are. The only people who can tell us where the gold is located are the same people who stole it. However, because they destroyed public property, and murdered thirteen police officers to get to it, a capital crime has been committed." The Mayor returned to his seat. "How do we find the people who knew that the gold was buried there?"

"As of this moment, I don't know, sir...." *I have a feeling that Ethan is going to show his ugly face sooner or later. And when he does, I will be waiting. To give the Mayor anymore details will be suicide. I only want to tell him enough just to clear myself if anything else goes wrong.* He was thinking. "Mr. Mayor, you can trust me, I am going to get to the bottom of this entire nasty situation.....My Department and this city, have suffered great losses. There will be no more incidents involving my officers, I promise!"

The Mayor smiled in a suspicious manner. "Be careful, don't promise anything that you can't deliver....You and I both know that whoever dug up that gold, they are not going to just hand it over because the police say so...If they were willing to blow up a damn precinct full of police officers, they sure aren't going to think twice about shooting a couple more of them. So, my suggestion to you is, whenever and wherever you locate the people with the gold, be ready to take them down! Or they will take you down."

"Yes sir, Mr. Mayor." Chief Martin responded as he stood to leave the office.

Mayor Townsend sat motionless, staring directly at the closed door that Chief Martin used to exit his way out his office. He thought about the many things that he knew about what had gone on involving Chief Martin, and of course Major Butler. The Major was dead, and apparently, from listening to the Chief, he took with him the secret to the whereabouts of a fortune in gold. If this got out to the news media and the general public, it would be a scandal that he and the Chief could never escape, especially if the gold finding mess hinged on the fact that they killed thirteen police officers in the process.

The question for him was, what, if anything that he could do about it? According to the Chief, he did not know the location of the missing gold, or who the thieves were who got away with it. What now? He stood, walked to the plate glass window overlooking downtown Atlanta, gazed at what many called a fantastic city. For eight years, he had ran the city like a magician working his magic. The people of Atlanta trusted him to run a good city government, especially the police department that was above and beyond reproach. Now this, after he and the Chief had denied the threat of terrorism, and made it clear that it was due to a gas line malfunction. But he is told now that thieves, including a police Major had planned, executed the worse terrorist act that Atlanta had on record.

Being Mayor of this great city, he had become familiar with the history of Atlanta. Especially the part on how General Sherman marched his troops into the city in 1864, chasing the Confederate soldiers. By the time Sherman and his men departed Atlanta, he had destroyed by fire every building that were standing in the central city. At the time, no one dared to question Sherman's motive for burning down Atlanta. After all, it was a war, and in war, it was to kill or be killed, destroy or be destroyed. That is the mission of a war. But now, they all knew, a hundred and fifty years later that General Sherman did indeed have a motive, and it was not for the safety of his troops or even to win the battle. It was all about the gold.

Now what? Again, he asked himself, but he had no answers.

Chief Martin on the other hand was asking a different question to himself. *Why can't the assholes that I send to do a job, get it right?* He had given very specific and clearly spoken orders to only follow John Sinclair and Seville. There was never an order to engage the pair. By departmental rules they were by law real cops. On the same night that the FBI agents were shot and one killed by people who could be linked back to him. Even the ones killed in a car crash on the freeway. *The Mayor is right. This is getting way out of hand!* And he knew that when it was all said and done, whether he was able to get the gold or not, it was going to fall squarely on his shoulders. *The Mayor will simply say, I should have known what was going on in my city and in my department.*

In a downtown parking lot on North Avenue, the Chief met with Bobby Turner. He was highly angered by the fact that every plan that he had tried to put in place had gone afoul. He stepped out of his car, met Turner away from the cars, just in case the Feds were trying to figure out what was going on. "Goddamnit, Sergeant, what in the hell happened last night?! I told you plain and simple, not to engage them. I wanted your people to follow them, find out where they go, who they talk to, and that's all. How hard is that to do, Sergeant? And how in the hell did your people end up getting smashed by a fucking big rig on the freeway?! Tell me, because I want to know."

Sergeant Turner could not answer the question. He looked off into the distance, wondering why he had taken on such a dangerous mission from the craziest police chief in the world. "Ah Sir, I gave them the orders that you gave me. Danny knew better. But for some reason, they got into a chase with a Hummer that apparently belongs to this John Sinclair,….." He paused. "I don't know how it happened."

"Yeah, I know. One of the beat cars ran his tag this morning. I had to call off the dogs, they know too much to be questioned. You on the other hand need to leave town."

Turner looked at the Chief strangely. "Why is that, Sir?"

The Chief laughed softly. "Because your people also tried to kill John Sinclair last night, but instead it was an FBI agent. And then, your people tried to run them off the road early this morning, but they missed on both counts! Do I need to say more?"

"That's fucking Calvin Gates!" ….*Danny Porter screwed up and got himself killed. Now this fucker wants me to leave town. Fuck it!* "How is he doing it?"

"How is who doing what? Oh, you mean John Sinclair. Well, you can thank your dead Major Butler for that. This was all his idea, the murder of Calvin Gates and the bombing of the precinct. At first, it sounded like a good idea, but now, I'm not so sure if this thing is going to work at all, especially if Calvin Gates remembers who killed him."

"So, you think he's going to remember that I was apart of what happened to him and his family five years ago?"

The Chief smiled. "Do you want to take that chance? I wouldn't. Look, whether Calvin Gates remembers you or not, there has been enough shit going on in this town for the last several months to send us all the prison for life if the truth is ever known. And unless you're willing to spend the rest of your life in federal prison, if I were you, when I give you the word to leave town, I want you to leave, okay?!"

"Okay, but what about you, Sir?"

"Right now, I'm okay. The Mayor believes what I tell him. But once he starts to see a problem with what I'm telling him, I'm leaving as well. Also, I've convinced Gates that his own half brother was the one who tried to kill him, and murdered his family. Right now, I think Gates is looking elsewhere. However, we need to find out where that gold is, or the cash that they were paid for the gold before Calvin does. That's our one and only mission at this point."

"You want us to continue the stakeout on Ethan Johnston's house?"

"Most definitely! Right now, he's the only man who can lead us to the gold or the money. It must be many billions by now."

Turner turned and started to walk away. The Chief stared at him for a moment. "Sergeant!" He shouted.

Turner stopped before getting back into his car. "Yes, Chief….."

"Try not to crew up the assignment this time…..Just watch the house until Ethan shows up. And then you call me, okay?"

Turner stared at the Chief for a few moments. He honestly wanted to tell his boss where he could take his assignment and shove it. But for time being, there was too much cash involved to just walk away. "Okay Chief, I won't crew it up this time….What about Calvin and the girl, you want my people to continue to tail them?"

"The Chief shook his head. "No…..I can't take any more chances with them. And besides, after that little stunt last night, I expect to see them real soon anyway."

Both cops got back into the vehicles and drove off. Chief Martin drove directly to his office. On his arrival, his secretary notified him that the Atlanta Field office Special Agent of the FBI was in his office. *What in the hell does he want?* He thought as he walked in. "Director Morrison, how are you? Which is it, Director Morrison, or Special Agent Morrison? I can never get those titles straight." He smiled as he took a seat at his desk.

Director Morrison stood. "It really doesn't matter, Chief, as long as you know that we, the FBI are in charge of this investigation from this point forward."

Chief Martin leaned back in his chair. "What investigation are you referring to?"

"Chief, I don't have time for your bullshit! Or this cat and mouse game that someone in your department is playing. I've got one agent dead, and another one low sick, and it all took place at the apartment where two of your cops are shacking up. Now, I want to know what in blazing hell is going on in this fucked up department?!" His voice was high pitched, and the secretary could hear him in the outer office.

Chief Martin was not fazed by anything that he was saying. "Director Morrison, go right ahead and investigate all you want to. And when you find out what's going on, then you come back to my office and tell me, okay? Because, frankly, I don't give a damn! I am up to my eyes balls with bullshit as well." He rocked forward in his chair. "I've done everything in my power to get to the bottom of this whole crazy mess, and I haven't gotten any place but deeper in trouble with the Mayor….By the way, I'm sorry about your agents."

Director Morrison sat back down. "You mean to tell me that you don't have the slightest clue as to what is going on? How is that possible, Chief Martin?"

"It's possible because I am being outsmarted by a bunch of brilliant assholes. That's how it's possible. Don't think for one moment that I haven't tried to get to the bottom of this mess, because I have. But every time I think I've got these assholes by the balls, they managed to pull a fast one, and no one sees them when they do it."

Director Morrison became a bit confused. "So, you're saying you know who blew up the precinct, and who killed my agent, but as far as you know now, they're gone?"

The Chief laced his fingers together, leaning on his elbows. "Lets' say, I have my suspicions as to what blew up my precinct. But right now, I am sticking with a faulty gas line. And, until my investigators can prove that it was an act of terrorism by a bunch of terrorist assholes, it will remain an accidental situation."

"It sounds like you need the investigative skills of the FBI....Look, I can bring three or four teams in here tomorrow, and we can get started on this thing right away."

"And what exactly are your people going to be investigating? A homicide of an agent, the bombing of a precinct, or the gold that your agents heard that was discovered buried underneath my precinct?...."

Director Morrison stared at the Chief with piercing eyes. Finally, he said, "Naturally, we would have to investigate the shooting of my agents first. Then we'll move on to the other aspects of this twisted situation. The two people who are presently working on this case, would you allow them to assist us? To just give us an idea as to what we are dealing with, or whom we are looking for."

"They're working for me, and I don't want them getting involved with the FBI.."

"Just for a couple of days, or until my people can get a feel of things, know who they're going after, and who they're dealing with."

Chief Martin smiled. "I'll think about it. Your other agents tried that, and you see where it got them. We don't need anymore cop killing in this city. And what you are asking me to help you do will guarantee more killing."

"Why, because of that so-called missing Confederate gold?"

"Yeah, I'd say so. I've seen people get killed for a lot less."

"But we're the FBI. The Federal Bureau of Investigation, do you know what that mean? It mean, we don't take no for an answer. We get results, because we have the United States Government standing behind us, that's includes the military. Do you see how powerful we are, Chief Martin?"

"Yeah, I see. But your people have been here what, two, three months, and they can't tell you one thing that they found out from their investigation.....Do you want to know why, Director? Because the people they're investigating are dead, they're ghosts, they're not real. And surely, who in their right mind is going to believe that a bunch of people, or cops blew up their own precinct, and killed thirteen fellow officers because they thought some gold was buried underneath the fucking the precinct? Come on, tell me who?! That makes no sense to you or anyone else that you might tell that story to."

Again, Director Morrison stood. "What about my agents, someone shot and killed one of my agents...Do you have any idea as to who did that?!!"

"If I did, they would be in jail waiting for trial in federal court." Chief Martin stood as well. "Listen, I'm not trying to sell you a bill of goods, but simply put, your super investigators will be doing nothing but running around in circles trying to make sense of what is going on.....The people who put this scheme together are much smarter than you and I put together....With that said, let my people contact your people whenever they come up with something solid, okay?"

Director Morrison immediately left the Chief's office in a quiet fury. *I am dealing with a complete idiot! Or he's putting on a serious act.* He thought as he was leaving.

CHAPTER TWENTY-THREE

Later in the day after John and Seville had visited Carolyn Butler and received the most shocking news of their lives together, telling John that he himself was partly the blame as to why things had gone so deadly five years earlier. He had thought about the conversation all that following afternoon. How could he have forgotten his relationship with another woman, that woman especially? Maybe somewhere during his recovery from memory loss, he had systematically selected the things in his former life that he did not want to remember. *That's it, I have selected amnesia.* He thought as Seville entered the family room where he was sitting staring at the wall.

"Do you think it was smart coming back here after what happened last night?" She asked as she sat next to him on the sofa, referring to their apartment. She handed him a glass half filled with scotch and water. "Maybe this will help ease your nerves."

He smiled as he took the glass and sipped from it. "We both are cops, we've got guns, and we don't run away from danger. I don't know what last night was all about, but there is one man in this whole city who knows exactly what's going on, and it's time that he do some serious talking."

"And who is this one man?" She asked as she drank from her glass.

"Chief Harold Martin." He was angry. "He has been talking out of both sides of his mouth long enough, and it's time that he gave us the real story about everything."

"And what make you think that he knows anything? I mean, he could be just as dumb as he's pretending to be."

"No….He's not that dumb. No one is that stupid. That's just an act. You see how he tried to make it seem like James Butler was in love with my wife when in fact it was me who was in love with his wife…."

"So, that places you in a whole different light of things doesn't it?"

John stared at her for a moment. "And what's that suppose to mean?"

"Well, it means, here we are thinking all along that you were the innocent bystander, when in fact, you were banging your boss's old lady which happens to be your sister-in-law as well. As Calvin Gates, you were a one man army, plus sex machine!"

"Are you angry because Carolyn said that she and I were lovers? Because if you are, don't be. I don't remember anything about being her lover."

"And what make you think that I'm mad about something that took place before my time? Hell, it was your brother who was pissed off, not me."

"Well, because anger or pissed off is written all over your face."

They both sat in silence for a few moments thinking about what Carolyn had said. "You know, what I don't understand about any of this is, as far as you and the Major are concerned,……" She started to say.

"I am already ahead of you." John said. "I was banging his old lady, and I was about to put his shit in the wind because he was a dirty cop. As a result, he tried to have me killed, but had second thoughts and saved my life. Now, the question remains, why?"

"If he were alive right now, would you ask him that same question?" Seville stared him directly in the eyes.

"Yes, I most certainly would, just before I'd kill him for what he did to my family. Saving me is all well and good, but he murdered my wife and daughter. There's no way I can forgive him, or allow him to live knowing that he was responsible for that."

"So, you're saying if our theory is correct, and he's alive as we suspect that he might be, are you still planning to kill him anyway?"

"Like I said, I can't forgive him for what he did. He took the only family that I had! He took all that I had."

"Even after learning that you and his wife were lovers, even before they were married? He apparently felt the same way about you. But he saved your life in spite of what happened to your family….Isn't it possible that he may have snapped, but came to his senses in time enough to save you? And that's the reason he stole the five million dollars from the city and gave you a new life. Something obviously happened to him inside that he would risk everything to do that. Rather than thinking about killing him if he's still alive, maybe you should try and think about why he did what he did for his only half brother."

John did not say anything for several moments. He knew that she was making a valid point, although he knew deep down within he would still kill his brother for killing his family. Finally, he turned to her. "I'm curious about something,....."

"Yeah, what's that?" She asked smiling, for she knew that he was getting suspicious.

"You,....." He looked at her as if he was looking straight through her.

"What about me?"

"They came to north Georgia, brought me down here and set me up in this fabulous apartment with all the money I can spend. Then, the Major brings you on board as my so-called partner. And you, being the brilliant woman that you are, you come right in, you don't ask no questions, you makes yourself at home, and immediately we are screwing like we've known each other for years. Again, being a beautiful and intelligent woman like you, that was much too easy. So, tell me, what is your stake in all of this?"

"What is my stake in all of this?" She repeated nervously, taking a drink before continuing. "You know, at first, I was against the idea. But the Major was very convincing. He made me a promise, he said if I could pull this off, crack this case the way they wanted us to, I'd be promoted to sergeant as soon as I went back to my unit. And, he said I would probably make lieutenant within the next six months. But in order for that to happen, I'd have to make this thing between you and I work like a marriage."

"So, this talk about you being in love with me, what was that about?"

"That's for real. Although I didn't plan for that to happen, but it did." She stood and walked to the middle of the floor. "You remember when the Chief said that we had been played from the very beginning, or something to that effect?"

John frowned for he did not like what he figured she was about to go with her statement. "Yeah, I remember him saying something like that."

"Well, you and I were put together as partners for one reason, and one reason only. We were not supposed to solve this case. We were to make everyone think we were working on the case in order to make it look good. It was supposed to take away from the real reason why that precinct was blown up, and we already know why that was done."

"And you knew this the first time you walked through that door, right?"

"Not about the gold. They said investigate, but at the same time, don't investigate. We were only supposed to be nothing but a window dressing for the Mayor, the Feds, the media, and the public. However, making love to you was never apart of the plan. I think the Major was shocked when he figured out that we were getting along so well."

"And what else did you know coming in?" John could feel the rage building inside of him, but he tried to maintain his calm and cools.

"I knew we were never supposed to have gotten this far, to where we have figured out everything that has happened, and why it happened. Major Butler getting killed was not in the plans either." She went and sat back down next to John. "Listen to me John, and believe me when I tell you this. You and I were only supposed to play the game, and at the end of the day, you go back to where you came from, I would return to my unit, and everybody else would ride off into the sunset and live happily ever after."

John knew from the tone of her voice that what she was admitting to was freely done. "Okay, other than trying to throw everyone off their trails, how are they supposed to get away with blowing up the precinct, killing all those cops, and escaping with a boat load of gold, which it seems like they have already done, except?....." John paused.

Seville eyes widened. "Except what?"

He pulled himself to the edge of the sofa. "Lets' you and I step back the in past for a moment." He handed Seville his glass. "Can I have another one while we're figuring this thing out?"

She immediately got up and went back to the bar and poured two more drinks. She rushed back to her seat to hear what he was about to say. "Okay, I'm all ears.....But first, are you angry because I led you on all this time?"

"Yeah!....But I'll get over it." He said as he took his drink. "Okay, lets' assume that Carolyn Butler was speaking the truth when she said that she and I were lovers, and James wanted me dead for that reason. And lets' assume that he plotted to have me killed by the three men whom I had placed in the county jail. Now, these four characters figured if they got rid of me and my family, all of their troubles would be over."

"As well as settling a score that he had carried around with him since you guys were kids,..." Seville added.

"Yeah, that too.....Now, I can vaguely remember that night. I remember wandering around in the woods after the explosion, dazed and bleeding. I also remember several men, hunters I believe. These same men rushed me to a hospital, and the doctors discovered that I was a cop due to pieces of my uniform that was still intact. Apparently, the doctors called the police department, and the dispatcher called Major Butler, telling him to go the hospital where I was."

"So, who pronounced you dead, the doctors?"

"Yes, based upon the Major's instructions. He convinced them that I was all that was left from a hit on me and my family, and that my identity should remain in strict confidential." John immediately realized that he could now recall that night clearly. "I remember being given medical attention there for a few days under tight security. And after that, I was transferred to another hospital out of the city where they reconstructed my face, performed plastic surgery, which ended up giving me a new identity."

Seville reached for his hand, pulling it to her and rubbing it. "I know from experience that Major Butler was a powerful man, but it's amazing how he was able to do all of this and no one, not even the Chief knew what was going on."

"Major Butler was a feared man. The Chief was afraid to attack him or accuse him of anything that he suspected was out of line with departmental procedures. In other words, Chief Martin was scared shitless of the Major….That's how he was able to just take five million dollars from confiscated drug money and spend it all on me."

"But why do that for you if his plan was to kill you in the first place?"

John stood. "Ah, again, we're back to the five million dollars question." He smiled.

"When you suggested that maybe he had a change of heart. Yeah, right!….No, he didn't have a change of heart, he had another reason. Now, what that reason was, I don't know. And I hope his ass is still alive because he's going to answer that question before I kill him."

Seville dropped her head before muttering. "Well, he's alive,….."

John suddenly turned to face her. "What did you say?!"

"I repeat; he's alive."

"How do you know that for sure?" He asked in a stunned voice.

She smiled as she said, "Why do you think Carolyn is going to Paris? She has heard from him, and she'll meet up with her new husband in about two weeks."

"How do you know all of this?"

"Because he called to give me the latest on what's happening. Plus, he wanted know what's going on here with you."

"And you didn't tell me this?"

She suddenly stood as well. "John, do you have any idea how hard it has been for me to pretend that I had no clue as to what've been going on with the Major?"

"No, but I'll bet you're about to tell me now.....And why are you telling me all of this now?!"

"I had to wait until the right time, like right now."

"Why now?" He was looking confused by her statement.

Without answering the question, she pulled out an automatic from the pocket of her robe. "My orders were, when you come to the point of remembering what took place the night that you were supposed to be killed, I am to finish the job." She pointed the gun at his chest as she stepped back.

He was not surprised by this turn of events. In fact, he was wondering what had taken her so long to get around to it. "Now I get it! Not only were you hired to do all the kinky girly shit with me, but my brother also sent you to kill me as well. Why am I not surprised by this move?" He went over to the sofa and sat down. "But why now?"

Seville continued to point the gun. "The idea is not to leave any loose ends dangling around that could come back haunt the Major. As long as you didn't remember what happened that night, it was left up to me to dispose of you or not. But now that I see you are remembering everything about that night, I have to take you out as ordered."

"Are you really going to do what you were told, I mean, take me out as ordered?"

"I don't want to, but I am being paid a lot of money for this job. I mean, I really do care about you, John...I really do, but I have a job to do, right?!"

"Well, in that case, I think you should follow your orders. Do it! In fact, I demand that you pull the trigger right now! Follow your orders, goddamnit woman, come on!"

Suddenly, her facial expression changed from mild to serious. "What did you say?"

"You were hired to kill me by my fucking half-brother, and I'm telling you to do as you were paid and ordered to do by him! If you don't pull the trigger, I'll do it for you."

"You really want me to kill you, don't you?!" She started to shake badly.

"Yes! Why not? He killed me once, now you kill me, again!" John yelled.

Without thinking, she did as he commanded her to do. She screamed as she pulled the trigger once, twice, and a third time. But nothing happened. Suddenly, she realized that no shots were being fired from her gun and that it was empty. She stared at the weapon smiling. "You sonofabitch!.... You knew my gun was unloaded, didn't you?!"

"Yes, and even if it had been loaded, you were not going to fire. When I kept telling you to shoot, my mama didn't raise no fool. I wanted to see if you had it in you."

She dropped the weapon on the sofa as she sat down next to him. "But how did you know that I would even pull a gun on you in the first place?"

"Remember earlier today when you left the room to meet Slim down in the lobby of the hotel? A little bird called me on the room phone and told me to be careful, because he figured you might try something like this."

"So, Slim called after I left him and told you what we had talked about.....?"

"Something like that. Yeah, but you also must remember it was Slim who helped me in gathering evidence on the bad cops, including Major Butler. So, naturally, when he learned that I was still alive, he was more than willing to help keep tabs on you. You see, he knew that this whole pretend love affair that we have was a set up by the Major."

"And you unloaded my gun while I was down in the lobby with Slim? What if I had pulled out my back-up weapon, would you have been so anxious for me to shoot then?

I bet you wouldn't have been shouting, shoot then. Your ass would be dead."

"First of all, you don't have a second gun. Secondly, I have suspected you since day-one....I mean, the sex is good, but I've always had a loaded gun under my pillow." He laughed softly. "But, as of this moment, since you failed to go through with your mission, you have to tell the Major one or two things; you either killed me, or my memory is still out in left field somewhere."

She shook her head. "No, I can't do that now. I've already confirmed that you had your memory back. And he expect for me to do as I was ordered and promised to do."

"How could you make that promise, knowing that you had feelings for me?"

"I really wasn't sure until after I met with Slim. You see, you, the Chief and Bobby Turner are the only three loose ends left that needs to be taken care of. And once that is done, we are to vanish in thin air and never to be heard from again. When I got back to the room, I suddenly realized that I am in love with you. Why do you think I wanted to have your baby?" She stood up. "Look, you and I can walk out of here right now. I can call the Major and tell him I've completed the job, dumped your body in the river, end of story. Later, I'll meet you, and we can live our lives like regular people."

"After all he has done to make this happen, do you seriously believe that we can just walk away that easily?" John stood with her, placing both hands on her shoulders, pulling her to him. "As much as I would like to believe that my half brother is a good man, I know he's not. He's an evil monster whose heart is cold steel. We both know that he has the money and resources now to do anything that he wants to, including finding out whether you really completed the job or not. He will not stop until he knows for sure that we both are dead."

Seville pulled away and sat down again. "Wow! I hadn't thought about that." She stared up at John. "So, what do we do now?"

He swallowed the last of his liquor. "First thing we should do is warn the Chief about the hit on him and Turner."

"Wait, wait, I thought you wanted Turner dead. Plus, the Chief knew all about the bombing of the precinct."

"Really?" John asked with a surprised look.

"I know, he was your friend as Calvin Gates, and you've looked at everybody as being apart of this elaborate plan except the Chief. Well, I've got news for you, he knew from day-one what was going on like the rest of us."

"So, what do you suggest, we let the Major kill everybody else, and then we go after him?" John sat back down as well.

"Why not?....That's the only way of making sure that they all are dead. You said it yourself, that's the only way we're ever going to be free of the Major."

"Wait a minute!...You're talking about going to Paris France, finding the Major in his new face, kill him, and then come on back home...What about his wife, Carolyn?"

"She's only going to be there for about a week or two. Then, she's coming back to the United States, pick up their two kids, and fly back to

Paris. By that time, we should know his new identity. And all we'll have to do is kill him. Then we fly back to Atlanta before she gets back." Seville said smiling. "When we arrive back in Atlanta, all the major players will be dead, and we will be home free."

John thought about her plan for a moment. "And you really think that will work?"

"Yes, I think it will work. But we'll have to make sure that we are in Paris when she arrives so we will know who's picking her up at the airport. If it's not him, we'll have to follow her to wherever she's going to meet him."

John smiled. "I like that. Have you been working on this plan long?"

"Yes, for the passed two days. Somehow I knew that it was going to come down to you and me against him and everybody else."

"Yeah, but you do know we are not dealing with the mind of an ordinary man. With the amount of money that he obviously has now, he's going to have round the clock security. He can't trust anyone now, not even his own partners in crime. So, in order to get to him after Carolyn leaves for the States, it's going to take some serious planning."

"Well, I guess we'll just have to improvise a way of getting to him." She turned up her glass swallowed. "You want to make love to me now?" She leaned over closer to him.

He grunted. "I don't know, is it safe, do you have a loaded gun somewhere?"

"You'll have to find that out for yourself....Are you scared?"

John thought about the offer and the challenge. "Oh, what the hell, as far as the Major is concerned, I am already dead. So, I guess if you end up killing me twice, at lease I'll die with a smile on my face."

"A really big smile too, my darling. Because I'm going to put it on you like you've never had it put on you before." She said as she stood and headed towards the bedroom.

"How can a woman be so lovely and be so dangerous all at the same time?" He asked as he followed her to the bedroom.

CHAPTER TWENTY-FOUR

Going to bed and making love, Seville tried her best to show John that her feeling for him was real, and that he did not have to worry about her doing anything to harm him. It apparently worked, for John and Seville fell sound asleep until around 4 o'clock in the morning when his cell phone began buzzing. He could barely open his eyes wide enough to locate the phone on the night stand. He picked it up, rolled on his back, eyes closed, and listened to the caller on the other end for a moment before groggily saying, "Yeah,.."

"Hey, old man, you need to wake your ass up! I've got a very serious tip to lay on you and Seville." Slim said in a loud and excited voice.

"Slim, why are you calling me this time of night?" John managed to get out.

"Because what I've got to tell you can't wait till daylight, that's why I'm calling you now. Wake up and listen old man! I'm going to say this slowly so you'll get it right."

John sat up in bed while Seville was still lay sound asleep. "Okay, you've got my attention, shoot!"

"Funny thing you'd say shoot, because that's exactly what's going to happen to you and my woman lying next to you. Your boy has put a hit on her, as of tonight. He wants her dead, you dead, and all the other fuckers you know! Are you feeling me?!"

For a moment, John refused to say anything, he stared in the darkness. Suddenly, he realized that he and Seville should have seen this coming. Why take a chance on leaving her alive as being the only witness who could identify him as the ring leader of everything that had happened up to this point? "Do you have any details about when, where, or how?" …..By the way, who has the contract?"

"I don't know when or where, but I can tell you how, by being dead. Who? Well, they are out of town folks coming in on a flight around five this morning. But you know what? I don't even trust him on that. They just might already be here as far as I know. Listen, I don't know what you did to piss this man off, but he want you and Seville dead like yesterday! So, if I were you and my woman, I'd get the hell out of there right now!"

"Slim, thanks a million… But let me ask you, what role are you playing in this?"

"Hey, I'm just a business man, that's all. I'm suppose to make sure that the contract get carried out…..Like I said, my nigga, don't be lying around there looking at that fine ass woman. Because if you do, she'll be the last piece of fine ass you'll ever see. Do you feel me, man?!"

"Yeah, I feel you, Slim. Thanks again. We're out of here."

"Peace!" Slim said as he stepped out of his limousine at his mansion. Shortly there after, a Yellow Cab pulled up to the gated property. The security guard notified Slim on his cell. "Yeah, I know who they are. Let them in." *And I'm keeping a close watch on whoever these bastards are. That Major is a tricky-ass motherfucker. Hell, he just might have taken out a contract on me.* He thought as he waited for the cab to arrive along with two of his men. "Guys, keep your eyes open on these clowns. And don't let them out of your sight. I don't know these guys, and I damn sure don't trust them."

John hurriedly got out of bed. He shook Seville, "Hey, wake up, we gotta go!"

Seville slowly opened her eyes as she mumbled, "Go where? Where are we going this time of morning? I just went to sleep." She sat up in the bed. "Oh, that was some wonderful loving you put on me, baby."

"Yeah, yeah…." John sat one the side of the bed. "Remember what you said about the Major tying up all his loose ends so there won't be anyone left to incriminate him?"

"Yeah, I remember, what about it?" She asked softly.

"Well, it seems like we're some of those loose ends that needs tying up."

"Wait a minute!" Her eyes suddenly wide open. "What are you talking about?"

"I just got a call form Slim, and the word is that a contract is out on you, me, the Chief, and everybody else. We've got to get ready and get out of town fast."

Seville smiled at John. "You sound like one of those old western flicks, where the outlaws say, we've got to out of town fast, the Sheriff is on his way!" She turned serious. "How do we know that this ain't one of Slims' practical jokes? You know, he loves pulling these kinds of stunts on people, especially you and me."

John stood, turned the bedroom lights on. "We don't know. But we can't just sit around waiting to see if one of his practical jokes will turn out to be the real thing."

"But why would the Major put a hit on me? As far as he knows, you're dead. I did what he asked me to do, so why kill me?!" She turned serious again as she got out of bed.

"When we get to Paris, and just before I kill this bastard, I'll let you ask him that question along with the hundred of others that I have for his ass, okay? But as of right now, we've got to hit the shower, get dressed, and get the hell out of here. I don't know who the number one target is, but I'm hoping Slim will help us out in that department." John turned and headed for the shower.

"Do you have any idea where are we're getting out of town to, I say there, my partner?!" She yelled, imitating the villains from the old western movies.

"This shit ain't funny, Seville!" John shouted back. "I don't know just yet. We'll probably head north for a few days. At least until we can figure out what our next move is going to be."

She rushed to the shower in the second master bedroom.

Twenty minutes later, they were dressed, packed and ready to travel. Seville slid into the passenger's seat this time for she had no idea where they were headed. "Are you going to warn the Chief that he's a marked man?" Seville asked as she settle comfortably in her seat as they drove north on Peachtree Street.

"I shouldn't, but I will. But, that doesn't mean he's going to believe what I tell him. Apparently, he has his own agenda about that missing gold, and he's not about to let the thought of somebody wanting to kill him stop him from searching for whoever has it."

She chuckled. "But if what Slim says is true, he needs to be convinced so he can have his people on the lookout for whoever is coming for him, don't you think?"

"Yeah, I see what you're saying, and I will try. But first, we have to look out for ourselves, and then I'll call the Chief." He thought for a moment in silence. "You know, you always hear about how crazy people can get over money. Some people will kill their own friends, spouses, relatives, and everybody for the love of money. Of course, in this case, it's all about the gold. It's gold fever! Remember those old western movies, in the gold camps and towns where the bad guys would kill the poor saps who had worked hard all of their lives panning for gold? This shit here really reminds me of those times. These people are suffering with that same mentality and greed."

"But why kill me?!" She asked, glancing out of the window. "I've been loyal to the damn man. I mean, I even played you all because he said there was going to be a big payday in it for me, plus promotion when it was all over with. But no! The bastard is sending his hit men to try and kill me.... Now, that's some low-down dirty nigger shit!"

"Okay, so we both have a score to settle with my half brother. Do you want to shoot him first, or you want me to shoot him first?" He said with a smile.

"Well, since you and he have the same fucked up father, I'll let you take the first crack at him." She laughed. "Sorry about that remark about your father."

"That's okay. I feel the same way. He had to be fucked up to plant a seed in a woman to produce a son like James Butler. The dude is bad to the core. Listen, God will have a big smile on his face when we off this monster."

"Amen to that, my brother!" She glanced at him. "Just suppose I had killed you for real. It would have been all for nothing. He still would have this contract out on me."

"Obviously, that was his plan all along. When Slim called,......" He hesitated for a moment. He repeated himself. "When Slim called,....."

Seville looked at him, wondering why he had suddenly stopped talking. "What's wrong?"

"Slim knew that you were supposed to kill me earlier, because he called me from the lobby to tell me that you had orders to do so."

"We already know that. So, what's the problem now?"

"But he didn't know that you refused to carry out the assignment, did he?"

She shook her head. "No....Maybe he suspected that I wouldn't, but I never said that I wouldn't. Why you ask?"

"Because when he called a little while ago, he obviously knew that you didn't carry out the order. Otherwise, why did he call me? He would've called you."

"Wow! I hadn't thought about it that way. You're right. But do you think he told the Major he didn't think I was going to do it?"

"I don't know. But even if he did, why would he then turn around warn me again that an out of town hit man was on the way?"

"So, you think that this contract was given to Slim?"

"Obviously not, because when he called, he was waiting for the hit guys to arrive by plane then….Sometimes I wonder whose side is this dude really on?"

"Right now, it looks like he's on our side." She thought for a moment. "So, this contract is supposed to eliminate me, you, the Chief, and the remaining three officers that you were going to arrest, right?"

"Yeah, and that was the other thing he said."

"So, apparently they do know that you're still alive…..You do know that we can't run forever. Sooner or later, we're going take a stand and kill anybody who is trying to kill us….You do know that, don't you?"

"Yeah, I know….As strange as it may seem, I really don't have a desire to kill anybody. But, you're right. It's either us or them, and I rather for it to be them!"

She pulled out an automatic from her overnight bag, and pushed in a fully loaded clip. "Well, Mr. Sinclair, I realized you've gone through a very traumatic experience over the past five years, and you can't seem to remember all the facts yet. But from this point on, forget your past, because there are people out there who are trying to kill us. And if we don't kill them first, they will succeed. And right now, I've got too much time that I've invested in you. I'm not about to allow either one of us to die just yet. So, man-up, big boy and get a fucking desire to kill, because this is some real shit!"

John looked at her smiling. "Where did you learn to talk like that?"

"See, I knew you thought that I was one of those nice, sweet little pretty cops. No, I am a long ways from that. For the last five years that I've been a cop, I've had dreams of being in a situation just like this. I've always wanted to be that female James Bond." She said laughing. "Have you ever wanted to be somebody other than who you are?"

John smiled. "I can't rightly remember. But as you said, this is serious, and I am up to the challenge. It's kill or be killed. And it would be a shame to not have anymore nights like we had last night."

"That's exactly what I'm talking about. You know, the Major didn't bring us together. We were destined to be mated up in a lovely, dangerous situation like we are right now. This is the work of God."

"You believe in God?"

"Sure, I believe in God, don't you?"

"I don't have much choice but to believe in Him. Look at me. I am a living example of what God can do. I am a walking, talking miracle."

"I can believe that." She said, letting the seat back. She placed her gun under her seat and closed her eyes. "I guess we'll be stopping for breakfast soon, you think?"

"We will as soon as we get out of the city, and get some distance between us and them." He said, continuing to check his rearview mirror for any vehicle that might be following them. They were at a point now where it was unsafe to go back to the city. It was unsafe to go to his north Georgia home, it was almost unsafe to travel any place. But they had to get to a place to sort things out. They still had to make plans on when they were going to travel to Paris. They had an idea about when Carolyn was supposed to fly out, but they did not know the exact date and time. Their plan was to leave a day or two before Carolyn left and be there when she arrived and follow her to wherever she was going to meet Major Butler. Within the next week, they had to figure out a way to get back to the city, find out the exact date she was leaving without drawing attention to themselves and sending a message to the Major saying that they were still in the game.

Approximately fifty miles south of the State line off I-75, John pulled into a parking space at a Waffle House. Before getting out, he scanned the area just in case they had picked up a tail along the way. He took out his cell phone and dialed the Chief, he remembered the number. He glanced at his watch, it was 7:35 a.m., and by his calculation, the Chief should have been in route to work, or getting ready to leave home. The phone rang several times before there was an answer. "Hello, ..." The voice said.

"Chief Martin?" John asked slowly, for he did not recognize the voice.

"No, the Chief is unavailable, can I help you?" The strange voice said.

John immediately closed the phone. His heart began to race to the point of fearing that the Chief was dead already. He shook Seville. "Seville, wake up!"

She opened her eyes slowly and let the seat forward. "Are we there?"

"Yeah, we're at the Waffle House....." He paused.

"What's wrong?" She blinked several times, trying to focus her vision.

"I just called the Chief on his cell phone and someone else answered. It was not a voice I recognize. I think they may have gotten to him already."

"But you can't be sure. That could have been anyone, maybe his son." She opened the door, and sudden felt a heavy downpour of rain. "Shit!.... Why didn't you tell me it was raining?"

John laughed. "I thought you knew it was raining." He reached into the back seat for an umbrella that he carried just for times like these and gave it to her. "Always be prepared."

As soon as they were seated in the restaurant, the waitress rushed over to take their orders. They ordered the special that was on the menu. John's cell phone buzzed. He knew it was not Maria, for she would never call this early in the morning unless it was an emergency. But as he stared at the caller ID, it said Chief Martin. He opened the receiver slowly as if he was afraid to answer it. "Yeah, this is John, who is this?!"

"Is this John Sinclair?" A strange voice asked. It was the same voice that answered the Chief's phone when he called earlier. "This is John Sinclair, right? Or is it Calvin Gates? Which is it?"

John looked at Seville as he was hesitant about responding.

She immediately knew that something was wrong. "Is that the same person?"

John nodded to her, and said into the phone. "You make the distinction. Where is Chief Martin, and why are you on his cell phone?....Better yet, why are you calling me?!"

"Oh, Mr. Sinclair, I see you haven't been watching the news....Chief Martin met with a terrible accident this morning on his way to work. In fact, it was a deadly accident. He was found floating in his car down the Chattahoochee River about an hour ago."

John closed the flip phone. He stood, went to the counter, and told the cashier to turn the television to a local news channel. Channel 2 was broadcasting a "Newsbreak". The announcer was giving the latest update on a strange and bizarre series of events that led up to the fatal accident of Chief Harold Martin's death. John started to turn around to go back to his booth, but he realized that Seville was standing directly behind him. "Look like we've got our work cut out for us, wouldn't you say so, baby?" She whispered.

John placed his arm around her shoulders and they went back to their seats. As soon as they were seated, they saw that everyone else in the restaurant had their eyes glued on the TV set with unbelievable stares. *If*

229

they only knew what was really going on. He thought. John opened his cell phone again and dialed the Chief's number.

"What are you doing?" Seville asked.

He did not answer her, he waited until the strange voice spoke with, "Yes, Mr. Sinclair....Are you a believer now? And by the way, you asked me, why had I called you? Well, don't you think it's obvious? My employer wants you dead! And it's my job to kill you since your partner you're with couldn't do the job." He spoke with a Russian accent.

"And who informed your employer that she had faltered in doing what she was supposed to do as far as her job is concerned?"

"Does it really matter who informed him?" The Russian accent was thick and bass.

"Yes! Because I want to know who all I have to kill, and that's including you!" John was now showing who he really was, the ugly side of Calvin Gates.

"Mr. Sinclair, the only thing that you need to know is, there is no place for you to hide. We will find you regardless of where you may go."

John's blood pressure was running at a very high level, he could only remember one other time that he had gotten this angry. It was when he received a call telling him to release the three cops, or his family would die. John stood because everyone in the eatery was now eyeballing him and Seville because his voice was rising with every word. He walked outside to complete his conversation. "Listen, you fucking dirt-bag, you've got it all twisted, I'm not running from you. I am going to find you, and I'm going to kill you. Then, I'm going to kill all your friends, your relatives, even your fucking dog if you have one. And then, you can tell that no-good half brother of mine, I'm going to blow his fucking brains out as well! Did you get all of what I said, or do you need an interpreter?"

There was no answer, it was dead silence. He glanced down to see if the phone was still on. He was not sure if his call had dropped, or the man with the Russian accent had hung up. "Yeah, you don't like the idea of being the hunted, do you asshole?" He said to himself as he re-entered the Waffle House.

By the time he got to the table to join Seville, the waitress had already placed their food on the table. Seville stopped eating momentarily. "So, what's the plan?"

"Find out if Slim is apart of the hit on the Chief and whoever else they might have a contract on. Think you can get a fix on him?" He said sipping his coffee first.

Seville did not hesitate she knew why he was asking. She paused from eating long enough to dial Slim on her phone. She waited three rings for Slim to answered with, "Hey, my sweet wonderful one, what can I do for you?"

"Don't you call me your sweet or wonderful, you, asshole, you know what I want!"

"Look, I just saved your life and that's the thanks I get?!" Slim snapped.

"Shut the fuck up, Slim! Now, you listen to me. If we find out that you had anything to do with the assassination of Chief Martin, I will personally cut off your balls and shove them in your mouth…..Now, did you have anything to do with it?"

"Seville! No way did I have anything to do any killing. All I did was furnish these white dudes some high powered weapons. That's all! That's the only thing the Major asked me to do."

"Well, if I were you, I would stay in my mansion for the next few days. Once we tell the cops you supplied the guns, your ass is grass. You got that? Unless,….."

"Unless what, Seville?! Anything you want, just name it!"

"Unless you can help us track down the people who murdered the Chief."

"You've got a deal!…Look, I don't know or like these assholes anyway. When do you want me to set this up for you?"

"I'll be in touch." Seville closed the phone. She looked at John. "He'll do anything to keep me off his slim ass right about now."

"I know the feeling." He laughed.

Seville twisted her mouth as she went back to eating.

CHAPTER TWENTY-FIVE

It was around 11:00 hrs. that morning before Mayor Clifford Townsend had all the details in his hands as to what had caused the Chief to run his car through the guardrail and into the Chattahoochee River earlier in the day on his way to work. He stood before a large gathering of news reporters in the City Hall Atrium. He was getting absolutely tired of standing before the news media, or anyone else for that matter trying to explain what had gone wrong in his city. He looked over the large crowd of men and women, holding microphones, pens and note pads, waiting for him to tell them and the world what he knew about what appeared to have been murder of Chief Martin.

"Lady and gentlemen!...." He began in a somber voice with tears in his eyes. "This is probably the hardest day in his life as a public official, to stand before you and the nation to explain that someone deliberately, with some kind high powered rifle, shot and killed our Chief as he drove cross the Chattahoochee. We know of no reason for this to have happened. This is a sad time for the City of Atlanta, all its citizens, and the police department. We all are deeply sadden by the suddenly demise of Police Chief Harold Martin. We have no suspects at this time, or eyewitnesses. But, it is my mission as Mayor to find the perpetrator, or perpetrators who were responsible for this deplorable act of violence against a good man and our police chief, and bring them to justice."

Police officers and detectives alike throughout the city, in their squad cars, standing on street corners, and sitting in donut shops were frozen in place, trying desperately to comprehend what was happening to their city. Each one of those officers began to count the number of cops who had loss their lives in the line of duty dating back to five years ago, starting with Lieutenant Calvin Gates. And the one thing they all had in common with the exception of the Chief, they all came from one precinct, and that was Precinct Three. There was a question mark on everyone's lips, was Precinct Three cursed by some unknown evil force?

Mayor Townsend ended his press conference without taking questions about anything that was related to the police department. Speculations flew rampant throughout the media world as who had placed a hit on the police chief. Some believed that organized crime was well and alive in Atlanta. Some even believed that the same people who were responsible for blowing up the precinct, they also killed the Chief. As for motives, no one had a clue, not even the Mayor, except for that wild story that the Chief had brought to him about gold being underneath the precinct. But then, as he began to think more about the possibility of gold being found, and the Chief being assassinated, the more he began to believe that maybe the Chief was not so crazy after all.

Lord, I hope this is not about some crazy story of finding gold, because if it is, this is not the last that I will hear about it. He thought as he returned to his office. As he entered his office, he remembered being informed by Major Butler that they were going to bring in an outside investigator to look into the bombing. *Who is he, and where is he?*

He picked up the desk phone and dialed the Deputy Chief over the Uniform Division. "Deputy Chief Cunningham, this is Mayor Clifford Townsend, I'm going to appoint you Interim Chief until I decide on whom my next Chief will be. However, in the meantime, I want to know who are working on the precinct bombing case. Major Butler brought in someone from outside of the department. I want to know who that is as soon as possible. And when you find out who that person is, I want him brought to my office."

Every unit commander in the department received an urgent call from the acting chief to come up with a name of the person working on the precinct case. Immediately after the alert went out, Captain Holloway from the Intelligent Squad called the new chief and advised him that Sevilla Patterson was transferred to Major Butler's command to work with a John Sinclair. Suddenly, several police units were dispatched to Seville's parent home to find out the location of their daughter. Their information led them to the apartment in Buckhead where they already knew about due to the FBI shootings.

A city-wide search began for the pair of cops who were still on the run from the same people who assassinated Chief Martin. Seville's squad leader, Lieutenant David Thompson had her cell phone listed and began calling it. Finally, she got tired of its' annoying buzzing, she opened the phone and said, "Yeah, Lieutenant, I know all about the Chief being murdered. And I suppose you and the rest of the department think that me and my partner are connected in some kind of way, right?"

"No, that's not the case yet. But if you and your partner don't get your asses in here very quickly, you just might become suspects. The Mayor is calling for someone's head on this one, and he really doesn't give a rat's ass whose head he gets. Do you get my meaning?"

"Yes, Lieutenant, I get your meaning. But we're running from the same people who murdered the Chief." Seville explained while sitting in the passenger's seat as they drove north into Tennessee. "Lieutenant Thompson, please do me a favor, tell the Mayor, we'll meet with him as soon as we can. But right now, we don't know who these people are, and we ain't about to get wiped off the face of the earth just so he can talk with us, okay?...I appreciate you, Lieutenant Thompson!"

"Okay, have it your way." The Lieutenant said and then hung up the phone.

The trip to the State line of Tennessee was to buy new weapons. John knew of a place just across the State line where he could purchase any kind of guns that they were going to need, and there were no questions asked. The way they were looking at their situation, it was deadly serious. And if they were going to shoot it out with some Russian hit-squad, they wanted to be prepared.

The rain had finally slackened by the time they arrived at Harvey's Gun Store off I-75, two miles inside of the Tennessee border. When they parked, John was deeply concentrating on something that the caller said on the Chief's phone. He asked the caller, how did his employer know that Seville had failed to accomplish her mission of killing him? The caller never said how his employer knew, which apparently was Major Butler.

"You know, I've been thinking,…." He said finally.

"Oh yeah?! About what now, other than the Chief being killed?"

"How did the Major know that you didn't kill me as you were instructed to do? Unless, there was someone in the room who knew that you didn't pull the trigger."

"Or, they could hear us talking about the fact I didn't do it."

They thought about the apartment for a moment before coming to the same conclusion together. "Our apartment has been bugged the whole time." John said.

"And someone has been listening to everything that we've said and done." She added. "And if that's the case, they also know that we were tipped off by Slim."

"Slim, don't trust the Russians!" John shouted.

Seville immediately picked up her cell phone and dialed Slims' number. He answered after two rings. "Yeah, what's up?"

"Slim!" She said strongly. "Don't trust the Russians! They know you tipped us off. Keep your eyes on the suckers, or you'll be dead too."

"Really now? I knew there was something that I didn't like about these assholes. Thank you my sweet! And I owe you and your boyfriend one." He hung up.

Inside the gun shop, Seville looked at several different kinds of weapons, especially the ones with a lot of fire power. When they were complete with their shopping list, on the counter were two Coonan .357 Magnums handguns. Two Glock model 20,10mm handguns. A Browning Auto-5 12-guage Magnum pump shotgun, and a M-16 5.56 mm assault rifle just in case, along with several boxes of ammo for each weapon. The cashier stared at the couple before ringing up the total amount due for all the weapons. He then said with chuckle. "Are you folks going hunting?"

"Yeah, you could say that." John said with a smile.

"We have a few dangerous animals running loose around the farm." Seville added.

"I see…." The cashier said. "They must be some mighty big animals."

"They are, about as big as you….." She said smiling.

The cashier quickly rang up the total which was close to ten thousand dollars. And as John and Seville were walking out of the door, the older white male cashier muttered, "I wouldn't wanna be the animals ya'll gonna be hunting."

Heading back south, John decided that Seville may have had a point. He wanted to check in on Maria. He was not sure if the Russians would travel that far north looking for them, but if they did, he wanted to make sure that his housekeeper was safe. Exiting the freeway and headed towards John's home, he began to get a gut feeling that they should not drive all the way up to the front door. His gut feeling also told him to park the Hummer in the wooded area about a hundred yards away from his house.

"You think maybe they have come looking for us up here?" Seville asked softly.

"The caller sounded pretty determined on making sure that we are dead. It sounded as if his employer is paying good money to make sure that he doesn't leave this country until the job is complete." John said as they emerged from the vehicle.

"It's still hard for me to believe that a once decent man like the Major would turn out to be such a murdering bastard." Seville said as she loaded one of her new hand guns to go with the one she already had.

John loaded up the shotgun along with the 357 automatic. "Remember that old saying; 'money is the root of all evil'? I always thought that it was the lack of it. But in this case, too much of it will make a person just as evil."

Once they were loaded with guns and extra ammo, they began to walk carefully inside the wooded area towards the house. From a distant, they could not see the vehicle parked in the rear of the house. But the closer they got, John could clearly see that there was a black Chevrolet mini van parked in the rear of his home. "Just as I thought," John whispered. "If the bastards harm Maria, I'll kill them all."

"I suggest that we kill them all regardless." Seville said, staring at the house.

"I'm down with that. But we need to keep one alive. We need some answers."

"Okay, after I shoot the sucker in both knees, then you can question him." She said with a smile.

John looked her. "One day, we're going to have a little talk about why you ever became a cop."

Seville looked back at him with a smile. "Okay. And I'll be glad to tell you."

From where they were situated, there was no way to approach the house without being spotted by the people inside. He figured by now Maria was probably being held hostage. With any attempt to rescue her from the front would get her killed for certain. *The one thing that these bastards have demonstrated, they don't mind killing people.* He thought. "The best way to approach the house is from the rear." He said.

Again, they began to follow the wood line that carried them to the far rear of the house. When they reached the rear of the house, he noticed that his dog Bo was not making any noise. Whenever someone was approaching the house, Bo would begin barking loud and constantly until he or Maria told him to be quiet. This could only mean that Bo was being kept quiet by Maria, or the intruders had killed him. "My dog normally would be barking like crazy by now. The bastards probably killed my dog." He said.

"If they kill people like dogs, than killing dogs don't mean a thing."

Approximately twenty-five yards into the woods from the edge of the back yard, John stopped, he stoop down and began remove leaves with his hand from a wooden door with a metal handle.

"Is that a door?" Seville asked surprisingly.

"At the time when I couldn't remember who I was, and when the builders were constructing this house, I had an escape tunnel put in. Funny thing, I didn't know why I was having it done, but there was something about having it done that kept eating at me. I guess now I know why." He explained as he pulled on the handle to open the door to the tunnel that led up to the house. "Back then, I was having serious flashbacks of what happened to my family." He climbed down a ten steps ladder. "Come on!"

"You're right. We do need to have that talk." She said as she climbed down the ladder. "It seems to me that you've got kind of futuristic mojo working for you."

From that point on to the house, they walked in total silence and darkness. A few moments later, John stopped to turn on a light switch that lit up the entire tunnel. Up ahead was the entrance to the basement. He knew that unless the intruders knew about the tunnel, the basement should have been clear. Not even Maria knew that the door to the tunnel was there. Quietly, he stepped on the ladder leading up into the basement. At the top of the ladder, he slowly and softly pushed the door upward. It opened. Before climbing completely out of the tunnel, he held the door just wide enough to get a good look around to see if anyone was in the basement. It was deserted as he and Seville very quietly climbed out of the tunnel, and closed the door.

They both stood staring upward and listening for any kind of movement, or voices upstairs. It was dead calm, too quiet for John. The basement was lit, apparently from the intruders checking it out. Suddenly, they heard steps in the kitchen area, it appeared that someone came into the kitchen, opened the refrigerator, took something out and went back to one of the other rooms. "I think these butt-holes are eating." John whispered.

Seville looked at him and smiled. "Bad guys gotta eat too." She whispered back.

They both pulled out their weapons and stood ready. Seville had an automatic in each hand. John pulled out his new 357 automatic and walked slowly towards another flight of stairs that led up to the kitchen. He suddenly remembered that one of the steps had a slight screeching noise when stepped on, but he did not remember which one it was.

He stopped, and with his hand, he pushed down on each step before stepping on it to see if it would make the creepy sound. He pushed down one step and step on one. It was so- far-so good with Seville following close behind him.

There was no sound made thus far. When they reached the top step, John pushed down, and a slight sound escaped from it. He let Seville know with his hand to step over the last one. A slow twist of the doorknob, he cracked open the door just wide enough to get a glimpse to see if anyone was there in the kitchen. Abruptly, he froze. Someone was entering the kitchen again. He eased the door close until there was only a slight crack. He could see a tall husky white man with blonde hair, apparently one of the Russian, opening the refrigerator again, bending over to reach a beer. He suddenly yelled out to someone else in Russian, "Do you want a beer?!" Someone yelled back, apparently replying yes.

John immediately knew that there were at least two Russians in his house. There may have been more, like someone standing guard, watching the front. John held up two fingers for Seville, letting her know that they had two intruders at least. The man removed two bottles of beer from the refrigerator and went back to where John assumed they were sitting in the living room. As soon as the Russian disappeared, John beaconed for Seville to move up and into the kitchen.

Quietly, they entered the kitchen, and Seville placed her back again the refrigerator that was located between the two doorways entering the kitchen from other parts of the house. She held up both guns, pointing in different directions, at each doorway. "Make a noise and stand back." She whispered.

John stared at her for a moment, observing her position. But then he realized what she was planning to do. He stood back, picked up a glass that was setting on the counter and dropped it, splattering on the floor, making a loud breaking sound. As she had figured, two men came rushing into the kitchen with guns drawn from both directions. As soon as they entered the doorway, they only saw John, but not her. Both guns in her hands began blasting, hitting both men as soon as they entered the doorways. They dropped immediately to the floor dead and in a pool of blood.

As soon as the Russians fell dead, John moved quickly through one door, Seville entered the other one. As figured, when they entered the living room, a third Russian was standing directly behind Maria who was tied to a chair with a clothe gag in her mouth. He held a gun to her head while speaking in Russian to his two comrades to see if they were still alive. But there was no answer. Then he began to focus on John and Seville. "So, you're the ones we are looking for?"

Before answering, John noticed Maria moving her eyes towards the front door, indicating that someone else was on the outside. Seville saw her eyes as well, and began to move towards the front door. "Stay where you are or I will kill her!" The man said.

Seville stopped moving. John looked at Maria. "Don't worry, Maria, it's going to be okay." He looked at the Russian. "Listen, you can still walk out of here alive. Our fight is not with you, it's with your employer. That's the asshole we want."

The Russian thought about the proposal, but then he thought about the amount of money he was going to collect if they finished the job. However, he was in an awkward position, there was no way he could get away with killing his hostage and still walk away alive. But, he believed that he still had an ace in the hole, his other comrade who was stationed outside the door waiting for someone to come out.

"You may as well call your partner inside, because you both are dead men unless you surrender." Seville said. "So, what's it going to be, Comrade?" She was still holding both guns out, ready to fire at the anything that moved.

John and Seville did not know what he was saying in Russian, but he told the other one to come in firing. As the other man swung open the door to burst in and open fire, he had no idea what was waiting for him inside. Both of Seville's guns were pointed at the door while John's was aimed at the one who tried to hide behind Maria. As soon as the door swung open, Seville began firing directly into the doorway, hitting the man several times before he could get one foot inside. The man standing behind Maria tried to duck down, but John fired, hitting him right between the eyes. He fell backward to the floor, dead on impact.

Seville carefully went to the door, guns pointing down at the gunman just in case he was still alive. She punched him with her foot, he was dead also. John untied Maria, and as soon as her hands were free, she pulled the gag out of mouth, and abruptly stood and began hugging and kissing John's on both sides of his face. "Mr. Sinclair!....I'm glad to see you.. Who were these men?" She looked at Seville. "Wow, she was amazing! Is she your partner you told me about?"

"Yes, this is Seville, my partner." John said quickly. "Maria, these four men, were they the only ones?" John glanced around quickly just in case.

Maria looked at him with wide eyes before answering. "There were five of them!....It's another one. When he heard the shots, he ran outside with this one. " She pointed to the dead man in the doorway. "He's outside somewhere!"

John turned and headed towards the rear of the house. "Stay here! Keep watch out on the front!" He shouted to Seville. He ran through the rear door leading to the back yard where he found the once parked car speeding around the house heading for the driveway at a high rate of speed. John took aim and fired several shots at the fleeing vehicle, but his bullets only penetrated the rear of the minivan. *Damn! I needed that one alive to get some answers from him.* He was thinking as he went back into the house.

When John got back to the living room, Seville was on her phone calling the local sheriff department. She filled the Sheriff in as much as she could as far as she and John were concerned. *When we arrived, we found four armed gunmen holding Maria Lopez the housekeeper hostage.* They all waited outside on the porch until the authorities arrived, equipped with homicide investigators and three ambulances. John was familiar with Sheriff Coleman Mathews, he was from the hills and impeccably country.

After an hour of telling the same story over and over again to one of the Sheriff's deputies, Seville was growing more and more agitated with them having a lack of big city investigative skills. She turned to John, "Are all country cops dumb like these?"

They all were still seated on the porch, and everyone involved in the hostage taking and shootout had to give their side of the story. John was sitting in between Seville and Maria said, "This is probably the most excitement that has been in these parts in about fifty years. Four dead Russians is a pretty big deal. They want to make sure that they get all the answers before they let us go. And then, you have to understand too, we ain't exactly the color they were expecting to find out here, with the exception of the Sheriff."

"Why did you say the Sheriff?" Seville asked curiously.

"Well, I met him about four years ago when he came out to see who were living out here. He wanted to make sure that I was an upstanding citizen, I guess."

"Yeah, right!" She said with a smiled. "He wanted to see who this uppity black man was living out here in this million dollar farm house." She glanced over at Maria. "And on top of that, of all things you've got the nerves to have a Hispanic housekeeper. Now, you know that is not the way we do things." She laughed.

Maria looked at Seville smiling. "You make a good point."

When the investigation was completed, John and Seville loaded up and headed back to city. In the meantime, Maria had a lot of work to do cleaning up the mess they had made. The Sheriff promised to keep check on Maria day and night just in case the one that got away decided to come back for more. John doubted seriously if that was going to happen. But he was sure that Maria would feel much better by having the sheriff deputies check in on her from time to time.

The way John figured it, unless the Russian got on the first plane out of the city, he would need a place to lay low for a day or two. But then, on the other hand, would he try to regroup, and find himself some more helpers? Apparently, the contract did not pay the full price until the job was finished. *However, knowing that four of his comrades were in wooden boxes now, would that be enough to persuade him look for employment elsewhere? I don't know about him, it certainly would convince me.* He was thinking as he continued to drive down the interstate towards Atlanta. *Plus, I owe this bastard just like I owed the others for killing my dog. Bo was a good dog and he didn't deserve to die. But that's okay, when this is all over and done with, I'm going get myself another one just like Bo.* He thought as he drove.

CHAPTER TWENTY-SIX

On their arrival back to the city, Seville called Slim to get the latest on what to expect from whoever was interested. "Hey, I saw it on the news!" Slim said. "Man, you guys are awesome! Well, baby, I always knew you were at the top of your game. Anyway, the one dude that got away called me just minutes ago, and he needs a couple more guns to help finish the job."

"What about the Major, have you heard from him yet?" She asked.

"Not yet, but I'm sure as soon as he learn that his Russian white boys failed to take you two out, he will be calling again. Listen, I don't know where the Major is keeping it low, but he certainly not showing his face in this town."

"Okay, now listen to this,…..we need to take the one that got away alive. This guy obviously knows exactly where the Major is hanging out these days. And he is the only one who knows where he is getting his instructions from. For him to finish the job, he'll need more people. We want to know what he knows. Unless,…." She paused.

"Unless what?!" Slim asked suspiciously.

"Unless you my old friend, can convince him to tell you where the Major is hanging out. Why don't you do that for a sista?" She said, glancing at John with a smile.

"Look, Seville, to be another man's woman these days, you are asking for a lot of favors…..Do you feel where this brother is coming from? I mean, I've saved your life, and I saved your boyfriend's fucking life, and now you want me to pimp on the Major?!"

"I want you to do as I ask you to do, my brother! Regardless of whose woman I am these days. You still owe me big time for wasting two years of my life hanging out with the likes of you! Which of course were probably the best two years of your life. Now, can I get an Amen on that?"

Slim laughed. "Yeah, you still know how to hit me where it hurt the most. Anyway, I'll do what I can. In the meantime, it's a safe bet that the Russian is going to be hanging out at the Gold Club. You want to check with your old boss, Egor on that."

After closing her phone, she looked at John and said, "The Russian is looking for help to finish the job. We'll probably find him at the Gold Club tonight."

Getting off the freeway, and driving directly to their apartment. John wanted to make sure that his suspicion was correct about the listening device. When they arrived at the apartment, they quickly realized that the front door had been busted from someone kicking it in. They quickly summarized that the Russians had done the damage before proceeding to his home in North Georgia. It was like they were told not to leave a stone unturned. On the inside of the apartment, they began a methodical search of all lamps, fire alarms, and wall mounting painting for something, or anything that resembled a tiny microphone.

Suddenly, Seville remembered their conversation about the Russians knowing that she had failed to kill John. She grabbed John by the hand and led him into the living room where they were when she pulled her gun on him and could not complete the job. She did not speak, placing her index finger over her lips, which was a sign to John not to talk. They began to carefully search for a microphone on all tables, lamps and chairs. Finally, John gazed upward at the ceiling fan and light combined. He could see what appeared to be a tiny flat-headed microphone, the size of a dime.

Seville saw him staring up at the light and knew that he had spotted it. She moved closer to him to see it for herself. John climbed up on the hardwood coffee table to disconnect the tiny microphone. *No, if I disconnect it, whoever is on the other end is going to know that we found it.* He thought. He then motioned to Seville to leave the living room and go back outside of the apartment. When they got outside, he said, "Lets' leave it in place. That way, they won't know that we know. However, who do you suppose is on the other end listening?"

"That's a good question, especially if the Major is supposedly in Paris France, or in Russia even....." She stared back inside the apartment. "It makes you wonder."

"Well, at this point and time, we can narrow it down to one of three people,......"

"Somewhere between Slim, Bobby Turner, and Carolyn......" She read his mind.

"Right! That is, unless,......" He looked at Seville smiling.

"Unless, the Major himself was on the other end listening. And if that's the case, he damn sure isn't in Paris." She was reading his mind once again. "Slick-ass bastard!"

"That is true....But it is because he want to get rid of everybody and anyone who will be able to link him to the gold and the killing of the thirteen officers that were inside the precinct. To him, it's a matter of simple logics. Leave no clues behind. But to us, it's a plain old case of murder in the worse way. And he knows that as long we are alive, we can prove that he and his people, along with the Chief discovered the gold and they are the ones who are responsible for all those murders." He reached in and pulled the broken door close. "Come on, we've got a date with the Mayor."

"Wow! That was deep...." She said as they walked back the vehicle.

"What was deep?"

"What you just said. It's kind of like we have finally narrowed this thing down to a simple case of greed and murder, which is almost like a scientific fact."

"In most cases it's that simple, my dear." He tried to speak like Sherlock Holmes.

"Okay, Professor Sinclair, the criminology expert." She said laughing.

"Hey, I'm getting good at this stuff, huh?"

"Yes you are, my dear. A female James Bond needs the mind of a Sherlock Holmes in order to do her job more effectively."

John looked at her smiling as he drove onto Peachtree Street heading south. "You're really serious about this female James Bond thing aren't you?"

"I sure am. And when we fly out of here to Paris, it will confirm my status."

"I can see it now, Jane Bond, a 002 secret agent from Atlanta." He laughed.

A few minutes later when they arrived at city hall, the entire block surrounding the building was still swarming with reporters trying to get the latest facts on Chief Martin's killers. The White County Sheriff office had called and confirmed that four members of the hit squad who assassinated the Chief were dead and lying in the morgue in their county.

No answers were provided as to who had done the killing, for the Sheriff did not really care if the media assumed that he and his people had pulled off such a feat.

Seville called the Mayor's office, informing him that they were there to see him, but the media mob outside was making it impossible to do so. The new acting chief of police personally led a five man squad from headquarters to escort the two cops into city hall to see the Mayor. Acting Chief Melvin Cunningham and his officers led the pair through a side door into the atrium and up to the Mayor's office. When they arrived, the Mayor invited the Chief and the two officers into his conference room for a talk, and with hopes of getting to the bottom of the situation.

Mayor Townsend was serving his second term as Mayor, and from all indications, it would probably be his last term. Looking at John and Seville, it became very clear that they were holding his political future in the palms of their hands. If they knew the whole connections between the bombing that killed thirteen police officers, the gold, and everything else that gone on in his city and was willing to tell the media, his political career was over. The media, the people of Atlanta, and the police officers, none of them were going to understand his explanation of how something so evil could have taken place without his knowledge? He could not believe it, so how did he expect anyone else to believe it?

The Mayor was seated at the head of the shiny redwood conference table. Chief Cunningham who was a thin, pale looking white man in his early fifties on his left facing John and Seville who were on right side of the table. The Mayor laced his fingers while looking at the two officers in total bewilderment. "Am I to understand that you two killed the four men who were responsible for assassinating Chief Martin?"

John glanced at Seville before answering. "I'm sure the Sheriff of White County told you that these men were in my home, armed with guns, and threatening to kill my house keeper. And to answer your question, yes, we killed them. One got away. But we hope to find him later tonight."

The Chief stared at John for a moment. "Do you work for my department?"

The Mayor cut in. "Ah, Chief, this is John Sinclair, a retired lieutenant from the New York PD who is on loan to us. He and Officer Patterson have been working on the precinct bombing case, independently of course. For now, you still work for us, right?"

"Yes sir, at least until we solve this case." Seville said sharply. "After that, I probably won't be."

"Okay!" The Mayor said. "Now, let's get down to the real nitty-gritty of this whole gruesome situation. Tell me and Chief Cunningham just how bad things really are. Do we stand a chance of coming out of thing with any kind of dignity left intact?"

John and Seville both were surprised by the question. But John waited for Seville to give her assessment of the situation. "To be honest with you, based on what we have learned, probably not. Your opponents are going to have a field day on you. But you have to understand that this thing started five years ago, maybe before then. But five years ago, a lieutenant named Calvin Gates and his whole family was murdered. We now believe that his murder was planned by Major James Butler. We also believe that the cops who were arrested by Lieutenant Gates were the ones who carried out the murders."

"Wait, wait a minute!" The Chief snapped, holding up his hands. "How can you sit here and accuse a man who was one of the best commanders in the department? Major Butler! No way are you going to convince us that the Major did something like that."

"Chief!" The Mayor said abruptly. "I want to hear what they have to say, not you."

"I'm sorry, Mr. Mayor!" The Chief responded respectfully.

"And Chief Cunningham, since you've only been on the job about two or three hours, we've got some more shocking news for you." John said smiling. "Not only was the Major responsible for Calvin Gates and his family murders, he also planned, plotted, and carried out the bombing of his own precinct that killed thirteen more police officers."

"And this so-called best commander, as you so eloquently called him. He's the same great cop who hired five big-ass Russians to kill Chief Harold Martin." Seville said.

The Mayor and the Chief both mouths dropped wide open. "What!" The Mayor shouted. "How in the name of God can that be possible? The damn man is dead for Christ sakes!" He stopped himself, for he was now acting like the Chief. "Okay, go ahead, let me hear the rest of it. I asked for it and you're giving it to me."

"I understand, Mr. Mayor that you thought the Major were dead, so did we. He had us all fooled, believing that he died in a burning car crash." She said. "But then, that's the way he planned this whole elaborate scheme."

Once again, acting Chief Cunningham could not fully grasp what was being said, he immediately cut in by saying, "Okay, lets say, you're right about what you're saying. What would be the motive behind Major Butler committing such acts as murder, and the bombing of his own precinct…? Nothing about what you two have said make any sense to me." He looked at the Mayor, then at Seville and John.

John looked at the Mayor. "Do you want to tell him, Mr. Mayor what this is all about, or should we be the ones to inform the uninformed?"

The Mayor twisted his mouth, looking away just for a moment. "And just how do you figure that I know what this is all about?" He said finally in an uneasy tone.

"When you asked the question about is there any way for you and the police department to come out of this one piece? And our answer was, and still is, it is highly unlikely. It's unlikely because all hell is going to break loose when the press and the public learns that two billion dollars in gold was taken from underneath a blown to hell police precinct that had thirteen cops inside standing roll call." John said.

Chief Cunningham looked at the Mayor. "Sir, what is this crazy man talking about? Has he gone mad or something, coming in here with a wild story about gold?"

"Yeah, he's as crazy as a fox." Seville said. "But we have proof to everything that we're sitting here claiming, Mr. Mayor. However, the question now is, did you know about any parts of this so-called elaborate gold discovery operation?"

The Mayor said finally, "I was kept in the dark about this. That is until a few days ago when the Chief informed me about what he thought had happened. But he never said anything about Major Butler still being alive. And what I told Chief Martin was, there's no way can we go public with such an outrageous story unless we had the gold in our hands. As of right now, everything that has been said is simply hearsay, or speculations. We don't have one ounce of proof that two billion dollars in gold ever existed."

"And you say you have proof, Officer Patterson?" The Chief asked Seville.

"We have proof, but not here, not now." She said quickly.

"So, where is this so-called proof?" The Mayor asked. "To be honest with you two, I hope you do have proof, because as of right now, the only thing we have is a bunch of dead police officers, and not one thread of evidence as to how, why, or who did the killing. And to add insult to injury, as far as we know, Major Butler is still dead as well."

"Right now, we think the evidence might be in Russia, or maybe in Paris, or he could in a lot of places. Whatever two billion dollars in gold from 1864 is worth on today's gold market, it can take a man anywhere in the world. Plus, he can become anybody he wants to on the planet, except who he was." John explained.

The Mayor stared at John for a moment. "I don't understand."

"Major Butler! He's hiding somewhere outside of this country. Maybe he's in Russia. That's where the hit squad came from. But then, his wife is preparing to fly off to Paris in a few days, and he'll probably be there to meet her. But, he's no longer the Major James Butler that we once knew. He has a new look, and a new identity."

The Chief stared at John for a moment. "How do you know all of this?"

"We cannot divulge our source of information." Seville cut in. "But trust us, we know about his little secrets.....That's why he sent those Russians to kill us because we know too many secrets about him."

"Wait!" The Mayor snapped. "He hired those men you killed to kill the Chief. After they killed the Chief, then they came to North Georgia to kill you two, but you ended up killing them, is that what you're saying to us right now?"

"Ah, you're catching on, Mr. Mayor!" Seville said smiling. "We still have one to go. Once we get him, hopefully alive. Maybe we will know who we're looking for."

"So, you have no idea what he looks like now?" Chief Cunningham asked.

"Ah, and you're catching on too, Chief." John said smiling.

"We don't, and that's why we need to keep this Russian alive tonight. But, it's no guarantee that he even knows." Seville said. "Here's what you must understand about James Butler. He's a brilliant man who has the mind of a criminal. He will stop at nothing to make sure that no one will be able to track him down. He's not leaving to chance that anything can be traced back to him. We think the wife will meet him soon."

The Mayor glanced at the Chief, then back to the officers. "And just how she is supposedly going to do that?" He asked.

"Well, we're hoping to find out when she is leaving, without her knowing that we are on to what's going on. And once we find out the date that she's leaving, we plan to leave a day or two ahead of her, and be there when she gets there. When she lands, we'll follow her to wherever she plans to meet the Major." Seville explained.

"How are you two planning to work in another country, you do not have any police powers to do that. If something happens, you're on your own." Chief Cunningham said.

John looked at the Mayor. "Sir, I know you have a lot of International pull, why don't you make a call to the authorities in Paris, or the Russian Government and inform them as to what is going on here and maybe there. That way, if something happens, or if we have to kill the Major or whatever, we'll be covered."

The Mayor thought about the request for a long minute. "Okay, I'll do it. But you two better be right. We've already had hell here in Atlanta, and the last thing I need is for you two to cause an International crisis. And if James Butler is still alive, I want him brought back to this country alive, if that's possible!" The Mayor paused for a moment. "Now I know Butler didn't pull off a plan like this alone, so who helped him?"

John looked at Seville, before admitting, "We don't know for sure, but we have a pretty good idea. We think it's a descendant of General Joseph Johnston, a Civil War general who fought in the battle of Atlanta in 1864, and his troops buried the gold."

"And what connection would a descendant have to the gold?" The Chief asked. He paused as he thought about his own question. "The descendant knew where the gold was buried from some kind of map that the General left behind in 1864, right?"

Seville smiled at the Chief. "Wow! You know, you just might make a pretty good Chief after all."

"Thank you for that vote of confidence." Chief Cunningham said sarcastically.

"You're welcome. And if I decide to stay on the force when we return from wherever, can I get a promotion. After all, I was promised a promotion to sergeant for going on this assignment in the first place. But now, after everything that we've gone through, I'm looking at lieutenant or above. Are you cool with that?" She asked.

The Mayor smiled and said, "Officer, if you pull this off successfully, I'll promote you myself to whatever rank you want."

John glanced at her and asked, "What about that female James Bond?"

"Trust me, if we bring James Butler back to Atlanta alive or dead, I'll be sitting where he's sitting." She nodded toward Chief Cunningham.

The Mayor stood. "Okay, from now no, I want you two to report directly to me. I want to know everything about your plans. I'll call the

French and Russian Governments in a few minutes. Listen, I'm depending on you, Sevilla Patterson and John Sinclair to save my ass from this major fuckup! If you do that, you can write your own tickets to whatever you want in this city, and that's a promise." He turned and left the room.

Seville looked at Chief Cunningham. "No offense, Chief, but why should I settle for being a sergeant when I can become the chief of police?"

The Chief also stood. "That will be a cold day in hell! No offense, of course." He said as he turned and left the room as well.

"I think you and the Mayor may have pissed off the new acting Chief." John said with a chuckle.

"Hey, why settle for hamburger when you can have steak?" She said laughing.

"Hey, that works for me."

"And I'm appointing you to my assistant chief right now."

They both stood laughing. "Hey, we still have a killer to capture." John said as they left the conference room.

CHAPTER TWENTY-SEVEN

The stage was about to be set. Seville made a call to Slim and told him to make contact with the Russian before he decided to leave the country. Slim complied with her request simply because as she had told him earlier, if he did not work with them in apprehending their suspect, he would probably go down for supplying the weapons that killed Chief Martin. And they both knew that the last thing Slim wanted to do was end up in jail for being a party to the murder of a police officer.

However, Slims' job definitely was not finished with just by dealing with the lone assassin. He first had to make contact with Major Butler. And if he was unable to make the contact, then he was to find out from Carolyn as to when she was leaving town for Paris. Seville knew that this was a possible mission for Slim to do because she knew the Major well enough to know that he would not allow for her to travel from wherever she was now staying to the airport alone. All but the one Russian were dead, and that only left the Major with the assistance of Slim and his crew as bodyguards for Carolyn.

Their plan nevertheless could only work if the Russian was still planning in some way to finish the job before he informed the Major that they had failed as far as taking out John and Seville. If however, everything went as they were planning it, Slim would then set the Russian up by offering a few of his own men to assist him with the hit.

"Are you ready for this?" John asked Seville as she completed dressing for the part of capturing the Russian. They had rented a room at a downtown hotel due to the bugging of their apartment. There could have been other microphones in the apartment besides the one they found. But

John did not want to take the chance of anyone knowing in advance what they were planning.

"I'm ready! I've done this type of thing a thousand times, I have no fear. And I made a lot of money doing it too." She said smiling.

"The greatest thing about you is, you're always up to the challenge…. Nothing deters you from doing whatever."

As she stood in front of the mirror adjusting her outfit, she glanced at him as he sat in a chair with his legs crossed. "Are you referring to as to how I led you on?"

John smiled. "Oh, yeah, I'm talking about that one as well. But it's your whole outlook on life in general. And that's including having my baby, remember?"

"Okay, I am down with that for sure. Are you ready to get started, right now?! Hey, I mean, we can hop to it before we go." She laughed.

"See, that's what I'm talking about! You're always up to the challenge." He stared at her for a moment. "You know, you're the only good thing that my half brother has done right lately. When he picked you, he picked a good one."

"Yeah, but he didn't realize he was picking a good thing when he picked me. He thought he was picking someone to kill you when the time came. But as we both now know, maybe picking me was probably the worse thing he has ever done."

"Anyway, after everything is said and done, and if we don't have anything else in life left to do, then we'll work on making a baby." John said in a blushing manner.

"By then, you may be too old to be trying to have a baby."

John laughed. "And how old is too old?"

"Well, you're forty-five now. I figure, by the time you're fifty, you should stop thinking about trying to get a baby. Now, that's just me talking, because there are a lot of old dudes out there who are hanging out with younger women and getting them pregnant. You know, like this old dude that was on CNN, Larry King. Man, how gross is that?!"

"And it could be some young studs getting the younger women pregnant for the old dudes. He was accused of having a young stud to take care of his old lady."

Seville went over and sat on John's lap, staring down in his eyes. "I don't think you have anything to worry about in that department. No younger man can outdo you."

"So you think I'm that good, huh?"

"Old man, you're better than good! You're all that a younger woman like me needs." She laughed, and then kissed him. "Are you ready to go?"

"I'm ready to go!!" He snapped with a grin.

"I mean, are you ready to go get this Russian dude?"

"Oh yeah, I'm ready for him, too."

Before John and Seville arrived at the Gold Club, Slim had gone ahead and arranged the set up with Egor Kolenka. The owner agreed to go along with the plan after learning that his countryman was wanted for the murder of Chief Martin. Meanwhile, Slim rented a private room and paid for a total of five strippers to join himself, the Russian, and two of his boys for a sex party. However, the sex party was not to start until Seville arrived to join in fun. She was counted as one of the five girls.

When they arrived, John parked the Hummer at the front door, and a police officer stood by at the front entrance waiting for it all to go down. Seville approached Kolenka when she entered the club. Kolenka was waiting for her at the front door, and he said, "Seville, the only reason I'm doing this is because I run a legitimate club here, and I don't want any problems with the police. I have to tell you however, that I'm sure he's armed, and I think he will shoot if he suspects that you're a cop."

John stood beside Seville. "Don't worry, we've got this." He said.

"Okay, I'll keep things rolling regardless of what's happening up there." He glanced up the second floor where the private room was located.

"Good, this is only going to take a minute or two." Seville said.

The Russian was getting very impatient, he did not want to wait any longer, he wanted to have sex right then and there with any one of the dancers, for he thought they all were very beautiful. He spoke very little English, so he made hand gestures to Slim as to what his intentions were. "Hey man, keep your damn pants on!....We still got another girl coming." Slim said, with little doubt that the Russian could understand anything that he was saying. "I know you don't understand shit that I'm saying, but you will in a little while….." He laughed while rubbing his hands on two of the dancers sitting next to him.

The two men with Slim acted as bodyguards, they stood by the door, saying nothing, and only staring at the women. Naked women were not unusual for the men who worked for Slim, for he owned his own strip club downtown Atlanta, and anytime they wanted to be with naked women, they could go to his club whenever they wanted to. It was already approved by their boss, Slim.

There was a knock on the door as the music played and other dancers performed on two separate stages downstairs. One of the guards cracked the door. He saw that it was Seville standing outside the room wearing only a black two piece G-string. "Hi boys, can I join the party?" She asked smiling and smoking a cigarette.

The guard stepped away from the door, glancing at Slim for confirmation. "Yeah, let her in!" Slim yelled. "Yeah, we need some of what she's got!" He laughed, winking his eye at Seville.

When Seville stepped inside the room and stood wide legged in the middle of the floor, the Russian immediately turned to her. He pointed to Seville with a wide grin. "That's the whore I want!" He snapped. *She's the kind of woman I want.* He thought.

Slim looked at the Russian with a surprised stare. "You told me you couldn't speak English, motherfucker!" He shouted at the Russian.

The Russian laughed, and then said, "I lied! All you Americans are just alike, you will believe anything." He picked up a bottle of Russian vodka, turned it up and drank several swallows before stopping. "Come to me, you fine, sexy whore!"

Slim waited for the fireworks to start as he cringed in fear. He knew what was about to come. And it would probably come a lot sooner than he expected if the Russian continued saying the word whore. Seville continued to stand with her legs open wide facing Slims' between the two guards. Therefore, it was impossible for them to see what was about to happen next. When she refused to budge, the Russian stood and was about to reach for her arm when she pulled an automatic that was taped to her back. She pointed the gun at the Russian's head. "Sit the fuck down, asshole!" She shouted to the Russian. "And placed your hands on top of your head.....This whore is your worse nightmare!"

Russian pretended that he did not understand English by shaking his head. "I don't understand." He muttered barely, turning to Slim.

Slim stood as John walked in the room. "This asshole Russian understands everything you're saying. He's playing you!" Slim and the dancers moved swiftly out of the way. "You may want to search this asshole. He has a gun on him somewhere."

John immediately walked behind the Russian and grabbed both hands and pulled them to his rear. The Russian immediately tried to strong arm John by pulling hands back forward and going for his own gun that in his waistband. Seville moved in like a bolt of lightening and belted the Russian across the face with the butt of her gun. At the same time, she grabbed his gun and pulled it from his waistband. "That vodka made you a little slow on draw, didn't it comrade?" She said smiling.

"Fuck you, you black bitch!" The Russian snapped, spitting in her face.

As John continued to hold his arms behind his back, Seville wiped the spit out of her face and immediately returned the favor with a brutal kick to his groin. The Russian screamed out, dropping to his knees at the same time as John held on to his hands. She was about to hit him again with the butt of her gun when John shouted, "Don't kill him, Seville! Remember, we need this one alive."

She stepped back, wiping her face while John placed the handcuffs on his hands.

"Damn baby, you're one mean woman!" Slim said as he held on to all the women that were with him. "Were you that mean when you and I were together?" He laughed.

She walked over and patted him on the cheek. "You never did anything to find out." She then walked to the door following John who was now pushing the Russian out of the room. She turned and said. "Thanks for your help." She then looked at the women. "Ladies, don't let him leave here before you take every dollar he has on him." She then walked out, still wiping her face with John's handkerchief, closing the door behind her.

Slim looked at the four women who were now surrounded him. "Now, ladies, you have just witnessed a real woman in action. And guess what? I taught her everything she knows….You see, she use to be my main squeeze, until I fired her ass….. But, my, my, my, she's some kind of woman!"

An hour later, Seville was fully clothed again. She and John were now in the suspect's interview room at precinct-two about four blocks from the club. They both sat on the opposite side of a metal table facing the Russian as the precinct commander and a lieutenant looked on from behind a one-way glass mirror. The Russian stared at the two cops wondering what would be their next move. The Russian was in his late thirties and looked very tough as if he could was a boxer. John also wondered why he did not put up more of a fight when he realized that Seville was not a real dancer. But there was a more pressing question that he wanted to ask.

"Was it you that I talked to, and who ordered the hit on the Chief?" John asked.

"My name is Cheslav,.. Brody Cheslav. And I'm not saying anything because I don't know anything. You may as well call me an attorney now. I know my rights."

"Not until you tell us what we want to know about who hired you and why?" Seville said. "You don't need an attorney to tell us who hired you."

Brody Cheslav looked at Seville for a long moment. He still liked what he saw although she was fully dressed now. "You're a very beautiful woman."

"Hey!" John snapped. "Yes she is, but that's not the question that I asked you. How did you get Chief Martin cell phone? And was it you who called to tell me that we were next on your hit list?"

"I don't know anything about no cell phone. And it wasn't me who called you. I've been in the city all day. I don't know anything about a Chief Martin! Who is that?"

Seville knew immediately what had to be done. She figured that if John left the room, maybe she would have better luck with the Russian. After all, he showed signs of a man who wanted to be alone with her. "John, I think Brody Cheslav would like to talk to me without you being in the room. Why don't you excuse us just for a minute or two?" She said to John.

Before John considered the idea of leaving her in the room with the Russian alone, although he would be right outside the room, he asked her, "Are you sure you want to be in the same room alone with this character?"

She looked at the Russian and then back to John. "Yeah, I can handle Cheslav…I get the feeling that he wants to talk to me without you being around."

John slowly rose to his feet. He pointed his finger in Russian's face. "I'll be watching you. And if you even think about getting out of here, or harming her, it will be your last thought. You better understand that too, I-no-speak-no-English!" He left.

The Russian waited until John out of the room before speaking. "He's very protective of you isn't he?"

"That's my partner. We look out for each other. He got my back, and I have his." Seville said glancing up towards to the mirror window. "Okay, you obviously wanted to talk me without my partner being in the room. You got me alone, now start talking."

He chuckled, glancing around at the window. "I know we're not a lone, but that's okay. I feel better talking to you without him. Look, I know what you're hoping to learn, but I can't give it to you. I was only the lookout man. You and your partner obviously killed the real shooters. I heard shots, I got scared and I ran. As for the cell phone, I don't know where Nicolai got it from. I thought it was his phone. He gave it to me after making the call. That's all I know. I had planned to fly back to my country tomorrow."

"Really?" Seville said sarcastically. "Now, you expect for me to believe that you and your friends flew all the way from Russia to kill the people on your list. And you were going to leave without finishing the job. But that's not the way the Russian mafia do things is it? When they're hired to do a job, they will keep trying to do that job until the last man standing. Am I right about that?"

"But this was not a Russian mafia hit. And I am the last man standing."

Seville smiled. "Okay, then tell me who put out the hit on the Chief and us?"

"I don't know....I was not in charge of knowing details. You killed my boss. Like I said, when the shooting started, I left, and came back to the city."

"So, even if you had gone back to Russia, you still would not have known who to contact to get your money for killing the Chief?"

"No, I would not have known. That's the reason I was going back. As far as I'm concerned, the job is over."

Seville stood. "Okay, lets say that the person who hired your boss, doesn't know whether you completed the job or not. Who is he depending on to tell him that the job is completed, if not the last man standing?"

"Two days from now, we were to receive a call, and at that time, we were to say that the job is complete. But apparently he has ways of knowing the outcome of whatever is going on already." He smiled, glancing up at the mirror.

Seville saw his eyes moving towards the window. "Why you keep looking up at that mirror, are you expecting someone to rescue you from the hands of the police?"

"You never know what might happen." Again Cheslav said with a smiled.

Suddenly, the door opened and in stepped John. "I'm sorry Seville, but apparently Mr. Brody Cheslav here has diplomatic immunity. And there's nothing we can charge him with. We have to let him go."

Seville stopped for a moment to lean on the table facing the Russian. "So, you and your comrades received diplomatic immunity before you left Russia just in case you were caught doing your dirty work, right?"

The Russian stared at Seville before saying, "I told you everything you needed to know. You know we were hired to do a job. Now, the question is who did the hiring? That's what you're going to have to find out for yourself." He stood. "I wish I could have gotten to know you better."

Seville did not respond, she stood straight and watched the Russian walk out of the room. She then turned to John. "I'm wondering, does James Butler have that kind of connection and juice in another country?"

John shook his head in disbelief. "James by himself, I'd say no! But we don't know who else he is dealing with. And someone else obviously has some powerful friends in high places. Remember we talked about what the gold would be worth on today's market, and how having that much gold could stabilize a small crumbling economy? Gold is solid everywhere, whereas the dollar is almost worthless in some countries."

Seville frowned. "So you're saying that the Major and whoever he's working with is still holding onto the gold, probably in Russia to help stabilize the economy there?"

"Yeah, and because of that gold, they can get any amount help to ward off any attempt to identify who they really are. I believe that the Chief was trying to figure out where the gold is being held. The Major decided that he was too much of a risk."

"Wow! You really believe that a country like Russia put that much stock in gold?"

"Yes. You have to remember, gold has stood the test of time since the beginning of the world. Gold goes all the way back to the days of Moses. Remember when God destroyed the world, it were the people who worshiped a golden calf as their god over the God who created them. That's why two billion dollars in gold a hundred years ago is worth probably twenty times that much today. Tomorrow, it will be even greater."

At that moment, the commander of zone two entered the room. "Too bad about what just happened. But as we all know, that's the way it goes on a federal level. If the feds say let him go, we have to let him go." He patted John on the shoulder. "So, what do you do now?"

"There's only one clue left to follow, that's the gold." John said as he nodded to Seville that it was time to go.

The Commander looked at John, then at Seville. "The gold? What gold?"

Seville smiled as she and John headed towards the door. "That's a little inside joke that we share between each other." She said.

The Commander frowned for he did not understand or saw the humor in the word gold. "Okay, whatever you say." He said finally as he watched the two leave his precinct.

Just as they were getting into the vehicle, Seville cell phone rang. She saw that it was Slim. "Slim, what's up my friend and used to be lover?" She laughed.

"Hey mama, that shit ain't funny!" Slim snapped. "But hey, that's okay. You and the old dude, y'all make a good couple…However, that's not why I called you. I've got a hot tip for you. Hey, remember that cop who suddenly disappeared from the radar?"

"Are you talking about Bobby Turner?"

"Yeah, that's the sucker!….But guess what? He just walked into the club with two of his cop friends. He's blowing big cash in here. And I'm wondering where all of a sudden he gets this kind of money?"

She held the phone in one hand while she turned to John. "Your third cop suspect is at the Gold Club spending heavily on the ladies. Slim is suspicious that maybe he has been paid off for something."

John suddenly turned the Hummer around in the middle of the four lane street and sped back south on Piedmont Road towards the Gold Club. "Tell Slim, for whatever he do, don't let that bastard leave before we get there!"

"Hold him in place, Slim….Don't let him leave, we'll be there in ten." She said.

CHAPTER TWENTY-EIGHT

Arriving back at the Gold Club, Slim met the two cops at the front entrance. Seville started to open the door, Slim said quickly, "Hey, don't worry, we've got him under wraps. I am in control of the situation."

"He's under wraps. And what exactly does that mean?" She asked curiously.

Slim stood back and pointed towards his Cadillac Seville that was parked in front of the Hummer. "He's out cold, and in the trunk of my car, that's what it means."

John leaned forward and said, "You ever think about becoming a cop, Slim?"

Slim laughed loudly. "Me, a cop? Hell to the no! You must have fell and bumped your head on something, man!"

John smiled as he sat back while Seville asked the next question. "Where to?...You know he's still a cop. So, don't be doing any crazy shit, okay, Slim?"

"Follow me. I know a spot a little ways from here." Slim said and then got into the back seat of the Cadillac and they drove off.

As Seville and John followed the Cadillac, Seville muttered, "I wonder how did he managed to get a cop in the trunk of his car?"

John smiled. "I guess we'll have to ask him when we get where we are going." John continued as he said. "This guy is either the police worse enemy, or their best friend. Some how, I haven't figured out which one he is yet."

Seville glanced over at him. "I guess we'll have to ask him that too." She said with a slight grin. "Anyway, now that you have your total memory back, do you care to discuss what happened the night your wife and daughter were murdered?"

John thought about the question a long while before saying, "Well, first you should know that my memory is not hundred per cent. But Yeah, I can talk about it. I mean, sooner or later I'm going to have to put it all behind me."

"If you don't feel up to it, you don't have to do it now. I prefer that you waited until you've had your talk with Bobby Turner." She said with no idea of how long the trip was going to take.

Suddenly, John had a strange feeling. "You don't think he's trying to set us up do you? I'm really not feeling what he is doing."

"Seville's eyes became wider. "Do I think who's trying to set us up?"

John pointed to the car they were following. "Do you think your ex-boyfriend is trying to pull a fast one? Remember what I just said, I'm not sure if he's friend or foe."

Seville pulled out her automatic, cocked it back and let the slide go forward, chambering a round. "Well, I don't know either. But he better have an unconscious cop in the trunk of that car, or he'll be a dead friend or foe, I'm feeling that."

Approximately three miles south of the club down Piedmont Road, the Cadillac turned onto a dark, tree limbs covered street. They drove until they reached a dead end. The Cadillac's brake lights flashed and then suddenly stopped. Immediately, John and Seville knew that something was about to go down, and whatever it was probably did not include a cop named Bobby Turner who was supposedly locked in the trunk. John slammed on brakes and yelled to Seville, "Get down!!" He saw the two front seat men getting out of the car and they appeared to have guns in their hands. "Oh shit!"

The Hummer was stopped about twenty-five yards back. The two men who obviously worked for Slim began firing automatic weapons into the windshield of the Hummer. Seville was crouched down in her seat, and John was desperately trying to shift the gear post into reverse. They both knew that they were at a disadvantage in terms of fire power. Fumbling with the gear shift and pushing on the accelerator at the same time, the Hummer suddenly lunged backward. They were in desperation to get out of range of the constantly popping sounds of the guns in order to have any kind of chance.

Raising his head up to get a glimpse of where they were heading backward to avoid crashing into anything that would impede their escape.

Suddenly, John felt that they were out of range as he leaned back up in the driving position. Peering through a bullet riddled windshield, he could barely see the two men running at full speed trying to catch the Hummer. "Seville, here they come!" He said. "When I say now, rolled out and fire on anything in front of our vehicle."

He stopped the Hummer abruptly. "Now!!" He leaped out to the pavement as Seville rolled from her crouched position on the ground, landing on her feet. Suddenly, she saw what John saw, two men still sprinting towards them as if they were made of steel, thinking that bullets would not harm them. John and Seville began firing on their targets with multiple rounds of rapid fire. The two men were obviously in total denial, for they did not believe that they could be hit, but suddenly dropped like bags of sand.

As the smoke was clearing from all gun fire in glare of the Hummer's headlights, John called out to Seville. "Are you okay, Seville?!"

Without responding, she walked around the Hummer with both hands still occupied with her two automatic. "Yeah, I'm okay."

They both began walk slowly towards the two men sprawled in the street. When they were up close, Seville slightly nudged the one her side with her foot. He did not move. "One enemy down, how about number two?" She asked John.

John did the same by examining the man's pulse on the side of his neck. "Number two is no longer among the living either."

They both then looked towards the Cadillac where the two men had left Slim who was in the back seat. "Slowly,....." John said. "He may be still sitting there."

They approached the Cadillac from both sides with guns pointed and ready to eliminate Slim from his misery if he made a move. But to their surprise, no one was inside the vehicle, front or back seat. "Damn!!" Seville shouted as she turned around and around hoping to get a glimpse of Slims' tall lanky ass running to escape what they had in store for him. "That's bastard! I knew he was no good. He has been playing both sides along. The only thing that matters to him is money. Whoever pays the most, that's all!"

They suddenly turned to the sound of the engine of the Hummer roaring as Slim backed away from the dead bodies that were laying in front of it. "That sneaky bastard is getting away!" John snapped angrily as they watched Slim steal the Hummer.

Seville turned to the Cadillac. "We've got his Cadillac!" She ran and climbed into the driver's seat while John got in on the passenger's side.

Now the chase was on heading south on Piedmont Road towards downtown Atlanta. "I wonder where does he plan to hide his face? We know all of his hiding spots." She said as she wheeled the Cadillac down the still crowded street. This was a close reminder to what had happened a few nights before, except they were the ones being chased. "One good thing about your vehicle, if he doesn't know what he's doing, he'll crash before we catch him." She said.

John did not want to see his prize vehicle all smashed up, he wanted to call for backup to block off the street. But he suddenly realized that their police radios were in the Hummer. He took out his cell phone and began to dial 911. "Police, Emergency!" He shouted into the cell phone. "Listen, this is John Sinclair and Seville Patterson, we're chasing a suspect in a black Hummer. He's wanted in connections to Chief Harold Martin's murder. We need back up, helicopters, and anything else you can give us!"

Within minutes, blue lights and sirens were coming from all directions, closing in on the Hummer as Slim approached the ramp that led to I-85 south. Two police cars were blocking the ramp, which forced Slim to continued driving on Piedmont for another two blocks where the entire four lane highway was shut down. He came to a halt in front of several police cars and many cops with guns drawn, pointed directly at the vehicle. To make another attempt to escape would have been suicide. He finally stopped and stepped out of the Hummer with a bullet shattered windshield, with his hands help over his head.

Just seconds later, John and Seville arrived on the scene. Seville got out of the Cadillac first and rushed up to Slim, standing face to face with the very tall black man. "What the hell was all that about, Slim, huh?!.... Have you lost your fucking mind?!"

He smiled, glancing at the scores of police officers. "You wouldn't understand."

"Yes I would. Just tell me why you tried to kill us?"

He leaned forward and whispered. "Watch your back. Anyone of these assholes might try to do the same thing. The Major owns all these cut-throat fuckers!"

Seville suddenly stepped back from Slim. "Like I figured, it's all about the money isn't it?.... So, he finally convinced you to turn against me?"

"Hey, you almost did the same thing. If you had not been fucking that nigger, you would have killed him a long time ago." He laughed as one of the officers handcuffed him and pulled him away towards a waiting patrol car.

John approached Seville, "What did he have to say, nothing?"

She smiled. "He said that your half brother is buying up the police department."

"Meaning that we can't even trust the cops anymore, huh?"

"That's exactly what it means." She turned and walked away.

John had a strange feeling that she was not going to just walk away from the fact that Slim had tried to kill them without having to say a few parting words to him. After walking a few feet away, she stopped, turned around and shouted to the officer who was placing Slim in the patrol car. "Wait!....I'm not finished with him yet." She then walked to where the officer was holding onto Slims' hands. "Take the cuffs off."

"What?!....Do you think that's a good idea?" The officer asked.

"Don't worry. He has no place to run." She then looked at Slim. "Do you baby?"

Slim looked at the officer. "Don't trust her, officer! She's mean. She just might shoot me right here."

The officer smiled. "Yeah, maybe that's not such a bad idea after all." The officer took the handcuffs off and stood by while Seville stood a few inches away from Slim.

"You know, every since I've known you, you've always had a bad habit of choosing the wrong people for friends. Expect for me, of course. But this time you chose the wrong side when you tried to kill me and John. Do you understand what I'm saying to you, old tall ass nigger?"

Slim stared at her for a moment. "No, I don't understand what you're saying. Look, you knew the kind of man I was when you met me. I am all about making a dollar bill, and I really don't give a shit who doing the paying as long as I get my money. Now, do you understand that, pretty-ass woman?"

"Really?!" She said as she came out of nowhere with a right hook that was so powerful until it knocked Slim back into the back seat of the patrol car. "Let's see will your money get you out of this mess." She turned to the officer. "I'm finished with him now." She walked back to where John was standing and observing. The officer laughed as he placed the handcuffs back on Slim.

When she got back to John, she muttered. "You know I just couldn't let them take him away without saying goodbye, right?"

John smiled. "Oh, yeah, I knew all right. But did you have to hit him so hard?"

Seville looked down at her hand, it had begun to swell. "Oh, shit, that hurt!" She shook her hand. "I hope it's not broken." She held it up to John.

John examined her hand making sure there were no broken bones. "I think some ice will take the swelling out of it. You'll be okay." He kissed her hand. "What you say, let's go home, I think we've enough fun for one night."

As John drove his shot up Hummer away from the scene, he thought about what had taken place. The police would pick up the two dead guys and try to make some sense out of the story that Slim would tell, if he told them anything. It was a sure bet that if Slim said anything, it would sound like something that he had read in a police mystery novel. In other words, they would have a difficult time believing his story. It was almost for certain that he would not reveal anything regarding the Russians or Major Butler. And if he did tell them that the Major was alive and well, no one would believe him anyway.

So, where did Slim really stand as far as the assassination of the Chief was concerned? *Right now, that's hard to determine. But if what he said to Seville was correct, he probably won't see the inside of a jail cell.* He thought.

Because of the electronic listening devices in their penthouse, John strongly requested and received a new temporary apartment two doors down from the old one. The layout was the exact same as their apartment. The only thing they required was a change of clothing, liquor, and food. All of that was transferred to the new apartment.

After showering and getting comfortable for the remainder of the evening, John and Seville were stretched out on the king size bed having a drink and going over what had taken place thus far on the case they were working on. Seville stared at the ceiling while holding glass with both hands on her stomach. She spoke softly. She was searching her mind while speaking out. "Why can't we just go to a news reporter, tell him or her our story, and be done with this? I mean, unless we go running after Carolyn to only God knows where, we're never going to get to the bottom of this."

John who was lying on his back as well glanced over at her. "Are you giving up that easy?"

She rose up, leaned over towards him. "John, everyone who was connected to the precinct bombing is either dead, or has disappeared. And we both know that Slim is the only one who knows what happened will never tell the police anything. Eventually, they're going to have to let him go. There's no evidence to tie him to anything."

John sat up and move back to lean against the headboard. He swallowed hard as he waited for her to join him against the headboard. "I must have been out of my mind to have allowed the Major and the Chief to talk me into coming back to this damn place to work on a fake-ass bombing. I should have known better!"

"In fact, you were out of your mind. You couldn't remember who you were, much less know that this whole thing was no more than a made up case for them to get away with that gold." She said smiling. "But I'm glad that you did come back. I mean, in spite of who, or what the Major might be today, he did one good thing by convincing you to work on this case. He brought us together."

"Yeah, and that was done because he wanted you to kill me when he gave you the word." John said. "But as far as going to the AJC with our story, even if they half way believed us, we don't have nothing to back this story up….As you said, they all are dead. And the only one who is still alive, we don't know who he is or where he is. So, going to the newspaper will be a waste of time."

"So, how do we find Carolyn Butler?" Seville asked sharply.

"I don't know. Slim was our only lead. But since he's in jail, we can't use him!"

Seville stared at John with a smile. "I wouldn't be too sure about that. I mean, he still has this wild notion that we were meant for each other, although he did try to kill us."

"But deep down inside, he really wanted to kill me, and not necessarily you. That's why all the bullet holes were all on my side of the vehicle."

She laughed. "You know, there must something special about me with all these men wanting you dead. Since I've been in your life, it has been one thing after the other."

"And this was supposed to be a set up for me. Bring me back into the picture to make a fool out of me on a case that doesn't exist. They bring you in to make me look like a bigger fool. Now, here you are, a young beautiful sexy woman, to make me want to stay here. We were supposed to hit it off, but not like we did. You fall in love with this fool, and then you can't do what you were really hired to do. Now, that's something!"

"So, here we are, two cops in love with each other, but we can't get on with our lives until we know for sure that the bastard who set all of this up is dead for real." She said as leaned over and kissed him.

"So, do you think Slim will give us what we want to know about when and where Carolyn is going to meet her dead husband?" John asked curiously.

"We can always make him a deal that he can't refuse."

"Yeah, like what?"

"It's a get out of jail deal."

"You think he'll go for it?....You did smack him pretty hard, you know."

"I know Slim, and he'll go for it. By then, he'll have forgotten that I ever hit him."

"Then, let's go for it." John smiled then kissed her sore hand.

"I wonder what ever happened to Bobby Turner?" She muttered.

"Yeah, I've been wondering the same thing myself."

"I guess Slim will tell us that as well." She said as she rolled on top of him.

She set the glass on the nightstand. She glazed down into his eyes as he stared back still holding his glass. "Okay, we talked about this once before, but I don't think you took me serious." She said frankly.

"What, getting married, or me getting you pregnant?" He said, figuring that her answer would be one or the other.

"Let not focus on either one right now. But I need to know what is in store for you and I when this case is all said and done? Can you see that far into the future?"

John sipped from his glass again, then said, "I'll tell you what, if this case, or whatever it is that we are doing, turns out to be a win, win situation for us, I'll do anything you want. That's including marriage, having a baby, or whatever, okay?!"

She frowned for just an instant. "Win, win situation. What exactly is a win, win situation?"

"If we locate the Major, if everything goes the way we hope they do, and if you and I come out of this alive, then I think it will be time for us to settle down. I mean, we've only known each other for a few months, and all ready, we've gone through hell and back again."

She rolled off him onto the bed. She then snuggled up close to him. "What would I have done if I had killed you?" She said glaring at him for a moment.

"I don't know. But then, since we both became a target, you might be dead alone with me." He laughed. "Now, we have to figure out how to stay alive."

CHAPTER TWENTY-NINE

John could not sleep due the nightmares that he was constantly having about that fateful night that he loss his wife and daughter. They would always come around three or four in the mornings. He would wake up by the blast that sent him into a coma. He would awake from the fear that he and his family died together in the abandoned house. This night was no different as he was startled by the blast once again. He sat up in bed with his eyes wide open, staring into the darkness, realizing that it was just another dream.

He gave a quick glanced at Seville, she was not disturbed by his sudden movement. He climbed out of bed slowly and quietly, then, walked to the patio sliding door that was in the living room. Rubbing his hands over his eyes, he could see that his hands were still shaking from the dream. While standing outside on the patio, he tried to steady his hands by holding them tightly to his face, he parted his fingers slightly only to see movement from a flashlight in their old apartment. *What the hell?! Someone is in our apartment. Can't be the maintenance man this time of night, no way!* He thought as he took his hands away from his face to get a better look. *Some asshole is in our apartment. Looking for us?*

He quietly went back into his apartment, put on his pants, shirt, and house shoes. He picked up his weapon from the nightstand on his side of the bed. Again he checked to see if Seville was awake, and she was not, still sound asleep. He knew that this was something that he had to look into personally. He eased out the front door, quietly tiptoeing to the door where they were living prior to that night. With his gun in his left hand, he stopped at the front door that was partially open. He stood fast for a moment listening for voices or any kind of sound. He heard no one talking, but he could not assume that the intruder was gone or alone. Slowly he pushed the door open wider, wide enough to step inside without alerting whoever was there.

As he stepped inside the doorway, he saw a shadow to his right, and there was movement with the shadow. The shadow came after him in an attack mode. John stepped aside and caught the arm that was coming down towards his head and jerked whatever that was attached to the arm across his shoulder and lifted the other part up and over his back and slamming the person to the floor. There was a loud grunt and a flashlight fell to the floor just before the body hit the floor.

At that moment, John slammed the butt of his gun into the head of the person sprawled on the floor. There was another loud grunt as if the person was in severe pain. John staggered backward to hit the light switch to see who was in his apartment. But just as he tried cut the lights on, a foot out of nowhere smashed into his face. The force of the blow spun him around and he hit the floor with one knee. *What the fuck! There must be two of them in here.* He was thinking as he tried to stand. Then there was another blow with the back of a leg coming across of his neck, knocking him to the floor again.

Suddenly the lights came on. He was dazed from that second blow, but he could see that it was Seville standing in the doorway with her gun pointed directly at another woman who appeared to be Oriental. "Lay another hand on him, bitch, and I'll light your ass up like a Christmas tree!" Seville shouted to the other woman.

John looked down at the one on the floor and suddenly realized that it was the cop that they had been looking for, Bobby Turner. Then he stood, glancing at the woman, before turning to Seville. "Thanks for showing up, but I had her." He forced a smile.

"Yeah, you're welcome, because to me, she was to kicking your ass." Seville said, glancing at the woman who was about her same build.

The Oriental woman stared at Seville for a moment. "And I'll do the same thing to you if you put that gun down."

Seville looked at John who was now standing with his gun pointed at Bobby Turner. "Now, I know she didn't just say what I thought she said." She said to John.

John smiled glancing at Seville. "Oh yes she did! She said exactly what you thought she said. She said will kick your ass too if you put that gun down."

Seville politely handed her gun to John. "Hold this while I show this Chinese checker-playing hack that she ain't the only one who knows how to kick some ass."

Both women began go after each other with all kinds of hand to hand combat. It was a martial art style of karate and judo combinations. The women hollered, kicked, hand chopped each other like nothing John had ever seen do before. It was a pleasure to see Seville do her thing in spite of having a sore hand. Seville obviously was trained by the best, someone much better than the woman she was fighting. The Oriental threw a drop kick towards Seville's head. Seville blocked her kick with a kick of her own and delivered a smashing elbow to the woman's jaw. And immediately, she swirled around with another round-house kick to the head, which sent the woman in a backward flip over the sofa, landing on top of the coffee table, and crashing it to the floor. After that, the Oriental woman did not move, which was an indication that she was out cold.

"Wow! Now, that's kicking some ass." John said excitedly, reaching down pulling Bobby Turner to his feet. "Get up before I let her beat the crap out of you."

Some of the residents called the police, but by the time the cops arrived, John and Seville had moved their two intruders down to their new apartment for questioning. Some how, some way, Bobby Turner and his partner were going tell Seville and John what they wanted to know. Someone had sent those two to search their apartment, they wanted to know who and why? It was obvious that they were not sent by Chief Martin because dead men do not give orders. So, why were they there, and looking for what? But on the other hand, they had been fairly warned by Slim, there was no way of knowing who were now on Major Butler's payroll in the police department, or elsewhere.

"We need to locate someone who knows the real value of gold that was worth two billion dollars in 1864." John said to Seville as they escorted the two intruders to their apartment.

"Why do we need to know that?" She asked.

"Because there are just too many things happening all around us, and one man so it would appears is pulling all the strings. The only way he's able to do that, the gold that we thought was worth ten to twenty billions is worth a whole lot more. We are talking about the kind of money would make the Russia government pay close attention to. Under ordinary circumstances, he should not be able to muster that kind of power."

"And of course, we don't know who he has working with him. But whoever it is, you can bet your last money they are not black like him."

John laughed. "Bet your last money! You sound like that dude on Soul Train! Don Cornelius. How old are you?"

"Hey, I know about Soul Train." She said laughing as they sat the intruders in straight chairs in the living room and handcuffed them to the chairs.

"You can't do this, I'm a cop!" Bobby Turner snapped, looking at John.

"So?! We're cops too. But that didn't seem to matter a few minutes ago." John replied just as stern. "If you two are cops, then you won't have a problem with answering our questions, will you?"

"I'm a cop, she's my civilian assistant." Tuner said, glancing at the Oriental.

"And what exactly does that mean?" John pulled up another straight chair and placed it in front of the two suspects. He then sat down. Seville remained standing next to John staring at the woman.

"Am I to assume that you are Lieutenant Calvin Gates?" Turner asked while trying to see the resemblance of his former boss.

"You can assume anything you like, but that doesn't make it true. Regardless of what someone told you, who is she? Does she work for the Major as well?"

Turner smiled before casually replying. "Major who?"

"Major James Butler, your former precinct commander. The man who everyone thinks is dead. Remember, he's the same asshole who ordered the hit on Calvin Gates and his family. Or would you like for me to refresh your memory?" John said very angrily.

Turner remained quiet for a moment. He then focused on Seville. "Are you a cop?"

"Just the answer the question that you were asked, and don't concern yourself with who I am." Seville replied sharply. "The one thing you can keep in mind, we don't care if you are a cop. You and your little sweet thing here are not leaving this apartment until you tell us what we want to know."

"Tell you anything like what?" Turner asked, pretending to be totally unaware of what was going on.

"For starters, why were you two searching our apartment, and who gave the orders to do it?" John said.

Turner twisted around in his chair as if he was trying to get comfortable. "Okay, first of all, no one ordered us to search your apartment. I was curious about who was looking for me at the Gold Club. And when I got word that it was you, Lieutenant Calvin Gates, I decided to come and ask you personally, why are you looking for me?"

John smiled. "And who told you that I'm Calvin Gates?"

"Does it matter who told me? You are Calvin Gates, aren't you?"

John stood. "Look, we're not getting anywhere with this twenty-twenty question bullshit. Now, you either answer my questions, or,...." He paused, glancing at Seville.

Turner knew well what the pause and look meant. And he did not want any part of Seville. He finally said, "Ah, Gates, or whoever you are. Right now, you are in the middle of something that you don't want to be involved with. Look, I heard about the Russians who killed the Chief. And I also heard about the gun battle up at your place in north Georgia where you and your kung-fu expert came out on top. But, do you realize that you, me, all of us are in the same boat? This two billions in gold that everybody keeps talking about has led to nothing but destruction! People are dead because of it"

John held up his hand. "Back up! You said, we all are in the same boat, explain that to me, I don't understand that part."

"Okay. Yes, Chief Martin was in on the digging of the gold, and we were supposedly going to hi-jack it for ourselves. But some how they figured that the Chief would try something like that, so they took the gold early, put it aboard a cargo plane and no one knows where they landed. But now, they are tying up all loose ends, meaning us."

John sat down again. "Let's take a step back. You said they, who are they?"

"They, mean that Major Butler didn't do this alone. As far as I know, there were at least two or three other people involved, maybe more by now, many more."

"Do you have names for these at least two or three other people?" Seville asked.

"Ah, the only two I know are Ethan Johnston and a dude named Sam Houston."

John turned to Seville. "This Ethan is a descendant to General Joseph Johnston who was in charge of burying the gold in 1864." He said with a curious look.

"And apparently, and this Sam Houston is the one who figured out the exact spot based on a map of some kind where the gold was buried." She said smiling.

"Are you all really buying into this gold bullshit?" The Oriental woman asked.

Seville glared at the woman. "I'm sorry. I didn't catch your name while I was kicking your ass. Who are you anyway?"

"Her name is Kim Lee. She was hired by the Major before he died. We got together after realizing that the Chief and the Major had worked together in planning the bombing, but the Chief wanted all the gold for himself. That's why he was assassinated. The others believed that he was too much of a risk to allow him to live." Turner explained carefully.

"And to answer your question, Ms. Kim Lee, the gold is real. We have at least twenty people who have died because of that gold. Trust us, it's real, or it's doing a damn good job of impersonation, and it's making fools out of all of us." Seville said.

"So, it's your belief that Major Butler is dead?" John asked Turner.

"I'm not sure. You see, we were ordered by the Chief to stake out the homes of Ethan and Sam Houston. We figured they would be showing up by now. Again, we figured wrong. Ethan or Houston has not shown up since they disappeared. So, if the Major is still alive, then they all are somewhere working together making sure that we don't live long enough to tell our stories to anyone who might believe it."

John chuckled for a brief moment. "So, you're saying that these two men who you know for sure, and if the Major is alive, they are somewhere in the world making plans, a calculated plan that you, me, and my partner don't make out of this alive?"

"That's exactly what I'm saying. And if you are Calvin Gates, you know exactly what I mean. Who do you think gave you the orders to release us from jail five years ago?

And who do you think set the trap for you when you walked into that abandoned house that night looking for your wife and kid? It was all planned by the Major. Now, I don't know how you lived through that explosion, but you can bet your ass that it was the Major who planned everything from start to finish."

John immediately stood and walked away from Turner. He was feeling a rage like he had never felt before. Why? Because he knew that everything Turner was saying was the truth. Now that his memory was back, he remembered the call that he received ordering him to release the three cops. He realized that no one else knew that he had arrested these cops. The call could have only come from Major James Butler. But the one major question that was still ringing in his ears, *why would he try to kill me, and then save me? And now, he's trying to kill me all over again. What's up with my half brother?*

Seville sat down in the chair while John proceeded to the Patio to clear his head.

"So, you were working for the Chief, trying to help him take gold from Major Butler?" She asked Turner.

"That was the plan. But nothing that he did worked out the way he planned it. The man seemed as if he was born under a bad sign or something." Turner chuckled. "Listen, do you have to keep us handcuffed to these chairs. We're not criminals, and we aren't going anywhere. Right now, our lives are hanging in the balance just like yours are."

"That all depends on how you answer my next question." Seville said, glancing with concern out to the patio at John. So far, he had taken the death of his wife and child without any emotional breakdowns at all. But for some strange reason, he was overwhelmed by what Turner had said. She wanted to wait until he returned before asking anymore questions. After a few moments had passed, she up got and joined John on the patio. "What's wrong?"

John turned to look at her, he was crying for the first time. "I'm okay. I guess for the first time, it just hit me all at once." He glanced inside at the two who were still sitting in place. "The thing that bothers me most is the fact that Carolyn said that James wanted revenge due to me being her lover that goes all the way back to when were kids."

"You think she was lying?"

"I know she was lying! I can now remember back to when I was a kid, and I don't remember dating this woman. You see, John and I didn't even know each other until we were teenagers. And even then, we didn't hang out with other like most brothers hang out. We just knew that we had the same father."

Seville frowned with confusion. "Why would she lie about something like that?"

"Why?!...Why is any of this bullshit happening? But I guess for the same reason he had all those cops killed in his own precinct. He's possessed by this whole idea that gold rules the world. And right now, he just might be right. At least, in parts, it does."

"So, which part do we fit in?" She smiled.

He looked at her with a smile as well. "Right now, I'd give anything to find out. But, I guess we'll just have to find out the hard way, we'll see when we get there."

They went back inside the apartment. He now stood while Seville sat facing Turner.

"Okay, we're back. And my question to you is this; bases on what you're saying, you believe that the Russians came into this country to kill the Chief, John and I, and who else that you know of?"

"And me." He said quickly.

"But why kill you? Did you know what was going on as far as the precinct bombing and the gold is concerned?"

"No, not in the beginning, I had no clue. But after the bombing, Chief Martin tried to get Ethan to kick the Major off the team, and make him their replacement. But Ethan wouldn't do it. So, he recruited me and some more to force them to go his way."

"Did it work?"

"Yeah, like everything else he tried to do, it all backfired."

"So, who blew up the precinct?" John asked.

"It were the two guys that you found shot to death out at the motel on Fulton Industrial. After they blew up the precinct, they were paid and told to leave town immediately. But they didn't. They stayed around spending lots of cash at the strip clubs. And like it has already been demonstrated, the Major and his people are not taking any chances of anyone telling anybody what took place, and implicating them as the culprits."

"Let me ask you this then," John continued. "Who is making the contacts for the Major and his people to perform his dirty work now, you?"

"Not me, it's that dope dealing Jeffery Carter, aka, Summerhill Slim. The same asshole who tried to oust you two by using me as bait."

"So, you were aware of that?" Seville asked.

"Yeah, I went to the club like he said I was. And he tried to get me go along with the idea to get you out to the club, and he would take over from there. I asked him, what was he planning to do? And he said, I didn't want to know. I said, no, I was not going to be apart of it. You see, I already knew that it was him who set the Chief up, orders given by Ethan, I assumed. But now, I'm thinking that maybe the Major is still alive and well."

"Good for you." John said.

Seville glanced at John. "Think we should cut them loose?"

John smiled. "I guess we can. Maybe they have an idea as to how we can locate the Major and his gang." John started to unlock the handcuffs on the woman first.

"Wait!" Bobby Turner said sharply. He looked scared. "We might be able to help you. We know that day after tomorrow, Carolyn Butler and Beth Johnston are preparing to leave Atlanta for Russia. From there, I don't know. Nevertheless, we can help you bring this thing to an end. If we don't go after whoever is trying to kill us, they will continue to send hit men after hit men until the job is complete."

"And you think just because your life is hanging in the balance, we should trust you and your friend here?" John asked having serious doubts about Turner.

"Listen, I know what happened five years ago was very tragic. But you have to believe me, the idea of killing you and your family was not my idea. It was not my doing, and I did not play a part in any of it. All I wanted to do was get out of jail, that's all."

"How do we know that you won't do like everyone else have done, they all jumped ship for the gold. They'd double crossed their own mothers if the money is right." Seville said. "Of course, they all are dead now. But, the fact of the matter is, the Major is offering big money to get rid of people. And if he got to them, he can get to you as well. That's including your girlfriend here as well."

Turner thought about what Seville said. "You're right. But right now, I am more concerned about living than I am about the money. And if we don't get to them before they get to us, we are all dead, plain and simple. Besides, you need Kim Lee she can speak five different languages, including Russian."

John was hesitant about allowing Turner and Kim Lee to join him and Seville, but he knew that they were going to need help going into a foreign country without knowing the language, or their way around even. He looked at Seville. "What do you think?"

"Well, as much as I hate to admit it, we do need them. However, can they afford to travel with us?" She looked at Turner. "Where we're going, it going to take a lot of money, can you afford it?"

Turner laughed. "Hey, I wasn't out there all those years pimping for drug dealers just because I was in love with the bastards. I did it for the money."

"So, you have money?" John asked.

"Yes, I have lots of money."

Seville glanced over at Kim Lee. "How about her, what she got?"

"Her father own one of the largest banks in Hong Kong. Trust me, she's loaded."

"Don't worry about me!" Kim Lee snapped.

"Hey, I'm not worried about you honey, because if you step out of line just one time, I'll kick your ass again." Seville said boldly.

"Okay, if we're going to be a team, you two have to knock off the rough stuff." John said as he took off the cuffs from Kim Lee's hands. Then, he took them off Turner's hands. "You say we have two days before these women take off?" He asked Turner.

"Yep, two days and they're out of here."

Seville remained a bit skeptical as to how he came about this information. "How do you know this for sure?"

He smiled. "I'm a good cop. The Lieutenant here can vouch for that. And any good cop on a stake out will plant listening devices inside if it's at all possible. A good cop must have the advantage of what's coming next. So, I see this fine looking black woman entering the Johnston's home. And this fine woman looks like the Major's wife, and I knew then that something was about to take place. And sure enough both women had heard from Ethan, instructing them where to meet him. The Major was probably there."

"So, in your opinion, you don't think that Russia is their final destination?" John asked.

"No way, by no means is Russia where they will stay. Russia is just the first leg of several cities. So, we'll just have to go wherever they go. And by the way, I have a contact with the airlines, and they'll be giving me heads up on where the women are going before they take off."

Seville glanced at John for his reaction. John did not respond, so she did. "Had you already planned this before we caught you searching our apartment?"

But instead of Turner answering, Kim Lee said, "We knew you were thinking what we were thinking. We have to get to them before they send others to finish the job."

"Lieutenant Gates, I've got a good woman here. And we don't want to spend the rest of our lives running from a ghost. Especially a man that everybody thinks is dead."

John looked at Seville. "They sound like us." John laughed. "Okay, the stage is set, so lets do it!"

Turner and Kim Lee left the apartment while John and Seville began their plans for the up coming trip in two days.

CHAPTER THIRTY

Around 9 o'clock that morning, Seville was still in bed while John was up in the kitchen sitting at the table drinking a cup of coffee. In spite of agreeing to bring Bobby Turner and Kim Lee on board to try and find the Major, he still had concerns about the way it all went down. They acted as if they wanted to get caught but put up a fight anyway. Even for a cop that was highly unusual in John's opinion.

A few minutes later Seville was up and about. John heard her rushing into the kitchen. "What's wrong?" He asked, noticing the expression on her face.

"My mother just called from the hospital, my father is in critical condition. He had a heart attack this morning." She turned and rushed back to the bedroom. "As soon as I get dressed, I'm going to the hospital." She said as she disappeared down the hallway.

John stood, still in his shorts, hurried to the bedroom where Seville was taking a quick shower. He yelled into the shower to her, "You want me to go with you?!"

She poked her head out through shower curtain, "No, you stay here and work on what we have to do. I'll be okay. I just want to make sure my father is okay. It may not be as bad as my mother says it is."

John went back to the kitchen and waited until she was dressed and ready to go. "If you want me to drive you, I will." He said as she entered the kitchen, poured herself a cup of coffee to go. She kissed him on the lips as she rushed passed him to leave. "I Gotta run, and I'll call you from the hospital." She disappeared out of the front door.

John sat back down at the table, continued drinking his coffee and hoping that everything would go well with her father. Half an hour passed, he was dressed casually, and still waiting for the call that Seville said she would make from the hospital, but had not received. He moved from the kitchen to the living room and was seated on the sofa when the doorbell rang. His first thought was; *why is she ringing the doorbell when she has a key?* Then he figured that it was probably the maintenance man checking on them in their new apartment to see if everything was all right.

John slowly set the coffee cup on the coffee table, got up and went to the door. *You can never be too careful.* He was thinking as he approached the door. As a precaution, he peered through the peek hole. A white man in a brown UPS uniform was standing outside holding a brown square box. He opened the door. He stared at the younger man wearing glasses. "Ah, you must have the wrong address I'm not expecting a package."

The delivery man glanced down at the label. "This is for a Sevilla Patterson. Does she live here?"

Even if she does, you still have the wrong address, asshole! He was thinking as he started to back away from the door. But as he did, two more men, one on each side of the door rushed in with guns drawn, slamming the door shut behind them. The delivery man dropped the box, and took out a black hood while the other two men grabbed John by both arms and held him tightly while the man in the UPS uniform placed the hood over his head and pulled a draw string only tight enough that the hood would not come off.

John struggled with all his strength to get free, but nothing that he did helped his situation. "Who are you, and what do you want?!" He shouted, although he knew well what this was all about. But he was more concerned about Seville. Was the call from her mother a fake call to get her out of the apartment? And why would they want to do that? Those were the questions that kept coming into John's mind. No one spoke a word.

Suddenly, John felt a needle piercing his right upper arm, and some kind of fluid was being pumped into his arm. Immediately he felt woozy, weak in the legs, and then there was total darkness, and unconsciousness. One of the three men picked him up and carried John over his shoulder to a waiting black Chevy SUV downstairs. A few minutes later, the vehicle and all its' occupants were leaving the complex and headed north on Peachtree Road for the Peachtree-Dekalb Airport.

Meanwhile at Piedmont Hospital, Seville rushed to the emergency desk looking for signs of her father and mother. She asked several nurses, doctors, and staff members for information pertaining to her father, and no one had any record of her father being admitted there. She called her mother at home. After a few rings, her mother answered the phone. Seville yelled into the phone, "Mom, are you okay!? Is Daddy okay?! Where are you?....Has he had a heart attack?"

Seville's mother was caught off guard with all the questions. "Yes, I'm okay...And your father is okay as well. We're at home. And what are you talking about, Sevilla?"

Seville suddenly realized that she had been set up once again. This time, it was to get her away from John. She immediately took out her cell phone again and called John. Impatiently she waited for him to answer, but there was no response. She knew that something was wrong as she ran out of the hospital and leaping into the Hummer with the still bullet riddled windshield. She sped out of the emergency parking area onto Peachtree and north towards the apartment. Thirty minutes later she pulled into the parking lot of the apartment, and was approached by the maintenance man Ben Thomas. "Miss! I saw some men take your husband away in a van. I wanted to stop them, but they had guns."

Seville stepped out of the vehicle and asked calmly. "Did you call the police?"

"Yes, I told the manager and she called them. What's going on?"

Seville glanced up at the apartment. "If I told you, you wouldn't believe me. What did these men look like, and how many were there?" She was angry at herself for falling for one of the oldest tricks in the book. She stomped her foot. "Damn!....Damn!"

"There were three guys, all white, and one was dressed in a brown uniform, the kind that the UPS delivery people wear."

She turned and walked away. "Let me know when the cops get here."

"Yes, Madam, I will. Will you be in your old or new apartment?" He asked as he stared at the perfectly shaped body in black tight jeans and a loose fitting white blouse.

"Does it matter? We live in both." She said as she entered the stairwell.

As soon as she entered the living room, she glanced around and there was no signs of a struggle. That could only mean that the delivery man in the UPS uniform pretended to be delivering a package. Glancing down to the floor, she noticed a brown box that had been opened. *The guy showed*

John the box, and John thought that either he was at the wrong address, or I had actually ordered something. She thought.

She pulled out her cell phone again and dialed the acting police chief. "Chief Cunningham, this is Detective Sevilla Patterson. We met in the Mayor's office, remember me from the other day?"

"Yeah, the one who wants to be chief. How can I not remember you? So, what can I do for you, Detective?" The Chief asked in a very stern voice.

"I want you to give the order to let Summerhill Slim out of the city jail. Or,….." She paused.

"Or, what?!" The Chief snapped angrily.

"Or, do I have to call the Mayor and have him to make the call to the city jail to get Slims' released?"

"You may as well make that call. Do you have any idea how long we've been waiting for an opportunity to get our hands on Jeffery Carter, or Summerhill Slim?"

"No I don't. But tell me anyway, Chief Cunningham?!"

"Years! And now that we finally have him in lock up, he's going to stay there."

"Okay, then I'll call the Mayor." As she started to close her phone, she heard him shouting something into the phone. She immediately said, "What was that, Chief?"

"I said wait. Don't call the Mayor. I'll do this one favor for you it this time."

"Thank you Chief…You may not be so bad after all." She hung up and got ready to drive down to the jail to pick up Slim before he could get lost in the hustle and bustle of the downtown traffic. As she was leaving, she met a uniform officer on the stairwell. She paused momentarily to tell him. "I'm Investigator Patterson, and I work out of the Mayor's office. The kidnapping call that you got, I'm working on it. You can advise your supervisor that I'm handling this case." She then walked on the Hummer.

The officer stared at the female cop as he talked into his shoulder microphone telling the dispatcher that he had been cancelled by a detective.

By the time Slim was processed and released, Seville was waiting outside of the jail on Peachtree Street downtown. When he walked out of the front entrance, he saw Seville standing beside the Hummer waiting and motioning for him to come to her. He knew right away that it was her who had sprung him. As he stood still for a moment staring at her, he hated to admit that he had a little fear in his heart of this woman. She was not the kind of woman that you wanted to piss off. And from the look that she was wearing, she was highly pissed off.

He walked slowly down the steps towards her and the vehicle. "Well, well, well, look what the cat done dragged in." He blurted out, trying to be amusing.

"And if you don't tell me what I want to know, look what the cops are going to drag back inside that hellhole you just left." She said without cracking a smile.

"Hey, black woman, why you always got to be so mean? Look, the shit that happened last night was not my doing. And by now, you should know that."

She looked at him standing a few feet away. "Come on over here and stand next to me. Listen, I know you're funky after spending the night and a half day in there. But, one phone call and your funky ass will go right back in there. Now, tell me who took John, and where did they take him?"

Slim stood back, waved his hands from side to side. "What the fuck are you talking about?! I was locked up in that place all night!" He turned and pointed to the brick building. "How in the hell would I know who kidnapped your man, John, huh?"

Seville smiled finally. She could tell that he knew something. "A very good choice of words, Slim,.... kidnapped. That's not a word you would normally use. Somebody told you there was going to be a kidnapping, didn't they?" She stood up straight and walked closer to him. "Don't lie to me, Slim, or I'll put your ass right back in lock up. Of course, you already know that the cops wants to send you away for a long time, right?...Tell me who took him, and I'll let you walk away right now."

Slim smiled as he turned around in circles twice. "Woman, you know who got him. The fucking Major, that's who, okay? Now where they took him, I'm not sure."

"Well, give me your best and wildest guess. And it better be a good one too!"

"Cuba. Havana Cuba, that's all I know, I swear to God!"

Seville stared at Slim for a few moments. "Cuba. Why go to Cuba?" She asked but not really expecting for Slim to know the answer.

"Who knows anything anymore? Maybe the man has gone loco or something. Nobody knows why the Major is doing what he is doing, except maybe that gold has made him a mad man. Come on, Seville, that's a lot gold, and it's driving them crazy!"

Seville paced the street for a moment searching her brain for some sort of answer. Then suddenly, she had the solution. She stopped, turned, and began looking at Slim.

"No!...No way am I getting involved with your bullshit!" Slim shouted.

Seville smiled. "Slim, you're already involved. You and I have been involved from the beginning. The problem was, you were being just a businessman, so you say. Remember that line of crap, or do you want me to refresh your memory? Okay, this is a business deal. I just got you out of jail, and its all business. Now, you have to pay me for keeping you from spending many years in prison. You have a brand new private jet plane, and I need a ride to Cuba."

Slim looked up at the glaring sun for a while before speaking again. "Damn! I knew there was going to be some shit connected to you getting me out of jail. Why do I let you talk me into doing stuff like this?!"

"Because you love me, and you can't help yourself, that's why." She smiled.

"And you really think that part is funny, don't you?"

"No. I mean, you can't help because you love me. But you know my heart is with John Sinclair, and you and I will always be friends. As long as you don't pull any more bullshit like you pulled last night."

Slim stood there in silence for a moment trying to figure out what options did he have at that moment. "And if I refuse to do what you're asking, then what?"

Seville grabbed him by the arm and started walking towards to city jail. "If you can't help me, then your ass goes right back to jail."

Slim stopped, pulled his arm away from her. "Okay, I'll do it. Now, you do know when this shit is all said and done, neither one of us are going to get out of Cuba alive."

"I know." She said softly. "But Major Butler won't be getting out alive either."

"Do I need to bring some of my boys?"

"You mean the two we killed last night?" She laughed.

"That's not funny!"

"I know, but they weren't funny when they tried to kill us either, on your orders!...No, I have some friends, one you might know very well."

" Oh yeah, who?!"

"The cop you tried to set up last night, Bobby Turner. Remember him?"

"Oh, him. Okay, when do we leave?"

"In three hours." She started to walk away, but then paused. "You need a ride?"

"No, I have my own ride." He pointed to a black Cadillac Escalade parked across the street.

Before turning to get into her vehicle, she said, "Three hours, we'll meet at your place. "And don't try to run out on me either. If you do, I will find you, and I will arrest you again. This time, you will rot in there, okay?" She pointed to the jail.

Slim smiled. "Okay!....I may be a lot of things, but the one thing I'm not, a liar." He walked crossed the street and got into the passenger's seat of his Cadillac. "Three hours!" He yelled at Seville.

CHAPTER THIRTY-ONE

In a small private jet that landed just west of the Havana, on a smaller airfield a few miles away from the International airport, Playa Baracoa Airport, the plane that was carrying John came to a stop and two black Chevy sports utility vehicles rushed up to the plane and several men, along with the two who were carrying John, who was still unconscious got off the plane and into the vehicles and drove away.

A short while later both SUVs' pulled into a parking deck at a downtown hotel in Chinatown next to an elevator. All six men rode the elevator up to the sixth floor, a spacious hotel room that was overlooking downtown Havana. The two men who were carrying John sat him comfortable in a leather chair and removed the black hood from his head. A different man went over to him and gave him another shot in the arm, and then stood back. "Give him a couple of minutes, he'll be around." He then left the room.

A couple minutes passed, and as the man with the needle had promised, John began to open his eyes, and the only thing he could see was fog, then shadows that were fuzzy. Then he saw figures of several people sitting around in the room that he could barely make out as being people. He shook his head vigorously trying to get the cobwebs to disappear. Finally, he spoke, "Where am I?....And who are you people?!"

No one responded to John's questions, they simply looked on as things began to come into focus. As he vision cleared, he began to turn his head rapidly from side to side trying to recognize the people that he now saw. There were approximately seven men in the room, some appeared to have been Cuban, and the others, he was not sure. He stared at each man one by one, hoping that one of them would say something, anything that would give him a clue as to why he was sitting in a room filled with men who all looked to have been carrying weapons. "No one wants to tell me where I am, and why have you brought me here?!" John snapped angrily.

Suddenly, a door from an adjoining room opened, and a man stepped in wearing a very expensive white suit, white shirt and a red tie, and was wearing white shoes. "You were brought here because I told them to bring you here!" The man said sharply.

John swiftly turned in his seat to see who was doing the talking. He was now staring face to face with a black man who he did not recognize, but he had a strong feeling that he knew the man who was doing the talking. *Could this be my half brother James Butler?* He was thinking. "And I suppose you're in charge?" He asked slowly.

The man smiled along with everyone else in the room. "Come on, John, you mean to tell me that you don't even recognize your own brother? I'm James, the man who saved your life, remember me now?"

John stared at the face as he remained speechless, for there was nothing about the Major that remotely resembled his old self. Finally, he spoke nervously. "It just now dawn on me as to why you went to the extremes to give me a new face, a new life, the whole nine yards. You were experimenting on me to see how it would work out for you.

You were planning this all along to pull off the same thing by changing your own identity. So, it was never about saving my life was it? You had bigger plans in mind that started approximately five years ago. Am I right, my old asshole brother?!"

The man walked around to another arm chair that was immediately put in front of John so he could talk to him. "John, a plan like this takes a long time to put into action. Everything that has happened, it had to fit just right, in the right place, at the right time. And it had to be done with the precision of a fine tuned and a well oiled machine." The Major sat down, facing John from a few feet. "With a hundred billion dollars at stake, my partners and I couldn't take any chances of anything going wrong. I hate what happened to you and your family, but you must understand, in order to be apart of something this big, you should be grateful that I allowed you to live this long."

John hesitated for a moment. "So, you killed my wife and my daughter for some lousy ass gold?.....Is that what you're telling to me to my face, James Butler?!"

"Yes! And I'm saying it to your face, Calvin Gates. And if you want to live to be a rich old man, you better understand one simple thing right here, and right now. I did you a fucking favor by allowing you to live. I gave you a young beautiful woman, you can start another family. But only this time, you can do it with one billion dollars in your bank account. Why do you think I stole five million dollars just for you? It was because I wanted you to get use to living the good life! Right now, you have a young woman, and if you do as I tell you, you can walk away from here as one of the richest men in America."

John glanced around the room, all eyes were on him. "Obviously, I don't have much of a choice but to do as you say. What with all the muscle and the guns?.....And by the way, you never said where I am, and why did you bring me here?"

James Butler crossed his legs as one of the men brought him a Cuban cigar and lit it. He puffed several times then blew out the smoke. "Okay, at the present time, you are in Havana Cuba. This is probably the safest place on earth for me and my people for the moment. You have to understand something, when you have in your possession the kind of loot that I have, you become a target for all kinds of treasure hunters. We don't have the pleasure of being protected by the federal government, so we protect ourselves."

John smiled. "So, the word is out that you and your co-harts are sitting on a shit load of gold, and they want a piece of the action, that's about right?"

"That's right." He turned to another man. "Get my brother something cold to drink." The man rushed out of the room.

"Can you trust all these cut-throats?" John asked.

Before Butler answered, he turned to yet another man. "Bring my two friends in."

The man disappeared and immediately returned with Ethan Johnston and Sam Houston, both with their hands cuffed behind their back and gags over their mouths. The two men stood in the middle of the room while a third man held on to them. "You see, me and these two assholes were supposed to split the gold three ways. But while I was having all this done," He pointed to his face. "They made the decision to take all the gold for themselves. They never once realized that I am smarter than the both of them put together. I had someone watching every move they made while they were planning to kill me."

John stared at the two men who had fear written all over their faces. "Okay, so now that you caught your partners in crime trying to take all the gold, what now?"

Major Butler smiled as he puffed on his cigar. "What now?" He laughed. "From here to Miami is ninety miles of the Gulf of Mexico. And anything can happen between here and there."

"So, you're planning to kill them. Then dump their bodies into the ocean?"

"Why not, that's what they were planning to do to me." He hesitated for a moment, glancing at the two men. "Get them out of my sight." He motioned to the man standing behind them to take them back to the adjoining room. He turned back to John. "The question is, why have I brought you here?"

"Yeah, I think that would be a fair enough question. Why did you bring me here, are you planning to kill me too? You've tried that a half dozen times already."

Major Butler laughed again. "John, you keep forgetting, if I wanted you dead, you would have been dead five years ago. Listen, I am sitting here with a hundred billion dollars in gold, safe where no one but me can find it. I have my own security people whom are all former cops from several cities around the world. After I take care of those two dirty rats in the other room, there will be no one left to connect me with anything that happened back in Atlanta, except for you of course. I've planned the perfect crime."

"Don't forget Seville. She's really pissed off because you sent Slim to kill us." John said glancing around once again. Everyone in the room was still staring at him as if they were waiting for him to make an attempt to escape. "Why so much security here, are you expecting something to happen?"

The Major smiled as he stood. "Like I said, right here in Cuba is the safest place on earth for me at the moment. However, as soon as my business is complete here, I'll be moving to an undisclosed location and there I will live happily forever after." He walked out to the balcony that was overlooking a main street in Chinatown. He waved his hand for John to join him. "Come, my brother! Lets' enjoy this moment together, for after today, we will never see or hear from each other again."

John stood slowly. He was allowing James words to sink in, which could only mean that whatever he had in store for him would all be over with at the end of this day. As soon as he had joined his brother, he carefully asked, "Why did you bring me down here? You haven't said why yet."

Instead of answering the question, he pointed outward. "This is a beautiful city. Think what this place might have been like today if the United States had not placed the trade embargo against Cuba in 1961…... Shameful!"

"Yeah, it is a shame. But Castro brought it on himself, and his people. Maybe if he had told the Russian to kiss his ass back then, Cuba would be a striving country today." John paused for a moment. "Are you going to tell me why you brought me here, or not?!"

The Major turned to John, placing both hands on his shoulders. "You mentioned Seville a few minutes ago. Trust me, when this is all over with, you and Seville will thank me. And by the way, she's getting ready to fly over here as we speak, thinking that she's coming to rescue you." He chuckled. "I have to give it to you, you've won her over. You had me worried there for a while. I almost thought she was going to kill you."

John backed away from the Major's hands touching him. "Hold it, you fuck! Does this mean that Bobby Turner and the Chinese woman are working for you as well?!"

James laughed loudly. "Come on, don't look so surprised! Look, like I told you, I planned this thing for five long years. Everything that you thought was happening to you, it was only make-believe. To make you believe that I really wanted you dead. And Carolyn, well, what can I say? She had you convinced that this was all about me hating you, and getting revenge. No, it was never about you. It has always been about the gold."

John shook his head in an unbelievable manner. "You murdered my family! And then murdered thirteen cops who were in your precinct just because you knew there was gold buried underneath it…...What a sick fucker you are! You're going to burn in hell!"

The Major laughed. "Don't judge me, John. You would have done the same damn thing if the situation was reversed. For a hundred billion dollars, I would have killed my own mother. I would have killed my wife if she had not agreed to go along with me. John, this is unlike anything you, I, or anybody else has ever seen, or ever dreamed of. Do you have any idea what having a hundred billion dollars in gold is like?!"

"No, I can't even imagine what it's like. But why don't you tell me, just to give me an idea of what it's like."

"Okay, it's like owning a piece of heaven. You see, the dollar bill is worthless compared to gold. Gold will never lose its' value whereas the dollar will loses its' value everywhere, even in America. On the other hand, gold was created by God. Gold will stand forever! And the man who has possession of it is king of the world."

John was in deep thought for a moment before saying, "Now, I know why you want to get rid of your two friends. They tried to buy you out with a couple of billions in cash. You found out that the gold was worth a whole lot more than what they were telling you. They tried to double-cross you by buying you out with cash money. You on the other hand double crossed them by hiring a bunch gun toting ex-cops to take the gold for yourself. Now, in order to be king of the world, you're going to drop them in the ocean, which is no more than doing to them what they were going to do to you."

The Major began to clap his hands. "That's brilliant, John! You figured it all out within a snap….." He puffed his cigar again. "Now that you have that part figured out, why don't you tell me exactly why I had you brought to Cuba?"

John thought for a long minute. "I don't have a clue. At first, I thought maybe you wanted to put a bullet in me yourself. But now, I don't think that's the reason at all. Why don't you tell me, and then we both will know."

The Major puffed once again. "Okay, your mission is very simple,……"

"Nothing is simple with you." John said bitterly

"This is simple. All you have to do is fly back home and do as I tell you to do. And you'll be paid one billion dollars for your efforts. Then, you're home free, forever!"

John smiled as if he knew there must have been some kind of trick that he had not yet mentioned. "So, who do I have to kill to get away from you?"

"Kill? No, I don't want you to kill anybody. Your killing days are over."

"You said Seville is on her way here. What about her?"

"When she gets here, you and she will then fly back to Atlanta, take care of my business, and you two can then ride off into the sunset, forever!"

"Okay, now tell me what do I have to do to gain our freedom?"

"It's a very simple task. Your job will be to convince the Mayor, the FBI, and anybody else who might interested in this so-called lost gold, that everybody connected with it are dead. The gold is lost forever somewhere in Atlantic Ocean that was on the plane carrying Ethan Johnston and Sam Houston. It crashed into the deep waters. The bodies and the gold were never recovered by the Cuban government or anyone else."

John frowned as he stared at the Major. "And, what about you, what do I tell them about you, that you just vanished into thin air?"

"Me, I'm already dead, remember? In fact you are too. From this point on, Calvin Gates and James Butler are dead and gone. There is no way anyone can prove otherwise." He laughed, puffing on his cigar. "You have to admit, this is some brilliant shit. It will take years before anyone can figure out what really happened. And even then, it will take an Albert Einstein like individual to figure out what happened to the gold. Maybe, you'll write a book about it one day, who knows….." James then turned and walked back inside. "Come my brother, lets' have a drink to our new fortune."

They both stood at the bar while the Major poured straight rum into two glasses. He handed John one of the glasses. But John did not drink the liquor. Instead, he said softly, "You know you'll never going to get away with this, don't you?"

James smiled. "And why won't I?"

"Because there is no such thing as the perfect crime; someway, somehow, someone will find out where you are, and they will do to you what have done to so many others for that gold."

James Butler smiled. "You see, my brother, I've thought about everything. Even if I die tomorrow, no one will ever find out where the gold is hidden. Unlike those white Confederate Soldiers, I did not bury it in the ground. It is locked away in the safest place in the world. The gold never left the United States, and I can put my hands on it anytime I want to. You see, John, I am the smartest criminal that the world has ever seen. And I am able to prove it by what I have done." He took a huge swallow. At that time, his cell phone rang. "Are you're here?...No, stay where you are, we'll come meet you." He closed his phone and looked at John. "It's show time, my brother!"

As they departed the hotel, the Major directed half of his security force to follow his instructions as far taking care of Ethan and Sam Houston. The other half traveled with them back to the landing strip where Slims' plane had landed. On their way to the plane, John sat in the back seat of the SUV sandwiched by two guards as the Major sat in the front passenger's seat. The Major turned to John and said, "All you have to do is tell them your story, and the case is closed. And in one or two days, check your off shore bank account, the money will be there, one billion dollars."

John looked at him point blank for a second. "Why are you doing this? You killed my family, you took my identity, you turned my life upside down, and now you want me to lie for you? Hell, everything I am is fucking lie! What if I decide not to do it?"

James laughed. "Like I said, John, killing you has never been a problem. Like all the others who died, you and Seville will be my next targets. That is, if you don't do as I have instructed you to do. And don't think you will be able to fake it. There will be some one watching you every second until you close this case. Do we understand each other?"

John glanced at the two men sitting on each side of him. "Yeah, I believe you. So far, you've pulled off the perfect crime. I have to give you credit for that."

When the SUV arrived at the landing strip, John saw Seville along with Slim, Bobby Turner and Kim Lee standing outside the plane. As John got out of the vehicle, he started to walk towards Seville, but Slim and Bobby grabbed her by the arms and escorted her to the SUV. John stopped in his tracks as the Major came closer to him. "I'm sorry John. I forgot to tell you that she's my insurance policy. If you fail to do as I have instructed you to do, she will die. It's as simple as that. You best believe me, John! You have already loss two women by being stubborn, so don't make the same mistake again."

John suddenly turned and tried to strike the Major with a hard right fist, but the two guards caught his hand as he swung. "You sonofabitch!....I will kill you if it's the last thing I do in this life….." John pulled away from the guards. "Okay, have it your way. But as soon as I do this, you let her go, you hear me, you lowdown bastard?! Or, I will hunt you down like the dog you are." John pointed his finger at the Major. "I know what you look like now, and I will find you no matter where you try to hide."

Kim Lee walked over and grabbed John by the arm. "Lets go, you've got work to do." He followed her to the second plane where a pilot was already waiting to take off. Two more security guards got on the plane along with Kim Lee. They were not taking any chances with John trying taking over the plane, or making an attempt to escape.

As the plane was taking off, the Major looked at Seville who was still being held by Slim and Bobby Turner. "You can let go of me now!" She said angrily as she jerked her arms free. "Where am I going here in Cuba?"

The Major turned and walked back to where Seville was standing, and looking very angry. "It's good to see you again, Sevilla Patterson. "You've done a good job on John. I had my doubts there for a while, but you pulled it off, congratulation!" He then got back into the vehicle.

"And fuck you too, Mr. Asshole!" She snapped as she was led to the vehicle.

CHAPTER THIRTY-TWO

Moments after the plane had been cleared to depart and was in the air, Kim Lee sat next to John. Before speaking, she carefully observed her two counter-parts to see if they were watching her as she talked to John. They were not. She spoke softly, "Listen, just do as you were told, and we'll take it from there…..I'm with the FBI, and we'll arrest James Butler as soon as he depart from Cuba."

John was stunned by her words as he glanced at her in disbelief. "What?!"

"Keep your voice down, I don't want them to hear what we're saying." She nodded towards the two guards. "I've been on this case since the Major faked his own death. We were just waiting for him to show his face again. Now that we know who he is, we'll take him down as soon as he land in Miami."

"Who says he's going to land in Miami?" John whispered back.

"We've got a man on his security team. We know where he's going next."

"Are your inside man going to stop him from killing his two partners?"

"Don't worry about them. It's all taken care of. The next time you see James Butler, he'll be in federal prison." She smiled, and then remained silence for the rest of the trip.

One and a half hour later, the plane landed at the Charlie Brown Airport, and John immediately called the Mayor, asking that he arrange a new conference so he could tell the news media what he had been ordered to say.

John and his three companions left the airport in a waiting limo, headed for city hall to give his made up information to permanently close the case on Major James Butler, the precinct bombing, and the gold. However, in spite of what Kim Lee had told him, he still had his doubts about the FBI's involvement. If they were involved, why had they not made it clear that Kim Lee was working on their side? But he quickly dismissed the thought, because he knew very well how law enforcement agencies operate, whether they are crooked or straight, FBI or local cops.

As soon as the limo arrived at city hall, Mayor Townsend and several high ranking police officers greeted John in the atrium where several news media personnel were on hand to hear what John had to say. Kim Lee and the guards quickly disappeared as soon as John emerged from the vehicle. He suddenly glanced back in the crowd of media people for them, but they were no where to be found. *Oh, what the hell let me get this lie over with so that nut can let Seville go free, she's the only reason I'm doing this.*

John was seated in front several microphones on a table, staring into the lens of many cameras rolling and flashing lights. "My name is John Sinclair, and I'm somewhat of a private investigator working for the City of Atlanta. I was hired several months ago to work along with police detective Sevilla Patterson who is not present at the time. We were working on the Zone Three precinct bombing case where thirteen day watch police officers were killed......

"As the case evolved, and the more involved we got into the case, we discovered that this was not just another act of terrorism, this was a crime committed to cover up something that was as valuable as gold. In fact, it was gold. Two hundred billion dollars in gold on today's gold market was buried underneath the precinct. That gold was discovered by three men, Major James Butler, the precinct commander, Ethan Johnston, the great, great grandson of Civil War General Joseph Johnston, and Sam Houston, a Georgia Tech professor in Civil War history. They committed the acts of murder and stealing the gold. General Johnston buried the gold just before end of the Civil War in 1864, and it was later discovered that it was buried underneath the Zone Three precinct.

"I know this may sound like one of those Indiana Jones movies, but trust me, the gold is as real as you and I. And, as in all Indiana Jones movies, the bad guys always end up dying trying to get away with the loot. This tail of greed, mayhem and murder took me and my partner a place no one expected them to be, Havana Cuba. And several months of following lead after lead, getting shot at, and anything else you can possibly name, all the players are now dead. On a plane loaded with the gold, Ethan, and his partner crashed into the Gulf of Mexico. Although the crash site is in International waters, the Cuban government declared the plane and everyone, including the gold are in too deep of waters for divers to salvage anything. Of course, as you know Major Butler died in a car crash.

"So, as I sit before you today, and I am officially closing the precinct bombing case.

Some of you might say that the gold is a myth. Well, whether it is a myth or not, we'll never know now. I thank you for your time!"

Although the reporters were yelling and screaming questions for him to answer, John refused to answer or say anything further. As he walked away from the table, he spotted FBI Special Agent Harvey Hill standing a few feet away. John immediately approached him and asked, "Have your people made the arrests yet in Miami?"

Agent Hill was startled by the question. "What arrests in Miami?"

"One of your undercover agents, Kim Lee said that the FBI was waiting for Major James Butler to land in Miami, and he would be arrested there."

Agent Hill turned and started to walk away. "Come with me." He told John.

They walked outside of the building, away from the crowd. "Now, what is this all about an arrest in Miami?"

Holy shit! John was thinking as the agent asked the question. "Obviously, you do not have an agent by the name of Kim Lee."

"There's no one in my district by that name. Wait a minute! Didn't I just hear you say in that press conference that Major James Butler died in a car crash?"

"Yeah you did hear me say that." John smiled. "And he is dead. I was just making a wild statement, that's all." John waved his hand as he walked down the steps, leaving the agent looking as if he had seen a ghost. "See you later, Agent Hill!" John yelled as he walked down the street away from the building.

As the rain began to fall heavily, he continued walking, feeling like he had been hit by a Mack truck. *I should have known that this was nothing but bullshit! They played me like I was a little school girl. I knew this was too damn easy.* He thought as he finally flagged down a cab after walking a couple of blocks in the pouring rain. The cab took him to his apartment in Buckhead. *Face it, it's over! There's nothing else you can do. She probably was in on it too, right from the beginning. She played me, but she was very convincing. And the worse part about it all, I fell for all her bullshit.* He was thinking.

90 MILES AWAY FROM MIAMI: HAVANA CUBA…..Major Butler was now packed and ready to board Slims' private jet to Paris as originally planned. Before leaving, he had one last chat with Seville who was seated in the hotel room along with several security guards. He sat across from her in an arm chair. "My dear, sweet Seville, it's time that we part our ways for good. But before I go, I'm going to keep my promise to my brother and your boyfriend." He snapped his fingers, and someone handed him and laptop computer. He opened it up and brought up a bank account. He immediately transferred one billion dollars to an account in John Sinclair's name and punched enter.

"What's that?" She asked sharply.

"That's the money that I promised you and John for being such good sports." He smiled. "I told you when I brought you in that I was going to take care of you. The only thing I regret is not getting some of that pretty pussy before I turned you over to him."

"Fuck you!" She snapped angrily.

"Oh yeah, that would have been nice. But, that's water under the bridge now. In fact, I can fuck all the pretty women I want who looks ten times better than you."

"What about your wife, what are you going to do with her?"

"In a few months, she'll be heading back to the States to start herself a new life, she and the girls. She'll be so rich until she won't give me a second thought. You have to remember, as far as everybody knows, the old corrupted Major James Butler is dead. And that's the way she has to live her life from now on, without me."

"Wow! You didn't miss a fucking thing, did you?" She said, shaking her head.

He wrote a number on card and handed it to her. "That's your new bank account, have fun kids! Oh, and by the way, the account is in John's name. So, in order to get your money, you'll have to go through John." He smiled. "Boy, I am brilliant!" He stood. "And, since you're no longer my concern, you can catch a commercial flight back to Atlanta. Tell the Mayor that Mr. Turner sends his best wishes." He glanced at Bobby.

"Now, that's low! You brought me over here, and now you're just going to leave me here by myself." She said in frustration.

"No, I didn't bring you here, you hi-jacked my boy Slim to bring you here to rescue John, so you thought. Now, John is back in Atlanta, probably thinking that you've fucked him again." He waved to her as he and all his security along with his two former partners who were still handcuffed being forcefully escorted out to the SUV. "See ya!"

"Wait!" Seville said suddenly.

The Major stopped and turned. "Yeah, you want to get it on with me before I go?"

"You wish. I just want to ride along with you and your people to the airport. Will you let me ride to the plane? Then, I'll catch a taxi from there to the regular airport."

He hesitated for a moment, wondering should he honor her request. *What harm can you do now, bitch?!...I've got five armed men with me.* He was thinking as he said, "I guess I can do this one last favor for you.... Providing, the next time I see you, you'll be appreciative enough to give your old pal some of that pretty pussy, okay?"

She smiled as she stood. "Okay, that's a deal. If you left a billion dollars for me and John, I'll give you as much of this pretty pussy as you want, when I see you again."

They all rode the two vehicles back to the airfield for takeoff. Slim was waiting with the plane. Everyone hurriedly and boarded the plane except the two vehicle drivers and Seville. She waited outside, standing next to one of the SUV'S as the plane was about to take off. As the plane was rolling down the runway, Seville walked over the one of the hangar and watched from there as if she was sorry that they were leaving her.

As soon as the plane was in the air, the two vehicles drove away leaving Seville alone. She could see that the Major was staring out of the window back down to the ground at her. He waved, and she waved back. But then he had the strangest feeling that something was terribly wrong. Why was she just standing there and smiling as if she was waiting for something bad to happen? Then suddenly as he watched her, he could see her raising her arm, holding something in her hand, high up in the air.

Suddenly, he realized that his greatest fears were about to come to past. He had allowed this young pretty bitch to bring his brilliant masterpiece of a plan to an end.

She was holding a remote detonator to a bomb that she had brought, and placed on the plane while they were in flight from Atlanta. "Yeah, you're brilliant all right. But you never once thought that someone like me would bring your sorry ass down. And like, I said, I will give you all the pretty pussy you want, in hell!" She said to herself out loud.

Immediately, he began yelling and ordering Slim to land the plane. "Get me down from up here! Land this motherfucker right now! That bitch put a bomb on this plane!"

Suddenly, everyone started looking for a bomb, and Bobby Turner found the bomb that was placed at the back of one of the seats. "I got it!..... I got it!" He shouted. But then they all suddenly realized that knowing that the bomb was on the plane and landing before it blew were totally two different things. They all began to panic and screaming in fear that the plane would blow before they were able turn around and land.

Seville saw the plane as it began to turn to come back to the airfield. She smiled, "Sorry boys, especially you, Slim, but sometimes the good must die with the bad." And then she pushed the red button. Suddenly, there was a red fire ball that blistered the day time sky. Then there were black and white smoke billowing outward, and then there was a red and orange flash. Followed by a mighty loud, roaring, thundering boom! While all that was going on, she walked over to a large trash can and dropped the black device in it.

As the airplane blew apart and debris began to fall from the sky as people ran out of hangars, and buildings not believing their eyes. A man asked her, "What happened?"

"I don't know. I've never seen anything like that before. It just blew up!" Seville responded as if she was as surprised as anyone else. She looked around and saw a taxi parked nearby, she walked slowly to the cab, got in the back seat. "Take me to the International Airport. I think I've changed my mind about flying on private jets."

As she rode to the International Airport, she thought back for a moment to see the look on the Major's face when he realized that she was holding the switch to his demise. *I absolutely loved it! Don't worry John, you didn't have to kill your brother, I did it for you. Plus, we got a billion dollars for killing his no-good ass.* She smiled as she stared out the window of the 1950's model Chevrolet sedan. "Wow! Now, that's what I call some real female James Bond shit for your ass." She said softly to herself.

CHAPTER THIRTY-THREE

It was later that afternoon and John was seated on the sofa, he was still in a bad mental state of mind, thinking about how everything had turned out for him. He was not sure what he wanted to do at this point. He had fixed himself a drink and decided to drink whatever liquor left in the apartment, and when he ran out, he would go buy some more. Suddenly the phone rang, he picked and said hello very softly. He heard Agent Harvey Hill's voice, and he apologized. "Agent Hill, I'm sorry about today....."

"John, forget that! Have you been watching the news today?"

"No, what's going on?" John said, quickly picking up the remote and turned on the television. He caught the tail end of a story coming out of Cuba. The newscaster stated that a private jet mysteriously blew up as it was taking off with eight Americans on board. All seven passengers, including the pilot, known as Summerhill Slim died in the explosion. "That was the plane I was talking about." He said to Agent Hill.

"That was the plane?! But how did you know?" Agent Hill was very bewildered.

John did not speak, he was quiet and saddened by the fact he was thinking that Seville was on the plane as well. "Agent Hill, call me later, maybe by then I'll be able to talk more about it, and possibly make some sense of all this." He hung up the phone.

At that precise moment he heard the key in the door of their new apartment. He suddenly stood, grabbed his gun from the coffee table and waited for whomever to enter.

The door slowly opened, and before completely entering, Seville called out his name, "John! It's me, Seville." Then she stepped inside the door. And to her surprise, he was standing the middle of the living room holding a gun, pointed at the door. "It's only me, baby!" She said, closing the door behind her.

John looked at her, then at the television. "I just heard the plane you were on blew up after taking off in Cuba…..I thought you were on it." He started to grin. "Boy! Am I glad to see you!" He placed his gun back down the coffee table, and reached for her.

She dropped her purse on the floor and rushed to John's waiting arms. "Oh, baby, I am glad to see you too." She kissed him on the mouth, and they held that kiss for several seconds. Then she stepped back. "Did they show it on the news?"

"Yeah, it was a newsbreak…..The FBI Agent Hill called and told me that it was on the tube." He sat down, pulling Seville down with him. "I thought,…..how did you get off the plane?"

Seville smiled as she stood to fix herself a drink. "Okay, let me start from the beginning." She sat down again next to John again. "When I got Slim out of jail, he agreed to fly me to Cuba. I'm thinking that we were going in there to rescue you. But then I began to get this weird feeling that they all were expecting me to do just what I did. I didn't know what was going to happen once we landed in Cuba, so I decided to take a little level the playing field along with me. I had a friend of mine to make me a ten pound bomb with a detonator, and I hid it behind my seat when we got airborne………

"Once we arrived in Cuba, and I saw them take you away on the other plane, I wasn't sure how this thing was going to turn out. But then, after they got the call saying that you held the press conference, they all got ready to go. Major Butler, I guess that's who he was. He didn't look like himself at all. Hell, I almost thought he was a white man. Anyway, he was going to leave me at the hotel and told me to get back home the best way that I could." She got up to get her purse, and she handed John the card with the account number written on it that the Major had given her.

"What's this?"

"According to your half brother, it's one billion dollars. He said that he made a promise to you before you left."

"Yeah, he did. But anyway, tell me what happen next." John said anxiously.

"As he was about to leave, I promised to give him some pussy if he would allow me to ride with them to the airfield, and I'd catch a cab from there to the main airport. But I really wanted to be there to see it for myself when I push the button on that detonator. For all the shit that he has taken us through for some fucking gold, I wanted to make sure that he didn't find a way to get off the plane before it blew up...And when I saw that explosion, a sigh of relief ran through my body like I've never felt before. Man! It felt good......"

John smiled. "Let me ask you this, did everybody get on the plane?"

She laughed softly. "Every asshole that was connected to the Major and that gold were on the plane when it blew up. That's including the two white guys who were being held hostage, I suppose. And of course, Bobby Turner was on board. According to the Major, they were flying to Paris where he was going to meet Carolyn."

"Wow!.....Baby, you did it, all by yourself, you pulled it off like no one else could have done. But what were you going to do if they had put you on the plane with them?"

"I don't know....No way was I planning to die with them. I guess God just worked it out that way, because I had no idea he was going to tell me to stay behind in Cuba. I mean, what were the odds that he was going to do that?"

"I would say a billion to one." John said smiling. "But I'm glad that you did what you did. Why did you decide to plant a bomb on the plane in the first place, knowing that you would probably be on board with them?"

"Again, I don't know what made me do it. But I did figure that sooner or later, I was not going to be on that plane with them. And whenever that opportunity presented itself, I was going to push that little red button."

"How did you feel about your old boyfriend, Slim?"

She thought for a moment. "I hated to see Slim go like that. But like I said at the time, he was connected up to his eyeballs. I just simply did to them what they were trying to do to us, kill everybody that could possibly come back to haunt us." She thought for a moment again. "What about the Chinese chick, Kim Lee, where did she go?"

John got up and mixed them another drink. "That, I don't know. When we got to City Hall, she and her two friends disappeared." He came back to his seat, giving Seville her drink. "On our flight back, she pretended to be with the FBI. Then, after the press conference, I realized she had lied about that." He thought for a moment. " But, I'm really glad that you blew up that plane, because if they had gotten away, we would have never seen or heard from them again…..My brother, James, what can I say about him?"

"Well, there is one thing you can say about him,….." She paused.

"Yeah, what's that?"

"This time he's dead for real. He couldn't fake his way off that plane before the explosion."

"I don't know about that. He believed that he was brilliant and that he could pull off anything. He thought that he had committed the perfect crime…..We may need to go back to Cuba to make sure that he didn't get out some kind of way."

"And speaking of the perfect crime, where did he hide that gold?"

"Don't know. I guess he carried that secret with him. Maybe after another hundred and fifty years have passed, it will turn up again."

"I'm sure somebody who is still alive knows where it is." Seville said smiling.

John turned to her with a question mark on his face. "There are two people whom I can think of might know or have an idea,……"

"Oh yeah, who are they?"

"Carolyn Butler is one. And then, there is always the Mayor….You think we should check them out just to make sure?"

"No way!" She snapped. "I'm tired of hearing about that fucking gold. What you need to do is check that account number to see if the Major really transferred a billion dollars into an account for us. That's the only thing that needs checking out right now."

"Oh yeah, I almost forgot that." He leaped up and went to the computer. Click it on and a few seconds later, he put in the account numbers. A few more seconds after that it flashed on the screen as having one billion dollars balance in a Swiss bank account. "I'll be damned! He really did do it." John said as Seville looked on with him. "We actually have a billion dollars in the bank….Maybe he wasn't so bad after all."

"Don't start feeling sorry for that bastard!" Seville said. "Hey, let's get all dressed up and go out on the town tonight. You and I are rich now. We can do anything, go anywhere, and buy anything that we want. And it is all because of that no-good brother of yours. Let's not disappoint him. This is what he would want us to do. We'll live like the rich and famous, and maybe have two or three kids in the process, okay?"

John stood and turned to her. "What about your wish to be this James Bond female type of character? Has the money suddenly curved your ambition to be super spy?"

"No way, we're going to do that too!"

"Okay! As soon as I take a shower, we'll start our life long adventure." John said laughing, and he kissed her on the lips. "Get ready, because here we come, world!"

"I love you, John Sinclair!" She said as she ran behind him to join him in the shower. She loved taking showers with John.

John on the other hand for the remainder of the evening allowed his thoughts to run free. He thought about this case from start to finish, and how ironic it had been to all the people who were involved. It almost seemed as if God himself was playing a game of chess to see who would yell checkmate first. James Butler, the half brother and mastermind of a criminal act that took five years of strategic planning, only to meet his demise by the very one who he least thought would bring him down.

John could only believe that after the billion dollar payoff, it was James way of trying to pay for a wrong that he knew God would never forgive him for. Killing his own half brother's family as part of a master plan to steal the gold was equal to the sins that King David committed murder in biblical times to steal another man's wife.

Nevertheless, in spite of all the wrong James Butler had done, he did two good things for John; he first introduced him to a woman who was totally unequal by any stretch of his imagination to any other woman that he had ever known, including his dead wife. Secondly, he left them both rich, and they would probably live happily ever after. What a beautiful ending to an ugly story. "Checkmate!" *I only wish that it was me who was holding the remote, pushing the red button, and watching the expression on his face.*